Misbehaving the Millionaire

KIMBERLY LANG
MARGARET MAYO
LEE WILKINSON

Published in Great Britain 2014
by Mills & Boon, an imprint of Harlequin (UK) Limited,
Eton House, 18-24 Paradise Road, Richmond, Surrey, TW9 1SR

MISBEHAVING WITH THE MILLIONAIRE © 2014 Harlequin Books S.A.

The Millionaire's Misbehaving Mistress, Married Again to the Millionaire and *Captive in the Millionaire's Castle* were first published in Great Britain by Harlequin (UK) Limited.

The Millionaire's Misbehaving Mistress © 2009 Kimberly Kerr
Married Again to the Millionaire © 2010 Margaret Mayo
Captive in the Millionaire's Castle © 2009 Lee Wilkinson

ISBN: 978-0-263-91187-9
eBook ISBN: 978-1-472-04482-2

05-0614

Harlequin (UK) Limited's policy is to use papers that are natural, renewable and recyclable products and made from wood grown in sustainable forests. The logging and manufacturing processes conform to the legal environmental regulations of the country of origin.

Printed and bound in Spain
by Blackprint CPI, Barcelona

Kimberly Lang hid romance novels behind her textbooks in junior high, and even a Master's programme in English couldn't break her obsession with dashing heroes and happily ever after. A ballet dancer turned English teacher, Kimberly married an electrical engineer and turned her life into an ongoing episode of *When Dilbert Met Frasier*. She and her Darling Geek live in beautiful North Alabama with their one Amazing Child—who, unfortunately, shows an aptitude for sports.

Visit Kimberly at www.booksbykimberly.com for the latest news—and don't forget to say hi while you're there!

For the women who made all this possible:

Andrea Laurence, Marilyn Puett, Kira Sinclair
and Danniele Worsham—who are more than just
my playfriends and the sisters-of-my-heart, they are
also some of the smartest, most talented, and infinitely
patient women I've ever been lucky enough to know;

Linda Winstead Jones, Linda Howard and Beverly
Barton—who let me learn at the feet of the
masters—I mean, mavens;

Pamela Hearon—who broke me of a lot of my bad
habits in the nicest way possible;

and,

Bryony Green and Lucy Gilmour, whose editorial
brilliance is matched only by their excellent taste.

CHAPTER ONE

"Evie is Bradley Harrison's daughter. I can't just lock her in the attic and pretend she doesn't exist!"

"You cannot continue to send her out in society as she is, either, William. She's an embarrassment to the family *and* the company."

Will Harrison poured another two fingers of Scotch and tipped the bottle in the direction of his late father's oldest friend and HarCorp's company attorney. So lunch at the Club yesterday hadn't gone as expected. It wasn't the end of the world.

Marcus Heatherton held out his glass for the refill. "Evangeline is a sweet girl, but Rachel let her run wild after your father died. You see the results. The child is a complete hoyden."

Now there's a word you don't hear every day. Hoyden. Much nicer sounding than "ill-mannered," "socially inept" or "tomboyish"—all of which had, unfortunately, been applied to his half sister.

The smile caused by Marcus's word choice faded. The image of a petit four flying out of Evie's wildly gesticulating hand and landing on the head of Mrs. Wellford's spoiled lapdog like a little hat flashed through his mind. That had been funny. The ensuing regurgitation of said petit four in Mrs. Wellford's lap after Shu-Shu swallowed it whole...well, that pretty much ended Evie's most recent foray into Dallas society on a distinctly low note.

At seventy, Marcus possessed old-fashioned ideas about proper upbringing for young ladies, but old-fashioned or not, he was right. Fifteen-year-old Evie had no manners, no social protocol and, as Marcus had been reminding Will for the last half-hour, *he* had to do something about it.

Or else the Harrison name would be gossip column fodder once again.

When his father announced his engagement to a company secretary half his age, everyone but him easily pegged Rachel for the gold digger she was. Bradley, though, either couldn't see or didn't care, and he smiled benignly in the background as Rachel ran circles around him, spending his money like it was going out of style and making him the laughingstock of the very society she'd worked so hard to infiltrate.

When Rachel tired of Dallas, Bradley officially retired and moved her and five-year-old Evie to the Caribbean, leaving Will in charge of the family company at the ripe old age of twenty-six.

And while Will dedicated the next ten years to running the company and expanding it into an international force, his father and Rachel frolicked on the beaches around St. Kitts and traveled the world, but made no attempt to prepare Evie for her place in Dallas society—or civilization in general, as far as Marcus was concerned.

Will hadn't heard much from Rachel in the last couple of years—after his father's death, she'd been little more than another issue for the accountant to deal with—but after the accident last month that had left her daughter an orphan, he'd found himself Evie's guardian.

So far, it hadn't been easy. Yesterday had just been the proverbial last straw for Marcus.

Will cleared his throat. "Mrs. Gray and her tutors…"

"Mrs. Gray is a housekeeper. She's kind to Evangeline and makes sure you both eat well and have clean clothes, but she is hardly the person to teach the child anything about etiquette. Evangeline's tutors, even if they were qualified, need to focus on her studies so she'll be ready to start at Parkline Academy in the fall."

Marcus could be remarkably and frustratingly single-minded at times, but he'd been the one unwavering pillar of Will's life, completely dedicated to the company and the Harrison family. Evie's arrival had given the old man new focus, and for that, Will was grateful. His own love life and the need for a new generation of Harrisons had been under Marcus's microscope for far too long. At least he hadn't re-visited the idea of Will marrying in order to give Evie a female role model. *Yet.* The night was still young, though, so he needed to think fast.

"William?"

"All right, I'll hire someone specifically to work with her on this—to teach her some manners and how to behave in polite society."

"You must do it *now*, William. People are already asking where Evangeline is and why you haven't introduced her to more of your father's friends or her own peer group. I've held everyone off for weeks now, claiming she needs more time to mourn her mother's passing."

"She does need time." His own mother had died when he was twelve; Will could relate to Evie's grief. At least he hadn't lost both parents so early in life. His father may have been distant, but he'd been around for the most part.

"Yes, but she has responsibilities that cannot be ignored now that she is back in the States."

"Responsibilities? She's fifteen, for God's sake. She doesn't *have* any responsibilities."

"Let me tell you this, William Harrison. Evangeline must

be introduced into society and take her rightful place in it. Everyone is expecting to meet her at the Hospital Benefit."

With that pronouncement, Marcus sat back in his chair and swirled the Scotch in his glass, seemingly amused by Will's sputtering.

"The benefit? That's three weeks away."

"Then you'd better get busy finding someone, shouldn't you?"

Dear Miss Behavior,

I told my best friend I was hoping this guy we both like would ask me to go to a concert with him. She goes and buys tickets and then asks him to go with her! I'm so mad at her, but she says that if he'd liked me, then he wouldn't have agreed to go with her. Now she wants to borrow my leather jacket to wear on their date. She says it would be the "polite" thing to do since she loaned me a pair of boots the last time I had a date. I think she's the one being rude. Since we both love your column, I told her I'd let you decide. Do I have to loan her my jacket to go on a date with the guy I like?

Thnx.

Cinderella

Gwen reached for her coffee cup. Empty. She'd need at least another cup before she was awake enough to deal with teenage angst. She swiveled out of her chair and headed to the kitchen for a refill to fortify her before she waded in to the dangerous waters of adolescent controversy.

In the nine months she'd served as Miss Behavior, Teen Etiquette Expert on the TeenSpace Web site, she'd been embroiled in enough melodrama to write her own teenage soap opera. She'd signed on thinking she'd be answering simple questions like who asks whom to the prom or who pays for dinner. How wrong she was. The complexities of seating charts were child's play in comparison to the day-to-day drama of high school.

The coffee carafe was still half-full as she pulled it off the warmer and poured another extra-large cup. Her experience with teenage dramatics had been vicarious at best. She'd been the "good" daughter—except that one time—leaving her sister Sarah to reap Mother's wrath over her outlandish behavior. Funny how now, after all these years, she was still standing on the outskirts of the fray and trying to mediate the peace.

A yowl was Gwen's only warning as Letitia jumped from behind the pie safe to attack the ears of Gwen's bunny slippers, only to land claws first on her ankle instead. Coffee sluiced over her hand as she jumped, splattering to the floor around the black and white cat. Letitia hissed at the coffee puddles, took one last swipe at the slippers and bolted out of the kitchen.

"You're going to get burned doing that, you silly cat." Or declawed. This was a new trick from the previously laid-back Letitia. A gift from her sister, the new slippers with their oversize ears had pushed the cat over the edge. After five days of this, her ankles looked like she'd been attacked by a ravenous horde of three-inch vampires. The slippers were comfortable, not to mention cute, but not worth the constant battle. She left the slippers in the kitchen for Letitia to attack at her leisure and went back to her computer.

Stifling the urge to start with *"With friends like that, who needs enemies,"* Gwen typed out her response for Cinderella and posted all five of today's questions and answers to the site before logging out of her Miss Behavior account and turning her attention to the mail on her desk. Miss Behavior had been an instant Internet success, tripling the hits to TeenSpace in the last six months, and her real-life consulting business was benefiting from the popularity of the column. As much as she hated it sometimes, practically every debutante in Dallas had her on speed dial.

In addition to bills and a few checks her bank account desperately needed, the morning's snail mail brought yet another plaque of thanks from the Victorian Guild for her work with the current debutante class. She'd *earned* a plaque this year; that group of debs had been the worst yet. Just getting them to spit out their gum and turn off their cell phones had taken most of her patience.

She scanned her office, debating where she had room for it. Wall space was at a premium as debutante class photos, thank-you plaques and other memorabilia competed for a place. There was space over her certificates from some of the best protocol schools in the country, but she really didn't want anything relating to her current work next to them.

She sighed. If her classmates could see her now. Those certificates—many awarded with honors as the top student in her class—hung next to her degree from George Washington, all of which needed dusting. She was trained to work with politicians, heads of state and corporate bigwigs; instead, she spent her time with debutantes and cotillion clubs.

One day, she'd be able to quit teaching spoiled, rich teenagers to eat without their elbows on the table and go back to working with grown-ups in serious business.

Please, God.

For now, though, the teenagers of Texas were paying her rent. She pulled her file on the group of Junior League members who would be taking their daughters to D.C. next month. Teenage girls meeting senators was at least *one* step closer to getting back on track. She should be counting her blessings.

The three short rings of her business line caught her attention. She sat up straight, smiled and answered before the second set of rings finished.

"Good morning. Everyday Etiquette. This is Gwen Sawyer speaking."

"Miss Sawyer, this is Nancy Tucker calling from William Harrison's office at HarCorp International." The voice was cool, smooth and undeniably professional.

Gwen's heart beat double-time at the woman's words. She'd been trying to get her foot in the door at HarCorp for *months*. That dragon in Human Resources seemed so hell-bent on ignoring her proposals, she'd almost given up. A squeal of glee wanted to escape, but she cleared her throat and concentrated on sounding just as professional as Ms. Tucker.

"Yes, Ms. Tucker, how may I help you?"

"Mr. Harrison would like to meet with you to discuss contracting your services. He realizes it's very short notice, but he could meet with you this afternoon at two, if you are available."

Adrenaline rushed through her system, and she began pulling files of proposals from her desk drawer. *Available?* She'd cancel a funeral to be there. Forget the HR dragon; the boss himself wanted to see her. "Two o'clock would be fine."

"Wonderful. I'll let the receptionist know to expect you." The carefully modulated tones didn't change.

"Thank you. I'll see you then." Only when the phone was securely in its cradle did Gwen release the squeal choking her.

This was it. Her days in debutante hell were finally over. After five long years of penance, she'd finally get the chance to restart her career. Ms. Tucker hadn't mentioned *what* kind of service HarCorp was looking for, but Gwen didn't care. If Will Harrison wanted to talk to her, it would have to be something important. Hadn't she seen an article in the paper not long ago that HarCorp was moving into the Asian market? Had someone passed along her proposals to the boss himself?

Talk about dream come true time… The Junior League file went back into the drawer, and she pulled out her folder on

HarCorp and the ignored-until-now proposals. She didn't have much time to prepare, but deep down, she knew one thing.

This meeting was going to change her life.

Gwen checked her watch. One-fifty. Perfect. She'd killed the last five minutes in the ladies' room on HarCorp's fourteenth floor, not wanting to arrive *too* early. One last critical look in the mirror confirmed that she presented the best image possible. The wind in the parking lot had teased a few wispy tendrils of hair out of the severe French twist she'd forced her hair into earlier, but thankfully, the damage wasn't too drastic. She powdered the freckles on her nose one last time and hoped the nervous flush on her cheeks would fade. Applying one last sweep of gloss across her lips, she studied the image in the mirror carefully. She wouldn't be winning any beauty pageants, but she looked responsible and mature—just like a protocol consultant should.

Camel-brown suit. Peach silk shirt. Closed-toe shoes with coordinating briefcase. Gramma Jane's pearls for luck. Gwen closed her eyes and inhaled deeply, willing herself to project cool, collected, *confident* professionalism.

Even if she was quivering so badly inside she thought she might be ill.

At one fifty-five, she opened the glass doors of the executive offices and presented herself to the receptionist.

"I'm Gwen Sawyer. I have a two o'clock appointment with Mr. Harrison."

The reception desk resembled the cockpit of the space shuttle: blinking buttons, keyboards and computer screens all within easy reach of the occupant. The nameplate on the desk identified the occupant as Jewel Madison, a detail Gwen noted so it could be added to the HarCorp file later. The Ms. Tucker she'd spoken to earlier must be Mr. Harrison's personal secretary.

Jewel consulted a screen. "Mr. Harrison has been held up

in a meeting and is running a few minutes behind. He sends his apologies. You can have a seat over there." She waved in the direction of a seating area. "Would you like a cup of coffee while you wait?"

Coffee was the last thing her roiling stomach needed. As she declined, something on the desk beeped and Jewel's attention shifted. Dismissed, Gwen went to wait. A leather couch nicer than the ones in most people's homes looked too squishy to get up from gracefully, so she chose the less comfortable, but much more dignified wing chair instead. Copies of the HarCorp Annual Report covered the small coffee table and for lack of something else to do, Gwen picked one up and flipped through it absently as she mentally rehearsed her pitch one last time.

As a "few minutes" turned into twenty, then thirty, her irritation level rose steadily. At two thirty-five, a forty-something dark-haired woman in a lime-green suit turned the corner and introduced herself as the Nancy Tucker of that morning's phone call.

"So sorry you had to wait. Mr. Harrison can see you now."

About damn time, Gwen thought before she checked herself. *Breathe.* Don't get irritated. This is too important to get all twitchy about punctuality issues.

Nancy was all business. She led Gwen down the hallway in silence, no small talk at all, and delivered her to William Harrison's office door. After a quick knock, she opened it, ushering Gwen in ahead of her.

A stunning view of the Dallas skyline greeted her, but the occupant of the office did not. Without breaking his conversation with whomever was on the phone, he waved her in and indicated he'd be with her in just a minute.

Nancy guided her to one of the chairs facing the massive desk, then slipped silently out the door. Gwen set her briefcase on the floor, crossed one foot behind the other, folded her hands in her lap and waited.

Lesson number one: Don't talk on the phone while there's a flesh and blood person in front of you. Taking a deep breath, she kept her frustration to herself. He was a busy man, and he'd at least acknowledged her presence. So she sat quietly, but uncomfortably, as the conversation continued. Gwen tried to keep her gaze on the view of the city as it would be rude to stare at Will Harrison.

And she knew for certain that it *was* Will Harrison. She'd seen his picture in the papers enough to recognize him. While she might not run in the same circles of society as he, her clients certainly did, and as one of Dallas's Most Eligible Bachelors, many of her debs and their mammas were quite obsessed with him.

She could easily see why they were swooning. If she weren't so irritated, she might feel a teeny-tiny swoon coming on herself. None of his pictures did him justice. In person, he didn't look at all like a buttoned-up and stuffy Fortune 500 CEO. His collar and cuffs were both *un*buttoned in fact, his tie pulled loose at the knot and his sleeves rolled up over his forearms. His dark hair hung a little longer than most executives', and the tan on his face said he didn't spend all of his time in the boardroom. Gwen could easily picture him as the outdoorsy type, and the broad shoulders and strong arms indicated it was something far more active than executive golfing. Maybe he was one of those weekend cowboys? The office lacked any Western-themed decor, so that didn't help. She tried to casually scan his office for clues to his hobbies, telling herself it was strictly for business purposes…

A deep, rumbling chuckle jerked her attention back to the man behind the desk. This time, he caught her eye and smiled. It was the smile that nearly did her in. The man had a dimple, for God's sake, and the total effect would give any live woman a pulse spike.

And, if her pulse was any indication, she was very much

alive at the moment. *Mercy.* Most Eligible, indeed. She stifled the urge to fan herself as the room grew a little too warm.

He was around the desk and extending his hand to her before she even realized he'd hung up the phone. "Sorry to keep you waiting, Miss Sawyer. Will Harrison."

Up close, the man was even more devastating to the senses. At this distance, Gwen could see that Will's eyes were hazel— not the murky hazel of her own, but a clear, perfect hazel. The hand he offered was strong and warm and sent a little tingle of electricity up her arm as she touched him. That swoon seemed more and more likely with each passing minute.

Focus, Gwen. She gave herself a mental shake. *You're not a groupie here to drool over the man. Pull it together because it's showtime.* "Not a problem." She opened her briefcase and pulled out several of her HarCorp folders. "Everyday Etiquette has a reputation—"

Will returned to his chair on the other side of the desk. "Nancy assures me you are the best at what you do, so I have no doubts you will be successful with Evie. However, we're on a deadline here, and I need to know you can work quickly. And, of course, your discretion is essential."

Irritation at being interrupted midsentence was tempered by the compliment that she was the best. She *was*, darn it; it was about time somebody took note. But how did Nancy know? And who was Evie? Discretion? What kind of training did HarCorp need?

"The Hospital Benefit is less than three weeks away. It's Evie's 'launch,' so to speak."

Confusion reigned. She knew exactly when the Med Ball was—it had been a major topic in one of her classes last week. But what did HarCorp have to do other than write a check? She cleared her throat, berating herself for not getting more details from Nancy that morning on the phone. "Mr. Harrison, Ms. Tucker didn't provide any specific information about what kind of services HarCorp needed, so I'm afraid I'm a bit at a loss as to what you are talking about."

Those black eyebrows shot up in surprise, but his computer pinged, and his attention moved to the screen. "Damn." His fingers flew across the keyboard before responding. "Evie is my sister—my half sister, actually."

Ah, the elusive Evangeline she'd read about. The society columns were buzzing with speculation... *Oh, no.* A bad feeling crept up her spine.

"She's living with me now, and her manners are atrocious. I need you to teach her how to be a lady. That is what you do, correct?"

Please let me be wrong. Please. "You need social training for your sister?"

"Table manners. Polite conversation. How to behave at a party." Another ping from the computer, and his eyes went immediately to the screen. "And she'll need help with her wardrobe as well."

Damn. Her heart sank as what was left of her hopes evaporated. HarCorp didn't need her—another spoiled debutante did. Just to be sure, she asked, "And how old is Evie?"

"Fifteen."

Gwen tried to keep her disappointment out of her voice. "Fifteen's a bit young for debutante training, don't you think? Surely you have a few more years before..."

That got his full attention. She trailed off as he pinned her with those hazel eyes, and his voice took on a sharp edge. "She's not a debutante. She's an heiress and a Harrison." He said "Harrison" like it was a synonym for "royalty." "Sadly, my father and stepmother didn't see to it that Evie learn how to behave properly in public before they died. Evie needs someone to teach her, and she needs to know enough not to embarrass herself or the family at the Hospital Benefit. It's pretty straightforward."

This time, it was the phone on his desk that beeped,

drawing his attention away again with only an offhanded "excuse me" as he answered it. Irritation bloomed again before she could help it. She dug her nails into her palm and bit her tongue. Good manners meant she couldn't call him on his rudeness—and busy man or not, he was starting to really fray her Miss Behavior nerves.

Good manners also meant she shouldn't eavesdrop on his conversation, and she needed a moment to think and regroup anyway.

She shouldn't be upset that he wanted her to do social training—it was, after all, her primary source of income at the moment, and she was very good at it. Her pride was just a bit bruised because she'd come in with such high hopes for something else. She should agree to work with his sister…maybe some of the lessons would rub off on him.

That thought kindled her hopes again. Maybe, just maybe, *this* was the way into HarCorp. The back way in, granted, but she'd take what she could get. She'd work with the sister and hope that the brother would be so impressed he'd listen to her proposals for business training…

"Well, Miss Sawyer, what do you think?" Will's attention was back on her, and she straightened her spine. Even with her irritation, she had to be impressed with how he could jump from one task to another and not lose track of either. Will steepled his fingers as he leaned back in his chair, one eyebrow raised in question.

"I'd be glad to work with your sister, Mr. Harrison, but three weeks is not a lot of time…"

"Exactly. You'll need every spare minute with Evie." He reached for a pen and scribbled something on a piece of paper before rounding the desk once again. This time, though, he leaned his hips back against it as he handed her the paper.

Dragging her thoughts from the long legs stretched out so close to her, she blinked and tried to focus on the bold scrawl.

An address in the elite Turtle Creek neighborhood.

"I've told the housekeeper, Mrs. Gray, to prepare the guest room. You can move your things in tonight and start with Evie tomorrow."

Heat rushed to her cheeks at the thought, and she struggled to find words. "M-m-move in? Are you—I mean, that's not—" She took a deep breath to calm the unprofessional stuttering caused by his presumptuous statement. "I have a business to run—other clients and responsibilities." *And the papers would have a field day.*

"Evie spends several hours a day with her tutors catching up on schoolwork. That would give you some time to take care of your other responsibilities. I'm quite willing to pay you for the inconvenience."

She had to call on years of training not to react at the outrageous figure he mentioned. He *was* serious about this.

"And, as I said earlier, your discretion is essential."

Discretion? For that amount of money he could silence *Dallas Lifestyles*'s gossip columnist.

She was younger than he'd expected. Prettier, too, in a wholesome girl-next-door kind of way. She lacked that brittle edge that often came with sophistication—a nice contrast from the women he was used to.

He'd been expecting a plump, gray-haired, grandmotherly type—or, at the very least, a Mary Poppins—if for no other reason he felt anyone calling herself an expert on anything should at least look old enough to drink. Miss Gwen Sawyer was neither plump nor grandmotherly and probably got carded on a regular basis. At the same time, she projected a kind of cool elegance that fascinated him and that Evie would benefit from learning.

She acted completely calm and professional, but he knew she wasn't as detached as she looked. While Miss Sawyer was capable of keeping a good poker face, she couldn't control those wide hazel eyes of hers that expressed each and every feeling the moment she had it. And she'd experienced several throughout their interview. Calculation, shock, confusion— she'd worked through them all. At least once, he'd even seen irritation there, but he wasn't sure why. But something *had* thrown Gwen off her game very early on in the meeting, and it had taken a few minutes for her to regroup. He still hadn't figured out what that had been about, either.

He expected the money to throw her off-guard. It was much more than such services could possibly cost, but it would assure she'd give Evie her full attention and keep her mouth closed to Tish Cotter-Hulme, the local society gossip columnist.

Gwen regained her balance much more quickly this time, covering her discomfort with cool politeness. Nice trick. Hopefully she could teach it to Evie.

"I couldn't possibly move into your home."

"Are you married?" He glanced down to where her fingers laced together in her lap. The white knuckles gave away her agitation as clearly as her eyes did, but from his position, he couldn't see if she wore a ring or not.

"Excuse me?" Her eyebrows flew toward her hairline in shock, and a flush stained her cheeks.

"Are you married? Do you have children or something?" Gwen took a deep breath before answering, and he realized he was a little *too* interested in her response.

"No, but—"

"Good." He let out the breath he'd been holding. "I understand the request is a bit odd—" Gwen gave him a wonderful *"you think?"* look that would have been funny in a different situation, so he forged ahead before she could mount a stronger rejection of his offer. "But Evie's still recovering from her mother's death. She's a little fragile at times and having a hard time adjusting. She needs someone who can give her undivided attention. It would be easier on her to have you there full-time."

He could see Gwen softening.

She played with the pearls at her neck, calling his attention to the flush rising from the collar of her blouse. "I guess I could—"

"Excellent."

Gwen took a deep breath, and her hand fell back to her lap. When she spoke, that cool professionalism was back. In a way he was disappointed; a slightly rattled Gwen was much more interesting.

"I'll prepare a contract and fax it to your secretary this afternoon."

"And I have a nondisclosure agreement that will require your signature as well. I don't want Evie embarrassed or details of my private life shared with the papers."

"Of course. I understand completely." She stood, and he rose to his feet. Although he topped her by a good seven inches, she pushed her shoulders back and looked him squarely in the eye for the first time since he'd rattled her with his unorthodox proposal. "I'll gather my things and be at your home tonight around six-thirty or so. Will that be acceptable?"

Her words caused a smile. He didn't know much about etiquette, but Miss Sawyer would make one hell of an executive if she put her mind to it. He was looking forward to seeing her in action with Evie.

"That'll be fine. I'll tell Mrs. Gray to serve dinner around seven."

She offered her hand. "I'll see you then. It was nice meeting you, Mr. Harrison."

"Call me Will."

"And I'm Gwen. I'll see you tonight."

With another of those cool, polite smiles, Gwen Sawyer showed herself to the door, allowing him the opportunity to observe what he'd missed earlier by being on the phone when she arrived. Long legs. Nice curves almost camouflaged by a conservative suit. A graceful and unhurried walk.

Hopefully Evie would take to her.

He couldn't help but think back to the evening two nights ago. After Marcus left, he'd found Evie on the stairs, tears glistening in the corners of her eyes. Evie took after Rachel with her auburn hair and high cheekbones, but she had her father's—*their* father's—eyes. Unsure how to handle a teary teenager, he'd joined her on the steps but said nothing.

Evie broke the silence first. "I'm sorry I'm such an embarrassment to you."

She must have overhead Marcus's comments. "You're not an embarrassment. You just don't know what it's like here." He patted her shoulder, feeling awkward as he did. He was still new to this big brother thing.

"I'm willing to learn, Will. I promise I'll work really hard." She swallowed hard as the tears overflowed. "Please don't send me away."

"Away?"

"To boarding school. I heard Uncle Marcus mention it last week. I don't want to go. Please, Will."

Guilt at even considering Marcus's suggestion nagged at him. "You're not going to boarding school. You're a Harrison, and this is where you belong."

Evie's tear-streaked face split into a wide grin as she launched herself into his arms.

Parenting a teenager still had him confused, but he'd bridged a gap that night with Evie. He barely knew her—partly due to the difference in their ages and partly because he'd simply been too busy to concern himself with a child several thousand miles away. But they were getting to know each other now and coming to an agreeable living arrangement.

He was getting the hang of this after all. With the addition of Gwen Sawyer to the team, his life could start working itself back to normal.

And, just to be sure, he'd be home for Gwen's arrival tonight.

CHAPTER TWO

"You *are* kidding me, right? *The* Will Harrison hired you? I didn't even know he had a sister."

"That's because you don't read the society section closely enough. And don't sound so surprised. As I've been reminded more than once recently, social training *is* what I do for a living." Gwen balanced the phone on her shoulder as she loaded her laptop into its case.

Sarah went into Sister Support Mode. "Temporarily, Gwennie, temporarily. Even if the kid eats with her feet, you'll turn her into Jackie O in no time. Then, big brother will *have* to listen to what you can do for his company."

"I can hope." Gwen consulted her list. Laptop. Dinner kit. Tea kit. Etiquette books for her new client. Her suitcase. Check, check, check and check.

The increase in background noise meant her sister was no longer alone. Hastily she added, "Listen, you can't tell anyone about this. 'My discretion is essential,' remember?"

"Ich verstehe." Sarah switched to German, a tactic they'd used for years when they didn't want others to understand their conversation. "Is he as handsome as his pictures?"

Better than his pictures. Yummy, actually. "Oh, grow up, Sarah."

"He's Dallas's Most Eligible Bachelor, you know."

"One of them, at least," she hedged.

"Seriously, what's he like?"

"Busy. A bit brusque. In need of one of my refresher classes." Gwen grabbed her address book and current client files and added them to the growing pile. Will Harrison might be the biggest client she'd signed on, but she still had to take care of the others.

"Well, maybe your lessons with his sister will rub off on him."

Gwen responded with an unladylike, but noncommittal "humph" as she dragged her suitcase down the hallway. "One more thing. Can you look after Letitia for a while?"

"Sure, Gwennie. Why?"

"This is where *your* discretion comes in. I'm going to be living with the Harrisons for the next couple of weeks." Gwen held the phone away from her ear in expectation of her sister's reaction.

"You're *what?*" Even with the phone several inches away, she clearly heard every one of the dozen rapid-fire questions delivered at the top of her sister's voice.

"Calm down. Good Lord, you sound exactly like Mother when you do that."

"That's uncalled for."

"Well, if the shoe fits…"

"You do understand that if that columnist from *Dallas Lifestyles* gets wind of this, she'll have a field day with you."

"There's nothing nefarious going on. I'm moving into the guest bedroom so I'll have total access to Evie. If *my* over-developed sense of propriety can handle it, so can yours." She consulted her list one last time. Surely she had everything she needed. It wasn't like she was going to Siberia or anything. "Since when do you care what people think anyway?"

Sarah sighed. "That's my point. I don't, but *you* need to. Let me remind you that the majority of your clientele is hugely conservative. Proper debutante trainers don't live with men they aren't related to."

"I know, I know. This is why you need to keep your mouth shut. Should anyone find out—"

"And you know they will, Gwennie. Will Harrison is one of that Hulme woman's favorite subjects for her column. Do you honestly think you can move in to his house and no one will notice?"

It was Gwen's turn to sigh. "I'll cross that bridge when I get to it. This is a business arrangement, nothing more. No one would question it if he'd hired a live-in housekeeper. This isn't any different."

"I'd keep practicing that statement, if I were you. I think you're going to need it."

"There's no need to sound so dire. It's not like there's paparazzi staking out his building or anything. If I just lie low and not call attention to myself, this should stay under the radar."

"Good luck with that." Gwen could almost hear Sarah's eyes rolling with the sarcasm.

"Jeez, thanks for the vote of support."

"You have my support—you know that. I also know how hard you've worked to build something here, and I'd hate for you to lose ground again."

"I know. But I just get the feeling this is the right thing to do. That it's my chance. I've got to try. If not, I'm afraid I'm going to spend another five years playing with place settings."

"Then I'll keep my fingers and toes crossed for you."

"Thank you. Now can you come get Letitia and keep her until I'm finished with Evie?"

"Of course."

"And speaking of Evie, can I bring her in to see you this week? Seems she's going to need a wardrobe."

She heard the clicks from the keyboard that meant Sarah was checking her schedule. "I'm free Friday afternoon," she finally said. "Will that work? Monday morning would be okay, too. Just let me know."

"Thanks. I'm already running late so I really have to go. I'll have my cell if you need me. And remember, *discretion*."

"*Genau.*" Sarah switched back to English. "Call me tomorrow. I want to hear all the juicy details."

"Good*bye*." *There will be no juicy details this time.*

The brief foray into German reminded Gwen to go back to her office for her Japanese dictionary and software. If she wanted to promote herself as an expert in Asian relations, she needed to get her fluency back in Japanese. Which meant she was dependent on software for the time being. Hopefully Evie *didn't* eat with her feet and she'd have some time to practice…

As she loaded her car, she questioned her sanity one last time. If all went well, this could change everything for her. If she could just get HarCorp as a satisfied customer, every company in Dallas would be lining up for her services. Heck, HarCorp could open doors for her all over Texas.

But if Evie wasn't ready in time…she could kiss most of her clientele goodbye. Sarah wasn't wrong about her business suffering if the gossip columns decided to portray her as some kind of immoral floozy. But the true Worst Case Scenario was if she didn't produce the results Will Harrison expected. Unhappy Harrisons spelled certain doom for her entire business— including the debs. No one would hire her for anything if the Harrisons blacklisted her. The Dallas elite were a close-knit group. Alienating one meant alienating them all.

This was make or break time.

Nothing like a little pressure to keep a girl on her toes. She shifted into Drive and tried to think positively.

On a map, Will Harrison's high-rise building might be only four miles from her funky M Street cottage, but in terms of wealth, Gwen felt like she'd traveled to the moon.

She stopped under the porte cochere where a doorman met

her at her car and introduced himself as Michael. She identified herself, half expecting to be told to move her simple
Honda to a less-affluent area.

"Miss Sawyer, of course. Mr. Harrison said to expect you.
Let me help you with your things, and Ricky will take your
car to the garage."

The helpful doorman made easy conversation as he gathered her gear from the trunk and escorted her to the elevator.
"The Harrisons are in Penthouse A."

Of course they are. Where else would they live? Michael
pushed the button marked P, and she gasped as the elevator
sped to the top floor in seconds and deposited them almost
directly in front of the door marked A.

"I cannot believe I'm doing this," she muttered.

"Excuse me?" Michael asked from behind her.

"Oh, nothing." With one last mental slap to the forehead,
she rang the bell.

She heard a voice shout "I'll get it!" before the door was
thrown open by a teenage girl she had to assume was Evie.

The girl's dark red hair was braided into cornrows tipped
with colorful beads that swung dangerously as she turned to
shout, "Will, she's here!" She waved Gwen in and smiled at
Michael as he returned to the elevator.

Evie's casual air and easy manner contrasted sharply with
the cool marble elegance of the foyer. Tall and thin in the way
only teenagers can be, she wore faded blue jeans frayed at the
hems and a gauzy white peasant shirt. While she was barefoot
and fresh-faced now, Evie would be a raving beauty once she
matured out of the gangly awkwardness of adolescence. Gwen
remembered the picture of Bradley Harrison that hung in the
HarCorp lobby; Evie must have inherited her amazing bone
structure from her mother. Neither she nor Will favored
Bradley Harrison at all, except for their eyes.

Just as she thought his name, Will appeared from a room

farther down the hall. Her breath caught in her chest. The suit and tie were gone, replaced by a pair of faded jeans and a snug blue T-shirt that clearly outlined the shoulders she'd admired earlier in his office. Tanned biceps flexed as he helped Gwen bring her suitcase in.

He, too, was barefoot, and she felt ridiculously out-of-place: overdressed in her suit and sensible shoes and totally dumpy standing next to such perfect specimens of beauty.

"Gwen, this is my sister, Evangeline. Evie, this is Miss Sawyer."

Pulling herself together, Gwen offered her hand to Evie. "I'm very pleased to meet you, Evangeline. May I call you Evie as well?"

"Ohmigod, you really are Miss Behavior, aren't you?"

Gwen ignored Will's uplifted eyebrows. "Yes, I am. I take it you read my column?"

Evie bounced on the balls of her feet. "Every single day since Mrs. Gray told me I had to learn some manners. Plus all the archive stuff, too. I've learned so much already. I can't believe Will got *you* as my teacher! Cool!"

"Then let's try this again." Gwen offered her hand to Evie a second time. "It's nice to meet you, Evangeline."

Evie took the hint and with a sideways glance at Will tried again. "It's nice to meet you too, Miss Sawyer. Please call me Evie." Evie shook her hand, but it was a timid handshake. They'd work on that tomorrow.

"Since we're going to be working closely together, why don't you call me Gwen?"

Evie grinned, and Gwen knew she had a winner on her hands.

"Evie, take Gwen's things to her room." Evie disappeared around a corner, dragging Gwen's suitcase behind her, and Will lifted an eyebrow at her. "Miss Behavior?"

"On the TeenSpace site. Kind of like Miss Manners." He finally guided her out of the foyer and into a living area with another spectacular view of Dallas. The man must really like looking out over the skyline. "That's why Evie knew what I was talking about there in the hallway. We went over introductions just last week on the site."

He nodded and changed the subject abruptly. "Mrs. Gray will have dinner ready in just a minute or two. Would you like a drink?"

Desperately. But she shook her head and declined. She needed her A-game tonight, and a drink wouldn't help. Perching carefully in the wing chair opposite his, she tried to make small talk. It wasn't easy.

Will picked up his glass from the coffee table and swirled the amber liquid. Scotch? Bourbon? she wondered briefly, then lost her train of thought as he leaned back in the chair and propped his feet on the edge of the coffee table. They were large and tanned, and for reasons she couldn't begin to explore, oddly fascinating to her.

"Gwen?"

She snapped back to the conversation and felt the guilty flush creep up her neck. She'd been staring at his *feet,* for goodness sake. What on earth was wrong with her?

She smiled an apology.

"You can get settled in after dinner. Please make yourself at home. If you need anything, just let Mrs. Gray know."

"Thank you."

"Now, let's talk about Evie."

Another complete turnaround. Will got bonus points for remembering the small pleasantries, but he remained focused on why she was here.

"What about me?" Evie came into the room and flopped on the sofa.

"I want to hear how Gwen's going to miraculously turn you into a lady before the Hospital Benefit. *You* should be sitting up straight and paying attention."

Evie straightened up and both Harrison siblings looked at her expectantly.

Good God. What have I gotten myself into? "Well…"

Mrs. Gray chose that moment to call them to dinner and Gwen sent up a word of thanks. This was the strangest situation of her career, and she wasn't sure how to proceed. Dinner would make this much easier.

How wrong she was. Evie chattered like a magpie, covering every topic that crossed her mind, from the TeenSpace site and Gwen's column to how much she disliked the food in America. Will said little, occasionally commenting on Evie's monologue when she paused for a breath, and when his BlackBerry beeped in the next room, he went to get it and brought it back to the table with him.

Gwen watched it all in a state of mild shock.

"So, how do you become a manners expert, Gwen? Is there like a school someplace or something?" Evie perched her chin on her fist and gave Gwen her full attention for the first time during the meal. Will even looked up from his BlackBerry to hear her answer.

Well, at least it was some progress. "There are several schools, actually. I have a B.A. in International Affairs, and I've attended protocol schools on both coasts. But my family was in the Foreign Service, so I've spent my entire life—"

"Really? Cool! Where did you live?" Evie spoke in a series of exclamation points, which wouldn't be too bad if she would stop interrupting.

"D.C., Germany, England, Japan. Asian culture is a special interest of mine." While she had Will's attention, Gwen debated adding more to that statement in hopes he'd make the connection to what she could do for HarCorp's expansion plans. The opportunity was lost almost immediately, though, as Evie sped on to the next topic of what was beginning to feel like an inquisition.

"Did you have to go to special classes and stuff so you wouldn't embarrass your parents?"

"Um, sometimes. My mother's a fiend for proper manners, and she taught me most of what I needed to know. Otherwise, I wouldn't have been allowed in public." She punctuated the statement with a grin, but Evie stiffened and glanced at Will. Okay, that may have been a sore spot for *her,* but she'd meant the statement to be funny. With the slight tightening of Will's jaw as well, she realized her attempt at humor had fallen flat. The light mood turned tense. So, it seemed *that* was a touchy subject in the Harrison household as well. She hurried on to cover the awkward moment. "But a lot can be learned from books, so I brought you some reading material."

Evie rolled her eyes. "More homework."

Will pushed his chair back from the table and stood. "You'll have to excuse me, ladies. I have a conference call in ten minutes. I'll leave you two to get to know each other." A second later, he was gone.

Evie merely nodded and went back to her dinner. Gwen, however, felt her jaw hit the table before she could stop it. Jeez-Louise. A certain amount of laxity was allowed at family meals, but this was ridiculous. She chose her words carefully. "Is this a normal occurrence?"

Evie poked at her peas. "Not really."

Gwen felt her shoulders sag. "Oh, good."

Continuing to push her peas around aimlessly, Evie didn't seem to notice Gwen's relief. "Will normally eats in his office if he's home. Sometimes we'll watch a movie or something while we eat." She looked around the dining room with interest. "You know, I think this is the first time I've eaten in here."

Gwen choked, then swallowed her lecture on the importance of family meals taken at the table. Her own parents had been such sticklers for family meals, partly due to Mother's abhorrence of the mere *idea* of a TV tray. One of the first things she did when she moved out on her own was to eat dinner in the living room. She'd felt so rebellious, she nearly had to call home to brag about her indiscretion.

Evie sat up straight in her chair, drawing Gwen's attention back to the situation at hand. "How am I doing? Am I hopeless?"

The earnest, expectant look on her face was so different from the usual teenagers that suffered through her classes, and Gwen's heart clenched at Evie's need to please. "You're not hopeless at all, just a little rough around the edges. Would you like to start your lessons tonight?"

Evie's eager nod would have been almost comical if Gwen hadn't seen that need exposed earlier. "Then sit up straight, feet on the floor…"

"It's taken care of, Marcus. Evie's lessons start today." The old man could be such a nag.

"Who did you hire? Did you check her references?"

Will hadn't; that's what he paid his secretary for. But Marcus didn't need to know that. "Gwen Sawyer came highly recommended. She does debutante training."

Nancy came in with his third cup of coffee and an armload of reports, giving him an excuse to cut the conversation short without too much guilt. "Unless you have some company business to discuss…"

"No, no. Get back to work. I'll be by Thursday evening to meet this Miss Sawyer."

That was the problem with working with people who'd known you all your life, Will thought as he hung up the phone and turned to the stack of reports Nancy left on his desk. *They never believe you're actually an adult.* He was perfectly capable of hiring a tutor for his sister without Marcus's oversight.

Evie was certainly thrilled with Gwen. He'd seen her briefly this morning, and she'd chattered on in her usual nonstop fashion about all Gwen had taught her after he'd left the table. And she'd thanked him again for hiring the one and only Miss Behavior.

Evie's excitement was the reason he was currently surfing TeenSpace instead of concentrating on the reports from Tokyo littering his desk. Well, it was part of the reason. He had to admit he was a bit interested in Gwen Sawyer as well. Too bad he had to leave the table last night for that conference call—he'd been enjoying himself.

Telling himself it was his responsibility as Evie's guardian to check up on Gwen, he'd headed to the Web site Gwen mentioned the night before. TeenSpace was a headache-inducing riot of color and graphics about TV stars and bands he'd never heard of. In the top right-hand corner of the home page he found the link he was looking for. The "Miss Behavior" page loaded and Gwen's picture smiled at him over the phrase "More Than Forks and Tea Cups…Etiquette for the Twenty-First Century."

"Etiquette" seemed a pretty broad term for what Gwen was dispensing in her column. Drama and angst outnumbered true etiquette five to one. Gwen was certainly trying, though. In addition to letters from her readers, she had column after column of basic behavior skills. He had to give Gwen credit; she seemed to give sound advice that her readers accepted at face value, and she was extremely, well, *polite* about every-thing. Any reservations he might have been entertaining evaporated. Gwen was definitely the right choice for Evie. Out of curiosity, he typed "Miss Behavior" into Google. An article from the *Tribune* popped up first.

"She's Not Your Mother's Miss Manners"
Miss Behavior, the new etiquette expert on the Dallas-based TeenSpace Web site, has taken more than Dallas by storm. Hits to the teen-centered site have tripled since she came on board nine months ago, and she gets

more e-mail from the site than any other columnist. Part Miss Manners, part Dear Abby, her answers to teens' modern-day etiquette dilemmas are succinct, sassy and spot-on. In real life, Miss Behavior is Gwen Sawyer, a Dallas etiquette consultant favored by debutantes…

Nancy buzzed the intercom, interrupting his reading.

"Mr. Harrison, Miss Sawyer is on line one."

Already? Had Evie pushed her over the edge in less than twenty-four hours? "Gwen?"

"I'm sorry to bother you—so I won't keep you but a minute—but I need to tell Mrs. Gray what time to serve dinner this evening. Is seven all right?"

"I'll just grab something on the way home, so…"

"I'm afraid that's not going to work." Gwen sighed. "I'd hoped to talk to you about this last night at dinner but you were, um, called away before I could."

Gwen sounded irritated. Evie must be giving her problems. "And?"

"If you want Evie to make progress, she's going to need to practice. But she needs to practice with someone other than just me, and dinner is a perfect time. Every night would be best, but you'll need to be home every other night at least."

"I'm very busy—"

"I know, but we only have three weeks until the Med Ball. Do you or do you not want Evie to be ready?"

"Of course I want her to be ready—"

"Then we'll see you at dinner. Seven o'clock. Goodbye, Will."

His hackles went up. Who did she think she was? *She* worked for *him*. He buzzed Nancy with the intention of having her get Miss Behavior back on the line so he could get a few things straight about this arrangement…

An unfamiliar feeling stopped him. This was important for

Evie; therefore, it was important to him. And what would it hurt after all? It would only be for a couple of weeks, and Mrs. Gray's meals were a lot better than the take-away bistro on the corner.

"Yes, Mr. Harrison?"

"Find Mitchell and move our meeting back to five o'clock. I have to be out of here no later than six-thirty today."

"Of course."

"And, Nancy?"

"Yes, Mr. Harrison?"

He could not believe he was doing this. "Go through my appointment book and reschedule any meeting in the next three weeks that will run later than six."

"Um…" He could hear the confusion in her voice, but she caught herself quickly. "Not a problem."

Oh, it would be one hell of a problem. His schedule simply wasn't that flexible. But he'd be able to assess Evie's progress and report back to Marcus on a regular basis.

And seeing Gwen in action wouldn't be bad, either.

"Sometimes, the dessert spoon will be above the plate, along with a dessert fork."

Evie looked confused for the thousandth time, but Gwen was pleased that she didn't show her frustration.

"So how's that different from the soup spoon?"

"Silver is always placed in the order it will be used. Start at the outside and work your way in with each course." At Evie's disgruntled look, Gwen added, "And you can always pause for a moment and wait to see which utensil everyone else picks up."

"No, I can do this." With her back ramrod straight and a determined set to her chin, Evie went over the place setting again. Granted, Gwen's teaching set contained enough pieces for the most formal of dinners—far more than Evie would ever be faced with unless she attended a state dinner at Buckingham Palace—but it didn't hurt to cover every possible base. From past experience, Gwen knew that if Evie felt like she had this under control, any regular setting would seem like child's play.

"Red wine, white wine, champagne, water. My glasses are to the right." She touched each piece as she spoke. "Fish fork, salad fork, dinner fork, bread plate and butter knife—"

"Good God, what are we having for dinner?"

Gwen looked up to see Will standing in the doorway, tie loosened and his briefcase still in his hand.

Evie paused in her recitation. "Baked chicken and green beans." Without waiting for a response, she continued. "Service plate, soup bowl, soup spoon, oyster fork…"

Gwen stepped from behind Evie's chair. "It's a teaching set. Every possible fork she might come across. I think Mrs. Gray will let us slide with a smaller setting for tonight."

She caught the amused smile playing at the corners of Will's mouth. "Well, that's good to know."

"Hey, Will, did you know there's a special fork just for oysters? I always thought you just picked them up and slurped them out, but Gwen says that's not the proper thing to do. Did you know that?"

"I think slurping of any sort is against the rules. But how you'd get the slippery little suckers onto a fork is beyond me." Over Evie's giggle, he added, "I'm going to take Gwen in the other room for a probably well-deserved drink while you check with Mrs. Gray about what forks she does need on the table."

Evie balked, and Gwen wondered if she'd ever help set a table before. A look from Will sent her scurrying for the kitchen.

"I'll come get you guys when it's time to eat."

"A drink, Gwen?"

"I'd love one, but not because Evie's driven me to it. She's done very well today."

"That's good to hear." Will stepped back and indicated she should lead the way. In the hallway, Will dropped his brief-case on a side table and fell into step beside her. She gasped as his hand went to the small of her back, the warmth seeping through her shirt to heat her skin. She swayed, her balance suddenly off-kilter.

It's just a polite gesture, nothing more. Still, the shock propelled her the last few feet into the living room and away from his touch.

She took a seat on the long, butter-soft leather sofa and watched as Will poured two glasses of wine from the bar. He handed her a glass and stepped away. She took a sip, glad to see her equilibrium had returned with distance.

Will seemed unaware of her discomfort. He took the wing chair opposite her and relaxed against its back. "I've never seen someone so excited about oyster forks and soup spoons."

"Evie's just eager to please right now. Everything is new and, therefore, fun. It'll pass in a few days. Believe me."

"So you're settled in okay?" He ran a hand through his hair, leaving it standing in funny spikes. She was still having prob-lems reconciling the Will Harrison from the papers with the one she was seeing in person. The corporate CEO didn't mesh with the man in front of her, the one who sputtered at the sight of a formal place setting and teased his little sister about oysters.

"Yes, thank you. Your home is lovely." Funny, this room felt smaller than it did when she and Evie were in here earlier. *Polite small talk. Come on, Miss Behavior, you can do small talk.* She took another sip of her wine. "Did you have a good day?"

"I guess you could call it that." Will removed his tie com-pletely and tossed it over the arm of the chair before unbut-toning the top three buttons of his white dress shirt, exposing bronze skin underneath. Although Will continued talking, she wasn't able to concentrate on his words. *Definitely some kind of outdoor activity.* The lack of a tan line at the base of his throat meant whatever he did outside, he did it shirtless.

Pull it together. She had no business pondering his shirt-free activities—whatever they might be. She should have known after her reaction to him in his office yesterday that moving in to such close proximity would be a very bad idea. Then she'd compounded the problem by insisting he be home every night for dinner. How long before he fired her for gawking at him? Not only was it extremely bad manners—and she should know—but it was unprofessional as well.

This adolescent mooning had to stop. She was *not* going down that path again. She'd learned that lesson the hard way. Or at least she thought she had. Obviously her libido was a bit of a slow learner. Maybe it was just because she'd been in a bit of a dating dry spell recently.

Fine. The day after the Med Ball she'd start dating again. She'd let Sarah set her up, hit the bars, try an online site—anything. She just needed to make it until then *without* making a fool of herself again.

Focus on Evie, and try to forget about her brother. Easier said than done, when even as she promised herself she'd find a man soon, she could still feel his hand on the small of her back like a brand.

Will sat on the balcony, his legs stretched out on the railing and a drink in his hand. The lights of Dallas spread out in front of him, twinkling in the darkness.

Evie and Gwen were both in their rooms and Mrs. Gray had long since gone home, and the apartment had fallen silent. At first, the quiet felt odd; he kept expecting to hear Evie's stereo or Mrs. Gray banging pots and pans in the kitchen. Funny how quickly he'd adjusted to having people around—Evie, Mrs. Gray and now, Gwen.

The balcony off Gwen's room angled his, and the glow

from behind her curtains meant she was still awake. He'd heard the unmistakable click of computer keys as he walked by earlier. Was she a workaholic, taking advantage of the quiet evening to answer the etiquette questions of the country's youth? If he knocked on her door, would she join him for a drink on the balcony instead?

When he'd opened the front door, he'd heard Evie's recitation of flatware and gone to the dining room expecting to find Miss Behavior in full form. He'd been struck speechless instead. Gwen's sensible suit had disappeared, replaced by a simple sundress that flowed over her curves intriguingly. Her hair hung loose around her shoulders, and as she'd passed him in the hallway, he'd caught a faint whiff of lavender.

The scent suited her: elegant, a bit old-fashioned and very feminine. He'd breathed deep and the residual tension of his day eased away. And while Gwen seemed to stay slightly on edge as they chatted, he'd found the wine to be an unnecessary additional relaxant.

He'd been charmed by her at dinner. When he agreed to be home for more family meals, he hadn't expected to enjoy it so much. Evie's presence seemed to melt some of the reserve he normally felt from Gwen, and he found her to be well-read and refreshing in her opinions.

And Evie! Gwen may have said it was too early to tell, but he could see the changes in Evie already. She did have natural charm, and under Gwen's gentle guidance, she was learning how to use it.

The light in Gwen's room went dark, and he'd missed his chance to offer her a nightcap.

It was probably just as well—getting involved with his sister's tutor in any way could only cause problems. If he'd learned nothing else from his father's late-life love affair, he certainly knew the folly of fishing in the company pond. At least the various women Marcus kept pushing at him as potential partners would never cause the same embarrassment Rachel had. They had their own wealth, their own family connections—they didn't need his in order to climb the social ladder.

Nope, he was better off enjoying the evening alone.

Then why did he have this lingering regret he hadn't asked her earlier?

CHAPTER THREE

THIS was definitely the way to work.

The guest room of Will's penthouse had its own private balcony, and Gwen had taken her laptop outside. Looking over the railing from almost twenty floors up had made her feel dizzy, but as long as she stayed away from the railing, she was fine. The small table and chairs had enough room for her computer and paperwork, and she could enjoy the summer breezes while she worked.

Mrs. Gray brought her a small pot of tea and some snacks about the time Evie went downstairs for her tennis lesson, and the apartment was quiet except for the jazz floating from the CD player inside in her bedroom. She loved her little 1920's cottage and the charm of M Street, but *this* she could get used to.

She posted her column to TeenSpace and answered a few e-mails. For the most part, she'd been able to either postpone clients or move them to the blocks of time she knew Evie would be with her tutors or at a lesson, but she'd sent a few to a friend and former classmate who did some deb training on the side. The obnoxious sum of money Will was paying her for this job more than covered the loss of income from those few classes.

She was just shutting down her laptop when her cell phone rang.

"You never called yesterday and I'm dying to hear *everything*." Her sister sounded as eager as Evie.

"I know. I was busy getting settled in, and Evie and I worked most of the day." The breeze on the balcony made it hard to hear Sarah, so she went inside and flopped on the sinfully wonderful bed.

"And…"

"The guest room here is nicer than that five-star hotel we stayed at in D.C. last year. The bathroom is the size of my bedroom at home and done completely in marble. The bedroom is huge, and I have my own balcony. It's *incredible*."

"Even the hired help lives the good life, huh?"

"That's for sure." Gwen rolled on to her back, felt the down duvet mold itself around her and stared at the hand-painted ceiling. "I swear, I feel like a princess in this room."

"What about the princess herself?"

"Evie's not bad at all. A little unsure of herself and the finer points of etiquette, but she's far from the mess I expected. I'm going to bring her in Friday, if that's still okay. I think you'll like her."

"Friday's fine. E-mail me her picture and sizes. Now, quit stalling and tell me about the Most Eligible Will Harrison."

Gwen nibbled on a fingernail as she hedged. "There's not much to tell."

"Gwennie!" Sisterly exasperation took over. "Details. Now. I'm holding your cat hostage, you know."

"Okay, okay. He's even more handsome than his pictures, and he can be quite charming when he wants to. Trust me, charm is not something the Harrison family lacks." So it wasn't the full truth, but Sarah wasn't ready to hear that Gwen was living with a man who oozed sex appeal. And she wasn't about to go into the details of what that was doing to her equilibrium. "He's really good to Evie, too, even though they're still figuring each other out."

"I hear a 'but.'"

"*But* he's terse sometimes and always seems to be thinking about something else when I'm talking to him. And if that damn BlackBerry rings one more time, I'll—"

Sarah's sigh interrupted her rant. "Not everyone feels the way you do about phones, Gwen. He's probably a very busy man. BlackBerrys just come with the territory."

It was her turn to be exasperated. "You know good and well that flesh and blood people—"

"'Always take priority over any message in any other medium.' Yes, Gwennie, I know. That speech is getting old, honey."

"That doesn't make it any less true." She knew she sounded huffy and defensive, but she also knew Sarah had been brought up better than that.

"Maybe you should work on some new etiquette rules for *this* century."

"The ones we have would work just fine if folks would only follow them." Sarah started to interrupt again, but Gwen cut her off. "He brought it to dinner."

"Oh." Even Sarah's lax rules on technology use included a moratorium on their presence at the dinner table. Mother had taught them too well. "So Will Harrison needs some work in the cell phone etiquette department. Big deal. He's handsome and charming and richer than God. You can over-look a couple of flaws."

"Sarah, I have no business even noticing his flaws. *Evie* Harrison is my business, not Will." *That needs to become my new mantra.*

"So? You're there. Living in his house. You're both adults, and you never know…"

Sarah was going to drive her insane. "Forty-eight hours ago you were telling me what a bad idea moving in here was. You've switched camps pretty suddenly."

"I just wanted to make sure you'd thought this whole thing through. Now that you're there…" She trailed off suggestively. "Anyway, you said you felt like this was the right thing to do. That it was your chance. Maybe it is in more ways than one. Couldn't hurt to keep your options open."

"You're jumping *way* ahead. Granted, Will is absolutely yummy—"

Sarah perked up. "Yummy? Really?"

Oh, for a different choice of words. Too late now. "This is business—and the future of my business. As you said, I've laid a lot of groundwork the last few years. I'm not going to screw everything up again with some silly crush on my boss."

"So he *is* crushworthy."

Gwen wanted to bury her head in the pillows and scream. "This whole conversation is ridiculous. Will Harrison barely knows I'm alive. I'm just someone he hired to tutor his sister. I doubt Evie's French teacher is having this conversation with *her* siblings."

"He didn't ask the French teacher to move in, now did he?"

Gwen heard the front door slam and the pounding of feet in the hallway. *Perfect timing.* She sent up a quick word of thanks. "Evie's back from her tennis lesson. I need to go."

"But you haven't told me anything—"

"I've *got* to go. Miss Behavior duty. We're going to work on introductions and handshakes this afternoon."

"Oooh, fun."

"Sarcasm isn't becoming of a lady, you know. Neither is that," she added as Sarah made a raspberry noise in her ear. She heard Evie call her name as footsteps approached her room. "I'll see you Friday, okay?"

"This conversation isn't over, you know."

"Yes, it is."

"At least think about what I said. Don't let past mistakes color your perception and cause you to miss out on an opportunity."

"Past mistakes are what's keeping my perception crystal clear." Sarah started to grumble again. To keep the peace she added, "But I'll think about what you said. Bye." She flipped her phone closed before Sarah had a chance to argue some more.

Sarah went through life like it was some kind of movie—which, for her, it often was. Gwen just needed to remind herself of that so that her sister wouldn't drive her into therapy or cause her to lose her job. If she limited her calls to Sarah over the next couple of weeks, she'd be able to concentrate much better on the job at hand.

Head in the game. Eyes on the prize. Hands to herself.

That should be easy enough to remember.

"*Konichiwa*." His tongue felt too thick to get the word out sounding anything like the voice on the computer lesson. Picking up Japanese in three weeks would be a challenge.

He looked over the notes Nancy had prepared about doing business with the Japanese. The business card thing was no problem; bowing wasn't that difficult to figure out. But he'd read how making an effort to learn a few words of Japanese—however badly pronounced—would go a long way in creating good feelings.

And good feelings were much needed. Expanding HarCorp's distribution of its luxury items into Asian markets had been his personal goal for the company for the last three years.

HarCorp's background was tied in Texas cattle, but the Harrison family didn't have ranch roots. His great-grandfather opened one of the first tanneries in the area, providing leather to the saddle and boot makers. When the demand for saddles waned, Harrison Tannery changed its name and began supplying leather to the automakers and eventually began supplying leather overseas as well.

The Luxury Goods arm of HarCorp had been a special project of Will's since he joined the family business. He'd championed it when the entire board had tried to nix the idea. It wasn't until his father retired that he was able to give it the attention it deserved, but Luxury Goods now showed a larger profit than any other department, and the naysayers were off his back. Now that Harrison Leathers had made a name for itself providing unique, high-quality items, it was time to expand their reach to the newly affluent Asian countries and their growing upper classes. Kiesuke Hiramine was his way into that market. The meeting scheduled for next month would be the make-or-break moment of three years' hard work.

"Konichiwa," he tried again. *"Dochirahe."*

The intercom on his desk beeped. "Mr. Harrison, are you ready for me now?"

He glanced at his watch. Three-thirty already, and past time for his daily meeting with his assistant. "Come on in, Nancy."

One second later, Nancy knocked sharply on his door and entered. With her usual efficiency—and he paid her handsomely for it—she went through his calendar and schedule for the immediate future as he signed the stack of papers she laid on his desk.

"Finally *Dallas Lifestyles* would like to know if you can schedule an interview and photo shoot."

A snort escaped at the mention of the magazine. Four-color gossip on glossy paper was still trash, no matter how the magazine tried to promote itself as something other than a gossip rag. He looked up from the contract he was initialing to see the corner of Nancy's mouth twitching in amusement. "Why on earth would I do that?"

Nancy feigned a look of innocence. "It's part of the whole 'Dallas's Most Eligible' package. Each Bachelor gets a spread. You're the only one left—are you sure you don't want to schedule?"

"Has hell frozen over yet?" That's all he needed: *more* encouragement for the fortune-hunting women out there on the dating circuit. Like he didn't have enough on his plate already between running HarCorp and raising Evie. Even if he had the inclination, he certainly didn't have the time.

"That's what I thought. But I told them I'd ask anyway. Maybe they'll quit calling now," she grumbled.

"We can hope, right?"

Nancy shrugged as she collected the now-signed papers from his desk. Knowing they were finished, Will turned back to his computer and clicked the file on Japanese business etiquette open again. He needed to figure out this bowing thing.

"Anything else I can do for you?"

He laughed but didn't take his eyes off the screen. "Yeah. Find me a Japanese expert to run my meeting."

His intercom on his desk beeped, meaning the lobby receptionist wanted to put a call directly through—which meant the call was either from Evie or Marcus. Nancy left as he answered.

"Hi, Will. I'm sorry to bother you."

Hearing Gwen's voice caught him off-guard. Jewel, the executive receptionist, must have been told something about their situation in order for Gwen to get connected to him directly. He hadn't thought about doing it, but Nancy obviously had.

"It's no bother." Surprisingly he meant that. "Is everything all right?"

"Oh, yes. Everything's fine. Marcus Heatherton called Evie today to say he'll be here for dinner tonight."

He'd forgotten about that. "I guess I should have warned you. Marcus is checking up on us."

"On me, you mean." He could hear the smile in her voice. Gwen was sharp.

"How'd you know?"

"After everything Evie's told me, I'm surprised he's waited this long." She sounded amused at the situation, which surprised *him*. Marcus was well-known, and it wasn't for his laidback outlook on life. Surely Gwen had at least heard of him in dealing with her debutantes.

His computer beeped, signaling an incoming e-mail. He glanced at the message and shot back a quick response.

"Mrs. Gray, however, is all atwitter. Something about Mr. Heatherton being impossible to please."

"Oh, well, there was that one night when the meat was a little tough…"

"So, it's going to be an interesting evening then." Gwen chuckled conspiratorially, and the sound was infectious. He liked this side of her. Gwen still seemed tense whenever he was around, and this was one of the few times he'd felt her loosening up.

"Oh, definitely."

"Actually I wanted to tell you that Mr. Heatherton plans to arrive around six-thirty. I'm hoping you'll be able to make it home a bit earlier tonight. I think he's eager to see you."

That comment brought a full-out laugh. "You *have* heard of Marcus. Don't worry. I'll be home in plenty of time to run interference for you."

"That's not what I was implying—"

"Yes it was." This was fun. How long had it been since he'd had an enjoyable and somewhat normal conversation with a woman? Years, possibly. He eased back in his chair and propped his feet on the desk. "Marcus will be nothing if not impressed by you—what you've done with Evie, that is."

"I hope. Evie's a bit nervous. You did tell her she wasn't going to be sent to boarding school, right?"

"Yep." His e-mail beeped again, and he glanced at the subject line. As much as he was enjoying the conversation, it was time to get back to it. "Anything else I can do for you—short of uninviting Marcus to dinner?"

"Actually there is one more thing. You mentioned before

that you wanted me to help Evic with her wardrobe. I'll be taking her to Neiman Marcus tomorrow."

Money. Of course. Everything in his life always came back to money. *His* money. Not that he minded spending it on Evie, but Gwen bringing it up had kind of dampened the mood. For a moment there, he'd forgotten he'd bought her time and attention. Her attention to Evie, he meant. "I'll take care of it. Anything else?"

"Guess not. We'll see you tonight." He heard Evie's voice in the background then Gwen's muffled voice as she placed a hand over the phone to answer her. "Oh, Will?"

His intercom was beeping. He didn't have time for this. "Yes?"

"Evie says not to be late. Mr. Heatherton frowns on tardiness, and it would be rude." That restrained laughter in her voice snared him again.

"Tell Evie I said she has to wear a dress." He waited as Gwen relayed the message and heard Evie's wail in response. The intercom's beeping got more insistent. "I have to go. I'll see you tonight."

He switched to the intercom line to find Nancy waiting impatiently. "Mr. Hiramine's assistant is on line three."

"Great. Tamishi, right?"

"No, Takeshi."

"Thanks. And tell Davis to just e-mail the sales figures. I have dinner arrangements with Marcus tonight, and I'll look them over at home. I'll be leaving early today."

Nancy's surprise registered, but he didn't have time to explain further.

"*Konichiwa,* Takeshi."

CHAPTER FOUR

"PAUL ANGERON tells me your backhand is showing great improvement, Evangeline." Marcus Heatherton wiped his small white beard with a monogrammed napkin and leveled a proud smile at Evie.

Evie brightened as she launched into a spirited rendition of the former Wimbledon winner's description of her tennis prowess. Gwen lowered her eyes to the table and hid a smile of her own. Evie had Mr. Heatherton eating out of the palm of her hand. A quick glance at Will and his half smile confirmed her thought.

Mrs. Gray had pulled out all the stops for dinner—once she'd finished grumbling, at least. Although the courses were uncomplicated, the food was plated beautifully on gold-rimmed china. The cream linen and the gleaming crystal seemed a bit over the top for a family dinner of salmon and potatoes, but Mrs. Gray had insisted Evie needed the full effect for this evening.

All of Evie's worries that Mr. Heatherton would find something wrong with her manners seemed to have evaporated. Although she still dominated the conversation a bit more than was correct, she hadn't interrupted anyone and proved she could tell an entertaining story for her guests.

No question about it. Evie was going to be fine.

Will's laugh brought her back to the conversation, and she

wondered what she'd missed with her woolgathering. Some etiquette tutor she was—mentally wandering away from a conversation was plain rude and she knew better. If only the Harrisons didn't give her so much to think about.

With Evie, she had an excuse—it was her job to correct, encourage, evaluate and decide what step was next in the run up to Evie's presence at the Hospital Med Ball. As for Will... well, she had no excuse other than her own unusual fascination with the man. In some ways, he was exactly the man she'd expected—businesslike, busy and often distant. More often than not, she found herself unsure of what to say or do when around him. Plus, she couldn't decide if his occasional rudeness and incessant BlackBerry usage was deliberate or not.

Regardless, she even found it difficult to follow her cardinal rule of "maintain eye contact," because staring into Will Harrison's eyes could turn any woman into brain-dead mush. And if he smiled...Lord, the man should carry a warning label. Plus he could also be kind and funny and completely approachable at times. Like when...

"Gwen?"

She looked up to see everyone watching her. Mr. Heatherton's frown had returned at her inattention. Evie stared at her openly in mild shock, and Gwen could practically hear her own lecture about attentiveness to others replaying in Evie's head. Will simply looked amused for some reason. She cleared her throat as she felt her cheeks heat. "I'm so sorry. I was thinking about Evie's shopping trip tomorrow."

"Gwen's sister is a buyer at Neiman Marcus. We'll be getting my wardrobe up to scratch. What color dress do you think would be most appropriate for the Med Ball, Uncle Marcus?"

"White or pastels, my dear. You're much too young for anything else. And remember who you are—avoid anything flashy..."

She could kiss Evie for that save. Whatever question Mr.

Heatherton had asked her was forgotten as he launched into a lecture on the horrid state of formal wear for young women. Evie was doing an admirable job of hanging on every word like he was the Fashion Oracle of Dallas.

Hearing a small snort of laughter from her right, Gwen looked over to see Will pretending to study his meal carefully. Without making eye contact, he leaned slightly toward her and whispered, "Tsk, tsk, Miss Behavior."

Buttering her roll kept her from winging it in Will's direction. Instead she waited until Will looked her way and winked at him. His eyebrows went up in surprise then, to *her* surprise, she felt his foot nudge hers under the table.

She nudged his foot in response, but Will had focused his attention on Marcus and seemed engrossed in his lecture on the importance of a modest neckline.

When Evie nudged her foot from the other side, Gwen's head snapped in her direction only to feel Will's foot reach over hers to nudge Evie's. She almost laughed out loud. Both Harrisons wore looks of absorbed interest on their faces while they kicked each other under the table like children.

Who knew Will Harrison could be playful enough to foot-fight with his sister under the dinner table? For the sake of Evie's education, she should put a stop to it, but there was no real harm. Marcus seemed completely unaware.

Another nudge from Will. This time Gwen retaliated more forcefully, only to miss her target and connect with the center table leg instead. Glassware rattled, and Marcus paused midsentence.

Oh, no. The heat returned to her cheeks.

"Sorry, everyone." Will covered for her smoothly, earning him a frown from Marcus and Gwen's eternal gratitude.

This was just dandy. She could hear her mother's voice chiding her for her behavior. Enough was enough. Time for her to remember she was a grown-up and act like one.

She cleared her throat. "Mr. Heatherton, will you be attending the Med Ball this year?"

"Of course, my dear. I try to attend every year, if only to put in an appearance. This year, however, it will be my pleasure to introduce Bradley's beautiful daughter to friends of the family." He patted Evie's hand fondly.

Evie beamed at the indirect acknowledgment of her social skills, but Marcus moved on.

"And you, William, will you be escorting Grace Myerly?"

Evie's eyes were as wide as Gwen's felt as they both looked at Will, who seemed to be having difficulty swallowing his salmon all of a sudden. Gwen thought she was up-to-date on all the society doings just by listening to her debs' conversations, but she didn't recall hearing Will's name connected to the great paragon Grace Myerly before.

"No, Grace and I aren't seeing each other any longer."

"That's a shame. You made such a lovely couple, and your families go way back."

She was still processing the Will and Grace connection when Mr. Heatherton turned his attention to her.

"Gwen, you know the Myerly family don't you?"

Gwen sat up straight. "Yes, I do. Not socially, of course, but both of the younger Myerly girls were in my debutante classes several years ago."

"Of course. Lovely girls, both of them."

If you say so. Personally Gwen felt the youngest Myerlys were spoiled, self-absorbed brats who'd made her classes hell for all involved. The older Myerlys hadn't helped the situation with their own self-important attitude. She was glad there weren't any other Myerly children at home ready to debut.

She nodded instead. "I haven't met Grace before, although I do know who she is." Everyone knew Grace Myerly. The woman was constantly in the papers for her charity work and her fabulous parties. Tall, willowy, gorgeous and seemingly gracious, she was the epitome of Southern high class and, by all standards, the perfect type of woman for Will.

Something unpleasant coiled in her stomach.

"Why don't you take Gwen, Will?" Evie piped up with that idea, sending Marcus's fork clattering to his plate. Will froze, his eyes locking on Gwen's face with a "Fix This" look, but she was too busy choking on her wine to do anything.

Evie, however, was oblivious to the change in atmosphere. "That way, Gwen can help keep me from messing up, and you won't have to deal with—what did you call it?—'the desperate cling of ageing socialites.'" When no one spoke, Evie looked at each face closely. "What? What's the problem?"

Evie looked genuinely confused. Will wanted to help, but wasn't sure he knew where to start. Marcus looked horrified, and Will knew at any moment Marcus would say something snobbish or classist and make the situation worse.

The grandfather clock in the hallway ticked in the silence as tears gathered in the corners of Evie's eyes because she didn't understand the currents swirling around her.

Gwen recovered first and placed her hand over Evie's. Will remembered that look on her face from their first meeting— the moment had passed and Gwen was back in charge. She'd know exactly the right thing to say.

He couldn't *wait* to hear it.

"Evie, honey, it's not appropriate to ask one person to ask another person to a social function like that. It puts everyone in an uncomfortable situation." Gwen's voice was gentle, with no trace of censure. "It puts Will in the position of asking me or risk insulting me or hurting my feelings, when he may have someone else in mind to ask. I take the risk of hurting his feelings if I have to say 'no' for whatever reason, plus it's embarrassing for the people involved to have such personal matters discussed in front of others. Understand?"

Evie nodded.

Bravo, Gwen.

"Remember, one of the most important purposes of etiquette is to make everyone feel comfortable and at ease. Quizzing people about their dating habits or trying to fix them up on a date never makes anyone feel at ease."

And that reminder was for you, Marcus. Score two points for Miss Behavior. Hopefully Marcus wouldn't bring up the topic of Grace Myerly again. It was only luck this time that sidetracked the conversation before Marcus had Will and Grace combining HarCorp and Myerly Cattle into one large family empire. Marcus and Peter Myerly had been pushing shallow, bubbleheaded Grace at him since Grace's debut.

If Gwen *had* intended that remark for Marcus however, she didn't show it. She seemed fully focused on Evie.

As Evie opened her mouth to say something more, Gwen's expression changed from one of cool calm to an unmistakable "We'll discuss this later." Evie nodded again in understanding, then turned her mother's megawatt smile on everyone.

"I see, and I'm very sorry if I made you all uncomfortable."

Gwen adeptly steered the conversation in a new direction, and the moment seemed forgotten. Marcus was soon pontificating on something—Will lost the thread quickly—and Evie and Gwen nodded in all the right places.

A weight lifted from his shoulders. Gwen was a godsend. Marcus was pleased. Evie was a new person—in three days, Gwen had not only improved her manners exponentially, but Evie seemed to be smiling more. For the first time in weeks, he really felt like this whole situation would work out. Nancy would be getting a nice surprise in her next paycheck for delivering Miss Behavior to his front door.

As Mrs. Gray served dessert and coffee, he nudged Gwen's

foot under the table again, and smiled his thanks. Gwen seemed to understand.

His BlackBerry chirped, indicating an e-mail. Probably Davis's sales report finally arriving. He fished it out of his pocket to check.

"You're not supposed to do that, Will." Evie's voice stopped him before he could open the message. He looked up to see Evie shaking her head at him in censure. He heard Gwen's shocked "Evie!" but Evie continued.

"Gwen says you're not supposed to have cell phones and stuff at the dinner table. It's rude to put technology before people. Right, Gwen?" Evie turned to Gwen for confirmation.

Gwen looked completely ill at ease.

Belatedly Will realized Evie—and by extension, Gwen—was right. He'd lived alone for so long, he'd gotten into lots of bad habits. He slid the BlackBerry back into his pocket and opened his mouth to apologize.

Marcus beat him to the punch. "Evangeline, William is a very busy man and the business needs his attention."

He tried to jump in. "Evie, I—"

"But Gwen says the rules apply to everybody all the time. It doesn't matter who they are."

Gwen went slightly pale. "Evie, we don't correct others."

"But you correct me all the time."

"That's because it's my job. What's rude is to correct other people in social situations. *Especially* your elders," she whispered.

"But, Gwen..." Evie's cheeks were getting flushed.

Marcus adjusted his cuffs and leaned forward. "Evangeline—"

"Why does everyone get to tell me what to do and tell me how wrong I am when they're breaking rules too? Will has his BlackBerry, Uncle Marcus is holding his fork wrong, and I'm the one getting yelled at!"

She had a point. She also had their father's famous temper, and that he knew how to deal with.

"Evie…"

But Evie carefully placed her napkin on the table and pushed her chair back. As she stood, he saw her take a deep breath to control herself. "Uncle Marcus, Will, I apologize for losing my temper and being rude. If you'll excuse me, I have a headache and need to go lie down. Good night, everyone." With that, she stomped from the room. Moments later, he heard her bedroom door slam.

Silence followed her departure. Gwen looked shocked and Marcus was frowning again.

With an attempt at levity, he said, "Well, she's certainly learned the art of the dramatic exit." *And a little bit of Gwen's "extreme politeness" trick.*

Gwen seemed to be calling on that same trick. "My apologies as well. If you'll excuse me, I'll go talk to Evie."

He caught her hand as she tried to rise and a little zing of electricity shot through him. The way her eyes snapped up to his had him wondering if she'd felt it, too. "Leave her alone for a little while. She needs to calm down first."

Marcus chuckled, and Will got to watch Gwen's jaw drop in shock. "She has the Harrison temper, that's for sure. William's right, Gwen. I've dealt with this before myself— with both Bradley and William, mind you. She'll need to stew for a while before she can calm down. There's no use trying to talk to a Harrison while they're angry." With that, Marcus pushed his own chair back from the table.

"But I'll leave you two to sort that out." He reached for Gwen's hand and shook it warmly. "It was a pleasure to meet you, my dear. You're doing a wonderful job with Evangeline."

Will walked Marcus to the door. "I must say, William, that's the most interesting dinner I've had with you in years."

"You can say that again."

When he returned to the dining room, he found Gwen gathering plates from the table while Mrs. Gray clucked at her to stop.

"Come on, Gwen. I'll get you a drink and we'll sit on the balcony."

She followed him to the other room but declined the glass he offered. *Guess a trip to the balcony is out, too.* Gwen didn't sit, either. Instead she gripped her hands in front of her and straightened her spine as she faced him.

"I'm sorry about that, Will. Really. I expected her to blow at some point…I just didn't mean for it to happen in front of you and Mr. Heatherton. I figured she'd take it out on me."

"You were expecting that?"

She nodded. "It's hard to have someone correct you all the time. How you walk, how you talk, how you hold your glass. Having every move you make critiqued and never getting it quite right." She laughed, but it was a bitter sound. "It gets old really fast. Trust me on this. I know how Evie feels."

There was a story there, but he had the feeling Gwen wouldn't want to go any deeper in to it, so he didn't ask. He'd guess Miss Behavior hadn't always gotten the forks right.

He sat and invited her to do the same. To his surprise—and pleasure—she chose to sit on the sofa with him.

"Believe me, though, when I say Evie will do fine—at the Med Ball and in general."

"I know she will. Like Marcus said, Evie really is showing great improvement. I'm very—I mean we're very pleased. Marcus said it was the most interesting dinner he's had here."

Gwen's shoulders slumped in what might be relief and she sagged back against the arm of the sofa before she caught herself and straightened back up. "Interesting is one way to put it."

"Go ahead and relax. You've earned it." She had. Evie's outburst aside, the evening had been a success, and he owed that to Gwen. "We'll let Miss Behavior take the rest of the night off, and we'll talk about something else."

Relax? He had to be kidding. She'd just experienced one of the strangest dinners of her career—make that her life—and he expected her to relax? The Harrisons were going to drive her insane.

She hadn't lied when she said she'd been expecting Evie's outburst, but when she'd snapped there at the table, Gwen thought her heart would stop beating. When Evie pointed out Mr. Heatherton's fork problems, she'd had a clear vision of her career going up in a puff of smoke. Again. And this time, it wouldn't even be her fault.

But both Marcus and Will seemed to have taken it all in good humor, and while it was a relief, it wasn't doing much for her nerves. And sitting this close to him on the sofa wasn't helping her composure, either. The easy smile caused adorable crinkles around his eyes and brought that devastating dimple out to play hell with her equilibrium. The deep breath she took to try to calm herself backfired when the spicy scent of his aftershave coiled through her and tied her stomach in an aroused knot.

Now he wanted her to have a drink and talk about something other than Evie and etiquette. What did that leave? HarCorp? She doubted he'd believe an interest in the actual business, and there wasn't exactly a casual way to broach the topic of her corporate workshops. No, her career had already teetered on the edge once this evening. There was no sense flirting with disaster again by bringing up *that*. The weather? Politics? Every topic of small talk fled her head as Will shifted to a more comfortable position and treated her to a full-out, heart-stopping smile.

"Are you sure I can't get you a drink? Wine?"

Was Will flirting with her? A drink? On the balcony? Small

talk? Her stomach fluttered at the thrill before common sense stamped it down. She worked for him, and she wouldn't believe for a second he flirted with his employees. Of course, this wasn't a normal employment situation, what with her moving in and all. Maybe…

Oh, no, she was doing it again. How stupid could one person be? She'd been down this path before, and it had ended in disaster, heartbreak, professional disgrace… None of which she planned on repeating. Sarah's little fantasy must have tripped some switch in her brain, turning her back into a complete idiot who let her libido lead her. She needed to put this evening back on its professional feet, and she racked her brain for an appropriate, *neutral* topic.

Will was saying something, but her heart thudded in her ears, drowning out his words as he leaned toward her. The couch seemed to shrink, moving him closer to her, and the temperature in the room rose several degrees. How'd she end up so close to him? So close she could see his eyes darken?

Her heartbeat accelerated. Rational thoughts clamored to be heard, but were easily brushed aside as those hazel eyes swept over her, affecting her senses as strongly as a caress.

When his hand reached out to gently brush her arm, she felt the hairs rise from the electricity before he even touched her.

"Gwen?"

The question was a whisper, his lips just inches from hers, and instead of answering, she let her eyes slide closed in response.

"Will? Gwen? Where are you guys?"

Evie's voice snapped them apart and sent them to opposite ends of the sofa moments before her head peered around the corner.

Damn, damn, double damn. Her heart was racing—from desire or adrenaline, she didn't know. While her hormones protested at the interruption, the logical, rational part of her brain kicked back in and sent up a word of thanks at Evie's perfect timing.

Evie looked confused. "Did I interrupt something?"

Only my latest attempt at career suicide.

Will coughed and dragged a hand through his hair. Gwen gave herself a strong mental shake and plastered a serene smile on her face. "Of course not."

"I came to apologize. For losing my temper, I mean. I hope I didn't ruin dinner for everyone." After a small pause, she added, "Is Uncle Marcus mad?"

Gwen decided to leave this opening to Will. He was the "parent" in this situation, after all, and she was just the hired help. *Remember that, Gwennie.*

"No one's mad at you. We were just a bit shocked. You will need to guard that temper of yours in the future, though. It might not fly well in the dining room of the Club."

Gwen simply nodded her agreement.

"But, Will, you know I'm right. You shouldn't have your BlackBerry at the table. If I have to behave, so do you."

Gwen cleared her throat, desperate for the chance to escape. "Um, I find that I'm really exhausted all of a sudden, and since Evie and I have a big day tomorrow, I'm going to head on to bed." She wanted to be out of there before Evie left; there was no way she was ready to deal with what almost happened. She then rushed for the safety of her bedroom before either Harrison could say anything.

That had been close. Too close.

CHAPTER FIVE

TAKING Evie shopping had seemed like such a good idea at the time. She'd even enjoyed the morning's activities—haircuts, manicures, pedicures, lunch in the Neiman Marcus restaurant. Evie's need for female companionship and her obvious enjoyment of such a girly day out kept a smile on Gwen's face.

But that almost-but-not-quite moment of the night before kept haunting her. She might have had more Will-free thoughts if Evie could go longer than ten minutes without mentioning him. Or if Evie didn't share so many mannerisms with Will that a tilt of her head or a certain phrase didn't make her think of him.

It was bad enough she'd spent hours staring at the ceiling last night replaying each and every second of her entire short history with Will in her head, trying to figure out when her professional working relationship with the man had veered wildly off-track. Spending the morning trying not to moon over the man while still spending time with his sister…well, that was a new exercise in personal torture.

And the torture wasn't over yet. The instant connection between her young charge and her sister should have clued her in. Their kindred shopping spirits recognized each other instantly, and Gwen resigned herself to a very long afternoon.

Sarah had commandeered a private room normally reserved

by the personal shoppers to Dallas's elite. Using the information Gwen e-mailed the day before, Sarah created a personal store for Evie where everything was exactly the right color, size and fit for her body type. Entire outfits, complete with shoes and accessories, hung on rolling racks lining the walls.

Evie started out hesitantly, seeming unsure of style and overwhelmed by the choices. It didn't take long, though, for her inner fashionista to emerge, and soon she sorted through the racks like a pro. Haute couture welcomed her with open arms, and Evie was still going strong three hours later.

She'd even worn out Sarah, who Gwen thought never tired of shopping.

Safely ensconced on an out-of-the-way couch, she kept half an eye on Evie's "yes" pile to be sure nothing violated the brief list of fashion taboos provided by Marcus and Will and spent the time brooding. Unfortunately she couldn't find any answers or reasonable explanations for her behavior.

Sarah eventually turned Evie over to one of the Personal Shoppers with the excuse that Evie would need one in the future anyway, and tiptoed carefully through the colorful mess to Gwen's sofa.

"The child can shop." Sarah slid her feet out of their purple slingbacks and wiggled her toes in relief.

Gwen laughed. "That she can. I'm exhausted just watching."

"She's a natural. Great sense of style and an eye for what works. She'll be a real trendsetter in a couple of years."

"I'm just glad Parkline has a uniform, or else I'd be sitting here for *days*."

Sarah chuckled. "All that's really left is formal wear and she only needs one or two right now. Chris from Lingerie is on her way, so it should wind down after that. Out of curiosity, does she have a spending limit?"

Gwen watched as assistants slid Evie's purchases into giant shopping bags. "I guess not. At least not that I was told." Waving in the direction of the growing pile, she asked, "Do y'all deliver?"

"Looking at the commission Liza is about to earn off Evie, I'm sure she'll work something out."

"Thank goodness."

Sarah handed her a bottle of water. "Speaking of working out, how's everything going with the handsome-yet-infuriating Will Harrison?"

Oh, great. Exactly the conversation she didn't want to have. "About the same. Evie called him on using his BlackBerry at the table last night."

"She didn't!"

"Oh, yes, she did. In front of Marcus Heatherton."

Sarah's jaw dropped. "You must have been dying."

"That's one way to put it."

"What'd he say?"

"Marcus or Will?"

"Will, silly. Like I care about what Pillar-of-Society Marcus Heatherton thinks."

"Nothing actually. Evie's remark kind of got lost in the whole temper fit she had, so I never heard him address it."

"But after dinner, surely one of you said something."

Heat rushed to her cheeks as the image of Will leaning toward her on the couch flashed in her mind. "Um…not really…um, we were talking about, um, other things."

"Gwennie…" Sarah tucked her feet under her and leaned in. "You're blushing. What aren't you telling me?"

Her sister knew her too well. "I'm not telling you anything."

"So there is *something* to tell."

"I mean, I'm *not* not telling you anything. Or nothing. Or…you know what I mean." Flustered, she unscrewed the top of her water bottle and took a long drink.

"Did you and Will…" Sarah glanced around quickly, but the assistants had moved on and Evie and her personal shopper were still chattering away in the dressing room. "Did you two, you know?"

"No!" Gwen's ears were burning from the blush. She probably looked like an overripe tomato by now. "I barely know him, Sarah. Jeez. Get your mind out of the gutter."

"But something happened or else you wouldn't be that attractive shade of red. Will made a play, then."

"No." Lord, was that tiny voice hers? "I mean, sorta. Maybe he did?" This was embarrassing.

"Ah." Sarah got to use her all-knowing worldly-wise Big Sister Voice. "I'm going to assume there was no actual physical contact, right?"

Gwen nodded.

"But from the tone of your voice, it sounds like you wanted him to. Well? Do you, Gwennie?"

Exhausted from asking herself the same thing, Gwen gave up trying to fend off her sister's questions and gave in to the desire to unload on someone. "Sometimes. Wait, let me finish," she said as Sarah started to interrupt. "God knows the man is handsome and charming and enough to make any red-blooded woman lust after him. But developing a crush on Will would be *bad*. Bad for me. Bad for this job. Bad for my whole career, possibly."

"But you never know. Maybe he's getting a little crush on you, too."

Gwen snorted. "Not likely. I simply train the Princesses—I don't get Prince Charming."

"There's a first time for everything."

She spared another quick glance around. "We both know what happened the last time I got involved with my boss. I lost my job. I had to leave *town*, for God's sake. I'm not stupid enough to make that same mistake twice."

"No, you let David offer you up like a sacrificial lamb to save his own sorry skin and you slunk out of D.C. with your tail between your legs."

"My reputation was shot. No one would have hired me after that fiasco."

"That's an exaggeration." Sarah held up a hand to keep her from interrupting. "It doesn't matter now. It's over and done with and you've established yourself here. You're older and wiser and you have a sterling reputation. I don't see any reason why you can't explore a possible romantic relationship with an attractive man—"

"Whom I just happen to work for?" Had Sarah lost her mind completely this time?

"This is a bit different. David was your boss. Will Harrison is your client."

"You're splitting hairs. And any way you look at it, it still leads to the same disastrous end." Gwen closed her eyes and took a deep breath. "I just need to start dating again. Got anyone in mind?"

"You mean other than Will?" she smirked.

"Sarah, *please.*"

"I'll think about it. Meanwhile—"

A flash of ice-blue caught her eye and she turned. "Evie!" How long had she been standing there? She searched Evie's face for a sign she'd overhead their whispered conversation, but Evie seemed to be fully focused on twirling in front of the mirror.

Sarah shot her a look that said the conversation wasn't over, and Gwen made a mental note to screen her calls for the next few days. She had enough on her plate without adding Sarah's overromanticized matchmaking.

But Sarah was right about one thing. She wasn't the same naive girl she was five years ago. Last night's odd moment with Will could be—would *have* to be—forgotten. She'd just needed a reminder of how far she'd come.

Will knew he should be more concerned about the fact Nancy was ill and less irritated because it threw his life into disarray, but it was increasingly hard to do so when the temp sent up from HR was next to worthless. Maybe "worthless" was too harsh of a word; Nancy spoiled him with her efficiency and her ability to know what he needed without him having to spell it out. The only task the temp, Jenni, managed to complete in the last five hours was ordering flowers for Nancy. Everything else lay in various stages of completion on her desk.

He sincerely hoped Nancy got well quickly, because, damn it, he wanted his secretary back.

Now Jenni wasn't answering her intercom. This was ridiculous. Cursing, he made a list of everything that absolutely had to be done today, carried it to Nancy's desk and stuck it to the computer screen. When Jenni came back from wherever the hell she'd disappeared to, she'd have no reason not to see it.

A folder labeled "G. Sawyer" caught his eye. Why would that be on Nancy's desk? He opened it and found copies of the contract and nondisclosure agreement inside, as well as a check from his personal account for the full amount of Gwen's services. Nancy must have written the check the afternoon before but not had time to give it to him for his signature. He removed the check and left a sticky note for Nancy explaining he would deliver it personally. He placed the folder back in Nancy's in-box, and went back to his office.

It was three-thirty on a Friday afternoon. Without Nancy, much of his normal daily business had come to a complete halt, and it made zero sense to try to work on anything important. The late summer sunshine streamed through the wall of windows.

What the hell. His e-mail in-box was empty. The silence from the offices surrounding his meant most of the executive staff had left early. He should give himself a break and cut out early as well. He could take Evie and Gwen out to dinner.

Whistling, he packed up and called it a day. His receptionist stuttered as he walked by and wished her a good weekend. The security guard in the lobby checked his watch, confusion evident on his face. How long had it been since he'd left the office early?

He called home only to be informed by Mrs. Gray that Evie and Gwen weren't back from their shopping trip yet. He gave her the evening off and tried Evie on her cell phone.

"Did you have fun shopping?"

"It was amazing, Will. I found the most awesome dress for the Med Ball, and Sarah and Liza had like the entire store in my size in the dressing room and all I had to do was try stuff on."

Evie bubbled over with excitement. Something else he owed Gwen for: making Evie smile. "Sarah and Liza?"

"Sarah's Gwen's sister. She's great, but not as great as Gwen. Liza's my new personal shopper."

Personal shopper? "Remind me I want my credit card back."

"Oh, no problem. Liza set me up my own account."

Gwen laughed in the background, and Evie kept chattering away. When she paused for breath, he interrupted. "Are y'all done for the day?"

Evie relayed the question to Gwen, and he thought he heard an "Oh, definitely" before Evie replied, "I guess so."

"How about I take you to dinner tonight? I gave Mrs. Gray the night off, and maybe we could catch a movie afterward."

"Can Gwen come, too?"

"If she'd like."

Evie's voice muffled as she invited Gwen to join them for dinner and a movie. He didn't realize he was holding his breath until Evie came back on the line.

"She says yes, but not any place fancy. She didn't pack any dressy clothes."

He was oddly pleased at the way this was working out. "That will work. I'm on my way home now, so I'll see you in a little bit."

"You're on your way home *now?*" Evie sounded shocked.

"Well, yes. Is that a problem?"

"No, you just never leave work early."

She made him sound like some kind of workaholic. Maybe in her eyes he was.

Traffic was light and he made it home in record time. The doorman looked surprised to see him and asked if everything was all right. Okay, he really was working too much.

The quiet of the apartment felt unusual now, whereas in the past he'd never noticed the silence. He turned on the TV for background noise—first to the twenty-four-hours news channel, then changed his mind and scrolled through the channels for something else. He settled on a bio-documentary on John Lennon and grabbed a beer from the fridge. He tossed his tie on the coffee table before propping his feet on it, sipped his beer, and waited for Evie and Gwen to get home.

He didn't have to wait very long. Evie burst through the front door still talking a mile a minute to Gwen about something called espadrilles before interrupting herself to shout, "Will, we're home! Come see what I got!"

Hard on the heels of her words, Evie and Gwen turned the corner into the living room, weighed down by what had to be a large portion of Neiman Marcus's stock. Ricky, the doorman, followed, his arms also overflowing.

Will flashed on a memory of Evie's mother returning from marathon shopping in the early days of her marriage loaded down in much the same way. Evie must have inherited the gene from Rachel. "Did you leave anything at the store?"

"Just the stuff that needs to be altered. It won't be ready until next week." Evie was already headfirst in one of the bags, pulling out clothes and shoes for him to see.

Gwen's smile was tired as she off-loaded bags and boxes and took bags from Ricky's outstretched arms. "Thanks for saving us another trip."

"My pleasure, Miss Sawyer. Miss Evie must've really enjoyed herself today."

"I think she did." Gwen graced Ricky with a smile that had Ricky blushing behind his freckles.

"I'm glad to hear it."

"So am I," Will added, as Ricky pocketed a hefty tip and left. "But you look worn-out."

Gwen sank to the couch and toed off her shoes. "Evie is a power shopper. I'm not. I'm *never* doing that again."

"From the looks of it, she'll never need to shop again."

Gwen closed her eyes and leaned her head back. "Just wait until the new spring lines come out."

Evie continued to rifle through bags, and clothing piled up around her.

"Evie, start taking all this back to your room."

"Okay. Gwen, do you—? Never mind. I've got it. You just stay there and…and…relax." She scooped up an armload and disappeared.

Gwen opened one eye. "What was that about?"

He sat next to her. "Remorse, maybe?"

"Trust me, the shopping elite care not who they exhaust in their quest." Her eyes slid closed again, and the corners of her mouth twitched. "My sister says she has a good eye for style. She's going to be a sensation."

For the first time since he'd met her, Gwen seemed fully relaxed. Since her eyes were closed, he allowed himself to study her, his eyes roaming freely over the arch of her dark eyebrows, the curve of her cheek, and the line of her jaw. Her hair fanned behind her, the loose curls snaking along the back of the couch toward his hands. She had a beautiful, elegant profile, and he mentally traced the line down her face, over a soft neck until the chain of her necklace drew his eye to a pendant nestled at the top of gently sloping cleavage.

He had no business ogling the woman, but she intrigued

him and stirred his blood in a way he hadn't felt in a long time. Unable to stop himself, he reached for the lock of hair that fell across her shoulder. He rubbed his fingers over its silkiness before tucking it gently behind her ear.

"*My* sister says you're the best. I think I might agree."

Gwen's eyes flew open at the quiet statement and a shiver slid down her neck from the touch of his fingers on her ear. She turned to meet his gaze, only to see a heat there she didn't expect.

Déjà vu. Same couch. Same desire pooling in her stomach, same fluttery feeling in her chest. As much as she'd tried to write last night off as an aberration, she couldn't deny the repeat of sensations that rippled over her when Will's eyes lit like that and the room shrank until there seemed to only be enough oxygen for one.

Will's hand slid down her jaw until his fingers cupped her chin. Heat moved over her skin, and she wanted nothing more than to curl into his hand.

Bad idea, remember? It would be oh-so-easy to fall into Will's arms, and every nerve ending in her body screamed at her to do so, but she couldn't.

Nothing good could come of this.

Oh, yes there could, her body argued.

Will's thumb stroked the sensitive skin under her chin, causing a shiver to run over her. She followed his gaze to the rapid rise and fall of her cleavage as her breathing grew shallow, watching in horror as her nipples hardened under his stare.

It took every bit of fortitude she had to pull away.

"Will, I…I…I need to go check on Evie. Excuse me."

Coward.

Will's confused look wasn't lost on her as she fled down the hallway. Music blared from behind Evie's closed door, so Gwen didn't bother to stop and knock.

In the safety of her bedroom, she collapsed across the bed

and tried to calm her rapid heartbeat. She stared at the ceiling and mentally recited her list of reasons why kissing Will would be a bad idea.

By the fourth time she made it through the complete list, she almost believed it. But once Evie was launched and she was back in her own house, she would *have* to start dating again.

She wasn't sure how long she lay there, but it seemed like only minutes later before Evie knocked at her door.

"Come in."

"Are you okay?" Evie's forehead furrowed when she saw Gwen on the bed.

"I'm fine. Just recuperating from your shopping trip. You nearly wore me out."

The furrow disappeared and Evie grinned. "Sarah warned me you were a lightweight. But it was fun, and if I haven't said 'thanks' already…"

"My pleasure, honey."

"Will sent me to tell you that he made dinner reservations, and we'll need to leave in half an hour to make it. So if you want to change or something…"

Gwen hesitated. She'd forgotten all about dinner. Considering what just happened, she should probably stay here. Better yet, she should pack and go home.

Evie picked up on her hesitation. "You are still coming, right? We're going to Milano's for pizza. I get to pick the movie, too. Please."

"Wouldn't you rather go with just Will? A little family time? You've been stuck with me all week."

"It'll be more fun if you come."

How could she say no when Evie looked so eager and hopeful? "All right. Give me a couple of minutes to freshen up."

"Cool. Will went to change, too, so we'll see you in a few."

Gwen fell back on the bed with a sigh. She was making way too much of next to nothing. She was probably no more than a blip on Will's radar—a "she's female, must flirt" kind of thing. She could control her hormones for dinner and a movie, and Evie would be there as a buffer.

Giving herself a hard mental slap to sort her brain out, she hauled herself off the bed and to the closet for something cute to wear.

CHAPTER SIX

"SO HOW am I supposed to eat this? Knife and fork?" Evie eye-balled the slice of pizza with everything like she'd never seen anything like it before.

"Easy. You pick it up and take a bite."

Evie giggled. "*Finally. Something I can eat with my fingers.*"

Gwen put on her best Miss Behavior voice. "But you must still eat with decorum." She winked, and Evie tore into the pizza with relish.

Will said something under his breath, and Evie erupted in another peal of giggles. He slid a piece of the pizza onto a plate and handed it to Gwen. She smiled her thanks, careful not to let her hand brush his as she took it.

So much for controlling her hormones. They'd been screaming at her when she'd run from the living room earlier, but they broke into new shrieks when she returned after changing. She'd known dinner would be a casual event and she'd heard Evie's remark about Will changing, but she hadn't been quite prepared when she walked in.

It was easier to remind herself of the distance she needed to keep from Will when he was in his suit and tie, but much harder when he appeared in a simple black T-shirt tucked in to body-hugging faded jeans. Her mouth had gone dry at the sight. He looked like the hero of some late-night movie, ready to peel the black T-shirt over his head and do something manly and sexy set to hard-rock music.

He was laughing with Evie, his dark hair falling across his forehead. When he turned that smile on her, she recited her mental list of Reasons This Would Be Bad until the flutters in her stomach calmed. And she kept repeating the reasons every time Will looked at her and started the flutters up again.

For the most part, it worked. Evie did make a good chaperone, talking nonstop and keeping the conversation in neutral areas. By the time they arrived at the restaurant, she felt she had it under control. As long as she avoided direct, extended eye contact with Will and kept a decent distance between them, she could act somewhat normal.

As she settled in to her second slice, Gwen realized—occasional shiver aside—she was enjoying herself.

They ate and talked about everything and nothing until her stomach hurt from laughing at Will's impersonations of Marcus and too much pizza. The movie theater was just down the block, and Evie suggested they walk off the monster dinner to make room for popcorn.

As Evie ran ahead to buy tickets, Will fell into step beside Gwen. They walked quietly for a moment down the tourist-lined streets of the West End. The night air was still slightly humid, but for a late summer night in Dallas, the weather couldn't have been nicer. The silence between them stretched with each step, until it changed from "companionable" to "awkward."

Searching for something to say, Gwen settled on, "Thank you for dinner."

Will nodded. "My pleasure. I'm glad you came with us." He shoved his hands into his back pockets and hunched his shoulders, a move so out of character with the man she thought she knew, she did a real double take. Will wasn't looking at her, though. His eyes were on Evie, and she got a lovely view of his strong profile.

"I guess I should apologize for earlier. I'm sorry I made you uncomfortable."

Why did he have to bring that back up? She'd been doing such a good job up until then. She took a deep breath. "Uncomfortable" would not be the word *she'd* have chosen, but she'd work with it. "Please don't worry about it. We'll just forget it, okay?"

He turned to face her, his features inscrutable, forcing her to stop walking. "Why?"

Why? "Because it will be easier for everyone if we pretend it didn't happen."

Will stepped closer to her, and she found herself eye level with the small hollow at the base of his throat. All she'd have to do is lean in…

"I mean, why were you so uncomfortable?"

"Oh." A dozen different reasons sprang to mind, but none seemed appropriate. She settled for a version of the truth. "Because I work for you, remember?"

"And?"

That wasn't enough? Maybe Will *was* the type to go fishing in the company pond. "It could also make it more difficult for me to work with Evie. You did want me to give her my full attention, correct?" Will didn't move, and every time she inhaled, the scent of him filled her. "Plus, it's hardly appropriate behavior."

"I guess I can't argue with that." Will's voice stayed bland.

You could try. No! What was she thinking?

Will stepped back and she could breathe more normally again. "Come on, Evie's waiting on us." He placed his hand on the small of her back again to steer her, and the heat made puddles of her insides.

Okay, so that went easier than expected. Case closed. Will seemed to agree with her, and as long as she kept her distance, she'd be fine. No more "almosts" and she'd get that embarrassing crush under control. She only had to hold it together for two more weeks.

Hopefully he'd have to work a lot and time would pass quickly.

Will didn't know if he should be insulted at the implication he could "just forget" the way she'd reacted to his touch and the desire he'd seen in her eyes or amused at how Gwen retreated behind that wall of politeness with some garbage about "appropriateness."

But he couldn't exactly push her any further while standing on the side of the street with Evie only a few yards away, either. He let Gwen put distance between them as she chatted with Evie and went to purchase popcorn and drinks. Evie produced the tickets to some blow 'em up thriller he'd never heard of, and he let her lead the way into the darkened theater.

Evie chose seats in the middle of the row about halfway up. When Evie sat, Gwen passed her to sit on the other side. Will flipped down the seat next to Evie and sat the vat of popcorn in her lap. As the trailers played, Evie fidgeted in her seat.

"Will, I can't see. Trade with me?"

The person in front of Evie didn't seem tall enough to block her vision, but he shrugged and switched seats. Evie handed him the popcorn and whispered, "Be sure to share with Gwen."

Evie could use some lessons in subtlety. He wondered which of her tutors could work that in to a lesson plan.

Not that he minded. His elbow brushed Gwen's on the armrest, and she pulled away with a whispered "Excuse me."

"Popcorn?"

"No, thank you." She fixed her eyes on the screen and ignored him as the movie started. Okay, so he couldn't honestly say she was ignoring him since watching the movie *was* technically what they were here to do, but she didn't look his way again.

He lost interest in the movie quickly, which was fine since he was far more interested in the woman sitting as far away from him as the small theater seat would allow. He didn't fully understand the magnetic pull of Gwen, but as he'd already discovered, it was nearly impossible to resist. His earlier resolve of not getting involved with his sister's tutor—much less a woman from outside his normal sphere—was rapidly eroding. They were both adults and the attraction was obviously mutual. As long as they kept things low-key, he couldn't think of a single good reason not to explore that mutual attraction—regardless of where it ranked on Miss Behavior's appropriateness scale.

Gwen continued to give him what he was beginning to call the Polite Treatment as they walked back to the car and during the drive home. An outsider would never surmise anything was wrong, and at no point could he say she was anything other than the perfect guest. She was just so stinking *polite,* and he knew it was a complete act.

Back at the apartment, he opened the door and held it for Evie and Gwen. Evie took a mere two steps inside before she stretched her arms over her head and yawned loudly.

"I'm pooped and going to bed. See you in the morning. G'nite, Will. G'nite, Gwen."

The kid was a terrible actress. But she was in her room with the door closed before her words quit echoing, and he was left alone with Gwen for the second time that day.

"I'm pretty beat myself," Gwen said a bit too brightly. "I think I'll head on to bed, too. Thank yo—"

He interrupted her, knowing full well how interrupting hovered close to the top of Gwen's list of pet peeves, but there was really no avoiding it. He wasn't going to let her retreat behind closed doors just yet. "There are a couple of things we still need to clear up."

"Really? What do you…" She trailed off as he closed the

slight distance between them, and she took two small steps backward only to find her back against the foyer wall. Her eyes flashed as he took advantage of her position and moved within inches of her body.

Reaching out, he captured the errant lock of hair that draped across her shoulder again. Twisting it around his finger, he played with the silky strand until her breathing became shallow, and she asked, *"What,* Will?"

"First, business and pleasure are two totally separate situations. I'm not one to confuse the two, and I'm surely not going to deny myself one because of the other. I hired you to work with Evie. This—" he released her hair, only to move his hand to the elegant column of her neck, pleased to feel the pulse thumping wildly there "—has nothing to do with that."

Gwen's eyes widened as his other hand slid up her neck to cradle her jaw. She leaned in toward him, and he felt his own heartbeat accelerate.

"Secondly, Miss Behavior, I don't give a damn about what's appropriate."

Oh. *My.* Gwen's thoughts scrambled, and her libido woke with a mighty cheer. Will's face hovered inches from hers, and for the first time in a long time, she didn't give a damn about appropriateness, either.

Yes, you do, her conscience argued, but it was a token protest rapidly smothered by the need that had been simmering all evening and burst to life at the touch of his fingers on her skin.

She lifted her hand to his chest, where his heart thumped heavily with excitement. It slid, seemingly of its own accord, up over soft black cotton until she found the warm skin at his collar. Will's breath hissed as her fingers moved around strong muscles to his nape and slid up to tangle in his silky hair. *Just one little kiss, that's all...*

That slight pressure seemed to be all the permission he

needed, and his mouth closed on hers. A lifetime of civility hadn't prepared her for the raw power of his kiss or the force of sensations that ripped through her. Heat. Hunger. Desire.

His tongue slipped across hers, tasting and tempting, and demanding a response, as lightning bolted down her spine and lit her on fire. Her hand tightened in his hair, holding him to her as she melted from the contact.

The man can kiss, she thought, before he trailed scorching kisses along her jaw to the soft spot at the base of her ear. All remaining rational thought fled when Will nipped the sensitive skin with strong teeth, and she gave over to the purely carnal thrill of his touch.

And, oh, oh, oh…his touch. Will's hands moved from her neck, massaging circles down the tense muscles of her back, to the indentation of her waist, where his fingers splayed for a momentary squeeze before pulling her body into complete contact with his.

Hard thighs. Powerful chest. Strong arms holding her against him. She rose on tiptoe, aligning her hips with the straining bulge in his jeans. Will groaned, his hand moving to the small of her back to hold her in place. Unadulterated want slammed into her, leaving her reeling on wobbly legs.

"Will," she whispered against his lips.

He broke the kiss, his breath coming in short pants and looked down at her with heavy-lidded eyes. A heartbeat later, he set her away from him, keeping his hands on her hips to steady her.

"I know." He exhaled and dropped his forehead to hers. "I got a bit carried away there."

Coherent thought eluded her. What? What was he talking about? *Why* was he talking? Her foggy brain wouldn't clear and she tried to make sense of his words. Will held her hand loosely as he led her down the long hallway to her bedroom door.

Twining his fingers in hers, he kissed her knuckles before

brushing his lips gently across her mouth. "Good night, Gwen. See you in the morning."

Good night? What? No! Clarity arrived moments too late as she watched Will disappear into his bedroom at the end of the hall.

No, no, no! Damn it! Needy nerve cells screamed at her to call him back, to bang on his door and demand he continue where he left off. Her skin tingled with electrical afterglow and she throbbed in sync with her heartbeat. She took a step toward Will's closed door.

Thankfully her sanity chose that moment to return. What on earth was she doing? Even worse, what had she done? Making out with Will Harrison in the hallway while his teenage sister was just footsteps away? Not to mention the whole "it would be bad to sleep with your boss" thing. She'd lost what was left of her cotton-picking mind with that one kiss.

One mind-blowing, toe-curling, too-good-to-be-real kiss.

She retreated to her bedroom and closed the door softly behind her. Kicking off her shoes, she left them where they landed and padded across the carpet to the cool marble tiles of the adjoining bath. Cold water splashed on her face helped bring her back to reality, and a sigh-by-sigh replay of what just happened flashed across her mind in Technicolor.

She closed her eyes and groaned. She'd practically climbed him like a tree. But, oh, what a fine tree he was, all heat and hardness....

Gwen forced her eyes open, banishing the visual, only to grimace at her reflection in the mirror. Her hair stood at crazy angles, and a vague memory of his hands tangling in it and massaging her scalp stirred. A flush rode high on her cheekbones. Her mouth looked swollen. Water droplets glistened at her temples, and she remembered how Will had kissed her there, too.

She could hear water running in the bathroom next to hers.

Will was in the shower. That was all her libido needed to roar back to life—the thought of Will warm and slick and soapy….

This had to stop. She visualized the place setting for a seven-course formal dinner that included a fish course and a cheese course. Keeping that image firmly in the front of her mind, she named each piece of the setting by course, hoping it would be unsexy enough to banish Will's kisses from her immediate memory. Gwen grabbed her brush from the countertop and attacked the tangles in her hair.

"Bread plate, butter knife, salad fork…" Six courses later, she'd managed to brush her hair and teeth and change into her pajamas without too much fantasizing. She turned off the lights and crawled under the covers. In the dark, fish forks weren't much of a distraction, and she returned to her list of Reasons This Would Be Bad and focused intently on reason number one: potential career suicide. Again.

Things had started out exciting with David, too—okay, he wasn't nearly as tantalizing as Will, but at twenty-two, she'd been much more naive and David had seemed so perfect. Handsome, successful, charming. As the top student in her class, she'd scored the most coveted of all possible internships: working for the most prestigious lobby group in D.C. When David offered her the chance to work on a plum project, she'd jumped at the opportunity, even if it did mean spending long hours after five in the close confines of his office—just the two of them. She'd fallen hard, and thought David felt the same, at least until *his* boss found them in a compromising position in the supply closet, and she'd become a Washington cliché in seconds flat. She'd found out then exactly how much David "loved" her. He managed to save *his* career by painting her as a grasping opportunist trying to sleep her way into a great job, and when the project went to hell days later, he let her take the fall for that as well—even though the blame should have landed solely at his feet. She'd been too heartbroken to fight back—even if she'd known how—and between the gossip about her personal life and the speculation of how she managed to flub such an important project, her job leads dried up.

Her broken heart had mended quickly thanks to the anger at being used, but it had taken a lot longer to get over the shame of it, and the five years she'd spent in Dallas building a spotless reputation had given her new perspective on the whole sordid affair. She knew better now.

Then *why* had she ended up in Will's arms, practically begging him to take her off to bed with him? She needed to be careful. Even if her heart could take another hit, her career certainly couldn't.

Sleep was a long time coming.

Cold showers always worked like magic in movies and books. But the characters in movies and books obviously hadn't been kissing Gwen, because the longest, coldest shower in the universe hadn't removed the lingering imprint of Gwen's body from his or chased away the haunting scent of her skin.

Will toweled off, scrubbing at the chill bumps on his skin, and tried to think of something other than the feel of Gwen's tongue sliding over his like a promise.

The fact he'd practically mauled her in the hallway popped to mind, followed closely by the realization that he'd have no one to blame but himself if Gwen packed up her tea set and moved out first thing in the morning. He hadn't intended for the kiss to go that far, that quickly. He just hadn't been prepared for the desire that had slammed into him at the taste of her.

Still…if she hadn't brought him to his senses when she did, he'd still be happily pawing her in his foyer. Or maybe they'd have made it as far as his room by now.

Gwen felt the attraction between them. That much he knew. She'd been an active and willing participant in that kiss, even if she was probably flogging herself with the inappropriateness of it by now.

Provided Gwen didn't hightail it out of here tomorrow at the crack of dawn, he'd start changing her mind about what constituted "appropriate."

That should prove interesting.

His body still wanted to knock on Miss Behavior's door and, well, *misbehave*, but it was under control enough for him to crawl under the covers and contemplate his next move instead. It wasn't often that Fate delivered an interesting, attractive woman to his door like a belated birthday present, and he wasn't going to waste the opportunity.

Vague notions he should use the late-night quiet to break out his laptop and work for a while intruded briefly, but, for once, he was completely uninterested in HarCorp and business problems. He chuckled. There was a first time for everything.

His plans for Gwen were *much* more interesting to think about. In no time at all, he found himself in need of another cold shower.

CHAPTER SEVEN

GOING back to her regular life in two weeks was going to suck. Gwen sat beside the rooftop pool of Will's condo building—a private pool only for use by the residents of the top three floors—and tried to read and relax.

A striped cabana shaded her from the sun, and as she leaned back against matching pillows with a cold drink, she half expected a cabana boy to show up with a bottle of suntan oil and offer to rub some on her.

Evie lay on her stomach in the sun beside the cabana, her feet moving slightly in rhythm to the music on her iPod as she conjugated a series of irregular French verbs. A Geometry text topped a pile of books next to her. Yesterday's shopping, dinner, and movie extravaganza must have put her behind on her homework. One of the etiquette books stuck out at an awkward angle from her pile as well; a ribboned bookmark indicated Evie was about halfway finished.

Fluffy white clouds spotted an otherwise clear blue sky, and a breeze fluttered the pages of the book in her lap. By all definitions, it was a perfect day. She would be relaxed and lost in her book by now if not for the constant sound of splashes coming from the pool.

The noise wasn't what was disturbing her. The *cause* of the splashes was. If she lifted her eyes from her book she wasn't actually reading, she'd see the pool and the powerful body making lap after lap. Will moved through the water like a pro, each stroke strong and sure. The sight of the water sliding over his body sent her mind back to the thought of Will in the shower the night before, which immediately sent her thoughts back to the kiss in the foyer.

Not that she needed much help remembering that kiss. The feel of Will was branded into her skin. She could still taste him on her lips. What little sleep she'd managed last night had only allowed her mind to carry that kiss to erotic extremes in her dreams.

After such a restless night, she crawled out of bed early to head to Sarah's house for coffee and a visit with Letitia. The spoiled cat curled into her lap purring and refused to move, keeping her pinned in the chair and under her sister's inquisition much longer than comfortable. *How* Sarah had been able to tell Gwen had been thoroughly kissed, she'd never know, but Sarah wouldn't rest until every last embarrassing detail was dissected to her satisfaction.

Yet Gwen still didn't have any concrete answers—not for why she'd kissed Will, not for what she wanted to happen next, nothing. After two hours and two pots of coffee, she'd finally been able to escape her sister—who really wasn't helping the situation *at all*—and headed back to what was beginning to feel like the lion's den.

Gwen hadn't thought to ask about how Evie and Will spent their weekends, and she'd returned to the condo to find them headed to the pool. Against her better judgment, she allowed them to convince her to join them. She regretted the decision instantly after Will stripped down to nothing but a pair of black swim trunks. Thankfully her sunglasses hid the unladylike and unflattering way her eyes had to have bugged at the sight of all that bronze skin and hard muscle. She'd run to the safety of the cabana immediately, very glad when Will dove straight into the water instead of taking the other lounge chair.

Now Evie was engrossed with homework, and she was having a hard time pulling her eyes away from Will.

It's rude to stare. But next to impossible not to, she told herself. She lost count of how many laps he completed long ago, but he showed no signs of tiring. That explained the tan. And the shoulders. And the chest... She reached for her water bottle, rolling it across the heated skin of her neck and chest before taking a long drink to try to lower her temperature. With a sigh, she tried to concentrate on the words in her book, thankful neither Evie nor Will were paying her any attention at all.

Water splashed at her feet, and she looked up to see Will, all wet and wonderful, standing in the shallow end of the pool, ready to send another stream of water at Evie.

"Hey!" Evie shouted, "You're getting my homework all wet."

"Aren't you two coming in?" Water dripped from his dark hair onto his shoulders before joining the rivulets running down his chest and over the muscles of his stomach. *Her* stomach contracted at the sight.

Mercy. The man should be on billboards.

Evie closed her notebook and took a running dive into the deep end. As graceful in the water as her brother—if not more so—she swam the length of the pool and surfaced not far from Will.

Cupping her hand, Evie expertly sent a spray of water straight into Will's face. He shook it off, sending droplets in all directions.

"Oh, big mistake, squirt."

Evie squealed as Will pelted her with sheets of water until she begged for mercy. For Gwen, it was a much-needed distraction from her brooding and drooling over Will. When he stopped, Evie sent one last spray his way, then swam quickly to Gwen's side of the pool.

Will's arm pulled back, ready to continue.

"Better not, Will. You'll get Gwen all wet."

Gwen laughed. "Oh, no, don't come running to me for protection. You're on your own, kiddo." She made a show of wrapping her book in a towel and placing it out of immediate water damage.

"Traitor," Evie wailed before she disappeared under a wall of water that drenched Gwen as well.

The cold water took her breath away. She pushed her sopping bangs out of her eyes to see a completely unrepentant Will grinning at her.

Something lightened inside of her chest, and she grabbed the feeling and the moment with both hands.

"Oh, you are so dead meat, Will Harrison. Come on, Evie."

That was all the warning he got before she jumped feet-first into the pool and joined Evie in sending as much water at Will as humanly possible.

She wasn't as good at it as Will and Evie, but at least two-against-one helped even the odds a bit. Will fought back, using both arms and hands to keep the water flying as he moved in her direction and backed her up against the pool wall, leaving her helpless under the constant fall of water.

Evie, that little traitor, switched allegiances and joined Will in dousing her.

She needed to get off the wall and back in the open. Gwen calculated her move, waited for the right second, then slid quickly to her left, planning to go under, push off the wall and slip quickly between them.

No such luck. Will moved at just the wrong—or possibly right—moment, and her push off the wall sent her barreling straight into him. Those strong arms locked around her and pulled her to the surface, keeping her trapped against his chest.

His wet, hard, stuff-of-fantasies *bare* chest.

Gwen's shout of outrage died in her throat as the bare skin

of her back burned where it pressed against his. She gasped instead. Every memory of last night's kiss and the fantasies it inspired flashed across her mind.

"You got her, Will!"

"Indeed I do." He lowered his voice and dropped his head closer to her ear. "Now what should I do with you?"

She shivered as much from the whisper of breath across her ear as from his words. Will answered her shiver with a squeeze that pressed her more firmly against him. Every inch of her—from shoulders to ankles—sizzled at the contact. The seconds stretched out as she reveled in the sensation. But the hard flesh nestling right above the swell of her bottom brought her attention rocketing back to his whispered question.

"I call for a t-truce."

Will chuckled in her ear and whispered, "Coward." But he did release her, and she sank into the cool water, allowing it to balm her burning skin. With a knowing wink in her direction that only scrambled her thoughts more, Will swam away to the other side of the pool.

Gwen climbed the ladder on trembling legs and retreated to the relative safety of the cabana. She would not take the bait of being called a coward, but she wasn't going to run and hide in her room, either. She placed her sunglasses firmly in front of her eyes, buried her nose in her book and tried to calm her rapid breathing.

Evie produced a Frisbee, and she and Will began a noisy game of catch, giving her a much-needed opportunity to mentally regroup.

Sarah had been brutally direct this morning with her analysis of the situation. *"Sounds to me like the attraction is mutual."*

Okay, so maybe it was. She couldn't deny or ignore Will's attraction to her, and she knew for damn certain she wasn't immune to him. Sarah had listened to the full list of Reasons

This Would Be Bad, but countered with romanticized possibilities that would ease any worst-case scenarios.

There was no romanticizing or outthinking the biggest Bad Reason, however, and that Reason was rapidly moving to the top of her list.

And that Reason would be how much she liked Will. *Really* liked Will. Irritating BlackBerry, bouts of overbearing arrogance and all, she'd finally found a man she liked to talk to. One who could surprise her and make her laugh at the strangest things. Everything she thought she knew about him had proved false; instead she'd found a handsome, charming, funny guy who was smart and successful and cared about his little sister.

She, thanks to the papers and her debs, knew a lot about his dating history. He wasn't exactly a playboy, but he did play the field one socialite at a time. That, coupled with what she knew about Will's workaholic tendencies and bolstered by some casual comments dropped by Evie, made *liking* Will a danger. Maybe Will wasn't looking for anything permanent, but could she enjoy what he did have to offer? It would be one fabulous ride—while it lasted. Could Sarah be right and the Worst-Case Scenarios actually be fixable? Could her heart and her ego take the hit if it didn't work out?

Evie, though, was still a sticking point. She didn't want Evie to get hurt. Had Will even given thought how his serial-dating technique might affect a fifteen-year-old?

And could she handle being the next installment in that serial? She remembered the feel of Will's skin against hers and the taste of him under her lips. The gooseflesh that rose on her arms answered part of the question: her body was more than willing to give it a shot.

"Gwen?"

Gwen snapped out of her reverie to find Evie and Will standing in front of her with identical puzzled expressions.

Evie had a sarong tied around her slim hips, and Will had a towel slung over his shoulders. Her eyes followed the thin line of hair down to where it disappeared into the waistband of his trunks, and her mouth went dry.

Oh, yeah, her body was more than willing.

"Book not any good?" Evie asked.

"Excuse me?" She tore her eyes from Will's abs and tried to focus. Both of them were merely damp, meaning they'd been out of the pool for a while.

"You're not reading it. You're staring at it."

"You seemed to be pretty far away," Will added.

She looked at the book in her hands. "Oh. Yeah. Um…" She fumbled. "I was dozing a bit there. I didn't sleep well last night."

Will's eyebrow cocked up and she realized where he'd gone with her statement. *Ugh.*

Evie, though, accepted her statement at face value. "Are you hungry, then? We're going to order some take-out."

"Sure."

Evie went for the elevator while Gwen packed up her things, very aware Will was watching her.

"You were thinking pretty hard there. Come to any conclusions?"

Good Lord, was she that easy to read? Or maybe he wasn't talking about *that.* She could have easily been thinking about a number of different problems in her life. Even the strictest tenets of etiquette didn't require her to give him a complete answer, so she settled for one that would give him something to think about.

If he'd been thinking in *that* direction.

"Maybe I did."

Since the day he'd brought Evie home, he'd never wished her gone. Not once. He may have briefly considered boarding school for her, but that was because he didn't feel like a suitable person to raise a teenager, not because of her. She had her moments when he could cheerfully strangle her, but he wasn't too proud to admit he adored the kid.

So he freely embraced the guilt that prodded at him when he wished Evie somewhere else tonight. Not *gone,* just not here in the room with him and Gwen. Her room would work just fine, but at nine on a Saturday night, he had no good reason to suggest she go there.

Even if he could come up with a good reason, he was hesitant to do so. Evie was having such a good time. So was he. Even Gwen had eventually relaxed and seemed to be enjoying herself. Take-out sandwiches and DVD movies, followed by Chinese take-out and now a game of Monopoly with no end in sight. He hadn't been near his BlackBerry all day, and the upcoming meeting with the Japanese seemed a long way away. It had easily been the best Saturday he'd had in ages, and as soon as Evie went to bed, it was going to get a lot better. That much he was sure of.

Gwen might try to hide behind that Miss Behavior wall of appropriate politeness, but he knew it was starting to crumble. Last night's kiss, the way her eyes had caressed him all day, the way he'd felt her shiver with desire against him in the pool today…the next step was inevitable. He knew it, and he was damn sure she knew it too.

So as much as he'd like to investigate that inevitability right this second, he could be patient and bide his time. He was content for the moment to relax against the sofa and nurse his beer while his sister beat them soundly at Monopoly.

Gwen sat across the game board from him, also on the floor, her bare feet with their bright red toes tucked underneath her. After her shower, she'd dressed in a pair of cutoffs and a white T-shirt, and her hair fell loose around her face. Without makeup, she looked even younger, and as she paid Evie for landing on Boardwalk, he wondered how old she was. At that moment, he realized he didn't know all that much about her.

Evie, of course, probably knew Gwen's entire life story by now; too bad he couldn't ask her. He settled for something simple and innocuous.

"So, Gwen, how did you come to be Miss Behavior?"

Gwen cocked her head, seemingly surprised at the question. "Well, that's kind of a long story."

He looked over at Evie, who was busy counting her piles of money with glee. "I think we have time while Miss Moneybags plays in her ill-gotten gains."

Evie stuck her tongue out at him. "You're just a sore loser. I'm going for another soda. Anyone want anything?"

Gwen shook her head, then settled back against a chair. "Well, I moved to Dallas five years ago after Sarah got her job at Neiman Marcus. I'd finished protocol training in D.C., done an internship and needed to land somewhere. I don't really have a hometown because we moved so much, and since my folks mentioned eventually retiring in Texas, this seemed like a good choice."

"I knew you didn't sound native."

"Nope. But my dad grew up in Houston, does that count?"

He nodded. "So how'd you end up on a Web site?"

She chuckled. "Accidentally, I assure you. I never planned to do anything with teenagers. But when I got to Dallas, I needed a job. I started working with a friend of mine who did some deb training on the side, and it worked out pretty well. I made a name for myself doing that without really meaning to. 'Miss Behavior' was a nickname my deb class gave me a few years ago, and when one of those debs started the TeenSpace site, she called and asked if I wanted to be one of the columnists. The rest is history."

"Sounds like you fell into the right job, though."

"Maybe. But I can't be Miss Behavior forever."

"Sarah says Gwen wants to ditch the debs and go back to working with grown-ups." Evie sat back in her place and eyeballed the stacks of money.

"Grown-ups?"

"Sarah needs to keep her mouth shut," Gwen muttered.

"Sarah says Gwen's going to bigger and better things one day, but she needs the debs right now because that's who's paying her rent," Evie continued.

That reminded him. Her check was still in his briefcase.

"Thank you, Evie. That's quite enough."

Gwen's carefully clipped tone made him laugh silently. He loved to watch Gwen wrap herself in politeness. Too bad he couldn't prod her more often.

"Gwen speaks Japanese, you know."

"Ev-ie!" Gwen looked ill at ease, but he didn't know why.

"Well, you do. I didn't know it was some kind of secret," Evie grumbled.

"You're right. It's not a secret." Gwen turned to him. "I'm not completely fluent, but I get by. I also speak German and a little French. No," she added as Evie perked up and opened her mouth to say something. "I won't conjugate those verbs for you. Madame Louise expects you to know them by Monday. Have you finished yet?"

Someone else might not have noticed the way Gwen subtly moved the topic away from herself, but Will did. And though he was more curious than ever to know more about her, he respected her desire for privacy—for the moment at least. Maybe it was some kind of lesson meant to teach Evie about polite conversation, and he shouldn't undermine Gwen's work to appease his own interest.

But he could use some help with his own Japanese lessons. Maybe Gwen would be willing to teach him a few phrases. The thought of private lessons with Gwen led him right back to his original wish that Evie would go to bed.

As if she'd read his mind, Evie stretched, looked at the game board pointedly and said, "If you guys will concede defeat, I'll go work on some French before I go to bed. I'm pooped."

Gwen's eyebrows went up as she glanced at the clock. It was still early, but he certainly wasn't going to argue with Evie's plan. It sounded great to him.

Once Evie left, Gwen began tidying up the game pieces. Her teeth worried her lower lip, and he wondered what she was thinking.

"Where does this go?" She indicated the box.

"Beats me. I didn't even know we owned the game." He took another long drink of his beer as Gwen rose up on her knees to place the game on the glass-topped coffee table and reached for her own glass.

She settled back in her original seat on the floor, her back against the chair and her legs stretched out in front of her. Silence stretched between them and without Evie in the room, the air became charged with electricity.

Only a few feet separated them, and he closed the distance easily, watching Gwen's eyes widen, then darken with unmistakable interest.

Will ran his hand down the silky skin of her arm and laced his fingers with hers. She didn't resist as he tugged her gently toward him, and when her pink tongue darted out to moisten her lips, what little blood was still circulating freely rushed to heat his skin.

Gwen cleared her throat. "Today was a great day."

He dipped his head to taste the soft skin on her neck and felt her shiver in response. "It's not over yet, you know."

She'd known this was going to happen. Her day of brooding may not have provided many answers, and she still wasn't sure this was the wisest course of action, but the tension inside her had her stretched to the breaking point. Will hadn't touched her since that moment in the pool, but the long, lazy looks that traveled over her as strongly as a physical caress had kept her on edge all afternoon.

She had two choices: turn tail and run or seize the moment. While retreat was the safer, far more rational choice, she'd lost the battle with her rational brain hours ago. She could be careful, try to safeguard her heart and her business, but she wasn't going to pass on what could be the most amazing man who'd ever crossed her path. Years of doing the prudent thing, of always weighing the benefits and minimizing the risks, hadn't netted her much beyond a job that didn't satisfy her and an existence that suddenly seemed rather blah and bland.

The sensation of Will's lips on her neck was far from bland, and she tilted her head back to provide him greater access. Heat rippled over her as his mouth traveled over her jaw and captured her lips.

Oh, yes. This was definitely worth the risk.

Gwen eagerly fitted her body against his, loving the feel of him, while his kiss wreaked havoc on her senses. She twined her arms around his neck, allowing her fingers to slide across the taut cords of muscles, and held on while the sensations tried to sweep her away.

She wanted to be closer, to feel more of him, to taste more of him. She pulled her mouth from his, gasping for air, and moved her lips to the same spot on his neck he'd found on her moments earlier.

She was rewarded with a hiss of pleasure as her tongue snaked out to taste his skin, and the hand that had been massaging her back in rhythm to his kiss moved down to her hip in a heat-filled caress.

Turning more fully toward him, Gwen slid her thigh over his, trying to get closer to the heat she craved. Will responded by capturing her mouth in another searing kiss, latching his hands around her hips, and lifting her until she straddled his legs.

Oh, *yesss*, she thought, as his hands locked over her buttocks and snugged her knees up next to his hips. Her new position gave her easy access to run her hands over the defined contours of his chest, over those wide shoulders, until she could bury her hands in his hair and hold his mouth against hers.

A growl of desire rumbled in Will's throat as his tongue mated wildly with hers. She gasped as his hand cupped her breast, his thumb dragging soft cotton over her distended nipple, and she arched back, allowing him greater access.

Will nuzzled her, and she cursed the T-shirt keeping his mouth from her skin. Every nerve ending screamed for his touch, and her body shook as pure want fired her blood. She wanted to feel his skin against hers, to revel in the magic his fingers worked on her, to let him soothe the ache growing deep inside her.

But not here. Sane thought clawed its way through her befuddled mind.

As if reading her mind, Will cupped his hands under her thighs and surged to his knees. "Not here. Evie might—"

She nodded, but he didn't release his hold on her.

"Hang on."

It took a second for Gwen to realize he meant that literally. Will got to his feet, and she clung to him like a vine on a tree as he padded quickly down the long hallway, past Evie's closed door and into the master suite at the far end.

Will barely paused as he entered, simply nudging the door closed with his shoulder before crossing what seemed like a huge expanse to deposit her on her feet next to the most luxurious bed she'd ever seen.

This is your last chance to back out, her conscience reminded her. She quickly stomped it back down. She wasn't going to worry about what might happen tomorrow—or the day after that. She could simply enjoy Will for the time she had him, and she'd have to trust she'd be able to make everything else work out.

That was her last fully lucid thought, as Will grabbed the hem of her shirt to pull it over her head. He thumbed the clasp of her bra open, tossing it to the floor with her shirt. Her shorts and panties quickly followed, and she stood naked in the half-light of the room.

Her breath came in short pants as his hungry eyes devoured her, and his fingers reached out to stroke across the slope of her breasts.

"Beautiful."

Emboldened, Gwen reached for the hem of his shirt and, with his help, it joined her clothes on the floor. She echoed his action, her fingers threading through the crisp hairs on his chest.

"I agree."

Will groaned as she touched him, the pads of her fingers finding his flat nipples and stroking over them. When she leaned forward to touch her tongue against one, he shuddered and grasped her shoulders.

Then she was on the bed, soft, cool sheets under her and the hard heat of Will covering her. *This* was heaven on earth, and she was beyond glad she hadn't talked herself out of experiencing it.

Those long, lean muscles bunched under her fingers as she traced them, memorizing their pull and play under the hot skin against hers. Shadows hid Will's face as he moved slowly down her body, making each touch of his tongue to her over-sensitized flesh an erotic surprise. In a daze, she closed her eyes and let the sensations ripple over her body unfettered as Will's hands slid over the muscles in her legs and his lips followed.

Strong teeth grazed the sensitive skin of her thigh, bringing her focus sharply back as Will draped that thigh across his shoulder and cupped her hips in his hands. One last feather-light kiss was all the warning she had before his mouth fastened on her and fire ignited in her veins.

She was mindless and shaking with need when Will finally settled between her thighs and slid into her in one smooth stroke. A hiss of pleasure escaped her as he settled into rhythm, one large hand resting on her hip to hold her in place as his body moved against hers.

Will caught her shout of pleasure in his mouth as she reached her climax, and moments later, he gave it back to her as he reached his. He relaxed on top of her, burying his face in her neck, and she could feel the pounding of his heart against her chest. Heart racing, breath coming in short gasps, she closed her eyes to enjoy the feel of his weight on her as she rubbed gentle circles on his shoulders.

Will finally lifted his head and kissed her softly before resting his forehead against hers.

"Can you breathe?"

She opened her eyes to see him staring at her, a bemused look on his face. Actual speech was out of the question for the moment, so she nodded.

"Good. 'Cause I may never move from this spot."

Warmth pooled in her chest before she could remind herself not to read too much into his words. But she relished them anyway and savored the afterglow of the moment.

When Will's breathing finally evened out, he rolled to his back and snuggled her against his side. His hands traced lazy circles over her arms and back and she relaxed into a delicious haze.

"Gwen?"

"Hmm?"

"You're not falling asleep, are you?"

Through her languor, she managed to crack one eye. Will's half smile and hooded eyes immediately chased her laziness away. "Nope."

The smile broadened briefly before his lips captured hers again and he pulled her atop him.

CHAPTER EIGHT

GWEN smeared aloe gel over the sunburn coloring her nose and cheeks a bright red. Looked like her ears needed some, too. The burn didn't hurt—yet—but it would before the night was out. She knew better than to hope it would fade to a tan; her fair skin only burned and peeled. Tanning was for people with better genetic luck.

From the other room, she heard her sister's ring tone for the third time in the last hour. Gwen ignored it as she examined the coloring on her neck and arms in the bathroom mirror. Sarah would just have to wait. She'd know something was up the second she heard Gwen's voice, and Gwen didn't feel like deconstructing the last twenty-four hours with her sister at the moment.

Of course, that would assume *she* knew what to make of the last twenty-four hours. Which she didn't. Not by a long shot.

She'd slept late this morning, waking only when Evie returned from swimming and pounded on her door with "Gwen! Are you alive?"

Gwen had a vague recollection of Will walking her to her own room in the wee hours of the morning. Exhausted and limp-limbed from Will's lovemaking, she'd crawled under the covers and slept like the dead. Or at least like the dead with very erotic dreams.

As she forced herself out of bed and crawled into the shower, she'd worried about facing Will in the light of day, worried about how she should act and what she could say. She worried about Evie figuring out how they'd spent the night before.

But her worrying had been for nothing. Will was friendly, but not overly flirtatious, and Evie, as always, made an excellent buffer. Her chatter made awkward silences impossible, and Gwen surprised herself at the ease she felt these days around both Harrisons.

So when Will handed her a cup of coffee and asked, "Do you like the Rangers?" she answered honestly and without thinking.

"I don't really know much about baseball."

Both Will and Evie gaped at her in shock. Will, it seemed, was a huge fan, and had converted Evie. Today would be Evie's first live game, and Gwen found herself dragged along as both of them tried to indoctrinate her to the sport.

She'd spent the afternoon at a Rangers game—just not in the HarCorp skybox as she'd assumed. Oh, no. Evie's first American baseball game had to be spent in the stands, under the searing July sun, so she could get the full experience— hot dogs, popcorn and a huge foam finger to wave.

And sunburned nose notwithstanding, Gwen had enjoyed it as much as Evie—although for slightly different reasons. She might not be a baseball fan after today, but...

Gwen stared at the phone as it rang, debating how much longer she could ignore it and how many more times Sarah would try to call.

"Sorry, Sarah," she muttered as she turned the phone off. She could call her tomorrow, when Sarah would be at work and have less time for analyzing Gwen's life.

Thirsty, Gwen went to the kitchen to get a drink. While she was there, she added sunscreen to the running list Mrs. Gray kept in the pantry. Then, out of curiosity, she peeked into the living room. Will and Evie sat on opposite ends of the couch, both of them tapping away at their laptops.

Well, everyone defines family time differently, I guess.

She should probably boot up her laptop and work some, too. Instead she thought about the massive tub in her bathroom. Just what she needed.

Gwen hit Play on the CD player and sank into the hot water with a sigh. She stayed there, letting the music hypnotize her while she tried to make sense of the wild turn her life had just taken.

Don't overanalyze. Don't overthink. Just take it one day at a time. She'd made her choice, and while she didn't regret it in the least—far from it—she didn't know what, if anything, came next.

She let her thoughts wander from the practical to the fantastical—and even through the possible repercussions—until the water turned too cold for comfort. She was rubbing lotion on her legs when she heard a soft tap at her door.

Slipping into her fuzzy robe, she glanced at the clock. Ten-thirty. How long had she been in the tub?

She opened the door, expecting to see Evie. Instead Will leaned against the frame. Her heartbeat accelerated as he grinned at her. A quick glance down the hall confirmed that Evie's door was closed.

"I need to talk to you about Evie."

Oh. So it was business he was here for, not pleasure. She tamped down the niggles of disappointment as she tugged on her belt, tightening it, and adjusted the collar of her robe. "Is everything all right?"

"Everything's fine. I just thought you should know Evie went to bed forty-five minutes ago. She has an early tennis lesson tomorrow." Will's hand toyed with the collar of her robe while he spoke. She wished she'd thought to bring a nicer one. This one had been with her since college. Yes, it was comfortable, but it fit like a comfy potato sack and the collar he toyed with was frayed at the edges. Not exactly the evening attire she wanted to be caught wearing by Will. The embroidered cats frolicking along the cuffs and collar didn't help the look, either.

Slightly confused and embarrassed, she prompted him. "And…?"

"And this." His hand closed around one of the frayed kitties on her collar and pulled her close until she pressed against his chest. Then his mouth closed on hers in a searing kiss.

That kiss brought every erotic sensation from last night back to the surface in amazing, gasping detail, showing her how faulty her powers of recollection really were.

In one swift movement, Will had them fully inside her room, and her back was against the door as Will loosened the sash and her robe fell open. She heard Will murmur his appreciation at finding nothing underneath, his words muffled against her skin as he sank to his knees, kissing a path down her torso as he went.

Gwen's knees buckled, her fingers first grasping his shoulders for support as Will tasted her, then scoring him with her nails as his tongue quickly sent her over the edge.

Holding her steady as the ripples ran through her, Will stood and kissed her deeply. Behind her, she heard the lock click into place.

"Now come to bed."

Gwen woke the next morning in a very good mood, but no one was around to share it. Evie had gone to her tennis lesson earlier, Will always left for work around seven-thirty and Mrs. Gray was walking out the door with a pile of what looked like dry cleaning under her arm just as Gwen emerged from her room.

"Good morning, Miss Gwen. I've left you some coffee and

rolls in the kitchen. I'm off to get more groceries—Miss Evie seems to have cleaned out the cupboards over the weekend. Can I get you anything? Do you need anything while I'm out?"

"No, but thanks." She did need a couple of things, but Gwen couldn't get used to the idea of Mrs. Gray doing it for her. Not that she should. Unless Letitia could be trained to shop, she'd be doing for herself again anyway in another ten days. This afternoon, while Evie was with her tutors, she'd run her own errands.

The morning edition of the *Tribune* sat on the marble countertop next to the coffeepot, along with the Monday edition of *Dallas Lifestyles*. Normally she'd take the time to flip through both over coffee, but she'd slept so late she really needed to get some work accomplished first.

Gwen poured herself a cup of the fragrant coffee blend Will preferred, grabbed a still-warm cinnamon roll and went back to her room to get dressed.

The coffee cleared her brain of residual sleepiness, and by the time she pulled on a pair of jeans and a T-shirt, she was fully awake. She caught herself humming as she pulled her hair up into a ponytail. Her amazingly good mood this morning had to be a residual effect of last night.

Ahh, last night. Her skin warmed as images flashed through her mind. She tried to focus on something else as she turned off the bathroom light—she *had* to or else she wouldn't get any work done today.

Her laptop sat on a small desk in the corner of the room, ready for her to log on and become Miss Behavior. A white envelope sat on top of it.

Her name was scrawled across it in a bold, male handwriting she had to assume was Will's. A small, fuzzy feeling settled in her stomach at the thought of Will leaving her a note.

She slid her finger under the flap, but instead of a letter, she found a check. A check made payable to her for an obnoxious sum of money.

The fuzzy feeling died and she sat with an unladylike thud.

Rationally her brain knew the check was payment for Evie's training. She had a contract with Will for her services, and here was payment in full. They had a business arrangement, after all.

Emotionally, though, she felt she'd been kicked in the stomach. Leaving a check in her bedroom after the weekend—hell, after the *night* they'd just shared—made her feel cheap. Like Will was paying for a completely different type of service.

Ugh. *I guess I should be glad he didn't leave it on the nightstand.*

The rational part of her brain tried again. *He had to leave it somewhere. Why mail it to your P.O. Box when you're living right here? He's not paying you for sex. Remember, he said business and pleasure were two totally separate things. Get it together, go to the bank, and deposit it so you can pay bills this month.*

She still felt a little sick, even with the "let's be rational" pep talk. She slid the check into her purse and sighed. This was yet another reason she shouldn't have gotten involved with Will.

Gwen refilled her coffee cup in the kitchen, then turned her cell phone back on. She really should return Sarah's calls before Sarah sent the police over to check on her.

She flipped open the phone and her jaw dropped in shock. Twenty-two missed calls? Twelve new voice mail messages? Eight text messages? Good God, did someone die? She started scrolling through the missed calls log, noting most of them had come in within the last couple of hours, and nearly dropped the phone when it rang in her hand.

"Hey, Sar—"

"Why haven't you been answering the phone? Are you okay?" Sarah's rapid-fire pace didn't leave her time to answer any of the questions. "I tried to call yesterday, and then after I saw *Lifestyles*—"

"Slow down. What are you talking about? I turned—I mean, my battery died yesterday, so I'm just now checking my phone."

"So you haven't seen *Dallas Lifestyles* today?" Sarah's tone made her heart drop.

"No. Why?"

"Page three, Gwennie. You made page three."

Oh, *no*. Gwen sprinted to the kitchen and grabbed the glossy magazine. Page three was Tish Cotter-Hulmes's page. Every Monday and Thursday Tish dished the hottest gossip and reported all the rumors on page three. No one wanted to make page three. Ever. Nothing good ever came of being on page three.

The headline stopped her heart. Is Miss Behavior Misbehaving With Dallas's Most Eligible?

"I'll call you back." She closed the phone on Sarah's sputtering and scanned the page. Oh, dear God.

Rumor has it that our own Miss Behavior may be vying for a new title. Sources tell me Gwen Sawyer moved in to Will Harrison's penthouse just last week, and there's no way she's only housesitting. In fact, Gwen and Will were spotted (along with Will's sister, the newly arrived and very elusive Evangeline) dining at Milano's on the West End and sharing popcorn at a movie afterward. Gwen and Evangeline were also spied having a very girly day of shopping and coiffing Friday, so I'm thinking there's definitely something going on. We all know how big a step shopping is. Personally, I'm intrigued. How did Gwen and Will cross paths and when? How have they managed to keep a low profile long enough for things to progress this far? Could Will be not-so-eligible any longer? Or is our Miss Behavior just flavor of the month? Anyone who can shed some light on the beginnings of this *affaire de coeur* needs to call me, quick!

In related news, the reports from Neiman Marcus say Evangeline spent a small fortune in a few hours with a personal shopper while Gwen supervised. Could this mean we're finally going to meet the Harrison heiress soon?

Several more paragraphs followed, each one more speculative than the last, all of them managing to put the worst possible spin on the slim details. Damn Tish! Gwen's fingers itched to wring Tish's scrawny, BOTOX-enhanced neck. Suddenly, the rash of missed phone calls made sense.

The anger receded as a chill settled over her. Not again.

Flavor of the Month? Her reputation could handle mild speculation about a possible romance, but to paint her as just another fling in a long line of flings? Especially one who had moved in? Once again, she was on the short end of the stick—Will's reputation was fine, while hers was tarnishing rapidly.

Romance or fling, one fact didn't change: the conservative elite of Dallas society wouldn't smile kindly on Gwen living with a man she wasn't married to. It didn't matter that it was the twenty-first century. As a debutante trainer, her moral compass needed to gravitate toward the 1950s—at least as far as her clients were concerned. It was unfair, yes, but a fact she'd come to accept as just part of the territory.

And Will would be livid. While his business—both personal and professional—ended up in the papers more often than not, she'd realized over the past week how much he tried to avoid the limelight whenever possible. In the past, Tish had limited herself to merely reporting Will's social life, but this time, she had moved to speculation and innuendo.

This was bad. At least Tish kept the speculation about Evie

to a minimum. It was one tiny point in Tish's favor. Still, though, this was *bad*.

Tish better hope she didn't need any favors from Gwen anytime soon. Old Money was a small and closed society, but then so was the world of those who made careers on the fringes of that society.

Damn, damn, damn! Sarah had been right from the beginning. She should have thought this through more thoroughly before she signed on. Now she was hip-deep in trouble. She paced the kitchen, berating herself and feeling like the world's biggest idiot.

Calm down. It could be worse. Right now, it was just speculation and gossip. There was no proof she and Will were any kind of item—fling or otherwise. No one, not even Sarah, knew their business relationship had crossed a line. Well, Evie might suspect something… It was only her own conscience reading damnation into Tish's column.

The one-two punch of Will's check and Tish's column made her want to crawl back into bed and start the day over again.

But she couldn't. She'd had five years to think about what she *should* have done when David hung her out to dry, and slinking away in disgrace had been the worst possible choice. She wouldn't make that mistake again. It was damage control time. Gwen shuddered to think what waited in her voice and e-mail boxes. And the messages on her business line at home…

She took a deep breath and let it out slowly. Neiman Marcus and the West End were both public places. *Anyone* could have seen them and tattled to Tish. Plenty of people had to have seen her coming and going from Will's building. Everything could be explained away easily—provided she could figure out how to explain without violating her nondisclosure agreement.

She'd have to call Will. Something she didn't look forward to.

Will didn't want to expose Evie to the possible embarrassment the implication having a personal etiquette tutor could bring. So how was she going to explain living here and taking Evie shopping? She needed to have *some* rationale or everyone would accept the most obvious explanation for their current living arrangement. And that was the absolute *last* thing she needed.

She'd call Sarah back and see which way the wind was blowing. Then, she'd check her messages and judge how bad the damage was.

She wasn't going down without a fight this time.

"We'll need to arrange a dinner for after the meeting. Something regional would be nice." Nancy, fully recovered from whatever kept her out of the office on Friday, was back and trying to get him to commit on several projects—including final arrangements on his meeting with Kiesuke Hiramine. And though he knew he should be far more involved in this conversation, he found himself oddly uninterested. Too many other things on his mind. Like the memory of leaving Gwen in a tangled heap of sheets early that morning. Like the knowing look Evie wore at breakfast. Exactly *what* Evie thought she knew was a question mark, though.

"Sounds good. And?"

Nancy shot him an impatient look. "I also understand Mr. Hiramine is a golf fanatic. I'm making arrangements for him to play at your Club and at Brookhaven."

"Tell Matthews he'll need to be there for the golf outings. He's good at throwing a game." His phone rang and he glanced at it. He'd had his daily phone inquisition with Marcus, so that left either Evie or Gwen.

"I already have. And Mr. Matthews has the final sales and profit projections ready for your review."

"Excellent. Anything else?" Evie should be with her French tutor. That narrowed it down considerably.

"Your phone is ringing." Nancy was secure enough in her position to lob one parting shot as she gathered her notes and made a hasty exit. "I'll just leave these reports for you to look over later."

"Will, it's Gwen. Do you have a minute to talk?" The easy warmth that moved through him at the sound of her voice faded at the tension he heard in her words.

"Of course." It wasn't an entirely true statement, but the reports could wait a few minutes longer.

"Have you read today's issue of *Dallas Lifestyles?*"

"I never read that rag, but—"

"Tish Cotter-Hulme has half a column about us. I mean, about you and me and Evie, and why we've been spotted together. I'm so sorry, Will. Tish is making all kinds of speculations…"

"Calm down. I'm fully aware of what she had to say this morning. I don't have to read it myself to get a full report of what she says about me. I have people for that." Gwen didn't laugh at his lame attempt at humor. "Just don't worry about it."

"*Don't worry?* Have you lost your mind?" Gwen's voice rose an octave, and he winced in pain. "You don't realize how many phone calls I've fielded this morning. Between people wanting me to confirm or deny Tish's rumors and my clients…"

"This is when the phrase 'No Comment' comes in handy." Why on earth was Gwen so worked up over a gossip column? "It's just gossip."

"Gossip kills careers like mine, Will. You may not read Tish, but other people do. And those people don't like the idea of a loose woman teaching their impressionable daughters." Gwen had herself worked up into a fine fit.

"A loose woman? Seriously?"

"I'm living in your *house*. The implication is that we are sleeping together."

"But we are…"

"That's beside the point." Gwen was practically sputtering.

"How is that—"

"I have to tell my clients something. *Some* reason why I'm living with you and Evie."

"Don't tell them anything. It's none of their business."

"Sadly, it is. Reputation is everything in this business, and mine is getting dragged through the mud. What am I supposed to…"

"Gwen, calm down. You can tell them you're working for me—I don't care about that. I just don't want people knowing the particulars. It would be embarrassing for Evie."

"*Hel*-lo, what else would I be doing other than tutoring Evie?"

"I don't know. You do business seminars, too, right? Tell them it's related to HarCorp." Gwen made an odd choking sound. He assumed she objected to the small lie. "We sponsor the Med Ball, so it's not that far from the truth."

"And why I'm living with you?"

"That's easy. You're living with *us* so you can concentrate fully on your current project."

"But—"

"What's that line you told your readers to use when folks want to confirm gossip? Something about assumptions?"

"'What an interesting assumption'?"

"That's the one. If someone wants confirmation of Tish's implications and you don't want to go with 'No Comment' then use that line. Or that 'How kind of you to take an interest' one."

"You read my TeenSpace page?" Amazement tinged her voice. It beat panic, hands down.

"Well, Evie lectured me on my BlackBerry usage, so I thought I should check on the etiquette laws."

"I think I'm flattered."

"You should be." He smiled. At least she was starting to calm down. "Now, are you finished hyperventilating over this?"

"I guess." Gwen sighed. "You don't sound very upset over Tish's rumor mongering."

"I learned a long time ago to ignore speculations made about me and my private life. Tish just hasn't gotten the hint yet." Although with Evie on the scene, he should probably make clear that his willingness to ignore was very limited when it came to his sister.

"I thought you'd be livid. Or angry. Or at least irritated." Gwen's outraged sails seemed to have lost their wind, and her voice lost the last of its bluster.

"Oh, I'm irritated all right. It just doesn't do any good. That said, I try to avoid being fodder for Tish—or anyone else— as much as possible."

Gwen sighed again. "I guess I can make do with the minimum amount of excuses. Whether anyone will believe them is a different animal entirely."

"Good. Now can we talk about something else?" He leaned back and propped his feet on his desk.

"Don't you have work to do?"

His e-mail pinged. "Of course, but I have a few minutes for you."

"Now I *am* flattered."

"You should be. I'm a very busy man," he teased.

Gwen's chuckle sent heat rushing through him and all of his blood south. It was hard to believe just a week ago, he hadn't known this woman existed. Seven days later, he was ignoring HarCorp just to talk to her.

"Well, I happen to be a very busy woman. *You* may have time to chat, but *I* have clients to soothe and teenagers to counsel."

Will was oddly disappointed. "Good luck with that. I'll see you tonight."

"Bye."

With the phone in its cradle, he opened his e-mail. Another file on Japanese business practices and culture from Nancy. He sighed; he really needed to get Gwen to help him with his language lessons.

Gwen spoke Japanese. That sparked a memory from Gwen's first dinner. What had she said? Something about a degree in International Affairs? Yeah, and a special interest in Asian culture.

Why hadn't he made the connection before? *Because at first you were only focused on Evie, and then you focused too much on Gwen.*

He'd ask Gwen if she'd be willing to help him with this meeting with Hiramine. That would save him a ton of work. Less work also meant more time with Gwen. Plus, the time he spent working with her on this project…well, that line between business and pleasure he'd bragged about was getting thinner by the minute.

CHAPTER NINE

THE next few days passed in a blur for Gwen. Sometimes it seemed like a rainbow-colored blur, so perfect she felt she'd stepped into someone else's much-more-exciting and perfect life.

First had been Will coming home on Monday with a business proposition for her: consulting on the upcoming meeting with the Japanese company HarCorp wanted to join with in its Asian expansion. She'd wanted to squeal with the excitement.

Suddenly there weren't enough hours in the day to be Miss Behavior, Evie's etiquette tutor and Will's consultant and Japanese tutor. But both Harrisons managed to excel at whatever she threw at them.

Gwen never had a doubt Evie would shine socially, but the surprise came as Evie took an interest in the family business and quickly showed business savvy was an inherited trait. Family dinners moved from the basics of table manners and polite conversation to proper discourse on current events and HarCorp company business. Evie managed to retain her natural exuberance and charm while acquiring a polish fine enough for the most critical of society's elite. With her good looks and intelligence, Evie was destined to set Dallas on fire.

While Will picked up Japanese with a speed that impressed

her, he chafed against the strictures of Japanese etiquette, his frustration at not being able to "cut to the chase" more than evident. But Will was a consummate businessman, and he didn't need any help in that department. Aside from a reminder to put the BlackBerry on silent, of course.

Both Evie and Will would be great successes on her résumé.

But for someone who'd always measured her happiness by professional success, Gwen couldn't deny that the best part of her day now came after Evie went to bed. Once Evie's door closed, Will transformed from charming boss and loving big brother into a bedroom-eyed Romeo intent on charming her in every way—including in her bed.

And she wasn't naive enough to believe Evie was ignorant of her and Will's relationship. No fifteen-year-old went to bed *that* early on a regular basis. Although she and Will tried hard not to make the physical side of their relationship blatant, Gwen knew Evie intentionally gave them privacy in the evenings.

Gwen didn't know where she and Will were headed—if they were headed anywhere at all—but she told herself she didn't care. Will never mentioned a future beyond the end of her contractual obligations, but they were all so focused on the events of the next few weeks, she couldn't read anything into it. She was living in the minute—enjoying what she could while she could. Gwen adored Evie, and her feelings for Will got more complicated every day, but she was taking her sister's advice to just take one day at a time. So far, that plan was working quite well.

Only one small problem flawed her otherwise halcyon existence—Tish's innuendos. She hadn't mentioned the column to Will or Evie since Monday night, but the fallout from Tish's gossip hadn't been pleasant. Two clients had backed out of their contracts already—one for a series of classes at a private elementary school and the other for a military wives' event. It took fancy footwork on her part to calm the sponsors of two of the debutante clubs that formed the backbone of her deb business. Half-truths and cajoling—and a little questioning of Tish's sanity and sources—managed to pacify the most conservative of her clients, if only temporarily.

She'd taken the opportunity to instruct her TeenSpace readers on the inappropriateness of speculation and evils of spreading gossip. She was also ignoring Tish's e-mails outright.

By Friday, the furor caused by Tish's column had calmed for the most part. Life was good. And when Evie returned from her afternoon swim with an enormous smile and an even bigger favor to ask of Gwen, she just couldn't say no.

At seven forty-five—the first time Will had worked late in two weeks—Gwen finally heard the front door open and close and the rattle of Will's keys as he dropped them on the hall table.

"Anybody home?"

"In here," Gwen called from the den where she'd been nursing a glass of Merlot for the last half hour and watching TV.

Will rounded the corner looking slightly disheveled and completely adorable. Her heart skipped a beat at his smile. "It's awfully quiet. Do I want to know?"

She laughed. "No drama." *Yet.* "Mrs. Gray needed to leave early, so your dinner is warming in the oven. Evie is in her room."

"Really?" One eyebrow raised with the question. "Then I can do this." Without warning, Will leaned down and kissed her. A simple "Honey-I'm-home" kiss that seemed perfectly right at the moment and sent a happy little thrill through her. "How was your day?"

"Great. And yours?"

He grunted.

"That good, huh? Can I get you a drink?" He nodded, and Gwen went to the bar feeling oddly domestic at the *Ozzie and Harriet* scenario as Will loosened his tie and got comfortable on the couch.

Will rubbed his temples. "Is Evie sick?"

"No. I'm pretty sure she's on the phone." That was almost a given, considering. "Why?"

"Then I'm not sure I want to know why she's in her room this early. Do I even want to ask?"

Perceptive man. She took a deep breath. "Evie wanted me to talk to you about something."

"Uh-oh." He took the glass she proffered and nodded his thanks. "I'm not going to like this, am I?"

"Why would you think that?"

"Because she'd be in here otherwise, pestering me to death if it was something simple like a new phone or clothes. Instead she's put you up to it." He cut his eyes sideways at her as she sat. "She's smart, you know. You can talk me into almost anything. Plus, she figures if you're on her side, I'm bound to give in to whatever it is."

Gwen shrugged. Good Lord, she was picking up Evie's bad habits.

"You might as well hit me with it. I promise not to shoot the messenger."

Gwen mentally crossed her fingers. "Evie met a boy—a young man, I mean—at the pool today. He's asked her to the movies tomorrow night."

Will sat his glass down carefully and rubbed his eyes. "And?"

"*And?*" Gwen wanted to hit him with something. "There is no 'and.' Evie's been asked on a date and she wants to know if you'll let her go."

"Who is this kid?"

"Peter Asbury. Evie says he's sixteen and lives two floors down."

He nodded, but his expressionless face kept Gwen from figuring out how he felt about this new turn of events. "I know his father. He's the head of something at the university."

"Dean of Students." Gwen supplied automatically. "Well?"

Will swirled his drink in his glass. "She's too young to be dating."

"She's fifteen. It's not out of the ordinary or anything." Will's dry tone bothered her. Evie expected him to go through the roof at the thought of her dating, which was why she'd conned Gwen into being the one to broach the subject. Gwen hadn't expected fireworks, but Will could be discussing the weather for all the lack of emotion in his voice. The idea of hitting him sounded better by the moment.

"What did you say when she asked you?"

"I didn't say anything." That wasn't entirely true. She'd shared Evie's teenage glee like Sarah had shared hers years ago. "You're the one who has to okay it, not me."

"I'm asking for your opinion, though. Do you think she should go? This is new territory for me."

Get used to it. Evie's going to have the boys eating out of her hand and you'll be beating them off with a stick for the rest of your born days. "Do I think she's old enough? Probably. Do I think she's ready? It's hard to say. Do I think she's dying to go? Yes, definitely."

Will sighed, the sound of a man who had resigned himself to the grim reality of a teenage sister teetering on the edge of boy-crazy. "I guess it was bound to happen eventually."

Gwen hid her smile behind her wineglass.

"I want to meet him first, though," he grumbled.

"Why don't you invite him to dinner tomorrow night before the movie. You can grill him on his intentions and put the fear of God in him before they leave."

Will perked up at her last statement. "Oh, I like that idea. Fear is a good thing. Anything else I need to know about before I talk to Evie?"

"Nope." Gwen wanted to do a little happy dance for Evie. Finally Evie could make some friends her own age.

"Evie! Get in here!"

Shocked at the heat in his voice, Gwen stared at Will.

Will winked at her. "No sense letting her think this is going to be easy."

She rolled her eyes. "Then I'll leave you to it."

Evie stuck her head around the door frame. "Yes, Will?"

"The Asbury kid?"

Gwen slipped past Evie and whispered "Good luck" as Evie fumbled for words. She repressed the urge to giggle as Evie straightened her shoulders but still seemed to slink in to the room to get Will's permission for something she desperately wanted. In the privacy of her room, though, she succumbed to the urge to both giggle and do her happy dance.

Feeling like the champion of teenagers everywhere, she logged in to her Miss Behavior e-mail, ready to sort out all the angst-ridden adolescents of the world. It kept her busy for the next half hour until Evie knocked on her door.

"He said I could go!" Evie's ear-to-ear grin was infectious.

"I'm so glad, sweetie."

Evie wrapped her in a hug. "Thanks, Gwen. I'm going to go call Peter and figure out what I'm going to wear tomorrow. G'night."

"'Night."

Chuckling at Evie's obvious glee, Gwen started work on her next column—about first dates in honor of Evie—and didn't look up until she heard another knock on her door.

She half expected Evie to come in with an armload of clothes, but seeing Will there wasn't exactly a surprise, either.

He closed the door and leaned against it. "You didn't come back out." She'd never heard him so disgruntled.

"Sorry. I didn't know you needed company."

"Evie disappeared to her room to call that boy back and you've been in here all night. I've been bored. And I had to eat dinner by myself."

This time she did laugh at his grumbling, and he looked at her sharply. "You find that funny?"

"For someone who ate either alone or in the company of his BlackBerry until a few days ago, you've certainly set up camp on the other side now."

He shrugged. He and Evie had so many of the same mannerisms that it had to be genetic. "What can I say? I'm getting domesticated."

Her heart flipped at the word "domesticated." It sounded so hearth-and-home and Will didn't sound the least bit upset with the idea. When he smiled at her and crossed the room to pull her into his arms, that little warm spot in her heart she'd been keeping alive but carefully corralled blossomed into something she could no longer deny.

Her rational brain argued it could be the biggest mistake of her life, leading only to heartache and regret. But rationality couldn't hold back the knowledge that raced through her with such clarity it couldn't be anything else.

God help her. She was falling in love with Will Harrison.

Intimidating the Asbury boy proved immensely enjoyable. Will didn't doubt for a second Evie would be home by curfew. Evie was shooting daggers at him by the time she left, and his shins would be covered in bruises tomorrow from Gwen's well-aimed kicks every time she felt he crossed a line at dinner.

From the feel of it, he'd crossed several.

If that's what it took to convince Peter Asbury to keep his hands to himself, though, then his bruised shins would be well worth it.

He helped Gwen clear the remnants of their dinner from the table. As she loaded glasses into the dishwasher, she shook her head at him. "You should be ashamed of yourself, Will Harrison."

"What for?"

"You know exactly what for. I hope Evie comes up with a suitable revenge for your behavior tonight."

"Hey, all she has to do to avoid it is not date. I'd be good with that."

She wiped her hands on a towel and leaned a hip against the counter. "You are in for a long, painful journey through Evie's adolescence. And I'm starting to think you completely deserve it." She tossed him the towel and indicated he should wipe off the counter behind him. To his utter amazement, he did.

Good Lord, he *was* becoming domesticated. He'd never held a conversation with a woman he was romantically involved with in a kitchen before—much less helped tidy it while he did.

Gwen was a far cry from the usual husband-hunting trophy-wives-in-training he was used to. Instead of Prada and diamonds, she wore faded jeans and a pukka shell necklace Evie had given her. And instead of the normal topics of conversation he was accustomed to, she was teasing him and talking about the kid. It was a cozy domestic scene probably being played out in millions of households across the planet.

It was odd. It was strange. Something nagged at him that he should be horrified, but he wasn't. It was oddly comfortable, and somehow seemingly natural.

Gwen cocked her head at him and raised an eyebrow. "Was all that big-brother caveman posturing *really* necessary?"

"Don't tell me you're going to side with Evie."

Her chin went up a notch. "On behalf of younger sisters everywhere, I think I should."

"You can't. We have to present a united front."

Her eyes widened, and he knew he'd said the wrong thing. Her next quiet words confirmed it.

"I don't get a vote here. I may side with Evie at heart, but I won't undermine your authority."

Not quite a slap in the face, but close enough for someone

who was feeling rather domesticated mere moments before. "I value your opinion, though."

"Thank you, but it's more important that you and Evie come to an understanding. Evie needs to learn to come to you with her problems, and *you* need to be ready to deal with them. I won't always be here to play middleman. Evie seems to be in denial of that fact, but surely you aren't."

Will was no novice when it came to women. He'd been propositioned in every possible way by women far more cunning than Gwen. He looked at her closely, but saw no artifice. Gwen didn't seem to be angling for anything. In fact, for all her tone indicated, she could be discussing the terms of her contract. Which in a way, he admitted silently, she was.

Maybe that was why her words left a hollow feeling in his stomach.

He hadn't gotten where he was today by playing dumb or avoiding risk, but he also knew when it was time to call his own bluff. Closing the distance between them in two strides, he backed her against the refrigerator and captured her mouth with his. He still wasn't comfortable with all these new emotions Gwen kept stirring in him, but he was willing to see where they might lead.

Gwen's arms twined around his neck as she leaned in to him. He heard her soft sigh as his lips moved to her neck, and something more primal than physical stirred inside him. He nipped gently at her earlobe and felt her shudder in response.

"Maybe I'm in as much denial as Evie," he whispered.

He felt her stiffen at his words, and her eyes flew open to stare into his with an intensity he hadn't prepared himself for.

She let a hand trail down his shoulder to his chest, resting her palm where his heart pounded.

A smile twitched at the corners of her mouth. "Sounds like you both need therapy." The challenge was there in her eyes and in her voice.

Only Gwen would mock him at a time like this. "If it's two against one, I'm thinking you're the one who's in denial. Maybe you should be seeking therapy."

"I won't argue with that," she said, as she rose up on her tiptoes to mold her body against his and kiss him again. Her odd choice of words bothered Will for a second, but the touch of her tongue against his chased those thoughts away.

His hand snaked behind her to cradle her head, and the backs of his knuckles brushed against the cold stainless steel of the fridge.

Conversation in the kitchen was one thing. Sex was a different story. Without breaking the kiss, he scooped Gwen into his arms and carried her down the hall.

They had several hours before he had to be standing watch over the front door so he could intimidate Evie's date some more. Having the free time so he could be alone with Gwen was almost worth letting Evie date in the first place.

CHAPTER TEN

"You made page three again, Gwennie." Sarah seemed to be struggling to not sound too pitying about it. "I'm so sorry. I'd like to break that witch's fingers for you to shut her up."

Gwen shifted the phone to her other hand and got comfortable on the couch. Sarah was worked up enough over Gwen's lack of regular contact, and the addition of another page three appearance hadn't helped. This could be a long conversation.

"Thanks, but I'd rather not have to bail you out of jail for your Assault charge." Gwen glanced over at the latest copy of *Lifestyles* containing Tish's newest column of salacious rumors about her. "It's just gossip."

Sarah practically sputtered, and Gwen had to fight back a laugh. "You're not upset?"

Gwen thought about her discussion with Will and Evie that morning over breakfast, and said, "I'm irritated, not upset. Let her speculate. I am curious where she's getting her information, though."

Much of Tish's column simply rehashed last Monday's speculations, with an update about the Ranger game the weekend before and more comments on their living situation, but this week she'd managed to ferret out information about Gwen's contract as well.

"Not from me, Gwennie. You know that, right?"

"Of course. It never even crossed my mind."

"Any fallout?"

"Actually Tish did me a huge favor by relaying the contract details. My clients now claim to understand why I moved in here in the first place, and no matter how she tries to twist the facts now to look more scandalous, it looks like a business decision. I should really call her and thank her as well for mentioning the 'exorbitant' amount of money Will's paying me. I can raise my rates." She tried for a lofty tone, but a giggle escaped and ruined it.

"Well, something good should come from the garbage Tish spouts. How's Evie handling it?"

"Pretty good. It was slightly embarrassing for Evie to realize most of Dallas now knew Will hired an etiquette tutor for her, but once she realized it wasn't that different from being sent through debutante training classes like any other girl, she got over it. Anyway, she's still floating from her date the other night. It will take a lot to burst that happy bubble."

"And you? How's your happy bubble today? Based on the message you left on my machine, you were totally floating last night."

A warm glow moved through Gwen and a tingle settled in her stomach. "I've never been happier."

"You're falling for him."

"Yeah, I'm pretty sure I am." Admitting it out loud was tough, but with that admission, the tingly glow in her stomach spread.

"And the feeling is mutual?"

"Will hasn't said anything directly, but I'm cautiously hopeful. We're in a strange situation now because we kinda skipped a few of those early casual-dating steps when I moved in here, but so far everything's just perfect."

"So this is going somewhere then?"

Gwen couldn't stop the smile, but her sister couldn't see it so she was still able to hedge a bit. "Hopefully."

"As in 'somewhere permanent'?"

In her secret heart of hearts, she might be thinking in that direction, but only a fool would share that kind of information too soon. Especially to Sarah. Her sister would have her in for a dress fitting before the echo of her words faded. "Let's not jump ahead of ourselves, okay? It's only been a couple of weeks. I promise you'll be the first to know if this…um…"

"Warrants further planning?"

"That'll do. Plus, there's Evie—"

"Evie adores you. I'm sure she's ecstatic to think you and Will might get…umm…'warrant future planning.'"

Like a djinn summoned by the speaking of her name, Evie bounded in through the front door. Gwen jumped at the sound. All those times she'd lectured debutantes about how to enter a room, she never thought she'd be thankful for the teenage inability to open a door noiselessly. Even Sarah heard it on her end of the phone line. "Speak of the devil."

"Indeed. I'll talk to you later."

"Bye. And Gwennie?"

"Yeah?"

"I'm so happy for you, honey."

"Thanks. Me, too."

One look at Evie's glowing face told Gwen Evie hadn't been lonely during her swim. "How's Peter today?" she asked casually.

Evie giggled, the unmistakable sound of a girl in a crush when the crushee returns the sentiment. Gwen knew the feeling well—especially since she felt a crush giggle trying to escape all the time recently.

Nothing like a new relationship to bring out a girl's inner fifteen-year-old.

"Go change. You can tell me all about it over tea."

* * *

He had piles of work to do, and therefore shouldn't be leaving the office early, but HarCorp had lost its monopoly on his time and attention. It was a beautiful, not-too-hot afternoon, and he could surprise Gwen and Evie by taking them out for an early dinner and a movie.

Will's new desire to delegate left Nancy gaping and his VPs scurrying, but that was one of the perks of being the boss. He'd hire Nancy her own secretary if that's what she needed or bring another VP on board to pick up the slack, but he finally understood what had pulled his father from the day-to-day grind of HarCorp. Thankfully Will himself figured it out twenty years earlier than Bradley had and wouldn't waste these years on a company when he had people at home who cared about him.

Silence greeted him as he opened the door to the apartment. No music blaring from Evie's stereo, no TV on in the living room, no sound of Gwen and Evie practicing small talk over tea or pretending to mingle.

Where were they? The pool? Shopping? Heading down the hall, he heard the faint sound of Evie's laughter. He veered right, into the living room, and noticed the balcony doors were open. Evie and Gwen were outside with their backs to the apartment, and they obviously hadn't heard him come in.

Gwen had her feet propped up on the balcony railing, those pink things women used when painting their toenails woven between her toes. What looked like the entire stock of a small beauty supply company littered the iron table next to her. Evie stood behind Gwen, a comb in her teeth like a pirate's cutlass, braiding Gwen's hair into cornrows while Gwen painted her fingernails.

He'd heard of girls doing stuff like this, but he'd never witnessed it live. As he watched, Gwen groped blindly beside her for a bottle of water while Evie kept a tight grip on the braid she held.

"Ouch! Easy there, Evie."

"Sorry." The comb clamped between her teeth distorted Evie's words. "But don't wiggle or I'll drop it."

Neither of them seemed to notice as he slipped out on to the balcony. He leaned against the glass door, oddly fascinated by this feminine bonding ritual.

Evie wrapped a rubber band around the braid and went to section off a new row. "So I'm still going to have to join a debutante class?"

"Not for a couple of years. Don't you want an official debut?"

He hadn't thought about a debut for Evie. He didn't even know where to start. Good thing he happened to have a deb trainer around.

"Hold this." Evie tapped the comb against Gwen's shoulder. "It just seems ridiculous. I mean, I understand why I needed instruction *now*. Dallas is completely different from home. What would I learn in a deb class that you haven't already taught me?"

"Ahh, there's more to being a debutante than just walking properly. Plus, you'll get the fun of the ball and everything."

"What kinds of different things?"

He wondered the same thing himself.

Gwen held up crossed fingers. "I can't tell you. It's Top Secret Debutante Information only learned in official debutante classes."

"Really?" Evie was obviously intrigued, and Will smothered a chuckle. He could almost see her brain trying to come up with possibilities. Gwen shrugged, and Evie's mouth gaped open. "You liar. There aren't any debutante secrets."

"You'll have to go to class to find out, won't you?"

"Will you be teaching the classes?"

"It depends. You'd have to ask Will where the Harrison family normally presents. If it's at Will's Club, then probably not. Theresa Hardin teaches that class."

"Maybe Will could get them to hire you instead."

He'd been thinking the exact same thing and was surprised when Gwen waved the comment away.

"Thanks, Evie, but no. I'm not looking to pick up any more deb classes."

"Oh, I forgot about you wanting to ditch the debs."

"It's not that I want to ditch them. I just want to do some different things. I'm trained to work with companies and professionals, and that's what I'd really like to do more of."

"Like stuff you're doing for Will's meeting?"

"Could you please quit saying 'stuff'? There are a thousand words in the English language far more accurate than 'stuff.' But, yes, exactly like the 'stuff' I'm doing for Will's meeting. In fact, I'd been lobbying HarCorp with proposals for months before Will hired me to work with you."

She had? It was the first he'd heard of it.

"Really?"

"Yep. I actually went to that first meeting with Will thinking it would be my big break into the corporate sphere. I got you instead."

Will thought back to their first meeting. Well, that explained a lot about Gwen's reactions that day.

Evie laughed. "That must have been a surprise."

"Definitely. But I took the job anyway—"

"Obviously."

"Sarcastic interruptions are unnecessary," Gwen teased.

"Sorry."

"As I was saying, I took the job anyway, because I hoped it might lead to more work with HarCorp. And it did in the end. The success of Will's meeting will be a big boon for my résumé. Working for HarCorp will open a lot of doors for me."

A cold rock settled in his stomach. Surely he'd misheard her and she wasn't just looking for a stepping stone.

"And the deb classes will go?"

"It depends. But *your* success, my dear, will be seen as due to *my* excellent instruction and means I'll be in high demand for social training. The Harrison name attached to my business will lift me to the top shelf."

Will couldn't believe what he was hearing.

"I thought you were the best already."

"*One* of the best, maybe. But as you've found out, the wealthy are a tightly knit social class that's hard to break into. Now that word is spreading that I'm the one doing Evangeline Harrison's social training, more folks will want to hire me just because Will did. I should really send Tish a thank-you note for her help spreading the word."

Evie laughed and started to say something more, but Will had quit listening. The cold rock had turned to an icy weight in his chest, and his fists itched to hit something. He slipped silently through the glass doors back into the living room.

That conniving little bitch. She'd been working him since day one; he just hadn't been looking carefully enough for the agenda. Damn it, he should have seen it. Gold diggers after his money and social climbers after his name were nothing new to him. Hell, he'd learned to spot them from the smiles on their faces. But a woman who used him simply to increase her business contacts…That was a new one. One he hadn't thought to look for.

What an actress. Gwen's good-girl-with-good-manners persona had him fooled. She must have thought she'd hit the jackpot when he stupidly allowed his penis to think for him. He'd never pegged her as someone mercenary enough to sleep her way into a better job—or a better bargaining position for her business. And he, stupidly enough, had thought her the answer to all his problems—first Evie, and now the Japanese expansion.

Oh God. Poor Evie. She adored Gwen. Practically worshipped her. She'd be crushed when Gwen left them both for fatter wallets or better connections.

"Mr. Will! I didn't hear you come in." He cut his eyes quickly to his left where Mrs. Gray stood in the kitchen doorway, but he was more concerned with the reaction on the balcony. Mrs. Gray had spoken loud enough for Evie and Gwen to hear.

Both of them turned enough to see him standing at the door. Evie waggled the three fingers not holding pieces of Gwen's hair at him. Gwen's face lit up with a smile that would have meant something to him five minutes ago. Now he knew it was just another part of her act.

"Hey, Will. Gwen's letting me put cornrows in her hair. They look good, don't they?"

He wasn't sure what to say. "If you say so."

"You're home very early today." Gwen tried to swivel further in his direction.

"Gwen, don't move so much."

"Evie—"

The ice continued to move through his body. "Evie's right. Stay where you are. I have a lot of work to do, so I'll be in my office."

Evie merely nodded, but he saw the confused look that crossed Gwen's face. *Good. Let her wonder.*

He retrieved his briefcase even though there was no work in it and retreated to his office even though he had absolutely nothing to do in there.

Dinner was a quiet, uncomfortable affair. As far as bad dinners went, it was almost as bad as the first one she'd sat through with Evie and Will—minus the BlackBerry and Evie's rough table manners. At least that first night, Will had a reason to be quiet and uncommunicative.

Something was bothering Will and she didn't have a clue as to what. Everything had been fine—better than fine—when he left for work that morning. Evie came to her wondering what was wrong, and the best she'd been able to come up with was a possible "bad day at the office." Evie wasn't convinced.

Will stayed locked in his office until Evie finally pulled him out for dinner. Since then, he'd said approximately ten words to Gwen and only when she asked a question to him directly. His answers were terse at best and monosyllabic at worst. Will did do better with Evie's attempts at conversation, but it had been so strained, Evie had lapsed into complete silence ten minutes ago.

Time to practice small talk. "I spoke with Mr. Heatherton today."

Evie pushed her peas around on her plate. Will merely grunted. Okay, this was going to be harder than she thought.

"He wanted a progress report on Evie. I told him he would be very pleased with all she's accomplished. Not only with me, but with her other tutors as well. Her French is really improving."

That earned her a weak smile from Evie. Will still said nothing. Evie, good student that she was, picked up the conversational ball.

"I like French. I'm still struggling with geometry, though."

Will cleared his throat. "I know you're working hard, Evie. I'm sure you'll figure it out."

Goody. Twelve whole words. It was a start.

"Mr. Heatherton would like to join us for dinner on Wednesday. I've already informed Mrs. Gray." With a wink at Evie, she added, "I didn't think we had much of a choice."

"Marcus is always welcome here," Will snapped.

Gwen choked. "Of course he is, Will. I wasn't implying otherwise."

Evie tried again. God love the girl, she really had learned well. "I'm happy Uncle Marcus will be here. I owe him an apology from last time. I hope he'll be impressed."

Gwen paused to give Will a chance to respond, but as

the silence stretched, she gave up. "I'm sure he will be, Evie."

So that topic was exhausted. Great. Gwen searched for another. "I made you an appointment for Friday afternoon to get your hair done. Patrick wants to do an updo with sparkles to go with your dress for the Ball."

Finally something managed to spark Evie's enthusiasm. "I can't believe it's almost here. Do you think I'm ready, Gwen? I mean, we've done a lot, but the mingling thing…"

"Don't panic. Just remember to be yourself and you'll do fine. You're as ready as I can make you, honey. You're going to be the belle of the ball. I promise." She reached across the table to squeeze Evie's hand in support.

"You're right, Gwen." Will spoke sharply, startling them both. Evie dropped her fork in surprise. "Evie *is* ready for the Med Ball, and I can't think of anything else you need to teach her." Something ugly tinged Will's words, making Gwen's stomach tie itself in a knot. "You've certainly done your job and then some. Therefore, I don't think your 'services'—" he practically sneered the word at her "—are required further. I know you're anxious to get back to your regular life and business, so we won't keep you here any longer."

His words hit her like a slap across the face. She opened her mouth, but no words would come out.

"Will!" Evie gasped, her eyes round in shock.

"Wh-wh-what?" she finally managed to stutter.

"Oh, don't worry, Gwen. You've done an excellent job with Evie, and I'm sure she won't mind being a walking recommendation for your business. I'm afraid, though, you won't be using my sister or riding my company's reputation in order to serve yourself any longer. Go write Tish her thank-you note."

Oh God. Oh God. No! Adrenaline surged through her veins, but she felt paralyzed as the full meaning of Will's cold words settled.

"It's over, Gwen. All of it. Pack your things and leave." Will dropped his napkin on the table and stalked out of the room.

Her chest felt tight, and she forced herself to take deep breaths. Tears burned at the corners of her eyes, and she closed them, but the image of Will's angry face still loomed in her mind's eye.

"Gwen, no. You don't have to leave. *Please* don't leave."

She opened her eyes to see fat tears rolling down Evie's cheeks. "It's okay, honey. Don't cry." If only she could follow her own advice. She felt a tear or two of her own escaping.

Will had overheard her conversation with Evie. His remark about Tish and the thank-you note at least gave her that much information. She tried to remember exactly what she'd said. A weight settled in her chest, making breathing difficult again. Evie's protestations were regulated to background noise as she replayed the afternoon on the balcony. She tried to put the worst possible spin on her words and realized exactly where Will was coming from.

Mrs. Gray stuck her head out of the kitchen to investigate and looked around in confusion at the sudden change in the dining room. She looked first at Will's empty chair, then wrapped Evie in a matronly hug. "What's wrong? What's happened?"

I feel like I'm dying. She took a deep breath to steady herself and swiped at her cheeks. "Just finishing up my business here. Thank you for dinner, Mrs. Gray. I have to go pack now."

"No!" Evie shouted.

Gwen stood and shook her head gently at Evie, trying to forestall another outburst.

"I hate him!" Evie ran from the room and down the hall. "Do you hear me, Will Harrison?" she shouted. "I hate you! I hate you!"

The slam of her bedroom door echoed through the apartment like a gunshot.

"I'm sorry to see you leave, Miss Gwen. You've been so good for Miss Evie."

"Thank you. And thank you for all you've done for me."

"My pleasure, Miss Gwen."

She didn't have much to pack. A couple of drawers, a few things on hangers, her toiletries. Her laptop slid easily into its bag, and her teaching sets fit back into their cases without a problem. She blessed the monotony of the movements as her brain was churning too much to allow her to concentrate.

The pain in her chest, though, nearly crippled her. Regardless of what Will thought he knew about her ulterior motives for working for him, he'd completely dismissed their fledging relationship like yesterday's gossip.

That was killing her. She'd either been played by a player who was simply taking advantage of a situation, or Will didn't care half as much about her as she did about him. Either way, she'd played the fool. Again.

And she'd be paying for it dearly.

CHAPTER ELEVEN

Dear Miss Behavior,
I was with a group of people from one of my clubs at school and they were talking trash about another girl I know (she's not in that club, btw). That girl found out about some of the things they said, and now she's really upset with me. I've known this girl since elementary school, and we're friends. I didn't mean for her feelings to get hurt. How do I apologize for something like this and get her to forgive me?
Signed, Big Mouth.

Gwen sighed. *That's the million dollar question this week. Wish I could help you, honey, but you're on your own.*

She'd called Sarah Monday night to tell her Letitia could come home now and promptly burst into tears. The rapid change of events left Sarah sputtering in shock, and she'd arrived half an hour later with Letitia in a carrier and vanilla fudge brownie Häagen-Dazs in hand.

Sarah's support helped a little, but not enough to soothe the ache that had settled in her chest. Tuesday morning, Letitia's yowling for her breakfast forced Gwen out from under the duvet with the unwelcome reminder that life goes on.

Throwing herself into her work passed the time but

provided little satisfaction. Several possible new clients contacted her, but Will's hateful words—*"you won't be using my sister or riding my company's reputation in order to serve yourself any longer"*—echoed in her head and stung her pride. These clients had indeed come her way citing her work with Will and Evie—as reported by Tish—as their source.

She was possibly the most popular etiquette consultant in the state at the moment, yet she was completely miserable. She was also well aware that if Tish got wind of many *more* details, her popularity would go in the toilet faster than she could blink.

By Wednesday afternoon, her depression started to give way to anger. Will jumped to a conclusion without even giving her a chance to explain. She'd been caught so off-guard by his anger, she hadn't been able to defend herself.

Granted, nothing she said to Evie on the balcony that day hadn't been true, but she'd been judged and convicted over her seemingly Machiavellian plans without any chance to explain. He'd taken everything out of context. She and Evie had been teasing each other all afternoon. He just came in too late to understand the joke.

Eavesdropping. Something she didn't realize she needed to explain the evils of to a grown man.

Anyway, how stupid did he think she was? If she had meant her words in the way Will interpreted them, why on earth would she admit that to his sister, of all people?

The anger finally fueled her and she shook off the self-condemnation—if not the self-pity. She wasn't the only guilty party here. Will's claim of keeping business and pleasure separate proved itself to be utter garbage. She was mad at him for feeding her that line, and mad at herself for swallowing it.

And she was disgusted with herself for falling in love with him and foolishly believing he might feel the same way about her.

Righteous anger and self-disgust for her foolishness kept her from calling Will and trying to explain. He certainly didn't know her at all, or else he wouldn't have believed the worst about her on so little evidence. And she obviously didn't mean very much to him if he were willing and able to just cut her out of his life without looking back.

So she was stuck in an impasse, unable to bring herself to call Will to explain and risk having him hang up on her, but unable to just move on because she loved him.

Therefore, she was just miserable.

Evie had taken to e-mailing her twice a day, keeping her up-to-date on her French lessons, her geometry struggles, her dress fittings and, most importantly, her budding romance with Peter Asbury. News of Will, however, came rarely, and was always prefaced with some kind of derogatory remark. Evie was still steamed at Will, and if she was treating him in person to the ire he received in her e-mails, life at the Harrison home was chilly indeed. She was doing her best to respond to Evie without dragging her into the middle of the mess with Will.

It wasn't an easy task, and it only compounded her misery.

Letitia stalked into her office carrying one of the ears formerly attached to her beautiful bunny slippers. She dropped it at Gwen's feet and meowed.

"A gift for me?"

Letitia batted the ear with a delicate paw, and meowed again, obviously proud of her kill.

At least it wasn't a real ear. "Thank you. I'm very proud of you for killing the big bad bunny." With a purr, the cat landed in her lap and snuggled down in a contented warm ball. Gwen scratched her behind the ears. "Good kitty. At least you still love and appreciate me."

Oh, God. I'm turning into one of those crazy cat ladies. I should just give in to the cliché and adopt ten feline friends for Letitia to keep me company in my lonely old age. She allowed herself to wallow in the misery and went for more ice cream. Who cares if it's only ten in the morning? She had nothing better to do than get fat.

With that, she burst into tears. Again.

Will looked over the documents Marcus had faxed to him, and the rock in his stomach gained more weight.

He wasn't Gwen's first attempt at sleeping her way to success. Fueled by the gossip swirling around—and Evie's complaints about Gwen's departure—Marcus had obviously done a bit of digging into Gwen's past. And he'd found something: David Seymore, Gwen's former boss and lover. On the phone, Marcus made it sound like Gwen had been the biggest scandal since Watergate, but in looking over the facts, it didn't seem to be more than a blip on the city's radar. If anything, Gwen had been the scapegoat for the gross misbehavior and poor planning of her boss. The size, scope or cause of the scandal didn't bother him, but the news Gwen had pulled this stunt before made him more than a little ill. Her first attempt had ended in disaster, but that hadn't stopped her from making the most of the situation when it rose again. She'd almost pulled it off this time—hell, for all intents and purposes, she *had* pulled it off. Even with the gossip, Gwen seemed to have landed on her feet *and* gained some nice business publicity for her trouble.

He heard the front door slam. Evie was back from her dinner with Peter's family. She passed by the living room without acknowledging him and down the hall to her bedroom.

He wasn't surprised. In addition to having the Harrison temper, it seemed Evie also carried a grudge with ease. She'd quit speaking to him unless absolutely necessary after Gwen's departure. Now, after three days of silence, Will actually missed Evie's usual nonstop chatter. Dinners were cold, silent affairs and Evie refused to be in the same room with him at any other time.

Tired of the impasse, he followed her to her room and caught the door before she could slam it in his face.

"How much longer is the silent treatment going to last?"

"Until you quit being a butthead." Evie flopped dramatically on her bed and turned her back to him.

Okay, that wasn't much better than the deep freeze. "Gwen was using both of us. Better to end it now."

Evie flipped over and sat up, eyes blazing. "Don't say that about her. It's not true."

"Trust me, it is. Do you think she's the first woman who's tried to ingratiate herself into my life? She won't be the last, either. *You* should be taking notes. The users and the gold diggers will be coming out of the woodwork after you soon enough. I'm just sorry I didn't see it sooner. Before you got too attached." *And before I got attached.*

"You're not only a butthead, you're a stupid butthead."

"That's enough, Evangeline."

"Don't 'Evangeline' me. You're not my father."

He could cheerfully strangle her. "But I am your brother *and* your guardian *and* you live under my roof."

"I should have gone to boarding school," Evie grumped.

"It's not too late, you know. I'll get the brochures from Marcus."

Evie gasped, then her mouth compressed to a mutinous line. "I hate you!"

"Excellent. It'll give you something to talk about with your therapist when you're older."

"I don't know why Gwen liked you so much. You're such a—"

"Butthead. Yes, I know." How had he managed to get pulled into this debacle of a discussion? Had he actually said the "under my roof" line? God. Teenagers obviously caused brain damage to adults. He took a deep breath and tried to regain control of the situation. "I'm trying to tell you that Gwen—

as wonderful as you *think* she is—was playing us for her own gain. I wouldn't be surprised to hear she was the source for all of that gossip in *Lifestyles*."

"And I'm telling you she wasn't. Wasn't using us *or* providing Tish with information."

As much as he didn't like the idea, maybe telling Evie what he'd just learned would help her see the truth. "Evie, this wasn't the first time she's done something like this."

Evie's eyes narrowed at him. "Do you mean what happened in D.C. with her boss?"

"You know about that?" What had Gwen been teaching his sister?

"Of course I do. It's not something she's proud of, but she says it's important to learn from your mistakes."

"Mistakes? This wasn't a 'mistake,' Evie. This is a prime example—"

An overdramatic sigh interrupted him. "You know, I heard her tell Sarah how getting involved with you would be a really bad idea. I guess she was right." With that, she turned her back to him.

Well, that was a waste of my breath. "Marcus will be here in half an hour. Change clothes and put a smile on your face before he gets here."

Evie merely huffed.

"And I promise you, if you call me a butthead or play that silent game at dinner, you'll really wish you had gone to boarding school. Here, allow me," he added, as he slammed her door.

He needed a drink.

Fighting with Evie, as frustrating as it was, at least beat brooding over Gwen. It was even slightly more productive. Gwen made a fool out of him and hurt Evie in the process. He wasn't sure which crime was worse.

If Tish and her column were to be believed, he'd broken his fair share of hearts. Karma must be trying to even the score. Making him feel like a fool was just a bonus. Fighting with Evie over it had to be part of his penance.

All he could do was hope Evie behaved herself at dinner. He did *not* want to hash this out in front of Marcus.

With a sigh of disgust over the shambles one small brunette had made of his life, he went to change for dinner.

CHAPTER TWELVE

IN ORDER to quit self-medicating with ice cream before she couldn't fit in her clothes anymore, Gwen switched to Retail Therapy. With Sarah's discount, she treated herself to a set of obnoxiously high thread count sheets—the kind she'd grown accustomed to in the last few weeks living at Will's. Tonight, she'd sleep in luxury.

In an effort to help, Sarah also provided a bag full of samples from the cosmetic counters, including decadent bath salts in her favorite fragrance.

She'd soak. Then she'd sleep. This horrible week would be over, and she'd have a fresh start for whatever she decided had to happen next.

Pushing the door open with her foot, she blocked Letitia's escape. From deep in her purse, she heard Evie's ring tone. Knowing tonight was Evie's big night, she'd been expecting a call all day. Evie, bless her heart, had to be a bit nervous. Heck, she was nervous for her, but she intentionally didn't call because she didn't want Evie to think Gwen had any doubts about her ability to shine.

"Hey, there! Are you ready for tonight?"

"Nooo, I'm not. I can't do this." Evie sounded on the brink of tears.

"Honey, what's wrong?"

"I'm going to screw this up. I know I am. I need you, Gwen. Please come with me."

Gwen dropped her bags to the floor and settled the phone more comfortably on her ear. "I can't, you know that. I'm not a contributor." *And there's no way Will wants me to show.*

"You can be my date."

"Evie…"

"Will has a meeting tonight and won't show up until late and Uncle Marcus has to go early and I can't walk in there by myself!" A sob broke through, and Evie drew a ragged breath.

"Yes, you can. You're ready for this. You're a natural and everyone is going to love you." *Okay, now I know how Sarah feels every time I go through a personal crisis.*

"Gwen, please." Evie was working herself up into a full-scale fit. "*Please* come with me. You told me about those companion women who used to go with ladies to balls to chaperone them. You can be that if you don't want to be my date. I need you there, though. Don't make me do this alone."

What to say? "Evie…"

"Please, Gwen."

She was both a sucker and a fool. Evie's pleas tugged at her heart. The poor kid had every reason to be nervous, and at the rate she was going, she'd be a complete wreck by the time she arrived at the ball.

I'm going to regret this. No doubt in her mind it was a bad idea. Of course, knowing something was a bad idea never stopped her before. Hell, bad ideas were what had put her in *this* situation.

"Okay. Just calm down. You'll get all puffy and blotchy if you keep crying."

"Then you'll come with me?" The relief in her voice made Gwen want to cry for her.

"I'll come with you—but just for a little while until you feel comfortable." *Hopefully, that will be before Will decides to show up.*

"Thank you, thank you, thank you."

"You can thank me by pulling yourself together and knocking them dead tonight." *Oh, hell, what am I going to wear?*

"I promise I'll make you proud."

"You already do, honey. Now, what time?"

"Uncle Marcus is sending a car for me at seven. I'll have the driver swing by and pick you up on our way, okay?"

"That'll work. I'll see you then."

"Bye, Gwen. And thank you. Really."

Seven o'clock? Yikes, it was after five already. She dumped food in Letitia's dish with one hand and dialed with the other.

Sarah answered on the first ring—she'd been on high alert all week with ice cream at the ready, but Gwen didn't give her the chance to go into Support Mode.

"I need a cocktail dress, but nothing too fancy. And possibly shoes, unless the dress will go with those black slingbacks I have. You know, the ones with the rhinestones? Oh, and I'll need jewelry, too." Leaving Letitia happily munching away, she sped down the hall to the bathroom.

Confusion crept into Sarah's voice. "Gwennie, what's up?"

"Oh, hell, just set me up with the full ensemble." She wiggled out of her jeans and left them where they landed. "Can you do my hair, too?"

"Of course, Gwennie. Whatever you need. Now, when do you want to come in? We could make a day of it, get our nails done..."

Gwen juggled the phone so she could peel off her shirt. She twisted the taps on her shower to full blast and the pounding water made it hard for her to hear. "You don't understand. I need this *now*. Tonight. Hell, twenty minutes ago would've been excellent."

"What? Why?"

"Just find me a dress and get over here with it. Please. I'm going to the Med Ball and I have less than two hours to get ready and I have *nothing to wear*."

"The Med Ball? Really? Oh, Gwennie," she gushed, "that's fantastic. So you and Will—"

"No. Me and Evie." Sarah started to say more. "Look, I'm getting in the shower now. I'll fill you in on all the details when you get here. Hurry."

"I'm on my way. I know just the dress…"

"Thank you. Bye, now." She flipped the phone closed and tossed it on the pile of clothes at her feet.

Somewhere between exfoliating and shaving, she realized this wasn't the relaxing bath she planned. And this evening…so much for a calming get-your-head-back-together night in.

She'd deliver Evie to Marcus, hang around long enough for Evie to acclimatize and realize she would do fine and then grab a cab home. An hour, max. Hopefully Will wouldn't decide to show up earlier than planned and make a scene. Her ego couldn't handle his derision twice in one week.

Neither could her heart.

"Gwen! You look amazing!" Gwen twirled a little for Evie and mentally thanked Sarah one more time. Her one-woman fashion army arrived forty-five minutes after her phone call, bearing a midnight-blue gown and ready to coif. Even the voice in the back of her head chanting "Bad Idea, Bad Idea," had been slightly beaten down by the results Sarah produced. If a girl had to risk looking like a fool, at least she could be gorgeous while she did.

"Now, let me see you." Evie turned full circle, and Gwen's breath caught. "Trust me, honey, you're the one who looks amazing. No one would ever believe you were a tomboy surfer girl just a couple of weeks ago."

Evie smoothed the ice-blue silk of her dress. "I know. Do you like my hair?" She patted the complicated curls and twists.

"It's beautiful. As are you. But I think I miss the cornrows."

"Me, too." Evie sighed dramatically at the loss.

"Well, I think you both look fantastic," Sarah gushed, snapping pictures like a proud mama on prom night.

A small wave of disappointment moved through Gwen at the thought. Had things worked out differently, she would have helped Evie get ready for tonight. Instead Evie had dressed for her big night out all alone. It just wasn't fair.

She forced a smile she didn't feel. "Let's go."

Limos didn't cruise her neighborhood often, and the one sitting in front of her house had her neighbors gawking. Evie slid in, saying, "I'm so glad we practiced sitting and standing and getting in and out of cars gracefully."

"See, I told you so."

Evie giggled, but not nervously. Instead Evie projected confidence and a youthful sophistication Gwen wished she could bottle for her debs. The stressed-out girl who had called her two hours ago was gone, replaced by a stunning young woman who seemed ready to conquer the world. Or at least Dallas.

As the limo coasted to a smooth stop in front of the hotel, Evie reached over to squeeze her hand. "You'll watch for my signal and step in if I need you, right?"

"I'll keep an eye on you, but you're not going to need me. You'll see."

Evie smiled, and her face lit up the inside of the dimly lit limo. "Thank you again for coming with me. The moral support helps."

"Knock 'em dead, sweetie."

A moment later, Evie stepped from the car with the aid of the chauffeur and into the waiting crowd.

Feeling very much like a Regency duenna chaperoning her charge, Gwen trailed slightly in Evie's wake. She scanned the crowd, noting she knew most of the faces: debs she once trained, the parents of her current and future debs, people she knew from their pictures in the paper. Evie held her head high and smiled as Marcus Heatherton broke away from a group of society pillars and met her halfway across the room.

"Evangeline! You look lovely, my dear."

Evie beamed as she turned a cheek to accept his air kiss.

"You look very dashing yourself, Uncle Marcus." Evie reached for Gwen and pulled her slightly forward. "And you remember Gwen, of course."

She bit her lip at Marcus's look of utter horror. No doubt Will had told him enough to make him believe the very worst about her. She plastered a smile across her face and brazened it out. "Mr. Heatherton, it's nice to see you again."

Marcus quickly schooled his features into benign friend-liness. "How unexpected, Miss Sawyer. I didn't realize you would be escorting Evangeline."

Evie stepped in smoothly before Gwen could answer. "I had to beg her to come. I wouldn't be here tonight without Gwen's help, and I wanted her to see how well I did."

Oh, Evie was good. Not much Marcus could say in response to that without sounding like a first-class snob.

"I'm sure Miss Sawyer knows many people here and will enjoy catching up with them. If you'll excuse us, I'd like to introduce Evangeline to some of her father's friends."

Well, that could have been worse. Dismissed, she watched as Marcus led Evie away, and then flagged down a server for champagne. Moments later, she was surrounded by familiar faces as her former debs greeted her with hugs and flashes of enormous engagement rings.

Tish Cotter-Hulme found her quickly as well. The friendly crowd dispersed rapidly as no one wanted to unwittingly provide Tish with fuel for Monday's column. Tish's graying hair was swept back from her surgically enhanced face, which barely moved as she smiled. "Gwen, dear, I'm so glad to finally see you at one of these functions."

That fake smile didn't fool Gwen for a second, and her former good mood turned sour. Gwen tried to find a light tone to cover. "No comment, Tish. I've been on page three enough recently, thanks very much."

"Oh, Gwen, don't be so harsh. You make it sound like I'm only after a story."

Gwen kept a surreptitious eye on Evie, who seemed to be doing better than fine at the moment. Bradley Harrison's friends and business cronies wore enchanted smiles, and since several had teenage grandsons Evie's age, Gwen wouldn't be surprised if Evie's social calendar filled up rapidly after tonight.

"If you weren't, you wouldn't be standing here." Gwen sighed. "For the record, there's no story to report. I was hired to help Evie transition from her old life into her new one. You know that. As you can see, she has done so beautifully. I'm only here because Evie asked me to come because she thought I might enjoy myself. I've grown very fond of her over the last few weeks, and I'm very pleased with how well she's handled all of the adjustments. Coping with the loss of her parents and a move here is a lot for anyone to handle and she's done beautifully." *There, print that on page three, you nosey witch.*

Tish cocked an eyebrow at her. "And Will Harrison? Are you fond of him as well?

Gwen lifted an eyebrow of her own. "I think you've beaten that dead horse long enough. Oh, I know how boring truth is compared to speculation, but you're just writing fiction these days." Evie was now being introduced to the president of the Dallas Junior League and the head of Parkline Academy. When she tossed her head back and laughed, Gwen knew tonight was a complete success. In another few minutes, she'd be able to head home without worry.

"But you—"

Inspiration struck. "I tell you what. You tell me how you found out about my contract, and—" she leaned in conspiratorially and lowered her voice "—I'll give you something for Monday's column."

Tish eyed her suspiciously. "What's in it for you?"

"I'm just curious."

"You're willing to violate your nondisclosure agreement just to appease your curiosity?"

How'd she know about that? "Let's just say there are some things I know about the Harrisons that won't put me in violation of anything."

"Don't jerk me around, Gwen. It won't be pretty. Rumors kill in your business, you know."

"Oh, trust me, I know. I've done plenty of damage control thanks to you."

"Fine. Will Harrison had a temp in his office one day while his normal tight-lipped secretary was out sick. The temp found your contract and your check. She called me."

Good to know. She'd make sure Nancy had that tidbit of info first thing Monday morning. HarCorp's HR was about to be hit by a hurricane.

"So what have you got for me?" Tish practically salivated at the idea of juicy gossip she could twist into something even more salacious.

Gwen thought quickly. "From what I heard—" she smothered a smile as Tish leaned in eagerly "—Will isn't dating Grace Myerly any longer."

Tish's face fell. "That's it? Everyone knows they called it quits months ago. Old news, Gwen."

"Really?" She feigned innocence. "*I* didn't know that. It was a surprise to me."

"Surely you have something better for me."

Gwen shrugged. "Sorry, no. I guess I wasn't in as tight with the Harrisons as you insinuated."

"Don't play stupid, Gwen. It doesn't suit you." Suddenly Tish's attention shifted to something over Gwen's right shoulder. Her face lit up in interest. "Oh, look, there's your boss now."

Gwen froze. *Oh, no.* Why hadn't she left earlier instead of standing here sparring with Tish? She turned to see Will make a beeline to the crowd surrounding Evie. Will bent to kiss Evie's cheek in greeting, but Evie's response lacked her normal exuberance. Thankfully only someone who knew them both well would notice.

There was much handshaking and backslapping going on around them, and Evie now wore a small, self-conscious smile. If she had to guess, Will was being made aware of how charming and what a success she was. Then, someone else said something, causing Evie to give Will a "so there" look, and Will stiffened slightly.

He knows I'm here.

When Will started to scan the crowd, Gwen knew he was looking for her. She really didn't want their first meeting to be here, in this crush of people. She hadn't yet figured out what she wanted to say to him.

"Who's he looking for, I wonder?" Tish's voice made Gwen jump. She'd forgotten Tish was still standing there, and the insinuation in the statement made Gwen want to smack her.

"Hmm, I don't know, Tish." She had to get away from that woman, so she added brightly, "If you'll excuse me, I think I'll get a refill on my drink."

Without waiting for Tish's response, Gwen headed for the bar. She cut around the dance floor, where couples moved easily to the band's music, smiling and waving to people like nothing was out of the ordinary.

She took a deep breath, and concentrated on slowing her rapid heartbeat. She hadn't prepared for this. Seeing him. Her chest hurt, and she vacillated between wanting to hit him with something heavy and wanting to run to the bathroom and hide. Leaving—while the obviously simple solution—wasn't an option now. Even if no one believed Tish's rumors of romantic doings between them, everyone knew of their business relationship. Etiquette required her to at least speak to him.

Sometimes, the rules really sucked.

The bartender handed her a fresh glass of champagne and she sipped at it gratefully. Each bubble, though, seemed to have taken on a sharp edge and made swallowing difficult.

"Gwen? You look pale. Is everything all right?"

It took her a second to focus on the speaker. When her brain clicked back on, she saw Megan Morris, the former debutante who gave her the nickname of Miss Behavior, staring at her with a worried expression.

"I'm fine now, Megan," she lied. "I just got a little over-heated in the other room."

Megan patted her arm. "It is a bit of a crush sometimes. Plus, I saw Tish Cotter-Hulme had you cornered there for a while. That's enough hot air to overheat anyone." She smiled, and Gwen's heart rate finally began to slow to a normal rhythm. "Now, come with me. I have some people I'd like you to meet."

She couldn't say no, so she allowed herself to be led to a group of twentysomethings where she made idle conversation for the next fifteen minutes. She tried to keep an eye on Evie, just in case, but Evie had made her mark and was taking a turn on the dance floor. She'd just managed to relax some when she saw Will approaching out of the corner of her eye.

She tensed as members of the group greeted Will. Finally Will turned in her direction, and she braced herself.

He won't make a scene in public, she reminded herself.

"Gwen, I didn't expect to see you here." There was no warmth in his voice, and her heart ached at the bland, yet polite, tone.

"It was a last-minute plan. Evie asked me to come." She watched the people around them carefully, but no one seemed to see anything amiss. "I assume Evie's having a good time, as I haven't had a chance to talk to her since we arrived."

"Evie seems to be enjoying herself, and she's certainly charming my father's friends. May I speak with you for a moment?"

"Of course." *Act normally.* "Excuse me," she said to the

others, hoping they'd see nothing out of the ordinary about Will's behavior.

"Care to explain what you're doing here?" So much for bland-yet-polite—Will's tone could refreeze the ice sculptures.

"Marcus had to come early and you were going to be late and Evie didn't want to walk in alone. She shouldn't have been placed in such an uncomfortable position, and I couldn't deny her such a simple and understandable request." She raised an eyebrow, practically daring him to rebut.

The arrival of the chief of staff from the hospital forestalled Will's response, and she listened and smiled politely as Will and HarCorp were thanked profusely for their support of the hospital's fund-raising efforts.

When the chief of staff moved on, Will grabbed her by the elbow. "Let's dance."

Gwen felt her jaw drop. "What?"

"Don't get uptight. I'd like to carry on this conversation without interruption, and the only place I can see to do that is on the damn dance floor."

She sputtered, but managed to put one foot in front of the other until Will found an empty space on the dance floor and pulled her into his arms.

Her stomach clenched and her whole body ached from the sensation of being close to him. His tux made him look even more breathtakingly handsome than usual, emphasizing the breadth of his shoulders and the lean-muscled length of his body. Gwen inhaled the scent of his aftershave with each breath, and the hand she placed on his shoulder itched to caress the warm skin only inches away. It was torture and her heart was taking the brunt of it.

If Will noticed, he didn't say anything, and he certainly didn't seem to have a similar response to her. He kept the proper distance between them and continued their earlier conversation.

"So this was Evie's idea."

"Of course. Why else would I be here?" Gwen glanced around. So far, no one seemed overly interested in their appearance on the dance floor, but again, based on their prior business dealings, it shouldn't draw undue attention.

She hoped.

Will moved easily to the music. "Evie I can understand. She's been your most vocal defender."

Gwen stiffened. "I haven't done anything that needs defending."

He continued as if she hadn't said a word. "Bringing you here is Evie's thinly veiled attempt at forcing a reconciliation."

"Do you think I—"

"I'd hate to even try to guess how your mind works, Gwen." He sneered.

"That's uncalled for." *Enough.* Her feet froze. She wasn't going to fight with him on the dance floor in front of hundreds of people.

Will's hand tightened on her waist. "Keep dancing. You wouldn't want to make a scene, would you?"

She was fuming, but he was right in knowing she wouldn't intentionally make a scene. She forced her feet to move. The song couldn't last more than a couple of minutes longer, and then she'd be able to leave without drawing undue attention.

"So, do you deny that you only took the job in order to drum up additional business?"

At least that was an easy enough question. "It's called good business sense, Will. Every business owner hopes the current contract will lead to future ones. Surely you understand *that*."

He shrugged. "Usually those contracts will be in the same general field. You decided to use my sister to infiltrate HarCorp. I checked with HR, Gwen. They had a file of your proposals."

"I'm not denying I lobbied HarCorp in the past."

"I just offered you the chance to do it in person."

"Which I never did! I agreed to work with Evie and that's exactly what I did. *You* came to *me* with the consulting job."

"Which was just what you wanted."

"Of course I did. It was the kind of opportunity I'd been waiting for for years." Will's jaw tightened. "Let me repeat— I lobbied HarCorp. I never once lobbied *you*."

"You didn't have to. You just crawled into my bed for the job."

She gasped and her fingers itched to slap him for that gross insult.

"You are a first-class bastard." She caught herself hissing and plastered a smile back across her face for the benefit of their audience. "You're not the only one who can separate business and pleasure, you know. And, just to refresh your memory, *you* crawled into *my* bed."

"You never answered my initial question, Gwen."

"Which was…?"

"Did you take the job with Evie so you could weasel your way into HarCorp?"

"Absolutely no—" She stopped, thinking back to that day in Will's office. She had almost talked herself into taking the job simply for the possible "in" into HarCorp *before* she got the full story on Evie and made up her mind. But it had been such a brief moment, and she'd gotten attached to Evie so quickly…

Will must have noticed her hesitation and decided it was a guilty conscience. She saw his eyes harden as he confirmed his suspicions based on her momentary lapse. She was doomed no matter what she said.

"And where did sleeping with me fall in your business plan?"

"If you remember correctly, I told you that would be a bad idea."

"Seemed to work out pretty well for you. Of course, you've had plenty of practice, haven't you?"

She sucked in her breath. Was he referring to David? The sarcastic tone answered her question. *How* did he know about that? *Oh God, could this be any more horrible?*

"You almost pulled it off. If you hadn't gotten cocky, you might have milked me for more."

She stopped dancing, well aware of the stares they attracted, but not caring any longer. All of her training and all of her studies failed her. None of the speeches or explanations she practiced over the week worked in the face of being called something only slightly better than an opportunistic whore.

She'd been so used to Will looking at her with kindness and an endearing smile, the hardness that stared back at her all evening was breaking her heart. But when his face cracked into a mocking smirk, she wanted to scream.

"You're good, but you're not that good." With that, Will turned on his heel and left her standing alone on the dance floor, her mouth gaping in shock.

Evie appeared in her line of vision, her eyes wide and her face pale. Horrified, Gwen looked around her. While some people tried to act nonchalant, like nothing had just happened, she could tell by the body language that every one of them had seen Will leave her standing there. And it didn't take a crystal ball to see what would happen next. A woman in a red cocktail dress leaned to the woman on her right and whispered. Anyone who hadn't witnessed Will's act of rudeness would have a full reporting in no time.

Hot-faced and humiliated, Gwen tried to hold her head up as she left the dance floor. She even tried a smile and a shrug as if to say, "oh, well." It didn't work. She could tell by the stares of shock and pity.

The band, as if aware of the drama and sensing the need to change the subject quickly, launched into an upbeat swing piece. Gwen skirted the couples making their way on to the dance floor and looked for the nearest exit.

Tish waylaid her departure. "Seems you do hold up your end of a bargain. You promised me something good for Monday's column, and you certainly delivered," she said with a smirk.

That was the proverbial last straw. Every pithy and etiquette-approved remark escaped her. Nothing Tish could print at this point could be any more personally humiliating or professionally damning than the scene she'd just provided for everyone's entertainment.

"Bite me, Tish."

She didn't take any time to appreciate Tish's openmouthed shock, choosing instead to make her exit on that small high note.

The doorman flagged a taxi, and Gwen barked her address at the driver. In no mood for small talk, she stared out the window and tried to calm her whirling thoughts.

She never should have let Evie drag her to the Med Ball. In light of Will's statement about Evie's matchmaking, Gwen wondered if Evie's earlier panic attack had been nothing more than part of a larger scheme.

I never learn, do I? Tonight's debacle just drove home how stupid she was. At least she wouldn't have to wait long for the fallout. Tish would help spread the word to anyone who wasn't at the Med Ball—and from the look on Tish's face, Gwen was going to pay dearly for her comment in Monday's column. By Monday afternoon her humiliation would be complete. And if her clients had been willing to drop her at

the first whiff of a scandal two weeks ago, the fact she was
on the outs with the Harrison family would have her black-
balled by Tuesday afternoon at the latest.

Tears burned behind her eyelids. She hoped she still had
ice cream in the freezer.

CHAPTER THIRTEEN

EVIE'S silent treatment was total and absolute, and Will almost felt like he was living alone again. While she'd kept her game face on at the Med Ball, only shooting him a few dirty looks after Gwen left, she'd shut down completely in the limo on the way home. Comments, questions, attempts at normal conversation—everything was met with stony silence. Even eye contact was out. He'd never been so completely ignored in his entire life. She stomped to her room without looking back, and had only left it to eat for the rest of the weekend. Mrs. Gray had weekends off, so Will rattled around his apartment alone in the silence.

And it was driving him insane.

He worked in his office with the door open, just in case Evie decided to call a truce. While it gave him a chance to catch up on the paperwork he'd let slide the past couple of weeks, he derived little satisfaction from the work. It didn't help that the majority of his time was spent working on his upcoming meeting, and that meeting made him think of Gwen.

The sight of her at the Med Ball had nearly knocked him off his feet. He'd grown accustomed to a down-to-earth look for Gwen—battered, curve-hugging jeans or sundresses that flowed around her luscious legs. He'd even gotten used to those frumpy Miss Behavior suits she insisted on wearing. But

Gwen as socialite, with her hair swept up to expose the long, lovely line of her neck and wearing a beaded blue cocktail dress that exposed just enough cleavage to remain classy yet still leave him salivating…that had set him back a pace, at least until the blood had started circulating freely again.

He tried to block the image of Gwen from his mind and concentrate on the work they'd done for the meeting. He had to give her some credit, however begrudgingly; she was more than a pretty face and amazing body. She was certainly good at her job. Gwen's notes on everything from the order of introductions to sketches showing where everyone should sit at the conference table were astoundingly thorough. Small notes written in the margins of his proposal outline in her precise handwriting showed she understood both the human and business aspects of successful meetings.

When he got to the page where she gave suggestions about what color ties he and his VPs should wear, he had to laugh. No detail was too small for her attention, it seemed.

He wondered if Gwen provided this level of service to everyone. If so, then her consultant's fee was too small. Thinking back to previous meetings and events, Gwen's expertise could have come in handy at HarCorp. Odd that HR never followed up on any of her proposals…

I lobbied HarCorp. I never lobbied you.

Gwen's words echoed in his head. That much had been true.

If he wanted to be honest with himself, he probably deserved Evie's silent treatment. He treated Gwen with unbelievable rudeness Friday night. He remembered one of her lectures to Evie: *"You don't have to be friendly. You don't have to be kind. But you do have to be polite. There's no excuse for flat-out rudeness. I don't care how angry you are."*

He'd let his anger take the lead and look where it had led him. She'd hurt him and he'd wanted to return the feeling. She'd used him to further her own ambitions—or at least he'd thought so. In the late nights after she left, he'd had a chance to rethink the events of the previous days and weeks and wondered if he'd jumped to an inaccurate conclusion. But seeing her at the Med Ball caused his anger to flare up again. All he saw was another woman riding his name—or in this case, Evie's feelings—for her own benefit. So he'd accosted her and blasted her with his worst suspicions.

The look on Gwen's face when he left her on the dance floor would stay with him for a long time. Whatever else she'd done, whatever her reasons were for working for him, she hadn't slept with him for professional gain. No one could fake the look of shock and hurt he'd seen in her eyes.

But if she was innocent of scheming and manipulations, then why hadn't she defended herself? She'd never had a problem taking him to task before. But she'd left without so much as a word and hadn't attempted contact since. Her silence should indicate she was guilty on all counts.

But now that he'd calmed down, he realized he couldn't have misjudged Gwen's character that completely. He wasn't a man easily fooled by anyone. His instincts had never been *that* wrong. He'd gotten his feelings hurt and jumped the gun in defense.

Which meant he may have screwed up big this time and run off the first woman who'd ever gotten under his skin.

In other words, he really was the butthead Evie accused him of being.

"I hope you're happy now, Will." Evie's first words since Friday evening blasted him as he came into the kitchen for his last cup of coffee before he left for work. She sat at the bar counter with a bowl of cereal in front of her and the newest edition of *Dallas Lifestyles* in her hand.

She couldn't have been more wrong. *Happy* wasn't in his emotional repertoire at the moment. But something had finally broken Evie's vow of silence—even if she was still angry.

He refilled his mug. "Good morning to you as well. I'm glad to see you're speaking to me again."

Evie snorted. "Hardly. I'm going to my tennis lesson." She tossed the open issue of *Lifestyles* on the counter in front of him. "There. You should be pleased with yourself."

Evie huffed out of the room and he heard the front door slam behind her as she left for her lesson.

He sipped at his coffee as he read the Society Column for the first time. As expected, the article covered the who-wore-what and the other basics of the Med Ball, but moved on very quickly to a far more interesting topic.

I hate to say "I told you so," but that doesn't make it less true when it comes to the Miss Behavior/Will Harrison situation I've been following the last couple of weeks. Despite protestations to the contrary from all sides, I've been firm in my assertions that Gwen Sawyer and Will Harrison had something going on when she moved in to his penthouse. Things have certainly turned interesting, and current events shed new light on the older facts. First, news trickled in that Gwen moved out very suddenly early last week, and the "friendly" relationship between all parties cooled considerably. Certainly, the lack of sightings about town seemed to confirm that. Miss Behavior's arrival at the Med Ball in the company of Evangeline Harrison might have thrown everything into question, but the Sawyer/Harrison showdown witnessed by yours truly and the other three hundred guests was nothing short of a lover's spat. No one has come forward with an account of what was said, but one thing was perfectly clear when Will left Gwen standing alone on the dance floor: her services—whatever she was providing—are no longer necessary or welcome. It leaves one to wonder if Miss Behavior has lost her magic touch.

He read on in disgust. Tish Cotter-Hulme was out for blood—mostly Gwen's for some reason. While speculation about his side of the story was kept to a minimum, Gwen got dragged in the mud both personally and professionally.

No wonder Evie had broken her vow of silence just to condemn him. If Gwen caught fallout from the earlier speculations and rumors, she was living on Ground Zero right now.

The last paragraph caught his eye.

Society-at-large finally got to meet the elusive Evangeline Harrison at the Med Ball, and she represented the Harrison family with style and class. Evie, as she is known to family and friends, is a breath of fresh air and a charming young lady. In an ice-blue silk…

Not that he'd had any question about Evie's success, but here it was in black and white for everyone to see. She should have been basking in the good press and enjoying her moment in the society column sun. Yet Evie hadn't said a word about it. After the crucifixion of Gwen in the paragraphs before, he could see why.

The morning traffic gave him even more time to think. The more he did, the nagging suspicion he'd not only judged Gwen harshly and unjustly but then compounded the issue by humiliating her in public intensified.

He could cheerfully wring that gossip woman's neck for her speculations. However true they were, it still wasn't for her to make them public. Plus, the viciousness in her attacks against Gwen went beyond the simple desire to sell papers. Tish's attacks were personal; Gwen had made an enemy of the woman somehow.

Legally there wasn't much he could do about it since gossip wasn't a crime—no matter how malicious he thought it was—and he couldn't go calling the paper without making the situation worse. But surely HarCorp's legal team and advertising department could stir up enough trouble at the paper to make that woman think twice before dragging Gwen through the mud again. It would probably keep her away from Evie as well.

The thought of turning his people loose on Tish Cotter-Hulme and her ilk gave him a great sense of satisfaction. That satisfaction sparked another realization in him he wasn't quite ready to deal with yet.

Gwen was more than just under his skin.

"Just quit answering the phone, Gwennie."

If I did, would you quit calling, too? Gwen didn't voice the frustration because she knew deep in her heart that Sarah only meant to help and console with her every-ten-minute phone calls. Didn't Sarah have actual work to do today?

But the headache pounding behind her eyes wasn't Sarah's fault, so Gwen tapped into her last reservoir of patience for her sister. "I can't. Silence is perceived as a sign of guilt. If I'm going to salvage what's left of my reputation and business, I have to have good explanations for Tish's accusations." Another message pinged into her in-box and Gwen sighed. "At least I can copy and paste the same thing over again in the e-mails."

To call the morning "hellish" would be an understatement. If she could keep reminding everyone how much Tish liked to blow the smallest of issues out of proportion and thereby make her "showdown" with Will seem like it was taken out of context simply for the dramatic effect, she just might make it through this with her career intact, if slightly battered. Thankfully many of her clients had been dragged through Tish's mud pit at some point, and they were proving somewhat sympathetic to her plight. Some carefully worded comments and a light tone helped.

So the hellish nature of her morning stemmed more from her own heartache than Tish's column. Yes, the damage control was taking its toll on her nerves and patience, but it was the constant discussion of Will that had her stomach in knots.

"How are you holding up, Gwennie?"

"Better than you, it seems."

"I can't help but worry."

Sarah sounded close to tears, and Gwen instantly regretted her snappish tone. "I know. And I appreciate it. But nothing has changed since last week other than the public nature and level of my humiliation."

"*Call him.* Call Will and explain."

Gwen sighed. "At first, I wanted to, you know, but I couldn't pull myself together to do it. But now I'm angry. *He* jumps to conclusions and berates me. *He* acts like a jerk and embarrasses me in public, yet I'm the one catching the flack. Even if he deserved an explanation, I'm not inclined to provide one anymore. I'm not sure I ever want to speak to him again."

"I don't believe that for a second."

"Start trying." When yet another e-mail pinged into her box, she saw the president of the Junior League's name in the sender line and cringed. She closed her e-mail program and headed for the kitchen for coffee.

"So you're willing to walk away from what could be the one guy you've been waiting for your whole life because of this?"

Gwen didn't have a ready answer. Letitia twined around her ankles and purred loudly as she refilled her cup for the umpteenth time this morning.

"At least when David hung me out to dry he had reason to—even if it was a purely selfish one. Plus, I brought a lot of it on myself with my naiveté. But this... There's just no excuse. Will doesn't trust me. He believed the worst about me and condemned me on the flimsiest of evidence, then compounded it by humiliating me in public." She'd followed her heart and her hormones and been so swept up by Will, the realization that crashed down on her was killing her. Her heart cracked and her voice broke.

"He's not the guy I've been waiting for."

CHAPTER FOURTEEN

"MR. HARRISON, I'm afraid there's a small problem."

Will looked up from the quarterly reports and saw Nancy hovering in the doorway between his office and hers with a worried look on her face.

"Just tell me it has nothing to do with Kiesuke Hiramine, the meeting, or anything Japanese in nature," he joked. Hiramine's flight was already in the air, and he and his team would be arriving tomorrow. Everything was in place for Friday's meeting, all the way down to the high-gloss shine on the conference room table.

"I'm afraid it does."

Damn. "What happened?"

"You asked me two weeks ago to find you an expert on Asian business and culture to assist with the meeting. When you hired Miss Sawyer as a consultant, I assumed she would be present and no one else would be necessary." Nancy took a deep breath. "I realized Monday that would no longer be the case, but I'm having a very hard time finding a replacement on such short notice. I've found a translator who's available Friday, but he has no other qualifications."

Nancy wouldn't be standing in his doorway if she thought a translator would be good enough, and she wouldn't be giving him the entire spiel unless she had a solution in mind.

He waved her into the room and leaned back in his chair. "So what do you suggest?"

"Bringing Miss Sawyer back on board is the simple and obvious solution. She is already familiar with the situation and she certainly has the expertise necessary. Unless, of course, your, um, personal relationship with her makes that a completely unacceptable choice."

"I see." Gwen *was* the obvious choice. The question was would she do it?

"I need to call the caterer back, so I'll leave you to decide. Let me know if you'd like me to call Miss Sawyer or book Mr. Michko simply as a translator."

Will tapped his pen on the desk. Hiring Gwen back would certainly solve his immediate business problem. And there were other benefits, too. It might not completely thaw Evie's cold shoulder, but she might lighten up. It would also help Gwen counterbalance the gossip about her and her business. Going back to work for HarCorp would make what happened at the Med Ball seem like a minor disagreement taken out of context—no one would believe the worst if he and HarCorp felt she was still the right person for the job.

Most importantly, it would give him the excuse to contact her.

He might not be able to fix the mess of his personal life, but he could solve both their business problems by simply extending an olive branch. Business he understood, and contacting Gwen would be a sound business choice with benefits to both parties.

He clicked open a new e-mail and chose his words carefully.

What happened after this…well, that would really be up to Gwen. He'd keep an open and optimistic mind.

Gwen,
HarCorp's meeting with Hiramine is still on for Friday at one. After all the prep work you put in on this project, I'm assuming you'd like to see it through to the end. HarCorp could use your expertise in making this meeting a success, and I'd consider it a professional favor if you'd be able to put our differences aside and assist as originally planned.

Gwen watched Sarah's face as she read the printout of Will's e-mail. She drummed her fingernails on Sarah's antique dining room table in impatience as she waited. Sarah's plan for a non-Will, get-back-to-real-life dinner had been sidetracked when Gwen produced Will's e-mail. Gwen needed a sounding board for this new development, but jeez, how slow did her sister read? "Well, what do you make of it?"

Sarah flipped over the paper as if more might be on the other side then looked at her in mild shock. "This is it? No explanation? No phone call?"

"That's it. Out of nowhere into my in-box this afternoon." She sighed and pushed at the potatoes on her plate. She appreciated Sarah's efforts at dinner, but tonight Gwen had little appetite for even Sarah's fool-proof comfort food.

"Do you think it's an opening? Some kind of attempt at reconciliation?" Sarah handed the printout back across the table to Gwen.

"I don't know what to think." Gwen smoothed her fingers over the words in the paper as if the answers might be in Braille. "That's why I haven't answered yet.

"On the one hand, he all but calls me on my contractual obligations—which he's fully within his rights to do so—but last week my contract didn't seem to matter. On the other…"

Sarah nodded. "It's tough to tell *what* he's thinking."

"Try 'impossible,'" Gwen muttered, as she moved the irritating e-mail off the table and pushed at her food some more.

"I meant," Sarah continued, "it's so vague. Someone needs to explain to him the great invention of the emoticon. I can't tell if it's just business or if he's trying to apologize."

"Welcome to my world." Gwen sighed.

"Are you going to do it?"

"I don't know. I did sign a contract, but I haven't been paid yet. I'd be in violation of the contract if I don't follow through, but other than losing the check, there's not much more professional harm that could be done. What's he going to do? Not give me a reference?" She snorted before she caught herself. "It's not like one is forthcoming at this point anyway."

Sarah's level look pinned Gwen to her chair. "But you want to do it. In a purely professional sense, I mean."

Gwen felt her mouth twitch. "Yeah. Kinda. It would be nice to see it all the way through, and it would be a nice feather in my cap. Plus, it would show that regardless of anything else going on, I can still do my job."

"Unlike before?"

"I wasn't given the opportunity before. When everything hit the fan, I was out the door before any of the other projects I was working on came to fruition."

"That was your own fault. You let David—"

She didn't need Sarah harping on that again. "Yes, I know that *now*. The thing is, no one's seen what I can really do. If I make it through the next couple of weeks with my reputation intact, my success with this meeting could open more doors for me."

"And on a personal level?"

There was that headache again, softly throbbing behind her eyes. "I want to, but I don't. I love him, but I can't just put myself out there for him to hurt me again. Being in the same room with him would be a nightmare."

Sarah nodded.

"But I know how important this is for him. I don't hate him enough yet to want him to fail." She sighed, the indecision eating at her.

"You're going to do it, aren't you, Gwennie? It's a win-win situation. You'd be making a sound business decision—and it will be good for your bank account as well. You should do it because it's the right thing for *you*, not because you're in love with him."

"Oh, no. I'm not considering doing it because I love him. Quite the opposite. He accused me of using him. Now it looks like he's using me. So we'll use each other, and we'll both come out ahead."

"And if this offer is more than just business?"

Gwen shrugged. "I can't infer that it is, and I won't get my hopes up."

"Smart girl." Sarah patted her hand. "But don't completely ignore the possibility."

"I guess I've made my decision, huh?"

"Sounds like it."

"Can I borrow your laptop for a minute?"

Sarah arched an eyebrow at her. "In the middle of dinner, Miss Behavior? Aren't there rules about that?"

Gwen lifted her own eyebrow in response. "Did you invite Miss Behavior to dinner or your sister?"

Sarah waved her hand in the direction of her desk and the laptop. "On you go. But the next time my cell phone rings, I get to answer it—no matter where we are."

"Hmm." Gwen grinned and scooted her chair back. "How about I won't mention to Mother that you offered me money to write your thank-you notes last Christmas instead?"

Sarah shrank noticeably. "You win. I'll open another bottle of wine while you're gone."

But she was already mentally composing her response. It had to be just as vague and businesslike as Will's.

Evie's natural exuberance couldn't be stifled forever, and Will was happy to see she was deigning to speak to him again. While she was still a bit cool, at least tonight's dinner wasn't the silent movie it had been recently. The tentative truce with his moody charge and the polite e-mail from Gwen waiting for him this morning informing him of her attendance at tomorrow's meeting had improved his outlook immensely.

"Parkline's open house is on Monday night. You'll get to sign up for classes and meet your teachers."

"Sounds great." Evie cut her beef with precise movements. "I'll need to go next week and get my uniform."

"The entire board of trustees will be at the open house," he added casually. "That includes Mrs. Wellford."

Evie started to nod, then froze midchew. Her eyes widened, and she swallowed with difficulty. "The lady with the dog?"

I will not laugh. "Yes, the lady with the dog. Its name is Shu-Shu, and you should probably be prepared to make amends."

Evie looked horrified. "It was an accident, Will, and I know better now. Surely Mrs. Wellford won't hold a grudge."

Evie paused, and when she winced, Will knew she was picturing Shu-Shu retching on Mrs. Wellford's white, lace collar. Lord knew it wasn't a visual he'd forget anytime soon.

"Oh, no, she will, won't she? I think I hate that dog."

"You and everyone else." He chuckled. "Just be prepared."

"Gwen says it's not polite to remind someone of past errors, so Mrs. Wellford would be rude to bring it up. But I'll apologize again anyway. Gwen said it couldn't hurt."

The mention of Gwen had him wondering if he should tell Evie about tomorrow. She'd be pleased, of course, and his making peace with Gwen would go a long way in warming her attitude, but he didn't want her jumping to any assumptions about Gwen being a part of his—or their—future.

"Just so you know, Gwen has agreed to help with my meeting tomorrow."

Evie's facade cracked, bringing the ear-to-ear grin he'd missed recently. "Really? So you two made up? Did you apologize? Is she—?"

"Evie, don't jump ahead. This is strictly business. Gwen has an expertise I need for this meeting, and we're simply sticking to the terms of her contract."

Evie's face fell. "Will, don't be a butthead about this."

"Evangeline, if you call me a butthead one more time, you'll be an old woman before you see the inside of a dressing room at Neiman Marcus again."

Evie closed her mouth with an audible snap. *Finally a threat with enough teeth.* He'd have to remember that one.

"Sorry. I just mean it's great that you've decided to work with Gwen on this. I know her pretty well, and I know she's going to do a great job for you. But—" she paused to lay her fork and knife down carefully before she leveled a look at him that was mature beyond her years "—I also know you pretty well now, too. If you keep acting like a butt—I mean, acting like this, you'll drive her away and she'll never come back."

"I know you miss Gwen and you were hoping she might be a permanent addition to the family, but this isn't about you, Evie."

"Oh, I know that. But I know Gwen cares about you—I think she might even love you. This is your chance to show Gwen how much you care about her. You do care about her, right?"

Evie's insight shocked him. As much as he wanted to steer her to a different, less uncomfortable, subject, he felt this conversation might be an important turning point in his relationship with Evie.

"I do care about her. And I know you'll be happy to hear I've realized that I may have been a bit hasty in my judgment of her. My only defense for my actions is wanting to protect you—and me, too. There are plenty of people out there who are only looking out for themselves."

Evie grinned at his revelation. "I know. But Gwen isn't one of them."

He returned the grin. "Hopefully not."

"So you'll apologize?"

"Yep." *As soon as the meeting is over and only if she seems to be open to it.*

"And you'll ask her to move back in with us?"

"Whoa, slow down there."

"But, Will—"

"We'll see how it goes."

Gwen dressed carefully Friday morning. Knee-length navy-blue skirt, light blue silk shirt, closed-toe pumps and understated jewelry. She started to twist her hair up into a French knot, but with the overly conservative outfit, it only made her look like a spinster librarian.

Normally that look would be considered fine for a meeting, but Will's presence at *this* meeting changed everything. She shook her hair out and let it fall in loose waves around her shoulders. Will liked her hair better this way, but the Japanese guests would find it odd. She compromised by clipping it at the base of her neck.

Gwen packed her briefcase and glanced at her watch. She'd meet with Nancy first to go over all the small details one last time. Then she'd meet with Will and his VPs for one last briefing before Mr. Hiramine and his group arrived.

She took a deep breath and checked her lipstick one last

time. An eerie sense of déjà vu settled on her shoulders. The last time she darkened HarCorp's doors, she'd been so excited and positive her meeting with Will would change her life.

How right she'd been. It had almost destroyed her.

She should have the same feeling today—and she did. Sort of. The feeling this meeting could change everything was there, only this time she lacked the excitement and hopeful expectations.

Unlike last time, at least she knew—somewhat—what she was getting into.

This time, she knew to guard her heart.

CHAPTER FIFTEEN

"WHERE the hell is Gwen?" Will paced his office and glanced at the clock again. Twenty minutes until show time, and Gwen was nowhere to be found.

Nancy bustled in carrying his suit jacket. "She's in the boardroom, briefing the others. You're late."

Will shrugged into the jacket and adjusted his tie. "Then let's go."

HarCorp's executive conference room took up the entire top corner of the building, and through the glass walls, Will could see his VPs lined up like school kids as Gwen lectured animatedly in front of them. Nancy opened the main door and he could hear her going over last-minute reminders.

"Remember—no big hand gestures while you talk. They won't call you by your first name, so don't ask. And remember to use 'Mr.'—this isn't the time to create false familiarity by just calling them by just their last names. All right?"

Silent nods answered her. Will could relate. When Gwen was in Miss Behavior mode, a man couldn't do much more. She simply projected an aura that made people want to be on their very best behavior. As several men noticed him and nodded, Gwen turned to see who was behind her.

One brief flicker in those hazel eyes of hers gave him a flash of hope that this meeting might be good for something other than HarCorp's profits. A split-second later, the look was gone, and her mouth curved into a noncommittal smile. "Good afternoon, Mr. Harrison. We're just going over a few last-minute things."

Her cool greeting irritated him, but he shook it off with a sharp mental reminder: *This is business. What did you expect? A big kiss?*

He inclined his head slightly. "Miss Sawyer."

Gwen indicated a chair at the table. "You'll sit here, Mr. Harrison. Mr. Hiramine and Mr. Takeshi will be over here."

He watched as she arranged people and water glasses to her satisfaction. He could tell she was tense as she looked everything over with a critical eye, but the rest of the occupants of the room would never be able to tell. Matthews from Marketing tried to pull him into conversation, and he answered absently.

His eyes feasted on her, forcefully reminding him how empty his bed had felt recently. As she laughed at something Andrews said to her, he felt a stab of jealousy in his heart. More than anything, he wanted to drag her to his office, tell her he forgave her and spend the next couple of hours showing her exactly how much he missed her.

But he had to make it through this meeting first. As he watched, Gwen demonstrated to his VP of Accounting how to bow, and he knew he'd been right to hire her in the first place. Even in some awful old-lady outfit complete with sensible shoes, she radiated poise and confidence.

The weight of the meeting lifted off his shoulders. With Gwen in charge, he had no doubt of the outcome. Just the sight of her filled him with surety of that fact. Gwen knew her stuff and had everyone and everything firmly in hand. Thank God he decided to use her for this.

Out of nowhere, his own words came back to him. *She was using us.* Guilt filled him. Was he any better? Was this any different? He was using her right now, after all.

Realization hit him like lightning. Utilizing someone's talents wasn't the same as using the person. Gwen's defense—

I lobbied HarCorp. I never lobbied you—made a lot more sense now. She may have been using the situation to her advantage, but she wasn't necessarily using him. And taking advantage of the situation wasn't a bad thing, either. If it was, he was just as guilty.

And with that realization, he could now admit Gwen was more than just under his skin without sounding like a gullible fool. Somehow, in the middle of all of this, he'd fallen in love with her.

He was out of his seat, fully intending to march Gwen out of the conference room for a private meeting of their own when she suddenly straightened and clapped her hands for everyone's attention. With a small inclination of her head toward the hallway, she brought him back to the situation at hand.

"It's showtime, gentlemen. Here they come."

Three years of work was about to be decided, and suddenly, Will couldn't care less.

Gwen knew the meeting went well. No major gaffes to offend the Japanese guests, and HarCorp's VPs kept their usual aggressive American business tactics to themselves. Mr. Hiramine's assistant, Mr. Takeshi, served as translator when needed, freeing Gwen to help steer the meeting properly. She couldn't have been more pleased.

But her stomach was still tied in knots, and had been since Will walked into the room and caused every nerve cell in her body to cry out to him. The long, level looks he kept sending in her direction were unreadable, and the uncertainty they caused made her slightly nauseous.

Her position at his left side kept her senses on overload during the meeting, and her focus shifted too often from the business going on around her to the smell of his aftershave and the sight of that place on his neck right above his collar where he liked to be kissed. Her ability to concentrate evaporated each time his arm brushed against hers or his leg bumped hers under the massive table. She had to call on every ounce of her pride, her professionalism and her training to keep the smile on her face and her head in the general vicinity of the game.

And then it was over. There was much bowing and shaking of hands, then the line of men in dark suits filed from the room. Will followed as far as the door and shut it behind them. With the meeting behind her and a safe distance between them, Gwen was able to draw a deep breath for the first time in hours. As she exhaled, she realized she'd made one last error.

"You should escort them as far as the elevator, Will," she whispered, moving in the direction of the door.

"They'll survive." Will perched a hip on the conference table. "So how do you think it went?"

"Good. Really good."

"You don't think they sounded unenthused about the idea?"

"That's normal. I warned you the Japanese could seem very reserved and formal. It doesn't mean they aren't interested in proceeding. It could mean quite the opposite. My feeling is that you'll hear good news soon." She tried for a bright smile, but it felt fake.

Will nodded, but didn't say anything. The silence, combined with that same stare he'd given her throughout the meeting, tightened the knot in her stomach even more.

"Thank you for your help. It wouldn't have gone as well without your input. I appreciate it."

"You're welcome."

The stilted, polite conversation was killing her. As soon as she could get out of here, she was getting a strong drink.

Will fished in his pocket and pulled out a piece of paper. "Here's your check." He slid it across the table to her.

As awkward as it was, she had no choice but to take it. "Thank you. You could've just had Nancy mail it. I—" She lost her train of thought when she caught sight of the numbers. That was more than her contract outlined. Like twenty percent more. She looked at Will in question.

"You did a great job, Gwen, especially considering the, uh, history we have."

Anger bubbled up inside her chest. It was a nice change from the nausea.

"HarCorp has always believed in rewarding good service from its employees. Consider it a bonus."

He sat there calling her just another employee while in the same breath he brought up their history? Anger continued to surge through her veins, warming her skin. She'd like to shove his "bonus" up his...

"Excuse me?" Will was the picture of shock.

Too late, she realized she'd vocalized the thought. *Oh God.* Her first instinct was to backtrack, but the anger fueled her forward instead.

"You heard me. I don't want your bonus." She ripped the check into small pieces, gaining great satisfaction from the look on his face. "You've embarrassed me publicly and insulted me personally, and you try to smooth it all over with a fat check?" She sneered the words. "Good God, you think you can just throw money at people to solve your problems. Grow up."

"I don't—"

"Yes, you do. First Evie, and now me." She was shouting, but she didn't care. God, it felt good to vent. She gathered up the last of her things and shoved them in her bag. "I'm not a whore, so there's no need to pay me for the sex, and if you're trying to salve your own conscience for some reason, it's really not necessary. Have Nancy mail me a check for the correct amount. I've fulfilled my end of my contract—both contracts, actually—and since I don't work for you anymore, I can now tell you what a first-class jerk you are." She looked at him levelly. "I don't want your bonus money."

The phone on the conference room table beeped. To her surprise, Will ignored it.

"I'm not paying you for sex." His mouth quirked upward. "I don't have *that* much money, you know."

Was that some kind of compliment? And what the hell did he find so funny?

"But maybe I was trying to salve my conscience." He slid off the table and walked toward her. "I know I cost you some business with my behavior. I was simply trying to offset the effects."

The phone on the table beeped again. Gwen glanced at it and noticed the red intercom light flashing. Probably Nancy. Will continued as if he hadn't heard it.

"I wasn't trying to insult you further."

He was close—too close for Gwen's comfort—and she forgot about the beeping phone as, once again, Will's presence managed to shrink her perception to just the two of them. The fire behind her anger cooled some, leaving her confused at her jumbled thoughts and emotions.

That half smile appeared again. "You know, I don't think I've ever heard you shout like that. Miss Behavior wouldn't approve."

As she calmed, the belated embarrassment at losing her temper crept in. Quietly, and surprised she had the guts to vocalize the thought, she whispered, "Well, you didn't hurt Miss Behavior. You hurt me."

"I know. And I'm sorry." He stepped closer and her breath caught.

The damn BlackBerry in Will's pocket chirped.

Will's eyes never left hers. "Gwen?"

It chirped again, the sound—and Will's lack of reaction—grating on her last nerve. When Will didn't move, she snapped. "Aren't you going to answer that? Nancy's probably—"

He shook his head. "It'll wait. This is more important."

What? "Huh?"

"'Flesh and blood people always take priority over any other message in any other medium.'"

Her shock must have shown on her face, because he laughed.

"I've been paying attention. And you are certainly my priority right now." His hand reached out to stroke the side of her face. The sensation, coupled with his quiet words, rocked her. "I miss you. I'd like the chance to start over, if you're willing to give it to me."

Her chest ached.

"You've civilized me and domesticated me. I'd like for you to love me."

The last bit of hurt pride propping up her defenses crumbled, and a happy, hopeful bubble inflated in her chest. "I do."

Will's face lit up. "Really?"

She could feel a big goofy grin pulling at her cheeks. "Yeah."

And then Will was kissing her, and every feeling she'd been trying to bury exploded back to the forefront. Her body sighed into his, and a feeling of *rightness* flooded her. His kiss turned hungry, and she responded, ignoring the strange knocking sound…

"Mr. Harrison!"

She broke away and saw Nancy standing in the now-open door, her fist frozen in midknock. Horror flooded through her as she saw Mr. Hiramine and his entourage standing behind Nancy. Oh God. They'd seen her crawling all over Will…

Will didn't even have the good grace to look embarrassed. Of course, her face was hot enough for both of them.

"Yes, Nancy, is there a problem?"

Gwen tried to step away from Will, but his hand on her arm stopped him. Short of looking like a fool trying to wiggle out of his grasp, she had no choice but to continue to stand there.

"You didn't answer my calls." Nancy was the picture of shock, but Gwen couldn't tell if it was from the scene she walked in on or Will ignoring his BlackBerry.

"I was busy."

"I see that now. But Mr. Takeshi wanted to speak with you."

Gwen stepped forward as far as Will's arm would allow. "I apologize for the, um, scene you witnessed. Mr. Harrison and I—"

"Please do not apologize, Miss Sawyer." Mr. Takeshi's young face was kind and slightly amused. "Mr. Hiramine was aware that you and Mr. Harrison had some kind of unfinished business and we are sorry to have interrupted your…reconciliation, should we say?"

Mr. Hiramine leaned in and said something in rapid Japanese, of which Gwen only caught a few words.

His assistant translated. "Mr. Hiramine says he looks forward to doing additional business with HarCorp, but we leave you now to settle your own matters. We will be in touch." With a shallow bow, he turned and led his group back in the direction of the elevator.

Nancy mouthed "I'm sorry" as she closed the door behind them.

Gwen sunk into a chair, her knees weak at the thought of how that scene could have easily undermined all of her hard work. She was just destined, it seemed, to be caught in compromising positions. "Well, that was embarrassing."

Will shrugged as he kneeled in front of her chair. His hands caressed her knees, sending shivers up her spine. "You care too much what others think."

She might as well get everything out in the open. "You know what happened in D.C."

He nodded. "Yeah. It wasn't all your fault, though. And I think you could have repaired the damage if you hadn't left town so quickly."

Sarah had said the same thing dozens of times, but for some reason hearing it from Will made her believe it.

"But it was a good thing you did leave."

She felt her jaw drop. "What?"

Will just laughed at her. "Because you wouldn't be here otherwise, and I wouldn't have a major business deal to celebrate."

Realization dawned. "What am I thinking? I should be congratulating you on sealing the deal."

Will's smile caused her heart to skip a beat. "With you in charge, was there ever a doubt?"

"You're just lucky we didn't lose it all right there at the end. I think we broke about forty-seven rules of etiquette with that display."

He stood and took hold of her hands. "Again, you worry too much, Miss Behavior. In fact, there's only one etiquette rule I care about right now."

"And that would be?"

"The one about 'flesh and blood' being the most important thing." Will pulled her out of the chair and into his arms.

With her body molded to his, she had no problem feeling *his* flesh and blood pressing insistently against her.

She giggled. "If you want to use the phone…"

"You're hysterical." Will's lips caught hers in a tender kiss, full of promise.

"Check your BlackBerry?"

"The only thing I need to check is whether the door is locked this time." With a groan, he lifted Gwen by the hips and settled her on the table. Standing between her legs, he moved in for a long, leisurely nuzzle down the sensitive skin of her neck.

Gwen put on her primmest, most proper Miss Behavior tone. "Sex on the conference room table during office hours is hardly proper etiquette. I thought you said you were civilized now."

Will didn't pause, and Gwen tipped her head back to give him better access. "Well, maybe it's time to redefine 'civilized behavior.' Some of your etiquette rules seem pretty old-fashioned. You should make new ones."

Her usual argument died in her throat as Will nibbled the magic spot beneath her ear. For once, Miss Behavior totally agreed with him.

"You know what? Forget the rules."

MARRIED AGAIN
TO THE MILLIONAIRE

BY
MARGARET MAYO

Born in the industrial heart of England, **Margaret Mayo** now lives in a Staffordshire countryside village. She became a writer by accident, after attempting to write a short story when she was almost forty, and now writing is one of the most enjoyable parts of her life. She combines her hobby of photography with her research.

CHAPTER ONE

SIENNA'S heart pounded as she stood outside the prestigious residential development, which was set in its own park alongside the Thames. Only the very rich could afford to live there. And the last time she'd seen Adam he'd definitely not been in that category...

When no one answered the intercom system, and it appeared that she had wasted her time, she felt strangely relieved. It had taken a lot of courage to come here and she was just about to leave when she heard Adam's well-remembered voice.

'Sienna?'

It was like velvet over steel. From experience she knew that it could be as soft as molten chocolate or as hard edged as a razor blade. She had felt both sides of his tongue, and as she stood there now Sienna gave an involuntary shudder.

She'd had no idea that a video camera was monitoring her presence. The thought that Adam knew she was there and that he had probably been watching the expression on her face as she waited chilled her blood.

Forewarned was forearmed, and she was at a definite disadvantage.

'Adam!' Was that really her own voice sounding scratchy and nervous when she had been determined to be strong? And why the hell was he keeping her standing here instead of allowing her entrance?

Was he taking some sort of perverse pleasure in it? Unless he didn't want to see her! After all, it had been over five years. 'I—I need to speak to you.' Her mouth had gone suddenly dry, swallowing became impossible.

'After all this time? How interesting. You'd better come in.' Again his deep, dark voice scraped over her nerves and as the barrier to the landscaped gardens lifted Sienna made her way slowly to the main entrance door of the complex where she was confronted with yet another see-your-visitor system. With a sigh she pressed the appropriate button and waited—and waited.

After what seemed like several minutes, though was probably only one, Adam's voice reached her ears again. 'You look impatient, Sienna.'

'Are you playing games with me?' She heard the sharpness in her tone but was uncaring any longer. Her anger was building and she was beginning to wish that she had never decided to approach Adam.

'I've been trying to work out why you're here.'

'And unless you let me in, you'll never know. In fact, don't bother, I've changed my mind.' She swung on one of her ridiculously high heels, heels she had donned to give her the height and the confidence to do what she was about to do, and was about to march back the way she had come when he spoke again.

'Wait!'

And she heard a click as the door opened.

'Top floor, penthouse suite. The lift's to your right.'

With his curt instructions echoing in her ears, Sienna approached the lift. It whooshed her swiftly and silently to the top of the building and she emerged in an entrance hall lined with beech panelling and lit by discreet, inset spotlights. Beneath her feet were exquisite tiles in varying shades of bronze and olive green. Glossy-leaved plants stood in corners and a mirror was directly opposite.

She looked, thought Sienna, petrified. Her wide blue eyes were burning like coals in her pale face, her chestnut hair awry, despite having taken care with it before she had left home. And having nervously nibbled her lips while she had waited to gain entrance, her lipstick was non-existent.

This was not the image she wanted to portray and she stood there a moment taking deep steadying breaths, pulling herself together, forcing a smile. She combed her hair, reapplied her lipstick and was popping the tube back into her bag when a door opened and Adam strode towards her.

Sienna took in a sharp breath. The change in him was dramatic. He'd gone from being almost too thin to broad-shouldered and well muscled. She could actually see his muscles rippling beneath the silk of his shirt. His waist and hips were still slender but he had powerful thighs, barely hidden beneath fine linen trousers.

Where had all this body development come from? she wondered. It looked as though he worked out on a major scale and yet from what she knew of him, and what she'd read in the press, he didn't appear to have time for exercise. Work was still his ethos. If there had been more than twenty-four hours in a day he would have worked most of them.

His strong jaw with its cleft beneath sculpted lips was

firm. His eyes, which were a dark, dark blue, were riveted on her face. Thick black brows jutted over them. The only thing that hadn't changed was his black, curling hair, which was as awry as it had ever been. It touched his shirt collar and looked as though it desperately needed trimming and combing.

'So—Sienna, I wondered if I'd ever see you again.' His deep voice rumbled into the open space. 'Actually, I'm intrigued. How did you know where I lived?'

Sienna allowed her fine brows to rise. 'You're in the news these days. A few enquiries and I had your address.'

Over the years it had been easy to keep tabs on what he was doing. He had gone from being a simple property developer to someone who bought ailing businesses, turned them around, and then sold them off at a huge profit. He had been voted businessman of the year on more than one occasion. To give him credit, he did a lot of charity work as well.

Wide shoulders shrugged. 'I always knew that I would make it.'

'Such modesty,' she flashed. 'But at what cost?' His driving force, his need to make millions, was one of the reasons she had left him.

Adam's lips thinned. 'Are you here to discuss my success? Or is it a share of my money that you're after? Is that why you've never asked for a divorce, so that you can lay claim to half of my worth? Well, I hate to tell you, Sienna—'

'That is not why I'm here,' Sienna said defensively, though in truth she could understand why he thought that. There were women who would go for the jugular under similar circumstances but she was not one of them.

She had struggled these last few years but she would never have asked Adam for a penny, not a single penny. She had her pride. And as for a divorce, she had liked the idea of being a married woman.

If she had met and fallen in love with someone else she might have demanded her freedom, but there had been no one, and clearly Adam hadn't wanted to remarry either—which hadn't surprised her. He enjoyed his life the way it was.

Inside his luxurious suite she stood for a moment looking around her. The large open space was entirely fronted by glass, which led out onto a wide balcony with a riven slate floor, studded with potted plants and cushioned cane furniture. It looked more like a courtyard than a balcony and the view over the Thames was stunning, but she had no time to give it more than a cursory glance before her attention was taken up with the room she was in.

The furniture was minimal. Chunky brown leather sofas and glass topped tables. A massive television screen on one wall. Everything in muted natural colours and the open-plan kitchen at the far end was to die for. Sienna couldn't help wondering whether Adam cooked for himself or sent out for food, or even used one of the restaurants she had seen along the riverside walk.

'Please—sit down.' Adam indicated one of the leather chairs but Sienna shook her head.

'I'd prefer to go outside.' Although the space was immense, she felt suffocated by Adam's presence. Strange when she had known him more intimately than any other man before or since.

'As you wish,' he said, leading the way. 'Would you

care for something to drink or would you prefer to say whatever it is that you came for?'

There was harshness in his voice and Sienna shivered. Adam had changed. He had always been a driven man, working hard, collapsing with exhaustion at the end of each day, but there was a hard edge to him now, a cutting edge. He clearly hadn't got where he was without being utterly devoid of emotion and manically ruthless.

Thank God she had got out in time.

'I'd like a drink, thank you.' Something to lubricate her still dry throat. This was going to be far harder than she had envisaged.

'Tea? Coffee? Maybe something stronger?'

'Yes.' Something strong and intoxicating, something to relax her tense muscles because otherwise she would walk out of here without telling him her reason for coming.

She had not imagined when she set out that Adam would be this coolly controlled man who had her at a disadvantage. She had known it would be difficult, she had rehearsed her little speech a thousand times, but this new Adam was making it ten times worse. She felt that he was toying with her, waiting for the right moment to throw her out and tell her that whatever it was she had come for he wanted nothing to do with it.

A dark eyebrow rose. 'Yes to all three?'

'I mean, I'd like…something stronger.'

His lips twitched but he didn't comment. 'Wine perhaps? Or brandy? How great is your need?'

His sarcasm wasn't lost on her and Sienna lifted her chin, her light blue eyes meeting his darker ones. She had almost forgotten how amazingly good-looking he was and for one small moment she felt a rush of heat between her thighs. Banished in an instant, deeply horrifying.

That part of her life was over. Not once since she'd left him had he tried to find her, proving that he hadn't been particularly disappointed or even worried. In essence it had given him a clear field to work even longer hours. To amass his fortune. She found it difficult to understand why anyone would let money be their god. There was surely more to life.

This apartment, for instance, was nothing more than a status symbol. Why would one man live by himself in a place like this? Unless he used it as a love nest. Did he invite lady friends here? Actually, she had not once seen him in the press with a female on his arm. He was either very careful or working his socks off was still his way of life.

'Wine would be perfect, thank you.'

Left alone for a few minutes, Sienna closed her eyes, wishing she hadn't felt the need to seek Adam out after remaining silent for so long. If she had any sense, she would blurt out her reason for coming here and then run.

Except that good sense seemed to have deserted her. All she could think about was the way she had looked into his eyes and felt an emergence of the hunger and longing she had always experienced when they were together. He had been an amazing lover, setting her whole body alight with a fire she had thought would never die.

But after their marriage Adam had quickly gone from being her knight in shining armour to working so hard, coming home so late, that he'd barely had time to speak to her before falling asleep each night.

'Here we are.'

Grateful for Adam's interruption, Sienna shot her eyes wide. As they cannoned into his she felt a further body blow. He was still devastatingly sexy, causing wave after wave of hot desire to flood her veins. Damn! All these years she had told herself that she hated him, so why was this happening now?

It had to be pure sexual hunger that she felt, it couldn't be anything else. She certainly didn't love him any more. How could she possibly love a man who thought more about his job than he did his wife?

The wine looked deliciously cool and inviting. Sienna watched as Adam poured the pale golden liquid, watching it swirl and then settle. Almost instantly a fine film of condensation formed around the outside of her glass and as she picked it up she stroked her finger down its side.

Adam watched her through narrowed eyes, making her wish that she hadn't done it because he was looking at her as though she had made some kind of erotic gesture. As though she was stroking *him*!

Heat fizzed through her and she took a long swallow, amazed to discover when she set her glass down that she had drunk almost half its contents.

'Is it such an ordeal coming to see me?'

The gruff tone in his voice sent her head jerking in his direction. She saw lips that were grim and eyes that were as cold as ice.

'Why don't you just spit out what's wrong and get it over with?'

How could she? They needed to be at ease with each other first. And getting drunk wasn't the answer!

'It's a very fine place you have here,' she said instead. 'Do you have someone to share it with?'

'If you're asking whether I have a girlfriend, the answer's no. You should know me better than that, Sienna. I have only one lover, and that is my work.'

'So you haven't changed.' Sienna let her eyebrows rise. 'You still work all the hours God made! Why, when you have this?' She spread her hands, taking in their impressive surroundings.

'It's precisely why I work, for security, and to have nice things around me.' His dark blue eyes watched her closely. 'I also have a pied-à-terre in France and an apartment in New York. It gives me a feeling of great satisfaction.'

'Or is that you have so much money now you have nothing else to spend it on?' Sienna queried, unable to keep the distaste out of her voice. It was as though he was deliberately throwing his wealth in her face, showing her what she had missed out on.

'If you've come here to question my lifestyle, I suggest—'

'It's not that,' cut in Sienna quickly. But she wasn't ready yet to disclose her real reason for being here. It was such a delicate subject that she had to get Adam into the right mood. 'It simply seems odd that you have these other places to live and no one to share them with.'

'Are you putting yourself forward?' He smiled grimly and his eyes locked with hers, sending a fresh scurry of feelings through her veins.

She had thought that over the years everything she had ever felt for Adam Bannerman had died. She didn't want to feel anything for him, she despised him and she wouldn't be here now if it wasn't entirely necessary.

There was ice in both her voice and her eyes when

she spoke. 'I've had a taste of what it's like living with a workaholic. It's no fun, I assure you, and I'm not entirely surprised that you haven't found another woman to share your life.'

'Are you suggesting that I should? Is it a divorce you're after? I occasionally wonder why you've never filed for one.'

The deep sarcasm in his voice scoured over her already tense nerves like sandpaper.

'I could say the same about you.' She held her head high and met his eyes. For several long seconds they challenged each other, Sienna not wanting to be the first to turn away.

'I've never had the time or the inclination,' he drawled, his eyes still not leaving hers. 'I knew that one day, when you were ready, you would start proceedings. What I didn't expect was that you would visit me in person. It's quite a surprise.'

'And a mistake,' she snapped before she could stop herself. 'I really think I should be going.' There was no way on this earth now that she could broach the subject that had made her come here. Adam was doing a very good job of letting her know that he liked his life the way it was. He wanted nothing to spoil it. She pitied him. He would become a lonely old man one day if he kept putting work first.

'You're not leaving until you tell me what brought you here,' he said, his tone sharp and authoritative. 'Why don't you finish your wine?'

Sienna glared at him, but she picked up her glass and downed the rest of its contents in one swallow. 'There, finished.' And she stood up.

Adam followed suit and Sienna was glad that she had worn high heels because they made her almost as tall as he was. She lifted her chin and looked into his eyes—and felt a wave of something she dared not think about pass over her. The word began with S and ended in X.

Why was this happening now, when she needed to be strong and in control? Was it the fact that he was the first and only man she had ever fallen in love with? Had her body retained those feelings even though she had been convinced that they had not?

Hell, what a situation to find herself in. Especially as Adam showed no sign of returning them. She couldn't believe how cold he was. It was as though she had never meant anything to him.

'So why are you here?'

Sienna closed her eyes. It looked as if there was no escape. And if the truth be known, she had to do it. She owed it to Adam, to herself, to— She stopped her thoughts there, drew in a deep breath, and bluntly and coldly stated the facts.

'I'm here to tell you that you have a son.'

CHAPTER TWO

ADAM felt as though he had been poleaxed. The words that had just left Sienna's lips sent him reeling across the courtyard.

She was saying he had a son!

A son!

A son who would now be…four years old!

And in all the time they'd been apart she had never had the decency to tell him!

The blood roared through his head like a hurricane and he wanted to hit out at her, shake her, ask her what the hell she had thought she was doing, keeping him in ignorance. This was a scenario he had never envisaged, not in his wildest dreams. It was something he was finding difficult, if not impossible, to take in.

He had never wanted a family, he was happy doing what he did. Happy, for goodness' sake! He didn't want a child in his life, disrupting his routine. The big question was, why had she told him now? Why not when she found herself pregnant?

His eyes blazed as a bigger scenario hit him. 'I'm not the father, am I? Why in heaven's name would you wait this long to tell me if I were? You're after money.

You're trying to take me for a fool. Get out of here, Sienna. *Get out!'*

Never in his life had he been so angry. If Sienna had thought she could pull this stunt on him, she was very much mistaken. If the baby really had been his, she would have wasted no time in coming back. She would have made him face up to his responsibilities. Even if she hadn't, no woman in her right mind would bring up her baby alone without seeking maintenance from the father. She would have insisted on that. She had to be lying.

Sienna's back straightened and her fantastic blue eyes flashed with indignant fury. She looked like a tigress protecting her young. 'He is definitely yours.'

'So you say.' He was not going to be so easily fooled. Words were easy. He had heard of women who did this sort of thing, who tricked their former partners or husbands into believing someone else's child was their own.

'Do you want proof?' she demanded. 'It can be arranged.'

Her eyes locked into his and held, and in that moment Adam saw nothing but blazing honesty. His brief suspicion was reluctantly relegated to the deepest recesses of his mind. Maybe it would resurrect itself. Maybe. Perhaps if he saw the child, he would know at once whether he was his or not. He'd had a strong resemblance to his own father so there was every reason to believe that he would see something of himself in this boy.

Adam folded his arms and looked hard into the blue of her eyes. *'If* the boy is mine, why have you waited so long to tell me about him?' He was aware that his voice was still harshly condemning, and filled with more than a little suspicion, but, hell, she couldn't drop a bomb-shell like this and expect no reaction.

His heart felt as though it was trying to escape from his chest and he was afraid to stand any closer to Sienna because he felt like shaking her. Why, for pity's sake, had she kept her secret all this time? Why?

She looked stunning in a black and white top and stylish black trousers, which hid none of the curves of her sexy bottom. Her black high-heeled sandals gave her added height, even though they looked dangerously dif-ficult to walk in. And her rich chestnut hair, which had always been her crowning glory, was cut in a short, chunky style that suited her elfin face.

She certainly didn't look like the mother of an ener-getic four-year-old. She was dressed to kill. She had come here to drop her bombshell—and she had cer-tainly done that. It was a wonder it hadn't exploded and brought the whole apartment block down around their feet. Above them the sky was blue and serene but inside his body a war was raging.

'My first instinct, when I discovered that I was pregnant, was obviously to tell you,' she said, her eyes holding his.

Intense blue eyes, eyes that he had once felt himself drowning in. Eyes which now warred with his but were extremely beautiful nevertheless.

'But as you'd told me enough times that you didn't want kids, not for many years anyway, I knew it would cause another unholy row between us.' Sienna lifted her shoulders and let them drop again. 'So I decided to bring Ethan up on my own.'

And still she looked unswervingly into his eyes.

Ethan! The boy's name was Ethan! He rolled the name experimentally on his tongue. 'So why are you here now?' he asked harshly, ignoring the unease he felt at her words. It was true he had never wanted children and he hadn't been afraid to say so. But he would never have ignored a son or daughter. They would have been given his love and he would have adapted his lifestyle. He would have had to.

Could he truly have done it, though? He hated himself for admitting that he would have been truly angry that his well-ordered life had been so rudely disrupted.

'You said it wasn't for money.' He pushed his thoughts to one side for the moment. 'What other reason can there possibly be?' He did not understand her, not one little bit. The shock still hadn't worn off and despite the fact that he didn't drink he felt as though he could do with a generous slug of brandy. He needed something to restore his equilibrium.

'Because,' she began hesitantly, for the first time lowering her lids and looking slightly uncomfortable, 'Ethan's been ill, very ill.' Then she looked at him again, a proud tilt to her head, trying to hide the pain in her eyes. 'He had meningitis and I thought I was going to lose him. I realised that if he had died and you'd never even known you had a son, I would have done you an injustice.'

Adam felt a band tighten around his heart. He felt physical pain. His son had been close to death and he had known nothing about it! The blood roared in his head and he quickly closed the space between him and Sienna, taking her shoulders, gripping them so hard that he saw her wince. But he did not care.

'What sort of a mother are you,' he growled, 'denying your son his father? Especially at a time like that. How could you? I'm presuming that he's all right now?'

Sienna nodded and swallowed hard but she did not try to pull away from him. She stood there and looked sadly into his eyes.

He saw tears, big fat tears that welled and escaped and rolled slowly down her cheeks. One half of him wanted to brush them gently away with the tip of a caring finger, the other half, the angry half, wanted to shake her to within an inch of her life.

In the end he did neither. He released her and, pulling a handkerchief from his pocket, pushed it into her hand. Then he turned away, contemplating the London skyline instead. Not that he saw anything. His eyes were blinded by fury, by disappointment, by the knowledge that his son, his own flesh and blood, had lain at death's door and he had been left in ignorance.

Adam felt a lump in his throat and an odd feeling he could not put a name to. He was not usually an emotional man, keeping an iron control over his feelings. He had a ruthless work ethic and it often crept into his home life as well. And yet Sienna had found a chink in his armour. She had hit him hard with this fresh piece of information.

Accepting the fact that he had a son had been bad enough, but to hear that he had almost died knocked him for six. How long he stood there staring into space he didn't know. It was not until he heard Sienna's tentative voice behind him that he snapped himself back to the present and turned to look at her.

Her eyes, which were sometimes more turquoise than

blue, were incredibly pale at this moment. 'I'm sorry.' And her voice was so low as to be almost inaudible.

'Pray tell me,' he growled, breathing hard and looking fiercely into her face. 'Would you have ever told me if— if my son—' he wanted to say the name Ethan but he couldn't get his head round it yet '—hadn't fallen ill?'

'I don't know,' answered Sienna quietly, still not taking her eyes away from his. 'I honestly don't know. But your reaction tells me that I did the right thing. You still don't want children, do you? You still put your work first.'

Adam didn't answer. She was so damned right that he felt guilty.

'Ethan would have had no father figure to look up to if we had stayed and lived with you. He'd be in bed when you got home and you'd have left for your office before he rose each morning. Not an ideal life for a child.'

She paused but he still didn't answer, he couldn't answer. Every word she spoke was the absolute truth.

'But,' she continued, 'I think he should know who his father is. Just as I think you should meet Ethan. We can still carry on living our separate lives.'

'In other words,' he growled, hating the scenario she had described, even though it was probably true, 'you will now be well within your rights to claim money from me. Just as I thought.'

'Damn you, Adam Bannerman! I want nothing from you except a father's love for his child. I might have known it was too much to expect.' Her eyes glittered as she swung around on her dangerously high heels.

The next second he heard a sharp crack and Sienna stumbled as one of her heels snapped off. He moved like lightning and caught her before she hit the floor, wrapping his arms around her and jerking her hard against him.

He had forgotten what she felt like. And what she smelled like. A summer's evening after rain. A delicate fragrance that briefly drugged his senses. She had grown into a beautiful, sensual woman.

He felt himself grow hard and quickly thrust her away from him. Damn! Sienna had just devastated him with her news. He should be hating her, not feeling raw hunger.

Neither did he want her to know that she still had the power to arouse him in case she used it to her advantage. He still wasn't entirely sure that her sole reason for coming there was to tell him about Ethan's illness. Why do something like that after the event? There had to be more to it.

Sienna felt stupid. If she hadn't moved so quickly she wouldn't have broken her heel. What was she to do now? Walk home barefoot? Hobble? Call a taxi—which she could ill afford?

She had borrowed the shoes from a friend, now she would have to pay for a new pair. But not only had she ruined a shoe, it was her dignity as well. She should have known it was a bad idea. Adam had reacted in exactly the way she had expected him to.

She glared at him as she slipped off her other shoe and marched indoors. She did not want to spend another minute in his suffocating presence.

'Where do you think you are going?' Adam's harsh voice sounded over her shoulder.

'Home.' That one single word was as much as she could muster.

'And how far are you going to get without shoes on your feet?' he wanted to know. 'Don't be ridiculous, Sienna.'

'So what am I supposed to do?' she asked angrily, turning to face him. 'Perhaps you'd like to pay for a taxi?'

'I could do that,' he said slowly. 'Or I could take you myself. And meet this boy I am supposed to have fathered.'

His eyes met and held hers but Sienna saw red. 'Supposed?' she queried, her eyes flashing hot sparks. 'Thanks for your offer, but no thanks. If and when you two ever meet, I want to prepare Ethan first. He doesn't know about you yet.'

'So who does he think his father is?' asked Adam, a sudden fiercely quizzical look in his eyes.

Sienna shrugged. 'He's not old enough to ask questions like that.' Actually, Ethan had more than once asked her why he didn't have a daddy but she'd always managed to avoid a definite answer, thankful that there were other single mothers at the nursery he attended. She believed that it would be best to tell him when he was older, when he could understand better.

'But he will have to know one day. So why not now?' Adam insisted.

'Because I need to prepare him,' she answered sharply. 'I can't suddenly introduce his father to him. I need to talk to him first, make sure he understands why you haven't been a part of his life.'

To her annoyance Adam's lips pulled into a brief, dry smile. 'And you will tell him—what? That his father's been busy making money? Actually, it should impress him. It does most people.'

'Most people don't know the agony it causes,' flared Sienna. 'It's no life living with someone who's rarely home.' She saw a pulse jerk in Adam's jaw and knew she had hit a raw nerve. Good! He deserved it. 'I'd be obliged if you'd phone for a taxi.'

Adam closed his eyes momentarily and Sienna knew that he was warring with himself as to whether to do as she asked or insist that he run her home himself. If only she hadn't broken her stupid heel. She did not want him anywhere near where she lived. She had been protecting herself as well when she'd said that she needed to prepare Ethan.

Just as she had begun to think that Adam was ignoring her request he reached out for the phone and barked a request.

'My driver is at your disposal.'

Sienna's brows rose though she said nothing, privately wondering whether there was anything this man could not organise at a moment's notice. Money spoke. And money ruined marriages! She compressed her lips and nodded her thanks.

'Before you leave I propose we arrange another meeting. We need to talk about our son and his future.'

Sienna felt her heart drop. It had been hard coming there, it would be even harder seeing him a second time. She had dropped a bombshell, which he would pick up and dissect and come back at her with suggestions that she would not like. Even though it was to be expected, even though she was the one who had started the ball rolling, she felt her whole body grow icy cold at the thought of seeing Adam again, of talking about Ethan, arranging for them to meet.

It was something she had shied away from for the past four years. She had known that Adam wouldn't want his life disrupted. But now she had done it, and she had to face the consequences. It was quite possible that he might insist she and Ethan move in with him. How disastrous would that be? On the other hand he might be happy to settle a sum of money on them. Wasn't money his god? Wasn't it all he wanted in life? His answer to everything?

Ethan would naturally be delighted to meet his father. He wouldn't know that Adam would remain a distant figure, seen only occasionally. So it would be up to her to stand her ground, declare that they were happy living as they were. She would allow him access, but as for anything else…

'What are you suggesting?' she asked stiffly. She was missing the extra three inches her shoes had afforded her. She needed to look up now into his face and it put her at a definite disadvantage. Nevertheless, she kept her chin high and her eyes cold.

'Dinner tomorrow night?'

'I thought you always worked late?' Her response came back with the speed of a bullet.

Even though Adam smiled, it did not reach his eyes. 'I'm prepared to make an exception.'

So miracles did happen! Or would it be a one-off? She'd like to bet that he would rarely make such exceptions. In the beginning maybe, but soon he would be back to his old lifestyle and poor Ethan would be left wondering what had happened to the father he had only just met.

'Very well,' she agreed reluctantly. 'I guess there are things we need to talk about.'

'I'll send a car for you.'

Sienna raised her brows. He would send a car! Not

he would pick her up. Oh, no, he didn't have time for that. He would send his driver. It would give him extra time at the office. Damn the man. She felt like slinging his suggestion back in his face, telling him that he didn't deserve to meet his son, he would be a failure as a father and she wished that she had never set eyes on him in the first place. But, of course, she said none of these things.

'Eight o'clock. You do have someone who can look after…Ethan?'

It was the way he said his son's name, the awkward way he said it, that made Sienna realise that the shock she had given Adam went far deeper than she had at first thought. It had shifted the earth from beneath his feet and he was having great difficulty in getting used to the idea.

Had she made a mistake? A big mistake? Nevertheless, she nodded. 'I have a friend who will look after him.'

'Good.' The word came out harshly. 'Till tomorrow, then.'

Within minutes Sienna was being driven away from the riverside development, sitting like royalty in the back of a gleaming black Bentley. In the rearview mirror she could see the driver's impassive face and knew he must be wondering who she was and what sort of a relationship she had with his employer. If only he knew!

Sienna lived in a rented two-bedroom ground-floor apartment in the north London suburbs and as Adam's driver pulled up outside she could imagine what he must be thinking. Nevertheless, she held her head high and her shoes in her hand.

Once indoors she flopped down on a chair in her living room. Tiny in comparison to Adam's oversized apartment, but comfortable. She had everything she needed here. Dropping her head back, she let out a deep sigh. It had taken a lot of courage facing Adam today and where had it got her? Precisely nowhere. OK, he now knew he had a son, and he wanted to talk about him, but he hadn't been exactly enamoured by the fact.

She went over their conversation in her mind and could see no part where Adam had shown enthusiasm or pleasure. Anger that she had kept him in ignorance, yes. But he had asked no immediate questions about Ethan, hadn't enquired whether she had photographs. She had to face him again to fill him in on the details he should have asked there and then. She guessed it was shock on his part, but even so…

And the outcome was that she would have to buy her friend a new pair of shoes. She glanced at her watch. Jo would be here any moment with Ethan. She had no children of her own and was always willing to look after him, even on a Sunday afternoon.

As if on cue, she heard the sound of their voices outside the door and jumped up to let them in. Ethan ran to her and wrapped his arms around her. Jo smiled. 'How did it go?'

Her friend lived in the flat above. They had both moved in at the same time and become firm friends. 'I broke your shoe,' Sienna said with a rueful grimace. 'It was a dumb idea, wearing them. I'm sorry.'

'What were you doing? Running away?' asked Jo with a laugh. 'And don't worry about it. They were stupid shoes. I could never walk in them.'

Ethan went to his room to play and Sienna grimaced. 'As a matter of fact, yes, I was running away. It was a waste of time going there. Adam didn't want to know.

He actually accused me of trying to get money out of him. He suggested Ethan wasn't his.'

Jo drew in a swift breath. 'He didn't! What did you say?'

'I suggested DNA.'

'And?'

'He backed down a bit.'

'And the outcome is?'

'I'm meeting him tomorrow night—for dinner.'

Jo raised her brows.

'He was in shock,' declared Sienna with a wry grimace. 'We didn't talk much, he needed time to get used to the idea. Can you babysit Ethan?'

'Of course.'

'You should see his place, Jo. It's out of this world. In fact, it's on top of the world. He lives in a penthouse suite overlooking the Thames. His driver brought me home—in a Bentley no less.'

'Then you should grab him with both hands,' said her friend with a wide grin. 'Why did you ever let him go?'

'It's a long story. Do you want a cup of tea?'

Sienna dressed carefully for her dinner date with Adam. She hadn't many good clothes; as a matter of fact, the trousers and top she had worn to face him were the best things she had, bought a few months ago to attend a wedding. But she couldn't wear them again or he would think she had nothing else to wear, so she matched a black strappy top—one she sometimes used to sunbathe in, but he wouldn't know that—with a black floaty skirt that was years old but nevertheless still looked good. She fastened a silver belt around her waist, added a silver necklace and slipped into black sandals. Her hair had been brushed until it shone, and with a slick of lipstick and a dusting of eye-shadow she pronounced herself ready.

Just in time. The car arrived. The impassive driver knocked on her door. Sienna slid into the back seat, inhaling appreciatively the rich smell of leather. And almost immediately wished that she was going any-where but to meet Adam again. It was going to be an uncomfortable encounter. There would be more recrimi-nations and almost certainly the suggestion that he wanted to meet Ethan.

But she wanted to feel comfortable with Adam first. She wanted Adam to feel at ease as well. Otherwise when father and son eventually met there would be an undercurrent and she didn't want that. It needed to be a happy meeting. She wanted Ethan to be ready, but even more than that she wanted Adam to treat his son in the way that a father should, with warmth and humour—neither of which were Adam's strong points.

She wished for the hundredth time that she hadn't gone to see him. It had been a huge mistake. One she might live to regret.

'Here we are, madam.' The driver jumped smartly out of the car and opened her door. Sienna felt almost like royalty. 'Mr Bannerman is waiting inside.'

Oh, he was, was he? Sienna felt like telling the driver to take her back home. Except just at that moment Adam appeared in the doorway of the restaurant. They were in Mayfair, in the heart of London's most exclusive district. Shopping, dining, living, all for the very rich.

Sienna felt distinctly out of place. Nevertheless, she

kept her head high and her eyes firmly on Adam's. He wore a grey suit and a white shirt with a grey and red tie and he looked the epitome of the successful business-man. While she felt like the poor relation!

'Sienna, you look good. I'm glad you made it.'

Liar! On both counts. She didn't look good, she didn't feel good. At least, not right now. She had when she had set out, but she hadn't expected to be wined and dined at one of London's most elite restaurants. She had thought, she had hoped, that it would be at one of the eating places she had seen near where he lived.

Nothing had prepared her for this.

However, she smiled her acknowledgement of his compliment and when he took her arm to lead her inside she felt a crazy awareness of the man she had once been so madly in love with.

It was insanity. They were here to talk about Ethan. Adam wanted to know more about him. She had brought photographs. But here she was experiencing a reincar-nation of the feelings that had once totally consumed her.

With an effort she dashed them away, relegated them to some safe place deep in her body. Hopefully they would never be restored. She was prepared to be civil with Adam, for their son's sake, but as for anything else—she would fight it every inch of the way. He had hurt her once, and she had no intention of letting him do so again.

far be the eventual to turn up that evening.

CHAPTER THREE

ADAM had half expected Sienna not to turn up that evening. He had thought she would despatch his driver, telling him that she had changed her mind. Her revelation that he had a four-year-old son had stunned him, sent his whole world out of kilter, made a mockery of every thought he'd ever had about not wanting children to interfere with his lifestyle.

After a night lying awake, thinking about its implications, he had not even gone in to work today—which was unheard of. His PA had had the shock of her life when he'd phoned to tell her. Without a doubt his life was going to be disrupted, changed for ever, and it would take a hell of a lot of getting used to.

After Sienna had walked out on their marriage he had buried himself ever more deeply into his work. He had been fiercely angry that she couldn't accept his need to create a good life for them. In a fit of rage after she had left him, he'd taken out other women to try to get over her.

It hadn't worked.

Despite what he saw as her failings, and despite the reason he had married her in the first place, he had missed Sienna more than he had ever thought possible, and he'd eventually felt guilty because he'd known that he hadn't given her the attention that she deserved. In equal parts he had experienced relief. Nevertheless, it had allowed him the space and time to build up his business without Sienna constantly complaining that she never saw him.

Now, though, he found it hard to believe that she had kept something of such monumental importance from him. A son! It did not make sense. It was a nightmare. How could she have done that?

His fingers curled and he wanted to wring her pretty neck.

Being a father would make a marked difference to his life. In the years since Sienna had walked out his business affairs had grown beyond even his own wildest dreams. Success had come to him and he'd embraced it with open arms. He needed no one. He was master of his own universe.

Or at least he had been.

Looking at her now, seeing how nervous she was, he realised that it must have taken a lot of courage to approach him yesterday. He had not thought of that at the time, he'd been too intensely angry to feel anything else. In fact, he was still angry, but he knew that he must hide those feelings if he was to come to any sort of an agreement with her.

'Would you like a drink before dinner?' he asked. Sienna not only looked gorgeous in black, she smelled divine too, and Adam felt a swift surge of hunger. The skinny straps of her top revealed velvety smooth, lightly tanned shoulders and the rapidly beating pulse in the long line of her throat gave away the fact that she was incredibly nervous. The swell of her breasts peeping over the top of her camisole made his fingers itch to touch, to feel their weight in his palms, to tease her nipples into tight, hard buds. As hard as he was feeling!

The crazy thing was that she was still his wife. He would be perfectly within his rights making love to her, and yet he knew that she was forbidden fruit. The sweetest fruit, the most tempting fruit.

Damn! It had been a mistake inviting her here tonight. They should have met somewhere far more austere, like in a solicitor's office, and let a third party work out the best way forward.

'No, thank you.'

Adam had almost forgotten his question. Sienna's fragrance was exciting him, her nearness drugging him. He was in danger of making a fool of himself. Instantly he channelled his thoughts away from Sienna's appearance, reminding himself that she had done the unforgivable. She had wronged him big time and he would find it difficult to forgive her—if he ever did!

They were led to their table and Sienna sat on the very edge of her chair, her back ramrod straight, her eyes wary on his, as though she was expecting him to declare that he was going to take Ethan from her.

Menus were handed to them and for a few moments they both pretended to be studying them. Twice Adam caught Sienna looking at him, her eyes quickly averted each time, and he gave a grim smile. She too was clearly wishing that she was anywhere but there.

Their food and wine orders given, Adam sat back in his seat and looked at her. 'Are you ready to talk?'

'About Ethan?' Sienna knew that the huskiness in her

voice gave away her inner tension. All day long she had been dreading this meeting, and with good reason. The stern look in Adam's eyes, the mutinous set of his chin told her that he was still furiously angry with her.

Adam nodded. 'What did he say when you told him that you'd been to see his father? Is he anxious to meet me?'

Sienna swallowed hard. 'As a matter of fact, I haven't told him yet.' She had been waiting for the right moment but had begun to have her doubts that there ever would be one. Ethan wouldn't understand her predicament. He would want to meet his father, he would be ecstatically happy, he would expect them to all live together like one big loving family. And if he discovered that Adam was wealthy enough to buy him anything he wanted, he would instantly become his best friend.

Adam's reaction was exactly as she had known it would be. He roared with rage. His eyes grew even harder, shooting swift bullets of anger across the table, making a mockery of its fine linen tablecloth and elegant silver cutlery. 'You have not told him? Why not? Why did you come to see me if it was not to acquaint me with my son?'

Sienna closed her eyes. 'I made a mistake. I—'

'*No!* I will not let you change your mind. You cannot hide him away from me any longer. I have a right to see him.'

Adam's voice roared into her consciousness, overpowering her, stunning her. She snapped her lids open and stared straight into the harsh blue depths of cold-as-ice eyes. A shiver slid down her spine, reaching out icy tentacles to every part of her body.

'And so you shall,' she said, horrified to hear the

tremor in her voice. This was not the way to react. She needed to be strong. Drawing in a deep steadying breath, she stared at him unflinchingly. 'Once I have told him about you.'

'And when will that be?' came the caustic reply. 'Today? Tomorrow? Next week? Next month? It's not good enough, Sienna. You cannot drop a bolt from the blue like that and then expect me to sit back and wait patiently. I demand to see him. In fact, I don't see why we shouldn't walk out of here right now and—'

'No!' Sienna's voice rose. 'I *will* tell him, but in my own good time. And he'll need to get used to the idea that he has a father before I introduce you. It will be a big thing for him.'

'No bigger than it was for me.' Adam's face contorted into a scowl that scored deep lines on his forehead and narrowed his eyes until they were no more than two silvery-blue slits. 'I'm still finding it hard to believe that you waited so long to tell me. You shouldn't have had to go through Ethan's illness alone. For pity's sake, Sienna, I'm his father. I deserved to be told.'

He was right, of course. And she would have felt so much better during Ethan's illness if she'd had Adam to lean on. It had been a terrible time, not knowing whether her son was going to live or die. As she'd sat for hours beside Ethan's hospital bed she had longed for Adam's strength, had told herself constantly that he ought to be here, that she should have told him about Ethan. The burden had been almost too much to bear.

Yet still it had taken immense strength to seek him out—and now she almost wished that she hadn't. His anger was doing nothing to make her feel any easier about the situation.

She was given a tiny respite while her wine was poured. Adam as usual touched nothing stronger than water. Nevertheless, he tipped his glass towards hers. 'Here's to a promising future.'

Tension tingled in the air between them. His eyes locked with hers and Sienna felt her heart beating heavily in her chest. When she had sought Adam out yesterday she had never envisaged that she would be sitting here with him tonight, drinking expensive wine, experiencing shock waves of sensation because feelings she had thought long dead were making themselves felt.

It was actually impossible not to feel. Her love for him had once been so strong that she began to wonder now whether it had ever died. Or was it because he was dynamically sexier these days? Success sat on his shoulders like an invisible cloak. And a successful man was always irresistible. At least, to some women. She had never put herself in that category but looking at Adam now, seeing the man he had become, she could not contain a frisson of awareness. It ran through her veins like molten metal, hot and swift and consuming.

'It might take Ethan time to get used to the idea that he has a father,' she said quietly. And she needed time too. Their meeting, when it happened, would be an emotional one, there would be a big change in her life. Also in Ethan's.

She didn't allow herself to think of the effect it would have on Adam. He had been absent for so long that all she could think of at this moment was herself and her son.

Clearly she hadn't been thinking straight when she

had decided to seek Adam out, and she had not reckoned on the enormous personal trauma it would cause. If only she could turn back the clock. But, of course, that was impossible. She had started this, so now had to suffer the consequences.

Their first course arrived and for a few minutes there was silence between them, Sienna cautiously tasting her vinaigrette of white asparagus with truffles. It was, of course, superb. Adam would not have taken her to a restaurant where the food was not first class. He moved in completely different circles to her these days. It was a life she could have once had but had chosen not to. And she did not particularly want her son to be brought up in this exclusive society.

'Does Ethan look like me?'

Sienna drew in a deep breath and nodded. 'I have photographs.' She reached for her bag and passed Adam an envelope.

He was silent for a few minutes as he scrutinised each photo in turn and Sienna took the opportunity to study him. She could see so much of her son in Adam that it was frightening.

Her lovable little boy was going to grow up in the very image of his father. Tall, devastatingly handsome, a real ladies' man. And she would worry herself sick over the years, wondering what sort of a life he would carve out for himself. Would he be as driven as his father? Would he put success and riches before everything else? Before human relationships? Human emotions?

There had been times when she felt that Adam had never loved her, when she had wondered why he had asked her to marry him in the first place. His goal hadn't been a happy marriage and children and she couldn't help wondering now whether his relationship with Ethan would suffer as a result.

'May I keep these?'

Sienna nodded.

'There's no mistaking that he is my son.'

The words were said calmly and with no malicious intent, but Sienna couldn't help flaring. 'If you thought that I would lie to you, you don't know me very well at all.'

'But you can surely understand? All these years and not a word.'

Their eyes met and held and Sienna was the first to look away.

'I'm going to enjoy getting to know him. I'll take him along the Thames on my cruiser, we'll fly over to Paris to see my place there and—'

'Adam Bannerman, don't you dare!' Sienna felt herself exploding. She felt sparks of white hot anger sizzling inside her head. If he thought money was the way to impress his son, he was sadly mistaken. 'A walk along the river, feeding the ducks, a ride on some swings is all Ethan needs. Even just sitting down and talking to you, finding out he has a daddy, will be the most exciting thing that has ever happened to him. You can't buy his love, Adam. Kids need companionship and love and caring. Doing little things together. And if you can't get your head round that then it might be better if he never finds out about you.'

'It's too late for that.' Adam's eyes glittered into hers. Hard eyes, cold eyes, that told her she couldn't back out now. That he would demand access to his son whether she liked it or not.

'Nevertheless, we need to set out some ground rules,' she declared sharply. 'I don't want you trying to impress him with your wealth. He needs to get to know you properly first.'

'I agree,' he answered with surprising quietness, 'and the sooner the better.'

The subject of their son drew them closer by an invisible thread. Adam's eyes had never seemed bluer. Or more fierce. Or more direct. They burned through into the very heart of her, making her wriggle uncomfortably on her seat.

'Do I have to come knocking on the door and announce myself? I could do that, you know.'

And he would, thought Sienna. He would turn up without warning and she would be left quivering with apprehension. What if the two of them didn't get on? Adam clearly knew nothing about children and their needs. He would overwhelm his son, maybe even frighten him.

'I'll tell him tomorrow,' she promised. 'But he'll need a few days to get used to the idea. I'll ring you.'

Adam threw her a look of disbelief. 'And how long will I have to wait? Maybe I should come back with you tonight and—'

'No!' yelped Sienna, then looked around swiftly to see if anyone had heard her panicked cry. Fortunately not. 'He'll be in bed, for one thing. I'll tell him tomorrow, I promise, and then I'll leave it up to Ethan.'

'What if he doesn't want to meet me?'

Sienna shrugged. 'That's something you'll have to deal with.' Though she couldn't see it happening. Ethan would be so excited he'd want to see his daddy immediately.

'If you think that I'm going to ignore my son now that you've told me about him, you're wrong.' Hard eyes met hers. 'Very wrong. But I appreciate that he'll need a little time. I'll give you two days then if I haven't heard from you I shall turn up on your doorstep.' He whisked a card out of his pocket. 'Here's my personal phone number. Use it.'

The rest of the evening passed in relative harmony. They had both chosen turbot for their main course, which was cooked to perfection, as were the accompanying vegetables. Sienna had never eaten such delicious food and she felt slightly sad that she didn't have room for dessert.

By the time Adam suggested they leave Sienna felt more relaxed than she had expected. He had regaled her with stories about his work life, some amusing, some deadly serious, and she had finished the whole bottle of wine.

Consequently she felt mellow and sleepy and when they left the restaurant she didn't even flinch when he put his arm about her waist.

'Have I told you how stunning you look tonight, Sienna?'

His voice rumbled from somewhere low in his throat, vibrating along her nerves, making her pull suddenly out of his embrace. What had she been thinking, letting him touch her like this?

Without warning his head bent down towards hers and eyes that were the colour of a sun-kissed ocean took her prisoner. And lips that she had sworn would never touch hers again captured her mouth in a kiss that revealed with devastating thoroughness that none of her feelings had gone away.

They had simply lain dormant, waiting like Sleeping Beauty for her prince to kiss her and bring her back to life. Her body felt on fire, electric sensations fizzing through veins and arteries. Emotions she had thought dead rose up and embraced the kiss, responded to it, filling her body with a hunger she had not felt for a very long time.

But it was madness. Allowing these feelings to surface was sheer madness. Adam would gain the impression that she was willing to enter into a sexual relationship and that was most definitely not the case. He had caught her unawares; it was not going to happen again. Not ever! That part of their life was over. They would be civil with each other for their son's sake, but that was all. She was not going to share his life or his bed ever again.

She jerked away, her eyes wide and fiercely angry. 'What did you do that for?'

Adam's smile was smug. 'How could I help myself? You're more beautiful than ever, Sienna. How could any man resist you? I bet they queue at your door. Is there someone special in your life at the moment?'

Sienna thought about lying and saying that there was. Except this was Adam, and no matter what had happened between them she found it impossible to lie to him. 'There is no one,' she said quietly.

'Has there been?'

'I hardly think it's any of your business. We've both been free agents these last few years.'

'We are still married,' he reminded her.

'And has that stopped you going out with other women?' she riposted, her blue eyes hard and challenging.

'Touché,' came the unblinking answer.

'So I suggest we stop asking each other invasive questions and go home.' Actually, she would have liked to know how many other women there had been in his life but since she didn't want him questioning her about her own love life, finding out that it had been non-existent, it was best they kept quiet on the subject.

'And home is?'

'If you're thinking it's back to your place, you'd better think again.'

'So I'm coming back to yours, is that it?'

Sienna shook her head, her eyes very blue and wide with horror. 'You know that's not going to happen. Where's your driver? He can take me.'

Adam grinned. 'I've given him the rest of the night off. I'll be driving you home myself.'

Sienna closed her eyes and gave an inward groan. 'That will not be necessary. I don't want you turning up at my house until I've told Ethan about you.' The very thought sent a chill through her veins. It was her worst nightmare come true. She could just imagine what would happen if Adam followed her in.

He would insist on seeing his son. And even though Ethan would probably be able to cope with finding out that he had a father after all these years, she certainly would not.

'I won't come in if you don't want me to.'

Sienna glared at Adam as he led the way towards his waiting car. Not the one she had been chauffeured in. Something small and snazzy, intimate. Not her idea of an easy ride. She would be sitting close and personal and her heart would inevitably play a tune of its own, maybe even loud enough for Adam to hear, make him aware of her plight.

When he opened the door for her and stood back, she slid silently and reluctantly into the seat. The fact that he was smiling made her even angrier, which in turn made his smile wider. It became a self-satisfied grin and she wanted to slap his face. Only good manners prevented her.

He leaned too close for comfort before he closed the door. 'Have you any idea how beautiful you look when you're angry? It makes me want to kiss you again, Sienna, feel some of that fire.'

'I don't think so,' she slammed back. 'The fire I feel is of a very different kind to how it used to be.'

'Really?' His brows lifted and he made no attempt to move out of her space. In fact, he was so close that Sienna could clearly see the outer dark ring around the incredible blue of his eyes, feel the heat emanating from him, but more poignant still was the citrus scent of his cologne, the musk of his skin. It wafted over her like a drug and she knew that if he did not move soon she would weaken.

'You know what I mean. I'm angry with you, Adam. You engineered this whole evening so that you could take me home and hopefully meet Ethan. Well, you're not going to set foot inside my house. Ethan will be in bed and I refuse to disturb him.'

'Sienna, you might be angry with me right now, but I won't go back on my word.'

Still the smile remained in place and Sienna was sorely tempted. But somehow she controlled her impulse. 'I'm glad to hear it. Let's go.'

It was with excruciating slowness that he lifted himself away from her and closed the door. For a few seconds she was allowed breathing space until he slid in beside her and the whole car was filled with his essence even more powerfully than before. Sienna closed her eyes, asking herself for the thousandth time whether she had made the biggest mistake of her life in seeking Adam out.

Never in her wildest dreams had she envisaged that she would still be attracted to him. She had thought only that he needed to know about Ethan. It had blinded her to everything else, in the same way that her love had blinded her all those years ago. But now, with her blinkers lifted, she was in grave danger. Adam still had the power to stir her innermost emotions. How cruel was destiny to inflict this on her?

The journey was accomplished in total silence, Adam seeming to know instinctively where she lived. She guessed that his chauffeur must have told him but it didn't please her. The contrast between his sumptuous penthouse suite and her modest little flat could not be ignored.

She held her breath as he pulled up outside, waiting for his comment, but none was forthcoming. Instead, he looked at her long and hard, giving nothing away now of the raw feelings she had seen earlier. 'Two days, Sienna. That is all you have. Two days. And if I do not hear from you I shall come to take my boy away.'

CHAPTER FOUR

ADAM knew that it had been the wrong thing to say. He had seen the flash in Sienna's eyes, that over-my-dead-body look. And she had every right. If he was honest with himself, he would not be able to cope with a lively four-year-old on his own. It would mean employing a nanny, which would be stupid when Ethan already had a mother who doted on him and looked after his every need.

He could, though, give him a much better lifestyle. He had been horrified when he had seen where Sienna lived and he wanted to move both her and Ethan into his own place straight away. But he knew that she would need time to get used to the idea; she wouldn't just up sticks and come. Persuasion had to be the name of the game. Persuasion and the promise of a better lifestyle.

He wondered how she had coped when Ethan had been in hospital. He couldn't bear the thought of her coming back to her miserable little flat every day after visiting him. It didn't even look a particularly safe area and it was certainly not somewhere where he wanted his son to be brought up.

Why the hell Sienna had chosen not to tell him about Ethan he did not know. What if she had never told him? What if he had never found out? It didn't bear thinking about.

He would have to make some pretty dramatic changes to his lifestyle once he had convinced her to move in with him, but he could do that. All men with families had to adjust—except they did it more gradually! They didn't have active four-year-olds suddenly thrust on them.

And he was taking things for granted! What if Sienna flatly refused to move? What would he do then? He could imagine the stubborn look on her face, the way her lovely lips would compress and her blue eyes narrow.

'Over my dead body.' He could hear her words in his head now.

Sienna was a force to be reckoned with. There was no way on this earth he could make her move in with him if she did not want to. He would have access to Ethan, she would not deny him his parental rights, but he wanted more. He wanted his son—and he wanted Sienna!

Both of them!

It hadn't struck him until this moment how much he wanted Sienna. Those few hours they had spent together this evening had made him realise exactly how much he had missed having her in his life. She had always been hot in bed, no other woman had matched up to her. But he hadn't analysed their love life until now, he'd always been too taken up with his work to think whether anyone else was a better lover.

His whole body began to ache for her. And Ethan was the one who could bring them back together! What he needed to do was tread carefully, not push her but let her think that she was doing what she wanted to do.

Adam went to bed that night and dreamt that Sienna was beside him, that they were making love, that he had never felt so physically aroused, so dynamically charged, so completely satisfied. It was hellishly disappointing, therefore, when he awoke to find the space beside him empty.

'I'm going to meet my daddy?' Ethan's eyes were as wide as saucers. 'Where is he? Did he come looking for me?'

Sienna had just fetched him from nursery and he jigged up and down with excitement. 'Not exactly, sweetheart. I went to see him. I thought it was about time you two met.'

She needed to be honest with Ethan, even if she didn't fill him in on all the details.

Adam had scared her when he had threatened to take Ethan away. She had lain awake all night thinking about it, and during the morning while Ethan was at school she ran the scenario through her head so many times that she felt dizzy.

Now there was no going back. She had set the ball rolling. Ethan was beside himself, he couldn't keep a limb still. He wanted to go and see his father now, this very minute.

Every pulse in her body throbbed, her heart beat so loudly she could almost hear it. All she had to do was arrange a meeting but what if Ethan didn't like Adam? What if Adam didn't like Ethan? What if they didn't get on? Had it been wrong of her to tell Adam after all these years? Ought she to have left things as they were?

'Can we go and see Daddy now?'

Sienna winced as she heard the easy way Ethan referred

to his father. He was so matter-of-fact about it. Almost as though he had known it would take place one day. On the odd occasions she had thought about them meeting she had expected Ethan to be shy and slow to accept.

It clearly didn't look as though that was going to happen.

She could almost picture Ethan running towards Adam and throwing himself into his arms. Of course it wouldn't be like that. They would stand off and size each other up first. Their coming together would be slow and calculated.

'Mummy! Can we?'

Ethan tugged her hand and looked up imploringly, his dark blue eyes so very much like his father's that her heart missed a beat.

'Your daddy's at work. I'll ring him tonight and arrange something. Don't forget he's a very busy man.'

But when she phoned Adam later and told him that Ethan was ready to see him, she was shocked when he suggested they come straight away.

'You're not at work?' Not for one second had she thought that he would be home.

'I finished early,' he announced abruptly. 'Just in case. How did Ethan take it?'

Sienna drew in a deep unsteady breath and was glad Adam couldn't see the pained expression on her face. 'He's excited. But I didn't mean tonight. It's still too soon.'

'Sienna,' he growled, 'if my son is ready to meet me, let's do it straight away. I'll send a car.'

'*No!*' Sienna winced when she heard the screech in her voice. 'I mean, I'd prefer it if you came here. I don't want Ethan being overwhelmed. Meeting you is a big enough deal without him seeing how rich you are.'

'You find my wealth obscene?'

His words were sharp and she could imagine the fire in his eyes. 'Since you put it into so many words, yes. Ethan's world is very different, and I want him to be impressed by you, not your money. You'd be his hero if he knew you could buy him anything in the world that he wanted. We have to count our pennies, Adam. I want him to grow up knowing that money has to be earned. Do you understand?'

'And you think that I haven't had to earn my money? Dammit, Sienna, I've had to work very hard to get where I am today. Nothing came easily. I admire your principles, you're clearly instilling into Ethan the value of money and that is good, but—'

Sienna did not wait for him to finish. 'Actually, I think it would be best if—'

'I'll be there in half an hour.'

The line went dead before she could protest further and Sienna suddenly realised that her son had crept up behind her.

'Does Daddy have lots of money?'

'Ethan, you should not have been listening.'

'But does he, Mummy?'

'It's not important.'

'Is he coming to see me?'

Slowly she nodded and wrapped her arms about her son. 'But he won't be staying long because it's almost time for bed. Do you understand?'

Ethan nodded, sucking his thumb, something he'd done as a baby but Sienna had thought he'd got out of it. Although he had claimed to want to meet his father, he was clearly as nervous as she was.

Ethan was looking through the window when Adam's car pulled up outside. 'Wow!' he exclaimed. 'Is this him, Mummy? Look at his car!'

It was the same black sports car that Adam had brought her home in last night and Sienna sighed. So much for her telling him not to show off. The whole street would be out looking at it in a few minutes. And she wasn't wrong. Even before he had reached her door a band of youths appeared.

She saw Adam say something to them and then hand over a note. It reminded her of a film she had seen. Pay them well and they would look after his car. This wasn't the impression she had wanted to create. Maybe it would have been better to go to Adam's place after all.

But too late now. The bell rang and she hurried to open the door, and even though she knew that all Adam was interested in was his son, she could not stop her heart from racing when they came face to face.

He wore a casual cotton sweater and jeans, and she appreciated that he'd dressed down for his first meeting with Ethan. He'd clearly thought everything through and did not want to overwhelm his son in a Savile Row suit and tie, but had he realised how much it would impact on her own senses?

It was all she could do to drag her eyes away from him. A whole range of feelings danced through her limbs as she moved back stiffly for him to enter. Why did he have to be the sexiest man on earth? Why hadn't she got over him? All these years she had thought her feelings dead and yet all it had taken was a steady look from those deep blue eyes to bring everything back to life.

Of course she must deny it, even to herself. She was

doing this for Ethan's sake. Her own feelings didn't enter into it.

'You'd best come in. You're causing quite a stir.' She stood back for him to enter. The door led straight into her living room and Ethan had disappeared. For all his excitement he was suddenly shy.

Adam brushed past her and the clean smell of him, the same musky aftershave that had aroused her senses last night, infiltrated her nostrils. Behind her back she clenched her fists.

'You are all right with this?' he enquired, pausing to look intently at her.

Would it make any difference if I wasn't? she asked beneath her breath. She hardly thought so. Adam was on a mission and nothing was stopping him.

She nodded.

'And Ethan?'

'He's anxious to meet you. I'm doing this for his sake, Adam, you do realise that?'

The look in his eyes told her that he was very well aware of the fact that she had agreed to them meeting only because she thought it was right for their son. That if it had been left to her, she would not want anything to do with him ever again.

'Where is he?'

He looked around the room and Sienna could almost imagine him comparing it to his own sleek apartment. Too tiny, too cramped, the furniture too old. She jutted her chin without realising it, already on the defensive.

Before she could answer Ethan's head appeared around the door from his bedroom, and with excruciating slowness he walked into the room, his eyes never leaving Adam's face. 'Are you really my dad?' he asked, a whole host of wonderment in his voice.

'I surely am.' Adam squatted so that his eyes were on a level with his son's, and Sienna drew in a swift painful breath. They were so much alike it was unreal. Her little man would grow up to look exactly like Adam. He would have girls flocking around him like birds after crumbs.

As she stood and watched Ethan edge slowly towards his father Sienna felt her throat close. It had been wrong not to confess to Adam that she was pregnant. He had missed all those precious first years of his son's life.

She was filled with dreadful guilt as she watched Ethan's serious face suddenly break into a wide smile.

'I always wondered what my dad looked like.'

'And do you approve?' asked Adam.

Ethan nodded, suddenly losing his voice again— until suddenly a thought struck him. 'Do you have lots of money?'

Adam glanced at Sienna and she frowned fiercely, wishing that Ethan had not overheard their conversation.

'I'm all the richer for knowing you, Ethan.' And he held out his arms.

With only a moment's hesitation Ethan walked into them, taking Adam at face value and clearly liking what he saw. Sienna guessed that whoever his father had been he would have approved.

All she could hope and pray for now was that Adam wouldn't let Ethan down. That he wouldn't disappoint his son by carrying on his exhaustive work lifestyle, leaving no time at all to spend time with him. That he wouldn't believe buying his son's love with expensive gifts would compensate for his absence.

'Mummy, can we?'

Sienna realised that while she had been deep in thought Adam and Ethan had been having a conversation. 'Can we what, sweetheart?'

'Can we go and see Daddy's house?'

'I didn't mean tonight,' said Adam quickly as he saw Sienna's swift frown. 'But perhaps the weekend?'

'It's too soon,' she retorted swiftly. 'Getting to know each other is far more important. You can visit here, or we'll go for walks, the three of us.'

Adam's frown gave away the fact that he thought she was being deliberately awkward. But Sienna stood her ground. 'You need to get to know your son before you impress him with your living standards.'

'But he's only a child, he would not understand the difference.'

Sienna's brows shot upwards. 'Really? I think it might be best if we talked about this some other time.'

He finally got the message and for the next half-hour Adam played with Ethan, who dragged him into his bedroom to show him his toys. Sienna was actually surprised by how good Adam was with his son. She had expected awkwardness, an inability to come down to Ethan's level, and yet he lay sprawled on the floor, letting his son climb all over him. They played battles, and had races with his cars, until Sienna decided enough was enough.

'Much as I hate to interrupt your fun, it's past Ethan's bedtime.' She stood in the doorway, her arms folded, but she was not feeling as tense as she had earlier. Her fears that Adam would let his son down had been unfounded, although she knew that there was still a long way to go.

Adam ruffled Ethan's hair. 'Time for bed, I guess. It's been fun, Ethan. We'll do it again.'

'Can't you stay and put me to bed?' he asked plaintively.

Adam looked at Sienna and saw the mutinous set of her face. It looked as though he had already outstayed his welcome. 'Not tonight, but another time perhaps.'

'Will you come again tomorrow?'

This time Adam did not look at Sienna but he sensed her objection. It was telling him loud and clear not to overstep the mark. 'Maybe, if Mummy agrees, we could go out somewhere at the weekend?'

'Yes, please,' said Ethan immediately. 'We could go to the park. You can push me on the swings.'

'We'll see,' declared Sienna. 'Now, tidy your room before bed.'

'Can Daddy help?'

'Daddy is leaving,' she said pointedly.

'But I'll be back,' Adam called. 'Goodnight, son.'

'Night-night, Daddy.' Ethan darted across the room and wrapped his arms around his father's legs, and Adam felt a curious sensation that he had never felt before. Pride and love. It welled in his throat and threatened to choke him, and at the same time he felt a resurgence of anger towards Sienna for keeping him in ignorance of his son for all these years.

When Ethan was safely back in his room with the door closed, Adam turned to Sienna. 'I've missed out on so much. I have a lot of making up to do.' He did not tell her that when he had first seen his son, when he had seen the strong family likeness, he had felt a pang of guilt for thinking that Sienna had been lying.

It had been wrong to doubt her. He should have known that Sienna was too honest and decent to do anything like that.

'Which you can't do all at once,' she said softly. 'No matter what you're thinking, you need to take things slowly. You can't overwhelm him.'

Adam frowned. 'He didn't seem overwhelmed. He accepted me instantly.' What was Sienna trying to say? That she was going to regulate his visits? Once a week only? Once a month perhaps? This was his son they were talking about, his own flesh and blood. He would see him whenever he wanted to.

Sienna looked totally gorgeous with her face aflame and her eyes shooting sparks. He was so angry with her and yet at the same time he wanted to kiss her. He marched across the room and the intent in his eyes must have been clear because she moved away, heading for the door instead, her hand on the handle.

'Dammit, Sienna, I'm not going yet. We need to talk.'

'And I need to put Ethan to bed.' Her eyes flashed beautiful outrage.

'He's a fine boy, Sienna. You've done well. But he needs a man in his life.

'I think you should both move in with me, as soon as it can be arranged.' It was the best solution. He hated the thought of them living here. He wanted to take them away, give them a lifestyle more suited to his wife and child.

Sienna's eyes widened into enormous orbs of disbelief. 'If we did that, Adam, I'm afraid Ethan would be disappointed by the amount of time you spend at work.'

'I would change.'

Sienna sniffed her disbelief. 'With your track record?

Don't forget I had a father like you. He was always at work, I rarely saw him as I was growing up. It's why my mother divorced him. I don't want that for Ethan. I'd rather he had no father than one who neglected him.'

Adam felt Sienna's anger. It shot over him in hot waves and he had never seen her look more beautiful. He wanted to pull her into his arms and kiss her senseless. Dared he try it? Would it work? Or would it make things worse? He guessed the latter.

'I could learn to delegate.'

'And I'm expected to believe that?' Sienna's beautifully shaped eyebrows rose dismissively. 'You never took time off for me, no matter how I begged or complained. Why should I believe that you'd do it for Ethan?'

'Because circumstances are different now.' He drew in a steadying breath. He wanted to fight anger with anger but knew that it would get him nowhere, so forced himself to remain calm. 'I'm established now, I can afford to take time off.'

Sienna tossed her head, her blue eyes flashing. 'You didn't think it important enough to save our marriage. And yet you'd do it for Ethan. Have you any idea how that makes me feel, Adam?'

Adam kept his temper—just, but his fingers curled into fists. 'Sienna, Ethan is a great boy and I want to get to know him better, but I want you to be a part of my life as well.'

A flash of blue was Sienna's response. He had hoped she would say yes, he had hoped she would realise that it would benefit both of them. But her answer was clearly negative. She was telling him that he didn't stand a chance. Well, he would see about that. There were always ways and means.

'Goodnight, Adam.'

It was the definite way she said it that made him kiss her. He hadn't meant to act so soon but how dared she dismiss him just like that? And once he had the taste of her on his lips, once he felt the soft warmth of her body, he could not contain himself.

He tightened his arms around her and deepened the kiss, feeling a surge of raw hunger. Sienna was all and more than he remembered. She smelled divine, like a breath of spring, and his heart began a manic beat.

Sienna felt as though every atom of air had been drawn out of her body. What was she doing, allowing Adam to kiss her when she was so angry? Why hadn't she opened the door and pushed him out? Now she was in danger of responding, and what a fatal mistake that would be.

But could she help herself? Heck, no. Her body had a mind of its own and her lips parted beneath his. Memories returned of kisses in the honeymoon stage of their marriage, deep passionate kisses that had led to hectic love-making.

Whoa! She forced herself to stop there. Would allowing this kiss lead back to the same place? She dared not let it. It was too dangerous. She did not want a repeat of the unhappiness she had felt when Adam had been absent. And she did not want Ethan to experience it either.

At this very moment his father was his new idol, but if Adam let him down then there would be tears and arguments, and it would be the same old thing all over again.

With a strength born of desperation, she pushed Adam away. 'This isn't part of the deal.'

'You can deny yourself what you so clearly want?' he questioned softly, though she saw something hard in his eyes, something that scared the hell out of her.

'I don't want it,' she claimed loudly. 'I want only my son to get to know his father. I want nothing for myself.'

Adam's brows rose slowly, sceptically. 'Doesn't Ethan's happiness coincide with your own? Don't the two come together?'

'That was not my intention when I sought you out.' But heaven help her, something was going on inside her body over which she had no control.

When she had first met and fallen in love with Adam she had found herself thrown into a kaleidoscope of feelings from which there had been no escape. Even when she had walked out on him, it had been tough love. And it had taken almost all of the time they'd been apart for her to reach the decision that she was no longer in love with him.

And now this! The heat in her body was overwhelming. Adam's kisses had re-ignited the flame that had once burned so brightly that it hurt, and it was going to take every ounce of her willpower not to give herself to him again.

'Then it remains to be seen.' There was a glint in Adam's eye as he spoke, as he opened the door and headed outside.

Sienna closed it quickly, holding a hand over her thudding heart, but she could not help a covert glance through the window.

Adam was laughing and joking with the youths who had guarded his car. He handed them another note.

Sienna shook her head. He earned big money but it

meant nothing to him. It had definitely been a wrong move going to see him. Her own life and Ethan's would never be the same again.

CHAPTER FIVE

SIENNA'S dream was disturbed by Ethan jumping on her bed. 'Wake up, Mummy, wake up.'

She opened her eyes sleepily. She had been dreaming about Adam, about the row they'd had that had ended their marriage. It was so vivid in her mind that she could recall it word for word...

'It's absurd the hours you put in at work.' Sienna had been virtually dancing on the balls of her feet. 'I've had enough. You never listen to what I say. If you don't change I'm going to leave you, it's as simple as that.'

Adam's anger had risen as quickly as hers. 'Don't you dare criticise me when I'm only doing it because of you.'

'Because of me?' Sienna had echoed, her eyes widening. 'Adam, I couldn't care less if we didn't have a penny. It's a simple excuse but it doesn't work. You're doing it for yourself and no one else.' Her body had been stiff with rage, her eyes almost spitting bursts of fire. They'd had this same argument over and over and it hadn't made one iota of difference.

'It doesn't become you, Sienna, screaming at me like this.'

'And neglecting me doesn't become you either,'

she'd snapped. 'Anyone would think you didn't love me any more.'

When he hadn't answered, when he hadn't even looked at her, Sienna had turned and stormed out of the room. And the next morning she had packed her bags.

'Ethan, Mummy's tired. Go back to bed.' She had been disturbed by her dream and wanted a few moments to herself. Their marriage had indeed been stormy and she had congratulated herself on getting out of it.

But now Adam was back in her life, threatening to turn it upside down again. And unhappily she had brought it all on herself.

What if Adam was an absentee father, the same as he'd been an absentee husband? The thought stayed with Sienna and she was not surprised when a few days went by and she heard nothing more from him.

Ethan kept asking where he was. 'Your father's a very busy man,' she told him. 'He has a big business to run.'

'But I want to see him again.'

'And you shall, but we must wait for him to find the time.' What a thing to have to tell her son, but it was true. This was typical Adam. He couldn't even spare a few minutes to pick up the phone.

It was totally unexpected, therefore, when he turned up on Friday evening and invited them to spend the weekend with him. Sienna was furious. Hadn't she already told him that it was far too soon for anything like that?

'I don't think so,' she said. 'We can go out tomorrow if you like, just for the day, for a walk somewhere, a picnic perhaps, but—'

'Oh, Mummy. I want to see Daddy's house.'

Sienna hadn't realised that Ethan was behind her, she had thought he was playing in his room, and although every instinct told her to refuse, she took one look at her son's face and knew that she could not disappoint him.

If Adam had phoned first she could have told him that it was a no-starter, but, no, he had to come in person, knowing that she would be unable to let Ethan down when they were standing face to face.

'I would have appreciated some warning.' Anger flared in her eyes and she felt like pushing him out and slamming the door on him. Instead, for Ethan's sake, she tried to keep some semblance of sanity.

'There was always the chance that you'd say no.'

'Exactly.'

'But now the matter's settled, I suggest you pack a few things and we'll be on our way.'

Again her eyes flashed, especially when he was looking so smug and satisfied. Without another word she marched through to her bedroom, throwing clothes into a holdall, doing the same for Ethan, then returning to stand in front of Adam.

Her eyes were filled with resentment and anger but he chose not to notice, smiling broadly instead. Ethan, too, was jigging up and down with excitement.

Adam's Bentley was waiting outside, his chauffeur standing beside it. Ethan's jaw dropped but he said nothing. It was so unusual for him to be at a loss for words that Sienna knew he was overwhelmed, and sitting between them his eyes were everywhere.

She was actually glad that Ethan shielded her from Adam. Despite her anger, she was very much aware of him. There was some infinitesimal spark inside her that refused to die out. She had sworn to herself after her dream, the dream that had reminded her of all that had happened, all the bad times, that she would not let herself get aroused by him again.

But how impossible was that?

He was still incredibly handsome and sexy. The first moment she had ever clapped eyes on him she had known that this was the man she had wanted to marry.

And she had never fallen out of love with him!

Oh, God, was that really true? Was she still in love with him? The answer was a miserable yes, though she would never admit it to Adam. It scared her to admit it to herself. He would never change. He might try, he might even succeed for a few weeks, but he would inevitably go back to his old ways and where would that leave her and Ethan?

He would strive to persuade them to move in with him, and it really would be tempting. But wise? She did not think so. All he wanted was his son. And if she was a means to an end then…

She must keep a level head on her shoulders, not let Ethan's enthusiasm or Adam's sweet-talking change her mind.

Watching her son's reaction as they approached Adam's home, seeing the way his eyes widened as they passed through the gates, watching the expression on his face as they were whisked smoothly up in the high-speed lift, she knew that these first impressions were what she had feared.

But Adam was heedless of the long-term effect this might have on his son. He smiled each time he saw Ethan's changing expression and over the top of his head he smiled even more complacently at Sienna.

And Sienna was yet further dismayed when she saw the toys that were piled up for Ethan in one of the bedrooms. It looked as if Adam had bought the entire shop.

'What are you doing, Adam?' she asked fiercely when Ethan was out of earshot. 'Are you trying to buy his love? You could have given him a drum or a football and he'd have been just as happy.'

'I have a lot of making up to do.'

'If you think spending money on him is the answer, think again. It's stupid. He wants you, not your money. Haven't we already discussed this?' She had been afraid that he would splash his money around to impress his son and she'd been right.

'You're incredibly sexy when you're angry, do you know that, Sienna?'

Her eyes flashed her displeasure, her whole body stiffening and rejecting him. 'This isn't about you and me.'

It was like water off a duck's back. Adam smiled, completely unperturbed by her words. 'You have the most amazing eyes. They tell me what your voice doesn't, do you know that? And at this moment they're telling me that you're wondering whether I'm going to kiss you again.'

Sienna shot him a blast of anger. 'Trying to butter me up will not change my mind about how I think your relationship with Ethan should go. I want you to stop believing that you can buy his love. It has to be earned. He wants a father. Not presents, not fancy cars, not houses that look as though no child would ever dare play in them, but a father's companionship. Can you give him that?'

By the time she had finished Sienna's breathing was all over the place but she didn't care.

But he either hadn't been listening or he chose to ignore what she was saying. He had edged closer without her even realising it, his eyes darkening and narrowing, and if she didn't move now all would be lost. For how could she not succumb to his kisses when her body was betraying her harsh thoughts? It knew only that this man could take her on an emotional roller-coaster ride, a ride that would tilt her into a world where nothing mattered except feeding her senses.

And what senses!

Even standing here, warring with him, every one of these senses was on red alert. It was as though the time they had spent apart had never happened. She actually wanted his kisses, her body called out for them, and yet the sane part of her mind warned her that to do so would be a huge mistake. One she might later regret.

But did she listen to the sane part of her mind? No! When Adam was so close that she could see each one of his incredibly long eyelashes individually, when she could, if she so desired, reach out and touch his jaw where already new growth was showing, when she could hear his breathing and see the sudden flare in his eyes, it was too late to back away.

A warm hand curved behind her neck and eyes that she'd once felt herself drowning in burned into hers, asking the question but not waiting for an answer.

Sienna's heart drummed an age-old rhythm. Each beat built up her senses, and when Adam's lips claimed hers she was totally ready. It was like much-needed rain after a dry summer. It was like finding water in the desert. It fed her inner needs and against her better judgement she returned his kiss.

It dived deep into the heart of her, arousing senses that had long lain dormant, sending thrill after thrill through her body so that she tingled and sizzled and did not want him to stop.

It was Ethan who put a stop to it, running into the room to show his father a toy boat. It did not faze him that they were kissing—he merely tugged at his father's sleeve. 'Daddy, I have a boat just like this at home.'

With her cheeks flaming, Sienna was thankful that her son saw nothing wrong. She guessed he thought it was what all mummies and daddies did. But it brought her to her senses, made her realise that spending any length of time with Adam was dangerous.

'Then you're a very lucky boy to have two boats,' said Adam. He too appeared untroubled by the interruption, though he did look darkly at Sienna, as if to say that they would carry the kiss on at another time. 'And guess what, Ethan? I have the real thing.'

'You do?' Ethan's eyes widened into two enormous orbs. 'A real boat?'

'A real boat.'

'Can I see it? Can I go on it? Where is it? Can we go now?'

'*Ethan!*' Sienna was appalled by Ethan's questions. 'You cannot go on your father's boat. I will not allow it. You're too young.'

'I can swim, Mummy, if you're frightened I'll fall into the water.'

'Of course you can, but it's different in the river from the swimming baths. Go back and play.'

Ethan looked crestfallen but did as he was told and as soon as he was out of earshot Sienna turned on Adam. 'You shouldn't have told him. Haven't I told you not to flash your wealth in front of him? You'll make him impossible to handle.'

'And why would that be?' Adam's thick dark brows drew together over eyes that were suddenly fierce. 'He'll find out one day, why not now?'

'Because it's too much too soon. He's only four, Adam. He doesn't really understand.'

'Exactly. Therefore I don't see what you're worrying about. Now, what were we doing before we were interrupted?' A faint smile twisted the corners of his lips as he moved in on her again, but Sienna was too quick for him.

If he thought she was going to slip back into a relationship with him because of Ethan, he was sorely mistaken. She might still fancy him like mad but she could get over that. She'd done it once, why not again?

Except that now, because of Ethan, he was a permanent part of her life. She could not introduce Ethan to his father and then never let him see him again. Somehow she had to ignore the emotions that flowed through her like a raging river. She had to pretend they did not exist. Adam was Ethan's father. Full stop. Not her lover any more. Just Ethan's father.

'It's time for Ethan to have a bath and go to bed,' she declared, hoping her voice sounded normal.

Earlier Adam had shown her the bedrooms. One room with twin beds that he thought Ethan could use, a room with a double bed, both rooms having their own bathroom, and his own impressive suite with its king-size bed and not one but two bathrooms and an inter-connecting dressing room.

Talk about excess, she had thought, though she had wisely kept her words to herself.

Ethan was totally impressed that he had his very own bathroom and Sienna thought that she might have problems getting him to sleep in a strange bed. But, no, he dropped off straight away, after persuading his father to read him a bedtime story.

Adam appeared a little awkward at first but soon his voice relaxed and he even managed to put on different voices for each character.

'Thank you,' she said. 'Ethan loves being read to.'

'He's a good child. You've brought him up well, Sienna.'

His voice dropped to a low husky growl and alarm bells went off in Sienna's head. Things were moving a lot faster than she had intended. It felt like only yester-day that she had faced him and told him that he had a son. Now they were staying with him and she was afraid that a weekend would lead to something more.

'I only wish that I'd known about him from the be-ginning.'

Then you shouldn't have ignored me and spent all your hours at work, thought Sienna. He had no one to blame but himself.

'But I intend to make up.'

Her eyes flashed a warning. 'All he wants is your love.'

'And how about you, Sienna? What do you want?'

The steady look in his eyes, the husky tone of his voice, warned her that she needed to be careful. 'I want

Ethan to be happy. I don't want him to get too close to you and then you let him down.'

'You think I'd do that?' Blue eyes darkened and narrowed, his chin lifted with familiar arrogance.

'You let me down and it destroyed our marriage.'

'Only because you didn't understand. You never made allowances. There was a reason I—'

Sienna's eyes flashed as fiercely as his. 'The fact was you neglected me. And if you dare do that to Ethan, I'll make sure you regret it to the end of your days.'

'There is one way you can ensure I don't neglect him.'

Sienna's heart drummed a little more quickly. 'And that is?' She knew what he was going to say and she had her answer ready.

'You can move in with me.'

'Not in a million years.' The words came out as quick as a flash. 'I've had one dose of living with you, Adam. It didn't work then and it wouldn't work now. Besides you can't cage Ethan in an apartment. It wouldn't be fair.'

'Then I'll buy a house with a garden. Problem solved.' He folded his arms and looked at her down the length of his nose.

If only it were that easy! Adam really had no idea what this was all about. It wasn't about them moving in with him. Despite what Sienna had said, she now knew that this wasn't about Ethan any more. It was about the two of them.

Their relationship.

Adam was as sexy as hell and there was clearly still an incredibly strong attraction between them. They would be spending more and more time together because of Ethan, and if things continued the way they were, Sienna knew, deep in her heart, that it wouldn't be long before she was sharing his bed again. But there was more to life than making love. Adam could declare as many times as he liked that he would change his working habits but she knew differently. Words were easy. Doing it was another matter.

He enjoyed the cut and thrust of business, it was his whole life, it meant more to him than a wife, and it would inevitably mean more to him than a child. Even though he would say he was doing it for Ethan. To provide for his future.

Heavens, he was wealthy enough never to work again. But work was his first love and his last love. She and Ethan would always come a poor second.

'I suggest we take things one step at a time, Adam,' she said carefully. 'Let's see how we get on. This is all very new for Ethan. He's excited now but—'

'But you're still afraid I'll let him down? Maybe not today or tomorrow, not even next week or next month, but in a year's time you're wondering what sort of a father I'll be?'

There was steel in his voice, which made her shiver. Nevertheless, she kept her tone firm and her eyes hard. 'You're forgetting I know your track record.'

'We also had a track record in love-making.' His voice changed, softened, and he took a step towards her.

Sienna held her breath. It would be so easy to melt into his arms, to let him kiss her senseless and carry her off to bed. That huge bed with its tempting gold and cream quilt. Not a man's colour, though it creatively relieved the brown carpet and curtains.

It was a sumptuous bedroom and everything inside

her quivered at the thought of sharing it with him. Their earlier kiss, brief though it had been, had rolled back the years, made her aware of the power Adam had once wielded over her. And when he looked at her from beneath those thick dark brows, the sort of look that would turn any woman's bones to jelly, she knew that that power had not waned.

It felt like a trickle of electricity running through her body, sparking and tingling and making her want to feed from his kisses. Which was crazy, considering their circumstances. But if he touched her now, if he attempted to kiss her, she would not be able to stop him. Instead, she would go up in flames.

'That was then, Adam. Things are very different now.' Somehow she kept her voice steady and indifferent.

Adam's lips quirked. 'A pity. It's been a long time since anyone shared my bed.'

Sienna let her brows rise upwards in a searching question.

'You think I've had a stream of women in your wake? Not so, Sienna. I've dated, yes, but I've brought no one here. This is my sole preserve—though I'm willing to share it with you.'

'It's a pity, then, that I don't want to.' Sienna kept her eyes steady on his.

'Maybe I could persuade you?'

Another step and he was so close that she could feel the warmth of him, see the intent in his sensational blue eyes, smell the rich male scent of him. It was a heady cocktail. A dangerous one.

She closed her eyes in self-defence, not wanting to see him, not wanting to feel. And was totally shocked when his arms slid behind her back and his mouth claimed hers all in one swift, devastating movement.

Unable to move or speak, unable to stem the tide of hunger that shot through her, Sienna kept her eyes tightly closed and allowed herself the luxury of feeling Adam's power, of experiencing a sensational explosion of feelings so strong that they stunned her.

Crazily she did not want him to let her go, she wanted to spend the night in his arms and in his bed, making amazing love. Adam had always been an innovative lover but she imagined that he would have improved, that he would take her to places she had never been before.

And her body cried out for fulfilment.

'So what is your answer, Sienna?' Adam lifted his mouth from hers and Sienna immediately felt that he had deserted her.

She shot her eyes wide. His kiss had disturbed her senses, made her forget everything except the thrill of the moment.

If he was going to carry on kissing her like this, turning her body into a mass of sensation that could only be relieved by making love, her answer had to be yes.

But if his intention was to win her over solely so that he could have access to his son, she would be foolish. There was no way on this earth that she was going to let Adam use her.

She pulled swiftly away from him, darts of sudden hostility shooting from her eyes. 'I need my head examined.' She needed more than that, she needed brain surgery. How could she have let him kiss her?

There were dark, dangerous thoughts going through

his head and if she wasn't careful she would play straight into his hands.

To her amazement Adam laughed, a cruel laugh that sliced into her heart, and his face was inscrutable as he moved away. 'Drinks on the terrace?'

Sienna wanted to be anywhere but with Adam. He had tested her and humiliated her, and unfortunately there was no escape. It might be a luxury apartment but there was no place to run. She was committed to spending the weekend with him, whether she liked it or not.

CHAPTER SIX

SIENNA chose to sleep in the same room as Ethan. Here she was safe. Here she could relax. Adam's continual assault on her senses spun her out of control. But also served as a timely warning.

It was total insanity letting him see that she was still painfully weak where he was concerned and she needed to be careful, to be on her guard at all times, to make sure that it did not happen again. Otherwise he would have her back in his bed. Not because he loved her, she knew that there was no chance of that, but because he wanted Ethan and he knew that they came as a pair. In effect he would have the best of both worlds.

After breakfast they walked along the river, they fed the ducks, they lunched at a riverside restaurant, and Ethan never stopped talking.

He was a welcome diversion. This was what the weekend was supposed to be about. Ethan and Adam getting to know one another.

To give him his due, he was very good with Ethan. They had long conversations and he didn't try to impress his son again by splashing his money around.

It was not until they got back to his apartment and

Ethan shot away to play with his new toys that she found herself once more alone with Adam.

He had discovered what a joy Ethan was. How good it felt to have a son, his own flesh and blood. A little companion. Sienna had denied him that pleasure and he made no attempt now to hide his resentment. 'I've enjoyed today with Ethan,' he said, 'more than I thought possible. But I'll never forgive you for keeping him a secret.'

'Perhaps I should have told you sooner, but do you remember what our marriage was like, Adam? What do you think you would have done if I'd told you I was pregnant?' Sienna's brows drew into a swift frown. 'Don't answer that, allow me to. You'd have been angry, furious, in fact. You'd have said it was all my fault. You weren't ready for children, or marriage for that matter.'

'Maybe I wasn't,' he agreed, ignoring the hint of guilt at the back of his mind. 'Nevertheless, you stole his first years from me, Sienna. I've missed out on seeing him learn to walk, to say his first words, all the cute little things that babies do.'

'Cute little things?' echoed Sienna, her eyes flaring. 'When have you been interested in cute? You had time for no one, Adam Bannerman. No one, not even me.'

'So how did we produce a baby if I had no time for you?'

She tossed him a scornful glance, one that could have frozen water. 'Because like all men there's one thing that you cannot do without. But rest assured, Adam, it will never happen again.'

Her demeanour, her whole attitude, fired him up and made him want to kiss her despite his anger. He knew that to do so would be fatal, but it did not stop him thinking about it. Sienna had grown spectacularly beautiful over the years. She had an added confidence about her now, a haughty look. He loved the way she tilted her chin, the way she challenged him. She'd been lovely before but the in-between years had turned her into one very stunning woman.

Her rich chestnut hair seemed to have thickened and he was sorely tempted to run his fingers through it. Snatch her face close to his and kiss her fiercely. Her blue eyes were clear and bright and they danced with fire. Hell, he could feel himself hardening.

It had definitely been a mistake suggesting they spend the whole weekend with him. He'd arranged it for his son's sake, because he wanted to get to know Ethan, but the power of Sienna was in danger of overriding it.

He had never expected to feel like this about her. He'd been as angry as hell when she had told him about Ethan, so angry he could have throttled her with his bare hands, and, yes, he still was angry. But now that he'd spent time again with Sienna he was beginning to realise how stupid he had been to let her go.

And stupid also to think that there might be a future for them, because she'd made it crystal clear that it was not what she wanted.

Even though she responded to his kisses!

There was certainly more to Sienna than he had ever thought. Not only had she improved in looks, she had more guts, more of everything, in fact.

Sienna did not wait for Adam's answer but walked away from him, out onto the terrace where she could look out over the Thames, throwing over her shoulder as she did so, 'Why don't you go and play with your son?'

She wished that her own body was as reassuringly calm as some of the boats making their way slowly towards their goal. Their earlier kiss still haunted her. It had been madness, letting it happen. On the other hand, it was a timely warning. One she must remember.

When Adam spoke softly in her ear she jumped because she had believed, had hoped, in fact, that he was safely with Ethan. She needed this breathing space to come to terms with what was happening. Had he deliberately trodden softly? Was he trying to home in on her thoughts?

She turned round swiftly—and found herself trapped between his arms. He was not touching her, not even a hair from his strong powerful forearms caressed her body. But she was his prisoner nevertheless, his hands either side of her on the safety rail. Judging by the way her body reacted, though, he may as well have been touching her.

The musky scent of his skin filled her nostrils and with her heartbeats accelerating to a million times a minute, a flood of heat gathering speed through her limbs, she stood in total shock, her eyes locked with his. 'What do you think you are doing? Ethan might—'

'He's asleep.'

'What?'

'I think his walk wore him out. He was lying on the floor with his toy boat in his hand. I've lifted him onto the bed.'

'I'd best go to him.' Sienna attempted to push past Adam but he was having none of it. He caught her arm and swung her to face him.

'He's fine, Sienna, you worry too much.'

She worried! What did he think mothers did? 'How

dare you tell me whether I worry or not, Adam, when you know nothing about children? When I've spent the last four years caring for Ethan, worrying about him. When I sat by his hospital bed for days and nights, not knowing whether he was going to live or die. They were the worst days of my life. If Ethan had died, I would have wanted to die too. So don't tell me not to worry.'

Adam's face became harshly angular, his skin stretched so tightly across his cheekbones that it looked as though it had been carved out of stone. And she had no idea what was going through his mind.

'You didn't have to be alone,' he said, his voice coldly damning now. 'You could have told me. I could have shared your fear. I would have been there beside you. Dammit! You should have contacted me.'

Words were easy, she thought. It would have taken an earthquake to drag Adam away from his business affairs. She certainly couldn't imagine him sitting for hours in hospital. His eyes, which were sometimes incandescently blue and dangerous, were now dark and accusing. His hand on her arm like a band of steel.

He didn't care about her, thought Sienna. It was only Ethan. She could walk out of here right now and he'd be perfectly happy—so long as she left her son behind. Fuming, she twisted herself free.

She went into Ethan's bedroom, pulling up short when she saw him safely curled in the middle of the bed. He looked such an angel when he was asleep, one hand outstretched on the pillow, his dark hair tousled. Adam had pulled a sheet over him and he hadn't stirred. Her little man! How she loved him.

'Are your fears allayed?' Adam's voice came softly

over her shoulder, all the harshness suddenly gone out of it.

Sienna spun around and almost cannoned into him She nodded, not trusting her voice.

When she walked from the room Adam followed. 'We've created a unique little boy.'

'Yes.' It was all she could manage.

'But he needs both parents.'

Shock waves rippled through her. Her words rattled into the air between them when she spoke. 'We need to do this gradually, Adam. Ethan's all over you at the moment, but it's new. Wait until he finds you're always at work whenever he wants to tell you something or do something exciting with you. The novelty will wear off.'

'You're not even giving me a chance.' The disapproval in his voice did nothing to calm her down.

Sienna felt her hackles rise. 'If you think I'm going to repeat this weekend, think again, Adam. It's turning into a nightmare.'

'Not from my point of view.' There was still a hard glint in his eyes. And his lips pulled into a straight grim line, his whole demeanour one of superb confidence.

Sienna felt like taking a swipe at him. 'You should be where I'm standing.'

Cold eyes condemned her, telling her clearly that if he had to he would fight for Ethan, and Sienna felt ice trickle down her spine, spreading its fingers until her whole body was frozen. He did have rights, she was aware of that, but even so...

She was the first to turn away, to walk stiffly out of the room, to turn her back on this man who had broken her heart once and looked set to do it again.

If only there was somewhere to run! She was effectively his prisoner here in this chillingly perfect apartment. And she had another day to go before they went home.

Sunday followed a similar pattern. Sienna had slept in Ethan's room again and now they were on the London Eye. She pointed out St Paul's Cathedral to Ethan. Big Ben and the Houses of Parliament. But he was more interested in the Thames itself.

'Look, Daddy, boats!' he exclaimed excitedly, pointing into the distance. 'Which one is yours?'

'It's the furthest away,' answered Adam, winking at Sienna. 'Can you see it?'

'I think so,' said Ethan, screwing his eyes up and concentrating hard.

Sienna knew that she was not going to hear the end of Adam's boat. Ethan would go on and on about it and wouldn't be satisfied until he had actually seen it close up and been on board. But it was not going to happen today. Once they had finished their ride and had had lunch, they were going home. She would insist on it.

But things did not work out the way she wanted. They had lunch at the riverside restaurant near Adam's apartment and afterwards he insisted on taking them both to see where he worked.

Actually, she was curious. Even when they had been together, she had never been to his offices. He had never invited her and she had never asked. So why he wanted her to see it now she had no idea. To impress, she guessed. Though Ethan was too young and she already knew that it would be state of the art.

She wasn't mistaken.

It was a different address from the one he had used

when they had first married. He had gone up in the world, of course. His offices were on the top floor—yet again—with views over London equally as impressive as those from the London Eye.

Everything was operated by the touch of a button and Ethan was in his element. Mirrors on the walls turned into screens for video conferencing. Monitors popped up out of desks. All the sort of stuff she had seen in futuristic movies.

'It's very nice,' she managed.

'Is that all you can say?'

Sienna shrugged. 'What do you want me to say? Your wealth doesn't impress me, Adam, and it never has. I wanted a man who cared for me, who thought more of me than he did his work. If you want my opinion, I think you're happier married to your work than you ever were to me.'

'So why didn't you divorce me?'

Sienna shrugged. It was a fair question, something she had occasionally asked herself. 'I didn't need a divorce. I had no other man in my life.'

Adam's brows rose. 'So if anyone asked where your husband was, what did you say?'

She would have liked to declare that she had told everyone she had walked out on him because he was more in love with his job than with her, but she didn't. She would have liked to say that she had told everyone that the love had gone out of their marriage, but she didn't. She would have even liked to say that she'd told everyone he was the lousiest husband in the world, but she didn't.

'I simply said that it didn't work out.'

A frown furrowed the space between his eyes, as if he had expected, wanted even, a better explanation than that.

'I don't believe in airing my dirty linen in public. What did you tell people? That I didn't understand you, that I didn't approve of your need to work so hard?'

'Something like that,' he agreed easily. *'Ethan!'*

They had both been so busy niggling at each other that they hadn't seen Ethan climb on a chair. They knew nothing until he fell over backwards and his head hit the floor.

Sienna screamed.

Adam bounded towards him.

She saw blood—and almost fainted herself.

It was during the next frantic few moments that Adam became her strength. She did not remember him phoning for an ambulance, she remembered nothing except cradling Ethan in her arms, trying to stem the flow of blood with the handkerchief Adam had swiftly pushed into her hand, soothing him when he cried that his head hurt.

In the ambulance he was sick, twice, and when they got to the hospital they were immediately taken into an examination room where he was sick again. She continued to hold the pad to Ethan's head and talked to him constantly because she was afraid of concussion. 'Where is everyone?' she kept asking, almost out of her mind with worry.

'They're very busy,' answered Adam, trying to look reassuring when she knew that he was as concerned as she was. In fact, he probably blamed himself for letting Ethan play on the chair, for even taking them to his office.

A nurse came to check on Ethan and confirmed that

they were doing the right thing in keeping him awake. 'A doctor will be with you shortly.'

'Can't you do anything?' Sienna asked Adam crossly when several more minutes went by and there was no sign of anyone.

'Relax, Sienna,' he answered calmly. 'He is in the best place and if they thought there was anything seriously wrong they'd be examining him by now. We just have to be patient.'

'Patient?' she cried. 'When my son's split his head open? I thought head injuries were always treated seriously.'

'I'm sure it's not as bad as it looks,' said Adam, trying to soothe her. 'I remember doing a similar thing when I was Ethan's age. Boys will be boys.'

But then a doctor appeared and after examining Ethan thoroughly he said that no serious damage had been done. 'He'll need stitches, of course, but you'll be able to take him home. Keep waking him every two hours throughout the night in case of concussion but otherwise you have very little to worry about.'

When they left hospital Adam's car was waiting outside. Sienna didn't bat an eyelid, she was too worried about Ethan to even think about how it had got there.

'We'll go back to my place,' he said decisively. 'I'm as worried about Ethan as you are. I feel totally responsible. And naturally you will stay until he is completely better. I'll take some time off to help you look after him.'

Was she really hearing this? wondered Sienna. Was this what it had taken to convince Adam that being a husband and parent was equally as important as earning a living? Wonders would never cease. But she wanted Ethan in his own bed.

'Thanks for the offer, I appreciate it, really, but I'd prefer to go home,' she told him firmly. 'It will be better for Ethan. He'll be more comfortable in familiar surroundings.'

Much to her surprise, Adam agreed. 'You're right, of course.'

But her comfort zone was shattered when they arrived at her flat and Adam calmly announced that he was going to stay the night. 'You don't think I'd leave you under the circumstances? I feel responsible, Sienna.'

Sienna began to panic. 'It wasn't your fault. We'll be all right. He's had cuts and bruises before.'

'But nothing like this, I'm sure. And he is my son. I want to be there for him.' The controlled look on Adam's face told her that there was no point in arguing.

Fear skittered down her spine. Adam would take over. His presence would fill her tiny rooms. But more worrying still was where would he sleep. The couch wasn't made for a six-foot-three hunk. And he certainly wasn't sharing her bed. She did have a sleeping bag, though. He'd have to make do with that, on the floor if necessary. And maybe he might find it so uncomfortable that he'd go home.

And pigs might fly. She knew Adam's gritty determination only too well. It entered into every facet of his life. It was what had made him the success he was. It was what would determine Ethan's future, and maybe even her own.

A scary thought. When she had announced that he had a son she had somehow believed that he would be a part-time father, seeing Ethan only when it suited him. Not for one second had she expected that he would want, demand even, that he play a big part in his son's life. And incidentally in her own.

Ethan was in his element, being the centre of attention, and he insisted that his father put him to bed. Sienna hovered and supervised and then sat by Ethan's side, holding his hand, while Adam read to him.

Adam had never, in the whole of his life, imagined himself taking part in such a cosy domestic scene. Seeing Ethan in bed in his own apartment was entirely different. This was Ethan's room, it was filled with well-loved toys, it had his own personality stamped on it.

And what a little personality he was. Already Adam was proud of his son and he'd been devastated when he'd fallen and cut his head. It had been the worst moment in his entire life. He felt totally responsible.

At the hospital it had reminded him of the occasion when he had been admitted with a suspected broken ankle—although it had turned out to be nothing more than a bad sprain. His anxious parents had never left his side, though, and he could now understand their extreme concern.

'The end.' He closed the book and looked at Ethan, but he was already asleep.

They crept out of the room and Sienna went in to the kitchen to make coffee. Adam wanted to follow but space in there was at a premium, and he also guessed his presence wouldn't be welcome. She still gave off very strong vibes that he wasn't wanted there.

He ended up sitting on the couch. A distinctly uncomfortable couch.

It had been a turning point in his life when he had found out about Ethan. And this was yet another one. Who would ever have thought that he'd be spending the night in a cramped little flat? He'd worked for years to lift himself above the ordinary. He'd reached the pinnacle of his career. And yet he felt happier here than he had for a long time.

It was the strangest feeling.

But it was only because of Sienna and Ethan. He could never allow them to continue living here. For one thing this place wasn't big enough, and he felt sure it wasn't safe. He'd been entirely serious when he'd said that he would buy a house with a garden. He had even phoned an estate agent friend of his and set the ball rolling.

Not that he had told Sienna. But if he presented her with a *fait accompli*, there was nothing she could do about it. She undoubtedly deserved better than this.

'You look tired,' he said, when she came in with their drinks, setting them down on a coffee table in front of him.

Sienna nodded. She *was* tired, tired of this game that Adam was playing. He was beginning to act as though they had never been apart, and Ethan was unwittingly drawing them closer together.

She sat in the chair and he watched every movement she made. The way she crossed her legs, the way she tossed her hair back from her face, the way she reached out and took her cup, holding it as though it was a barrier between them.

Adam didn't fit into this place. She had never for one moment thought that he would stay. And now there was no way she could get rid of him.

'Ethan's quite a little soldier, isn't he?'

Sienna nodded. 'He's always been a battler. He shrugs off wounds in the same way that we shake rain-drops off our clothes.' And how she wished she could shrug Adam out of her life the same way.

In the confines of her living room the air had thick-ened until every breath she drew became painful. At least in his apartment there had been acres of breathing space. Here there was nothing. It was like being caught in a trap with him.

'I don't mind admitting that he scared the hell out of me when he fell. What if anything had happened to him, Sienna?'

She looked at him with wide, pain-filled eyes. 'It doesn't bear thinking about. Ethan's my whole life. I love him so much that it hurts.'

'You do know that if I'd known you were pregnant I would never have let you go?'

'Perhaps not,' answered Sienna. His words were soft and all the more plausible because of it. 'It happened, though, and we can't put back the clock.'

'You shouldn't have had to bring him up on your own. Every child deserves both of its parents. And you certainly shouldn't have had to cope with him being seriously ill. I wish you had told me, Sienna.'

Sienna wasn't sure that it would have helped matters, nevertheless she could see that Adam was seriously affected now by Ethan's accident. It had given him a taste of what it had been like for her when he had been seriously ill. It was something she never wanted to go through again.

'We've both grown up a lot since I left,' she said. 'I'm not sure bringing up a baby would have been a pleasure as far as you're concerned. We'd have probably had more rows than before.'

Adam groaned. He did not actually say that he agreed but she could see it in his eyes. 'And now I need to make up. You've suffered enough on your own, Sienna. In future I'm going to take the weight off your shoulders.'

Quite how it happened she didn't know, but her cup was taken from her and she was hauled to her feet and held in a powerful embrace. Unable to stop herself, Sienna buried her head in his chest, feeling the throb of his heart match her own. Tears filled her eyes, the events of the past few hours finally catching up with her.

When Adam lifted her chin to look into her eyes he gave a groan and held her even more tightly. 'It's all right, Sienna. It's all right to cry. You've been strong for Ethan but you can let go now.'

He stroked her hair back from her face and kissed her brow—just as she did Ethan's when he fell and bumped himself. Except that this didn't feel like a mother's kiss, or even a father's. It felt like a lover's…

And she had run out of strength. There was nothing that she could do to stop him. It actually felt good to be held against someone as strong as Adam. For the past five years she had had no one to support her. She had been the strong one, the capable one. Now, though, it felt as though all her trials had come together and she was unable to bear up any longer.

'I think I'd like to go to bed,' she said quietly, adding, when she realised exactly what she had said, 'By myself.' If she stayed in Adam's arms any longer, she would melt. She would give in to the urges that were already beginning to form. Dangerous urges that ought to have no place in her heart.

'If that is your wish.'

'You know it is, Adam.'

'And I am to sleep—where?'

'The couch, the floor, the choice is yours.' She struggled out of his arms. 'There are only two beds in this house. One is Ethan's, the other is mine. I have a sleeping bag somewhere you can use.'

'That should be fun!'

It was his tone of voice that made her smile. 'You knew the set-up before you invited yourself. You've no one else to blame.'

'Have you no heart, Sienna? Are you sure that I cannot persuade you to share your bed? After everything we've gone through today, can't you take pity on me?'

His expression reminded her of Ethan's when he was trying to wheedle something out of her. It made her laugh.

And Adam jumped in.

With one swift movement she was back in his arms and he was carrying her through to the bedroom. Their coffees sat congealing on the table. She thought of nothing except the heat of Adam's body next to hers.

CHAPTER SEVEN

'ADAM, we shouldn't be doing this,' insisted Sienna. 'Not while Ethan's so poorly.'

He merely grinned. 'You can't get out of it that easily, Sienna. And since we have to keep waking him, there's no point in us going to sleep. We have to fill in our time somehow.'

His kisses became more demanding, more urgent, as though he had been waiting all day for this very moment. Not that he could have expected they would end up here, and neither had she!

With a sigh she gave herself up to Adam's kisses, his magical, heart-stopping kisses. Kisses that had more fire in them than ever before.

Feelings that had been buried rose as swiftly as a bird in flight and when Adam began to remove her clothes she made no attempt to stop him. With each inch of flesh that was exposed Adam covered it with kisses, her arms and shoulders, his tongue finding the pulse at the base of her throat, resting on it, feeling its frantic beat.

In fact, every one of her pulses throbbed. Sienna felt as though her whole body had been taken over by this man. He was making it his own and there was nothing that she could do to stop him.

She felt uplifted. As though something had been missing from her life and now she had found it again.

And this was only the beginning!

When Adam turned his attention to her breasts, when he cupped them in his capable hands, when he took her nipples between his teeth, nipping gently at first but then biting and sucking each one in turn into his mouth, her whole body was in danger of igniting.

Unaware that tiny groans kept escaping the back of her throat, Sienna gripped Adam's shoulders. A smile softened his eyes but his mouth never left her nipple.

Sienna wanted to smile herself but was feeling too much going on inside her body to do anything other than grip Adam's shoulders and dig her nails deep into his firm flesh. She wanted more of this man who had once been her whole life, who could arouse her more magnificently than any other man she knew.

A trail of kisses to her belly button had her squirming and writhing, and when he flicked the button on her jeans and dragged them off in one swift economical movement, her tiny black lace briefs following suit, she felt freedom as never before.

She lay back and closed her eyes, her legs parting involuntarily. Adam's mouth continued its course, his fingers twirling and gently pulling the dark hairs that covered her femininity.

She heard the groan of satisfaction in his voice, a groan that continued as his tongue replaced his fingers, as it sought and reached the very part of her that was hot with need.

Involuntarily she lifted her hips, offering her now throbbing and parted core. It was her ultimate gift, born of desperation. Adam had reached deep into her emotions, he had brought them back to vigorous life, and she could not go on unless he made love to her.

At first it was his tongue and expert fingers that brought her to the edge, and it was almost more than she could bear. 'Don't do this to me, Adam,' she cried, her nails clawing his back. 'Don't torment me like this. Make love to me.'

She was hardly aware of uttering the words, she knew only that she would be the one taking the initiative if he didn't hurry up.

But in seconds he was out of his clothes, obeying her command, and Sienna's world exploded. Making love in the past had been good but never this magnificent. She had thought it was, she had been eminently satisfied, but time apart had taught her that Adam was even more knowledgeable now in what women wanted.

When they were both fully sated, when their bodies lay limp, he held her closely to him, stroking her hair, letting her know without words that he too had experienced something uplifting and wonderful.

It was not until their bodies cooled and her breathing returned to normal that Sienna began to have doubts about her sanity. Their love-making had been intense and fantastic, she could not deny that, but how could she have let this happen? What had got into her? They hadn't even used protection. And why was Adam a better lover now than he had been before?

Because of all the other women he had bedded in her absence!

It was a bitter pill to swallow.

Or had she been more receptive, forgetting the bad times, conscious only that Adam had the power to turn her into someone she hardly recognized?

Already she could feel her body springing back to life, ready for another assault on her senses. But it would be wrong to allow it. She had let herself down. It must never happen again, good though it had been. More than good actually. Remarkable, incredible, out of this world!

Adam's hold on her relaxed. He had fallen asleep! With a grunt of satisfaction he settled more comfortably. Was he dreaming about what had just happened? she wondered. Did he feel as fulfilled as she did, but without the self-recrimination?

Adam would never blame himself for anything he did, she knew that for a fact. His actions were always calculated and deliberate, whether he was making love or finalising a business deal.

It was herself she had let down. She had given in too easily. Without words she had told him that she was his for the taking whenever he felt like it.

Heat of a very different kind flooded her body now and she rolled away from him in disgust, giving a little huff as she curled her knees up to her chin, vowing never to let him touch her again.

'Sienna? What's wrong?'

So he was not asleep!

'This is wrong,' she hissed fiercely, pushing herself up. 'Me and you. After everything that has happened between us. You never loved me, did you, Adam?' At last she asked the question that had troubled her ever since she'd walked out.

Adam sat up too and looked at her for several long seconds, seeming to be reflecting on her words, wondering how to answer, and when he did it was not what she expected.

'It's true, I didn't love you.'

Shock waves rippled through her. Agonising waves! So she was right! It wasn't good hearing it but before she could respond he spoke again.

'I liked you, Sienna, a lot. I was very fond of you. But…' He fought for the right words. 'I don't know how to say this, but…I'm afraid to love. I made a promise to myself many years ago never to do so.'

His words made no sense and Sienna shot him a sharply suspicious glance. 'So why did you ask me to marry you? Why did you let me think our marriage was a love match? No wonder it fell apart. What's there to be afraid of?' The situation was getting more bizarre by the second.

Adam drew in a long, slow breath and let it out again even more slowly. Sienna began to think he was not going to answer until he finally said, 'My father loved my mother very much. So much that when she died he lost control of his life, couldn't focus. He became a broken man and went from being someone I respected to someone I could hardly recognise. He turned to drink and eventually that became his crutch, his reason for living.'

Sienna's fingers fluttered to her mouth, her eyes widening. She had met Adam's father and had known of his drinking problem, but had never thought about the cause of it until now. The news that it had followed the death if his wife shocked Sienna terribly and she understood now why Adam had never talked about the issues before.

'Is that why *you* never touch alcohol?'

Adam nodded, his eyes dull and sad, making her wish that she had not asked the question. 'I did not want the same thing to happen to me. If losing the person you love causes such pain that you lose control of your life, change beyond recognition and feel the need to blot it out with drink, then it is better to never love at all.'

So Adam had never loved her and never would! It was a sickening, saddening thought. He was a strong man and it was ironic that he could make such spectacular love, and yet not be *in* love with her. And more incredulous still was the fact that she still loved him.

And Adam would never let her go now because of Ethan!

'I'm sorry,' she whispered, her heart aching for him. 'Sorry for you and sorry for your father. I didn't know that that was why he drank.'

'And why would you?' he asked sharply, swinging his legs off the bed and standing up. 'It's not something I shout from the rooftops. My father became a liability. A sad, drunken old man. His death was a merciful release.'

'And your grandfather, how did he take it?' She knew that Adam and his grandfather weren't on the best of terms. She had heard them having a terrible row just before their wedding and Adam hadn't spoken his name again.

Adam's eyes grew icily remote. 'I'd really rather not talk about him.'

Sienna nodded, she could see how painful his memories were. 'Perhaps you'd like to go and wake Ethan? Check that he's OK?' She felt that he needed something to do to take his mind off their unfortunate conversation. She dearly wanted to check on her son herself, but Adam's need at this moment was greater than hers.

Immediately his face softened into a ghost of a smile and he pulled on his pants before swiftly disappearing from the room.

Sienna struggled with the information Adam had given her about his father. She had only met him a couple of times and his drink problem had been strongly evident then. She had often wondered why Adam had not persuaded him to seek help but had never dared ask, as it had seemed such a touchy subject. Now she realised that he must have tried, he'd probably been in despair, but his parent had been beyond help.

And all because of love!

In an odd sort of way she could understand Adam's reasoning about not wanting to fall in love. Understand it, yes. But not agree with it.

'Mummy.' Ethan seemed none the worse for wear as Adam carried him into her room. In fact, he seemed proud of his injury. 'Daddy says I'm a brave little soldier.'

'And so you are, sweetheart,' she said, smiling. 'And so you are.'

'And Daddy says we can go on his boat tomorrow.'

Sienna frowned and looked at Adam, who simply shrugged and tried to look innocent. 'Oh, Daddy did, did he?' she asked. 'And what about school?'

Adam answered for him. 'I thought Ethan deserved a treat for being so brave.'

It sounded as though she had no say in the matter and although she was cross and intended telling Adam when they were alone, Sienna nodded briefly. 'I wasn't going to send him anyway, so perhaps yes. I'm sure Ethan will enjoy it. So long as he's careful.'

'And how about his mother? Will she enjoy it too?'

Sienna did not know how to answer. Travelling the Thames on a private cruiser had never been within her range. She had done the occasional river cruise but always with dozens of other passengers. This would be a totally new experience. And if Ethan hadn't hurt himself she would not have agreed to it, at least not this early in Adam's relationship with his son.

'Won't you be going to work?'

Adam shrugged. 'I can afford to take a few more days off.'

Which he had never done for her!

Because he didn't love her!

So why had he married her in the first place? Why had he needed a wife? Sienna wanted to ask him but now didn't seem the right time. 'I think Ethan should go back to bed. In fact, we should all try to get some sleep.'

'I want to sleep with you and Daddy, Mummy.'

Sienna hadn't the heart to say no and actually it would be easier as they had to wake him frequently. So Ethan snuggled down between them, a smile on his face, and although Sienna had thought she would not sleep, not after what had happened between her and Adam, and certainly not with Ethan sharing their bed, she somehow managed it, and when she awoke she had the bed to herself.

She had dreamt that they were making love again, desperate, uninhibited love. Her heart was still racing, her body bathed in sweat. She was a fool. She was setting her own fate by letting Adam get close. It was giving out the wrong impression.

Ethan deserved to get to know his father, yes, he deserved to spend time with him, but she knew that Adam wanted them to live together and she didn't see how that scenario could ever work—not again. Her mind would constantly dwell on the fact that it was a loveless marriage. Always had been and always would be.

Hearing Adam and Ethan talking in the kitchen, she silently slipped through to the bathroom. After showering, she dragged on clean jeans and a white T-shirt with a broken red heart on it. There were no words but she guessed that Adam would get the message.

When she joined them in the kitchen, though, Sienna couldn't help smiling. Ethan was busy laying the table while Adam whisked eggs. It was a perfect domestic scene. When had he become a dab hand at cooking? she asked herself when he presented her with perfectly cooked scrambled eggs on toast. It was not something she could ever imagine him doing. His eyes rested on the message on her T-shirt, and he looked at her questioningly but said nothing.

After breakfast she washed up while Adam took his shower, and after she had got an excited Ethan ready, Adam's driver appeared as if by magic. When they arrived at where his boat was moored Ethan jumped up and down with glee.

Sienna was a little concerned that his over-excitement might have a detrimental effect. The stitches didn't seem to be worrying him, though. He never even mentioned them.

She did her best to keep him calm while silently admiring the cruiser's sleek lines. There was nothing modest about it and she had expected no less.

Adam was very much the man of the moment, taking charge with smooth efficiency, letting Ethan sit between his legs and pretend to steer.

But he never ignored Sienna. He included her in their conversation, looked across at her constantly with promise in his beautiful blue eyes, managing to keep her in a constant state of arousal—much to her annoyance.

She didn't want to feel. She didn't want this man back in her life, not like this, not when he was behaving as though it was a foregone conclusion that they would become one happy family.

He was undoubtedly doing his best to achieve that status but it was not so simple. Adam was hard to resist, as last night's love-making had proved. Nevertheless, his confession that he had never loved her really had knocked the ground from beneath her feet.

As far as he was concerned, though, nothing had changed. And the stakes were high.

Adam wanted Ethan. And if Ethan came with his mother then so be it. She was good in bed and that was enough.

It was all he had ever wanted her for! It was a disheartening thought. And the more she thought about it, the truer she knew it was.

They stopped for lunch at a riverside café but as they made their way back afterwards Ethan began to complain of a headache.

'I knew it would be too much for him.' Sienna's eyes flared as she faced Adam.

'Sienna, he'll be all right.' Adam kept his tone calm, his whole demeanour suggesting that she was worrying for nothing.

'I'll take him into the cabin and see if he'll go to sleep,' she announced, her eyes flaring a magnificent blue. 'He's over-excited. Didn't the doctor say he should be kept quiet?'

She did not wait for Adam's answer, holding her son's hand as they descended into the cabin. Here she laid Ethan down on one of the couches and sat beside him, smoothing his brow and singing softly.

Within a few minutes he was fast asleep.

'I didn't realise you could sing. You have an amazing voice, Sienna.'

With a start she realised that Adam was standing at the top of the steps, looking at her. And she realised also that the boat was no longer moving. 'Why have we stopped? I want to get Ethan home.'

'I thought I'd check that he was all right.' He came slowly down the steps, his eyes never leaving her face. 'But now I'd like you to sing for me.'

'I don't think so.' Sienna looked defiantly into his eyes. 'Let's go, Adam. It was kind of you to suggest this boat trip but I was crazy to agree. Ethan's clearly not up to it after his accident. '

'I guess the little guy's just tired after his disturbed night.'

He was probably right but she didn't need him telling her what was wrong with Ethan. 'I want to get him home.'

'Have you any idea how fantastic you look when you're angry, Sienna?'

If he thought flattery would get him anywhere he was grossly mistaken. 'You never used to think that. You always said I made myself ugly when I shouted.'

'I said many things I shouldn't have said,' he

admitted with a rueful grimace, his eyes shadowed for a brief moment. 'But I've grown up too, Sienna. We're two different people now.'

Maybe they were, but it didn't mean that they were going to get back together.

Almost as though he had read her mind, Adam said softly, 'I meant what I said last night, I can't change that, but for Ethan's sake I think we should give our marriage another try. He deserves both parents.'

'You mean you're going to *try* to fall in love with me?'

Anger flared from his eyes then, fierce blue sparks that spelled trouble. 'I didn't say that. You know my feelings on the matter. But we make a good pair, Sienna.'

'You mean in bed?' she tossed hotly. 'And that's all you really want me for, isn't it? Go to hell, Adam.'

'Mummy, why are you shouting?'

Sienna groaned. She flayed Adam with her eyes and turned to her son. 'I'm sorry, my darling. How are you feeling?'

'My head still hurts.'

Again Sienna turned a recriminating stare on Adam. 'We need to go home.'

Another glare and he had gone.

Adam had thought that for Ethan's sake Sienna would jump at the chance of reviving their marriage. Last night in bed she had proved that the spark between them had never died. It had ignited into glorious passion and he wouldn't be human if he didn't want more of the same.

God, she excited him. It was a different Sienna who had embraced their love-making with open arms. Either that or he'd never realised her full potential. Maybe he shouldn't have admitted his inability to fall in love. Was it this that was holding her back now? Would she never walk into his arms again? Never share his home?

And how he wanted her!

Every time he thought about last night a treacherous hunger filled his body. In fact, he had only to look at Sienna, to catch her eye, and he was ready.

He wanted her back in his home and in his bed. Tonight preferably.

Today had started with such promise that he felt cheated when they arrived back and Sienna barely spoke to him as he tied up the boat, and when he suggested that they go back to his apartment as it was nearer she flatly refused.

'Ethan needs his own bed,' she declared emphatically.

It was always Ethan, thought Adam, and he couldn't help wondering whether she was using their son as a barrier to hide her own feelings. He smiled inwardly. If it was her feelings she was afraid of, it was all to the good. Time would tell. All he needed was patience.

The trouble was patience wasn't one of his strong points. When he wanted something he usually went all out to get it.

When they reached Sienna's flat and he made to follow her indoors she turned to him. 'I want you to go home, Adam. I want peace and quiet for Ethan—he's had quite a day.'

Even though she wanted him out of the way he was determined not to go. He could see no reason why he should not stay a while.

And in the end Sienna gave in. She decided that here was no sense in arguing in front of Ethan, who by this time looked very pale and tired. But she ignored Adam as she gave Ethan some medicine for his headache then undressed him and put him to bed.

Adam waited patiently, putting on the kettle and making tea because Sienna looked as though she needed it.

'It was too much for him today,' she said quietly.

'It was my fault.'

She said nothing, she did not want to start another argument. Instead, she sipped her hot, strong tea, which was just as she liked it, and slowly began to relax.

After they had finished and put their cups down on the table, Adam took her into his arms and fool that she was she let him. She needed comfort, she needed reassurance. Last night and today had taken their toll.

Adam stroked her hair back from her face with warm, gentle fingers, and his closeness began working its magic. Already she could feel herself relaxing, feel the heat of him warming her, the clean male smell that was essentially Adam filling her nostrils.

But then amazingly, surprisingly, he announced that he was leaving. 'You need your rest too, Sienna. You look tired.'

He was right, she was tired. Contrarily, though, she could think of nothing better than Adam joining her in bed tonight.

He smiled, as though he had read her thoughts. 'Goodnight, Sienna. I'll be in touch.'

CHAPTER EIGHT

IT WAS almost mid-morning and Sienna was keeping Ethan home again. He had looked pale when he had woken up and she didn't think it fair to send him to school. They had just finished breakfast when the doorbell rang.

'Don't tell me you're taking another day off?' were her first words when she discovered Adam on the doorstep. If one small boy had made this much difference to his life then maybe they should have started a family straight away when they had first married. And maybe their lives would never have changed. She would not have walked out on him.

Maybe!

'How's Ethan?'

Sienna appreciated his concern but she couldn't help wondering whether Adam had an ulterior motive in turning up here today. He had made it clear that he wanted them to give their marriage another go and that he wanted them all to live together as one big happy family.

Which was not what she wanted. Even though she had longed for him in bed last night. Even though she had imagined him at her side, and replayed in her mind the amazing way he made love.

It had been a frustrating exercise. It had made sleep impossible and left her feeling tired and out of sorts this morning.

And now he had turned up again!

'You could have phoned to ask that.' She didn't want Adam calling on them at any odd time. It was disrupting for her and had to be the same for Ethan.

Not that Ethan minded. He heard his father's voice and came running. Adam scooped him up in his arms with a big grin on his face. 'How's my injured soldier this morning?'

'I'm good, Daddy. Have you come to take us out again?'

'No!' It was Sienna who spoke. 'You need a quiet, relaxing day, Ethan. And I'm sure your father has much better things to do. Shouldn't you be at work?' she asked Adam pointedly.

He wore a blue short-sleeved shirt that matched his eyes and did nothing to hide his muscular chest, and a pair of navy linen trousers that sat low on his narrow hips. There was a raw sexiness about him that triggered an unfortunate response.

Sienna dashed it away. 'Adam?'

'I'm going in later,' he told her, his lips curved in a mysterious smile. 'There's something I want to show you first. Both of you.'

'Then I suppose you'd better come in.' She turned back into the room, hating herself for feeling anything other than animosity towards Adam. 'What is it?'

Another secret smile as he put Ethan down. 'We need to go and take a look.'

Ethan looked at his father. 'Where are we going?'

'It's a surprise.'

'I like surprises. Will I like it?'

'I jolly well hope so.'

'Come on, then, let's go.' And he tugged at his father's hand.

Sienna was less eager. There was something about Adam that worried her. He had an air of the cat who had stolen the cream. He was planning something and she couldn't help feeling that she was not going to like it.

'So where is this surprise taking us?' she asked, attempting to keep her tone light, aware that she failed miserably.

Adam grinned again, one of those grins that seriously creased his eyes and made him look as sexy as hell.

Sienna felt like hitting him.

'You'll have to wait and see.'

'You're worrying me, Adam, do you know that?' she asked as soon as they were alone, whilst Ethan went to grab his things. 'Are you the same man who would never take a day off?'

'The very same,' he agreed. 'But I have a family to look after now.'

'To look after?' Her eyes widened. 'We don't need looking after, Adam. I only told you about your son because—'

'Because he almost died and your conscience was bothering you,' he cut in swiftly and harshly, his smile fading. 'But the fact is that now I know about him I intend behaving like a responsible parent. You cannot take that away from me. I will not let you.'

He would not let her! Sienna felt like telling him he

couldn't stop her, but at that moment Ethan came running back. 'I'm ready, Mummy. Can we go now?'

With reluctance she nodded, trailing them out of the house. Little though he was, Ethan had the same walk as Adam, even his shoulders squared in the same manner, and she couldn't help feeling proud of him.

Adam had driven himself here today and Sienna lifted her eyebrows when she saw that a child booster seat had been fitted into the back of a silver limousine. She was impressed but not for the life of her would she admit it.

He drove no more than a few miles before pulling up outside a house in a leafy cul-de-sac where houses had walled gardens and electronically controlled gates.

Ethan's jaw fell when the gates opened all by themselves and Sienna wondered what they were doing here, who it might be that he was taking them to see.

It was with great astonishment, therefore, when they walked up to the front door of an imposing red brick house and he presented her with a key. 'Take a look at your new home.'

'*My* new home?' It was all she could manage. Her thoughts were racing at a mile a minute and her heartbeat was erratic. What the devil was he talking about? She knew he didn't like her living where she did—but he wouldn't really buy her a new house, would he?

A host of questions flitted through her mind, each one tumbling over the other in their haste to be heard. She turned on Adam with a questioning stare. 'You'd better explain.'

'I've bought it.'

It was a plain statement of fact. But all the more devastating because of it. 'Why?'

'I've bought it for us.'

Us!

It was the one word that registered in her mind. Us! Adam, Ethan and herself. The three of them. Living together. Here. Permanently.

'You're out of your mind.' They were the first words she could think of. 'I have no intention of living with you.' Was he crazy or what? Did he really think she would agree to move in with him? Had he no real idea how she felt?

'Not even for Ethan's sake?' His eyes locked with hers. Serious eyes, a serious face. 'He needs both of us. And I need to get to know him better.'

'Which you can do, gradually. It doesn't mean we have to move house. You cannot manipulate me like this, Adam.'

'It's not manipulation, Sienna. It's logic. It makes perfect sense.'

Sienna closed her eyes, praying she was dreaming, that the house and the situation were not real. Adam was being so reasonable that she wanted to scream. But she knew it would get her nowhere. She needed to meet calm with calm, especially with Ethan hopping excitedly from foot to foot.

'Is this where we're going to live?' he asked excitedly.

Sienna put her hand on his shoulder. 'I don't know yet, sweetheart.'

'Can we go in?'

Sienna realised she still had the key in her hand. Reluctantly she inserted it into the lock and pushed open the door. Ethan raced inside. She stepped over the threshold more slowly. The entrance hall was huge, lofty and beautiful. Much as she was determined not to like this house, the immediate effect was one of awe.

The floor was tiled, the walls pale, and there was a profusion of pot plants. A staircase curved upwards from one side and several doors opened out on the other. There was a dark green leather settee and a table with a telephone and a lamp on it.

It was picture perfect and she guessed that the whole house would be the same.

'What have you done, Adam? How could you buy this without consulting me?' Ethan had skipped off to explore so she didn't fear that he would overhear their conversation.

'I don't like where you are living.'

'And you think that gives you the right to—to do this?' Her throat felt tight and panic began to set in. 'It's very generous of you but—'

'Generosity doesn't come into it,' interrupted Adam. 'I will not have Ethan living in that lousy flat of yours.'

'Lousy? We have managed fine there up until now, thank you very much,' Sienna said, and glared into Adam's eyes, which were almost navy and dangerously fierce. But deep down she knew that a part of what he said was true. Her flat was small and cramped and the area certainly left a lot to be desired. A number of times recently she had worried at how safe it really was for her and Ethan, but she couldn't allow Adam to railroad her like this.

How she wished again that she had never gone to his damned too-grand penthouse that day. Adam had gone up in the world whereas she had gone down, but at least she'd been happy. Now he was taking that happiness away from her. He was making it his business to organise their lives.

'Look, you've done a fantastic job with Ethan,' he answered, his voice surprisingly calm. 'But sometimes you need to accept help when it is offered. It isn't always easy to see what's best for us.'

'And you're saying that you know best?' she asked, finding it difficult to keep her tone down. She did not want Ethan to hear them arguing, but on the other hand how impossible was it not to get irate?

Adam lifted his wide shoulders and spread his hands wide. He did not speak.

Sienna pushed herself to her feet. 'I suppose I'd better take a look round while I'm here.' She needed to put distance between them and to her relief Adam let her go. He did not even follow. She explored each room— the fantastic kitchen, the three separate living areas, a massive conservatory overlooking a garden with a swimming pool and a tennis court, and that was only what she could see! Upstairs there were six bedrooms and the same number of bathrooms, all furnished to a very high specification.

And he had bought it! He'd clicked his fingers and it was a done deal. What did it feel like to have power like that? Money like that? And did she want to be a part of it? As far as she was concerned, money did not buy happiness.

She and Ethan had been very happy until Adam had appeared in their lives, and they had had nothing. Happiness was a state of mind, not how much money you had to spend.

'Mummy, are we going to live here? *Mummy?*' Ethan had trailed after her, running in and out of rooms, jumping on beds, so excited that she feared he might fall and hurt his head again. At the very least she feared his headache would come back.

'Mummy's thinking about it.'

'We'll have to persuade her to say yes.' Adam's voice came from very close behind, a rough, deep growl. His persuasive voice. One that had once turned her limbs to jelly.

It seemed a long time ago now. When they had first married. She had thought he was the sexiest man on earth.

Actually, he still was sexy, but he was also aggravating and so damned sure of himself that she wanted to scream. If this was what money did, if it empowered him to such an extent that he thought he could do whatever he liked, have whomever he liked—which in this instance meant her—then she wished he was a pauper.

The man she had fallen in love with had had very little money. It had only been when making it had become his obsession that their marriage had failed.

Ethan ran away to explore some more and Adam turned her to face him. 'Ethan loves it already.'

Sienna nodded. That was one thing she could not dispute.

'So here's the deal.' He took her hands and although she would have dearly loved to snatch away Sienna remained still and silent, listening to her heart beat with sudden frantic haste. She wasn't sure whether it was because of his nearness, his touch, or the thought of what he was going to say. Or maybe a combination of all three!

'You and Ethan move in here and I pay all the bills.'

So he wasn't moving in with them. It was as if a whole weight had lifted from her shoulders.

But her pleasure was short-lived.

'In exchange we give our marriage another try.'

Sienna's heart stopped beating. Her eyes fixed themselves on Adam's face. He looked very pleased with himself, as well he might, but if he thought she was going to agree, he was seriously out of his mind.

'You really think I'd do that?' she asked, her eyes suddenly hostile. 'It's an impossible proposition. I'm wasting my time here, and I'm afraid you've wasted your money.' There was the gravest danger that she would lose her heart to him again, only to have it once more broken when he went back to his old ways. It was something she dared not contemplate.

She loved the house and the area, it was such a far cry from where she lived now, and she would have no more financial worries. But as well as worrying about her heart she had Ethan's emotional well-being to take into consideration. If it didn't work out between her and Adam, she would be the one left picking up the pieces. She couldn't do that to her son. She simply couldn't.

She turned and was about to call Ethan to tell him that they were leaving when Adam spoke. 'You're making a mistake, Sienna.'

'Am I?' She drew herself up to her full height, which was still a few miserable inches shorter than he was. How she wished for high heels. But she met his eyes bravely, telling him without words that she did not agree.

'You're not thinking about Ethan.'

'Oh, yes, I am,' she declared firmly. 'I'm only thinking about him.'

'In which case you'll realise that he'll be far better off here.' Adam's eyes bored into hers. It was almost as if he was trying to hypnotise her into saying yes.

'Not with an absentee father,' she retorted, hearing

the sharpness in her tone but not caring. Adam was being impossible. How could she live here happily? 'He's already beginning to idolise you, Adam. You'd break his heart if you let him down.'

Adam's eyes flickered a savage warning. 'I have no intention of doing that.'

'Easy words. You don't know what you're doing half the time. You think that putting food and money on the table is the be all and end all. You have no idea that it's relationships that count.'

'So you'd rather our son be bought up in a slum than—'

'My flat is not a slum,' cried Sienna, aghast that he should think that and deeply offended. And yet she could see why his thoughts went along those lines, living the way he did.

'No, it isn't, Sienna. You keep it beautifully. It's the area you live in that worries me.' His voice dropped to a low growl. 'You could keep this house beautiful. Doesn't it appeal? Would you like me to—?'

'Of course it appeals,' she cut in speedily. 'It's lovely. It's the nicest house I've ever seen. But I...' Sienna stopped her thoughts. She was looking a gift horse in the mouth. She really would be crazy to turn him down flat. Maybe they could make it work.

But on her terms!

'But what, Sienna?' prompted Adam, a faint smile flickering at the corners of his mouth.

She met his eyes with her head high and a similar smile on her own lips. 'Actually, I've changed my mind. I *will* move in with you.'

She saw the triumph on his face and took pleasure in

knowing that it would be immediately wiped off when he learned what her conditions were. 'I'm willing to give our marriage another go.'

'I knew you'd see sense, Sienna.' Her made a move towards her but Sienna backed away.

'Provided that you take our marriage and your role as a father seriously.'

He nodded. 'You have my word on that.'

Sienna seriously doubted it. Words were easy. Actions were harder. 'In return, I shall expect you to leave your office at five o'clock every night. No working late. And every weekend we'll spend together as a family.' She watched his smile fade, though it didn't go altogether. Perhaps he thought she wasn't deadly serious. Perhaps her next request would tell him exactly how determined she was.

'And if you break your promise just once—I shall leave and take Ethan with me.'

The pause that followed told her that she had read him correctly. He would never agree to this. He could not possibly give up so many of his working hours. She may as well call Ethan and leave now. It was a nice dream, thinking they might live here, but it would never happen.

Goodness knows what Adam would do with the house. Sell it again? Move in himself and get rid of—

'I'll do it.'

Sienna stopped breathing.

Adam smiled.

Her heart thudded. Had she heard him correctly? Never in her wildest imaginings had she thought to hear those words.

'Have you nothing to say?' he prompted now, still with an irritating smile on his lips.

'I...' Sienna swallowed hard. 'I wasn't sure that—'

'That I would agree?'

She nodded.

'I'll do anything to keep my family together.'

The proprietorial way he said 'my family' stunned Sienna. He sounded like a proper family man and yet...

'It will be much safer for Ethan, for one thing,' he continued, cutting into her thoughts. 'But it also means I'll have my wife back. And I won't let you down this time.'

Sienna struggled to come to terms with the fact that she was now going to be trapped in a house with a man who did not love her. He might say he wouldn't let her down but that wasn't the point. He had already done that. He had already proved that she didn't really mean anything to him. It was Ethan he wanted now, and since they came as a package...

Fate was cruel. She had thought that she was doing the right thing on the day when she told Adam he had a son. And now she was going to be locked back into a loveless marriage simply so that he could have access to him. She had somehow walked right into his trap.

Half expecting Adam to take her into his arms, Sienna was relieved when he did nothing more than smile complacently, as though he had known all along that she would agree to move in. It would have made him look pretty silly if she hadn't.

In truth, she was grateful to him, not that she would ever admit it. There had been times when she was a little bit scared living where she did. This was going to be an exciting new future for both her and Ethan.

* * *

The speed with which Adam moved her out of her flat and into the house left her breathless. She took few possessions with her—clothes, photographs, Ethan's favourite toys. Nothing else was of any value. The only person she told that she was moving out was Jo upstairs, who wished her the best of luck and said she had known, from the second she had seen Adam, that it would happen.

Adam did not know why he wasn't feeling as happy as he should that Sienna had left her dreadful flat and moved into the house he had bought for her. Was it because she wasn't as thrilled as he'd hoped? Had she thought that he wouldn't agree to her request that he make time for them? Or was it because he had a sneaky feeling at the back of his mind that he had somehow bullied her into it?

Their love-making had always been amazing. Even when he had been tired and brain-dead from a hard day at work she had always managed to entice his libido into life. And he was looking forward to a future with her back in his bed every night.

She had crept beneath his skin in a way he had not expected. He was still damned angry that she hadn't told him about his son, but Sienna herself was sexier than ever, even in those dreadful jeans she insisted on wearing. He wanted to see her in something more feminine, something alluring. He wanted to take her shopping and buy her rich splendid clothes that showed off to perfection her spectacular figure.

And what had that damned T-shirt with the broken heart on it meant? Was she trying to tell him that her heart would never mend? That she would never truly be his again?

The thought crossed his mind that now she had found

out that he didn't have it in him to love someone uncon-
ditionally, she might try to back off. She might not keep
her promise to share his bed.

It had taken a great deal of courage to admit the truth
to her, but he had felt that if she was to become a major
part of his life again then she deserved to know. Otherwise
she would expect more from him, she would expect dec-
larations of love, and that was never going to happen.

After his mother had died he had been grief-stricken.
They had had a very close bond and having to put up
with his father's anguish as well as his own had shown
him how dangerous it was to love someone so completely that they became your whole life. That you could
not function without them.

Neither did it sit easily on his shoulders that he had
shown his vulnerability to Sienna. He had thought it
would help, but actually it looked as though the whole
thing had spectacularly backfired.

She knew now that he had never loved her, that he
couldn't love her!

Sienna had been shocked by his confession but there
had been no time for questions. Ethan had interrupted
their conversation and he had actually felt relief. It had
been a hard enough thing for him to do without an inquisition following.

He felt fortunate now that Sienna had agreed to move
into the house—even with her conditions. For a while
he had thought she was going to refuse altogether.

'Do you have everything you need?'

Sienna nodded. 'You've been very kind. I cannot
believe you've done all this for me.'

'And Ethan,' he added curtly.

Of course! Sienna's thoughts were suddenly bitter. It was for his son, not her, that he had provided this magnificent house. He would have left her to rot in her flat if she hadn't borne his child. In point of fact they would never have met again because she certainly would not have gone to see him. They might even have been divorced by now.

'Then I'll leave you to settle in. I need to call in at the office as well as packing a few things for myself.' He gave Ethan a hug and a kiss. Seemed to contemplate doing the same to her, but changed his mind, striding to the door instead. The next moment he had gone.

'So, Ethan, what do we do now?' It was more a rhetorical question than anything else because there was nothing to actually do. The house was beautifully furnished, the fridge and freezer well stocked. She was going to rattle round in it like a dried pea in a pod, and more especially when Ethan went back to school.

'I'm going to ride the rocking horse,' he declared loudly. One of the rooms had clearly been a children's room and a huge rocking horse had been left behind—unless, of course, Adam had bought it! That was something she hadn't thought of. Nevertheless, Ethan was totally impressed and happy to sit and rock.

Suddenly the front door opened and Adam appeared again. 'I meant to give you this.'

It was a store card. A major, expensive department store. Sienna's eyes widened. 'Why? What for?'

His brows rose as if it was a stupid question. 'For whatever you need. Clothes, toys, anything you like. Go shopping, Sienna. Have fun.'

She hadn't even thought about clothes but clearly

Adam had. She was his wife and he would want to show her off. Trying to bring Ethan up on a shoestring had left little or no money to spend on herself.

Living here, she would seriously need to update her image—was that what he was saying? He wanted a wife to be proud of, not someone who walked around in jeans and T-shirts.

'You don't approve?' His voice cut into her thoughts, his tone hardening. 'Have I made a mistake?'

'It's not that,' she cut in swiftly. 'It's just I'm used to my own money. I—'

'You don't feel you can take anything from me? That's ridiculous, Sienna. You are my wife. In a few days you will have a bank account in your own name. Meanwhile, I want you to use this card. Treat yourself.'

'And what else do you plan doing for me, Adam?' she enquired sharply. Everything was moving too quickly. How many days ago had it been since she had gone to see him? Eight! Eight short days. And look what had happened in that short space of time.

'What else do you want?'

It was the impossible tone in his voice. The way his blue eyes looked as though they were made of ice. The way he held his body stiff and formidable, looking nothing like the lover who had shared her bed. And whose bed she was going to have to share again!

'I want nothing.' He thought she was being ungrateful. Which in a way she supposed she was. But she did not like the fact that she been uprooted from her comfortable flat into this monster of a house that looked like a show home. A beautiful home admittedly, but a lifeless one. She would make it hers eventually, she would stamp it with her own personality, but at this moment she felt as though she had been lifted up and dropped into a soulless building.

Strangely, she had not felt this way before Adam had left. Which meant, she supposed, that he had such a big physical presence that it filled every room.

It had felt as though something was missing when he had walked out. Her whole life had changed in a matter of hours and she wasn't sure that it was for the better.

CHAPTER NINE

'DADDY.' Ethan heard Adam's voice and came running down the stairs, launching himself into his arms. 'Come and see me on the rocking horse.'

Instantly Adam picked Ethan up, glancing at Sienna over his shoulder as he climbed the stairs. 'Are you joining us?'

It was Ethan's 'Please, Mummy' that persuaded her. She had been relieved by Ethan's interruption and would have preferred some breathing space, but she didn't want Adam acceding to any more of his son's requests. Whatever he asked for he would get, she knew that, and it wouldn't be good for him.

After a few minutes' rocking, encouraged by his father shouting, 'Ride 'em, cowboy,' Ethan grew tired of the horse and took them into his new bedroom. 'Which is your room, Daddy? Is it next to mine?'

'If that's where you'd like me and Mummy to sleep.'

Sienna drew in a shocked breath. It made the whole moving-in process sound so final.

'I do, I do. I want you near me in case I wake up in the night. It's a big house, Daddy. I might be frightened in the dark.'

'You have nothing to fear, Ethan. I shall be here to look after you.'

Sienna still struggled with the fact that she would be sharing Adam's bed. She wanted him and yet she didn't. She wanted to be free of him and yet their lives were inextricably woven together. Could she really spend the rest of her days with a man who did not love her? The fact that he was a spectacular lover was a point in his favour—but would it be enough?

When Ethan had settled down to play with his toys they went back downstairs and Adam declared that he really was going this time. 'Don't miss me while I'm away,' he said, his mocking expression making her grit her teeth.

Miss him? She wanted to lock and bolt the doors. It was hard finding out that her life was no longer her own.

'And when you're ready to go shopping call my driver—he will take you. Here's his number.'

Sienna glared as the door closed behind him. He really did think money was the be all and end all of everything. He had no idea that it was just as easy to be happy without store cards and big houses and posh cars and chauffeurs.

She did not go out. She hung her clothes instead in the built-in wardrobe in the room she was being forced to share with Adam. 'Forced' felt like an appropriate word, even though she had agreed to this arrangement.

Then she and Ethan toured the gardens. The pool was set into raised decking with inset lights and easy chairs for relaxing. There were even lights in the pool. Sienna was glad that she had taught Ethan to swim at a very early age. He was like a water baby, he loved the water, so she had no fear for him living here.

He wanted to jump in right now but she persuaded him against it and instead they explored the rest of the garden with its massive lawns and a shrubbery and a small wooded area where Ethan could hide. It was paradise as far as he was concerned.

It seemed like only minutes before Adam returned, although it was actually about three hours, she realised when she glanced at her watch.

'I don't know about you but I'm starving,' Adam declared. 'Do we eat in or out? The choice is yours.'

'In,' she answered swiftly. She'd given Ethan a sandwich for his lunch but she'd had nothing for herself and she was hungry now too. 'There's enough food in the house to feed an army.'

Ethan became the buffer between her and Adam as she prepared their meal. He never stopped talking to his father and she was able to laugh and even enjoy herself.

'So what did you buy?' Adam asked when they finally sat down to eat.

'Nothing. Ethan and I explored outside instead. The garden's amazing. The pool's amazing. Ethan wanted to swim. I told him that—'

'But I wanted you to get new clothes.'

Sienna's chin set in a mutinous line. She had changed into a clean pair of jeans and a plain pink T-shirt and had thought she looked OK. 'Are you ashamed of me?'

'I'd never be that,' he answered softly, his eyes resting for a few seconds on the soft swell of her breasts.

Annoyingly she felt a faint response, a faint hardening. Her nipples tingled and she glared.

'Every woman likes new clothes. I thought you'd be off like a shot. I thought you'd have a mad spending spree.'

'Then you don't know me very well at all, Adam.' Blue eyes met blue. Sienna was the first to look away. 'I will shop, but in my own good time.'

She remembered now that Adam liked his women feminine. He liked floaty dresses and low-cut tops. He didn't approve of jeans. They had their place, he'd once said, but he preferred to see a woman's legs. He was definitely a legs man. He had once complimented her on her legs, which were long, and when she wore high heels they seemed to go on for ever. Or so he had said. But that had been then and this was now. Jeans were more practical.

After dinner it was Ethan's bedtime and Adam again read him a story. He seemed to enjoy doing this, it had become a ritual now, and Sienna sat quietly and listened and watched. It actually felt good to see him bonding with Ethan in this way.

Ethan's eyes never left his father's face and every now and then Adam looked at him and smiled, such a soft, gentle smile.

And it was not only Ethan he held in thrall. The deep tones of his voice were mesmerising. She had always found his voice sexy, especially when it went very low, and tonight was no exception. She didn't listen to what he was saying, just the cadence. It reverberated through her nerve ends, heightening her tension until in the end she got up and walked out of the room.

How could she sit there and carry on listening when he was doing unmentionable things to her body? How could she hide the very real emotions that were careening through her veins? Fortunately Ethan had his eyes closed by this time, he was probably even asleep, so he had no idea that she'd gone.

What she couldn't understand was why she felt like this when she had been forced into the situation. No—that was wrong. She hadn't been forced. She had brought it all on herself by her ludicrous suggestion. How the hell had she been supposed to know that Adam would agree? She ought to hate the very sight of him. She ought to feel nothing. And yet, conversely, she felt everything. All her old feelings were tumbling back with indecent haste.

Which was good in one way as she'd talked herself into sharing his bed. If she had no feelings for him, if they remained dead, it would be hell. In fact, it would be impossible. There was no way on this earth that she could let any man make love to her who she didn't have strong feelings for.

Adam finished the story, kissed his son, and then went in search of Sienna. The intervening years had done nothing to stem the hunger he had always felt for her. He had buried it somewhere deep down inside him, concentrating on building up his empire, and it hadn't risen again until the day she had come to see him.

When he'd first seen her standing hesitantly outside his apartment, her face on his monitor a picture of unease and impatience, he had felt a swift surge of desire race through his body. There and then he had wanted her.

And now she was his!

Today was only the beginning. Today had actually been easier than he had thought it would be. He had been prepared for her to flatly refuse to leave her home. He had expected a challenge on his hands.

But it hadn't happened, and she was here now, and

with Ethan fast asleep she would have to spend time in his company.

When Adam joined her out on the terrace Sienna's heart began an erratic beat. He had a look in his eyes that worried her. He wanted her and, yes, she wanted him too, very much so, every bone in her body ached for him. And yet it didn't feel right.

Their marriage had been a lie. Even now it was hard to believe that he had never loved her. He had been an attentive lover but that had been all, and she had been drawn into his web with the same unerring skill as a spider catching a fly.

And the question still remaining was why he had married her in the first place. Had it been for her body? Had she simply been a conquest?

It looked like it and she ought to despise him—yet her spark was still there, the hunger, the need. It didn't please her but there was nothing she could do about it. Her body had a mind of its own.

'Ethan's fast asleep,' he said softly.

'He was very tired—he's had an exciting day.'

'And your day? Has that been exciting too? Do you like your new home?'

Adam's eyes never left hers as he waited for her answer. But what could she say without hurting his feelings? She could hardly tell him that it wasn't to her taste. That it was too big, too pretentious. Not when he had made this magnificent gesture for his son's sake. She was not stupid. She knew that everything he did was for Ethan.

'It's a fine house,' she managed at last. 'You've been very generous, too generous. It's going to take some getting used to.'

'Ethan loves it.'

'He can't believe all the space he's got,' she said with a fond smile as she thought of her son's pleasure. 'It's a little boy's dream.'

'But not your dream?'

Her dream was of a man who truly loved her, for herself, not because she happened to be the mother of his child and they came as a pair. Not simply because he wanted a woman in his bed, available to him whenever he felt like it. 'I was happy in my flat.'

'And you think that you won't be happy here?'

Adam's eyes narrowed and Sienna knew that she needed to be careful. It was not only herself she had to think about but Ethan as well. 'I'll get used to it.'

'I want you to do more than get used to it, Sienna, I want you to enjoy it. I want you to feel relaxed and happy. I want us to be a family here.'

How could they ever be a proper family? He was asking the impossible.

'Sienna?'

'It will take time.' She evaded his eyes, turning away instead, walking across the lawn towards a summer-house. As a child she had always wanted her own play-house and she was thinking now that this might be somewhere where Ethan could play. Not that he needed any extra space, but children loved hiding and this would be a perfect den for him.

She heard Adam's phone ring and looked back, expecting it to be something to do with work. His expression changed from anger to concern as he listened. 'Yes. OK. I'll be there immediately. Thank you.'

But it was not his office who had called. He looked

at Sienna. 'My grandfather's been taken ill. He's in hospital. I need to be there. I haven't spoken to him in years but I cannot ignore him now. I'll try not to be long.'

'Of course.' Sienna felt compassion as well as relief. She had never had much to do with his grandfather, she had met him a few times but for some reason he had seemed to disapprove of her. And she actually hadn't known whether he was still alive, but it was important that Adam go to him now.

Adam had mixed feelings as he drove to the hospital. There was no love lost between him and his grandfather and he couldn't help wondering whether his visit would be appreciated.

What would the old man say, for instance, if he told him that Sienna had borne him a son? That he was now a father and he and Sienna were back together? It would probably finish him off altogether. His grandfather disliked Sienna intensely for the simple reason that she was too much like Adam's mother, and in his own warped mind he actually blamed his daughter-in-law for dying and ruining his own son's life.

It didn't make sense that he hated Sienna for this reason, but when Adam saw his grandfather lying pale and lifeless in his bed he knew that he couldn't open up old wounds. So he said nothing about her being back in his life. In fact, neither of them spoke very much at all. The old man kept his eyes closed, although Adam felt sure he wasn't asleep. But he didn't feel that he could just get up and go, he had to stay a decent length of time.

Sienna had been thinking of going to bed when Adam's car pulled on the drive. There were taut, tired lines on his face and she wondered whether she ought to suggest making him a drink of hot chocolate before he retired. Except that Adam probably wasn't a hot-chocolate man. He never had been in the past, whereas it was her favourite bedtime drink.

And she was right. Adam wanted strong coffee. Any sort of coffee. Instant would do.

'How is your grandfather?' she asked tentatively, putting the kettle on to boil and spooning coffee granules into a mug. He did not look as though he welcomed questions and she guessed that even his grandfather's illness had not bridged the gap between them. Which Sienna thought was sad.

'He's had a heart attack. A bad one. He may be in hospital for some considerable time.' His tone was clipped, his words concise, and it was clear that he did not want to talk about him.

'I'm sorry.'

'Even in his illness he did not welcome my presence. We barely spoke.'

Sienna felt even sorrier. 'I didn't actually realise he was still alive. He must be a great age.'

Adam shrugged. 'Late eighties He's made of tough stuff without a doubt. I wouldn't be surprised if he doesn't pull through.'

'Does he live by himself?'

'He has a housekeeper. She keeps him under control—or tries to,' he added with a wintry smile. 'He's a cantankerous old devil. But enough about him. I appreciate you waiting up for me, Sienna.'

'It was the least I could do.'

Without warning, without so much as a change of expression, he slid his arms around her waist and urged her against him.

Sienna had no time to protest, no time to lift her arms in defence. She was effectively his prisoner. The throb of his heart against her breastbone echoed the sudden frantic beat inside her.

It was fairly clear where this was going to lead. Adam needed something, someone, to take his mind off his hospital visit—and losing himself in her body would be the perfect solution. Already she could feel him growing hard and every sane emotion in her body told her to push him away before it was too late.

And yet she was committed. There was no escape. Even if she wasn't a magnet pulled and held her against the steel hardness of him. A magnet stronger than herself.

Adam appeared bigger and darker and extremely dangerous. Already every pulse in her body leapt into life. Her heartbeat was loud and irregular, thudding against her ribcage, echoing in her ears, tightening her throat.

This was what it was going to be like. They would settle into happy family life—on the surface at least. Ethan would believe his parents loved each other and loved him. He would be in his element. Yet there would be no love involved.

For all Adam's money, for all his success, he had denied her the one thing she really wanted.

Nevertheless, Sienna found herself leaning further into him. The scent of his body, his individual male scent that reminded her of when they had first met—when she had fallen in love with this impossibly good-looking man—stung her nostrils, swept a flash-flood of desire through her entire body.

Adam groaned, sensing her acquiescence, and his lips swooped down to claim hers in a mind-blowing kiss that sent every sane thought into outer space. The heat of him, the taste of him, both contrived to spin her senses, to leave her reeling, to want more!

How stupid was that when their marriage was over and the only reason he was being nice to her was because of Ethan? He had let her walk out of his life once before and had not once tried to find her, but now, now that he had a son, he wanted her again.

His coffee forgotten, Adam swung her up into his arms and carried her upstairs, kissing her senseless as he did so, giving her no opportunity to protest. Not that she wanted to. And once in the room they were to share his arms relaxed and she slid slow inch by excruciating slow inch down the length of his body until her feet touched the floor.

There was no disguising the fact that he was ready for her but he seemed in no hurry now. Sienna had thought that he would drop her onto the bed, rip off her clothes, and make love without any preliminaries.

How wrong she was. Instead, he traced the contours of her face with warm fingertips. 'You're incredibly beautiful, do you know that, Sienna?' His eyes were an amazing blue, a deep, dark navy, and Sienna felt herself drowning in them.

They sent dangerous signals through her sensory system. Was it because Adam had looked so tired when he'd come home that she felt sorry for him? Or was it because once he had touched her she couldn't help herself? Whatever, the feelings were crawling all over her body.

Adam's arms tightened around her. And his kisses

became more demanding. Sienna felt an explosion burst from the very centre of her, reaching out to fill her entire body. Sensations that exceeded everything she had ever felt before.

She had been young and immature when she had married Adam. Now older and wiser, she knew the power of his kisses, how they could trigger a potent response.

Arching her body into him, Sienna returned his kisses with fire, fire in her body, fire in her mind. Every sane thought had fled. And as soon as he felt her response Adam groaned, a deep, agonised growl low in his throat, and his kisses deepened, their tongues entwining, their hunger spinning them out of control.

For just a second his mouth left hers while he dragged off her T-shirt and unclipped her bra. His eyes were drawn to her softly moulded breasts with their dark pink nipples standing proud and ready, aching for him to touch them.

She felt no shyness, no distress. Everything was forgotten except the power of the moment. Her breasts swelled and seemed to surge towards him of their own accord, and when he lowered his head to take her nipples into his mouth, when his tongue and teeth nipped and teased, Sienna's head fell back, her eyes closed, her mind taking her into a world where only sensations mattered.

Her fingernails dug into his back as she urged her lower body deeper and harder against him. The heat and power of his erection only added to the hunger sweeping through her. She did not want to wait, she did not want foreplay, she wanted him to take her now, swiftly and fiercely.

Even though she was unaware of it she must have groaned and wriggled even more fervently against him because Adam's response was to rip off his shirt and let the muscular hardness of his chest with its springy dark hairs take the place of his hands and mouth. His body hair was like a whisper over skin, over her breasts, over her nipples, and yet its very softness created an entirely new sensation.

Hips ground against hips now and with trembling fingers he unfastened her jeans and slid them downwards. With a quick hop and a skip Sienna was out of them. He wanted to touch her then, he wanted to feel for himself the urgency pounding inside her, but Sienna wanted to free him of all restrictions as well.

Her fingers were equally as shaky as she undid his trousers and he was out of them so swiftly that it was a miracle he didn't fall over. Underpants were disposed of, thrown across the room, haste was the word. And now their liberated bodies came together.

It was all heat and passion, fingers exploring, mouths tasting, tongues teasing. Sienna felt as if her world was being blown apart. She could feel her heart thudding against her breastbone, feel the strength going out of her legs, and as if aware that any moment she would collapse Adam lifted her up and laid her down on the bed.

'You're beautiful, Sienna. You always were, but you're different now. You're a woman who wants to be made love to. I've never seen you more lovely, more exciting, more...' His words faded as he lowered himself over her.

'I need you, Sienna,' he groaned. 'I need you *now*!'

As she needed him.

Their coming together was powerful and instant, like thunder and lightning. Like a firework exploding. Like a rocket soaring.

A sheen of sweat covered Sienna's body as she lay exhausted by Adam's side afterwards. He was on his stomach, one arm draped over her, and she felt the heat of his body too. It was several minutes before their breathing returned to normal, before she felt able to move.

Then she shivered and Adam was instantly alert. 'You're cold?' He pulled her into his arms, his hands massaging her back.

'You're really something, Sienna, do you know that?' he questioned softly, his mouth against her cheek, caressing her skin with more kisses. 'Why did I ever let you go?'

His touch evoked fresh emotions, renewed hunger, and before Sienna could answer, before she could even think of an answer, he was making love to her again. More slowly this time, more eloquently. Except that the slowness became torture and Sienna gripped his shoulders hard, moving with him, driving them swiftly into a further climax that shattered her body and left her gasping for breath.

For several minutes she was too sensitised to move, she lay there in a haze of pleasure, marvelling at such exquisite feelings. She hated to admit it but it got better every time. There was no going back. Not now that she had tasted heaven.

CHAPTER TEN

SIENNA felt amazingly lonely when she discovered the bed beside her empty. It was almost as though she had dreamt what had happened. And yet how could she have dreamt such magic? It had been real all right. They had woken in the middle of the night and made love again. It was as if the years she and Adam had spent apart had never taken place. Their love life had suddenly blossomed and deepened again—and her body hungered for him.

Except—that all it had really been was sex. What was she thinking? There had been no emotions involved. She and Adam were no closer together. She would be as well to remember that and not let herself get carried away.

The house was quiet, too quiet. Ethan! Where was he? He always woke early and jumped on her bed. She looked at the clock and saw to her dismay that it was almost half past nine. Adam would have left for work so where was Ethan? With a groan she leapt out of bed. The first thing she thought about was his injury. He'd been extraordinarily brave about the whole thing but perhaps the excitement of moving had been too much and he—

She skidded to a halt when she saw his room empty. Her stomach felt hollow. Then she heard voices in the garden. When she looked through the window she could not quite believe her eyes. Adam and Ethan—in the swimming pool.

So Adam had not gone to work!

Wonders would never cease.

She swiftly showered and dressed and ran downstairs. Adam grinned when he saw her. 'Come and join us.'

In the brief second she looked at him Sienna saw Adam as she had never seen him before. A man in his element, relaxed, his normally unruly hair plastered to his well-shaped head. He looked happy, and she hated to use the word, but he looked human. He was not a machine who went to work and came home late every day. He was a family man. A man who cared for his son.

Amazing. Totally amazing. She actually felt the prick of tears in her eyes. This was something she had thought never to see.

'Mummy,' called Ethan. 'Look at me, I can swim on my back. Daddy showed me.'

'Why don't you join us?' suggested Adam. 'Work up an appetite for your breakfast.'

'No, thanks,' she said. She did not want to spoil their time spent together. Ethan looked so very happy swimming with his father. It was easy to see that he idolised Adam. 'I'll get breakfast ready instead while you two continue your swim.'

By the time breakfast was cooked Adam and Ethan had showered and dressed. She had heard Ethan giggling as his father tried to dry him. Ethan was like an eel, especially when his ticklish bits were touched. It did her heart good to hear them laughing together.

She had cooked Ethan a sausage sandwich, which was

his favourite food, and when Adam saw it he said that that was what he wanted too. So the two of them munched on their sandwiches while she ate a bowl of cereal.

Afterwards, when the dishwasher was loaded, Adam opting to do it, he suggested they take a ride out to Hampstead Heath where Ethan could run around to his heart's content. 'Have you ever taken him there before?' he asked Sienna.

'Actually, no. I've never had a car, for one thing.'

'Then that's something I must see to,' he declared. 'There's always my driver at your disposal but sometimes you'll want to be able to drive yourself.'

He was being too understanding for Sienna's peace of mind. But she quickly forgot it as she packed a picnic and it turned out to be a day that she would never forget. Adam was like a boy let out of school. He and Ethan kicked a ball, they all played hide and seek; they even caught a butterfly. And Ethan spent the whole day giggling.

She felt totally relaxed. She had never seen Adam play like this before. He had always been such a serious man that she had thought he must have been born that way. But with Ethan he let his hair down and did everything on his son's level, as though he was trying to make up for all his missed years.

A streak of guilt ran through her. When she had discovered that she was pregnant she should have gone back to him. Or at least let him know so that he could have been a part of his son's early life.

'Look,' said Adam suddenly and quietly. They were standing by one of the ponds, looking for fish, when a kingfisher landed on the far side.

Even Ethan held his breath. 'Daddy, he's beautiful,' he whispered.

'And you're very lucky to see him.'

'And I'm lucky, Daddy, that you brought me here.'

It was a special moment between them. Sienna felt a lump in her throat as father and son hugged, and she felt certain that Adam too was welling up inside. He kept his face turned carefully away from her.

Afterwards they ate their picnic. They had sausage rolls and egg sandwiches, crisps and pork pie, even tiny individual trifles that Sienna had found in the freezer and were by now perfect to eat.

'My parents used to bring me here when I was a child,' she told Adam. 'That was before they separated. I had such an idyllic childhood, it's a shame it all—' And then she stopped, suddenly realising what she was saying.

'It's not too late,' Adam said softly. 'Ethan has his best years in front of him. I bet you can't remember what you did before you were four?'

'I can't remember much,' she agreed. 'I do remember a tricycle I had and I got lost. My mother panicked. My father was at work. But I hadn't gone far, I was soon found.'

Adam smiled and stroked the back of her hand. It was the lightest touch yet it sent tremors down her spine. 'I did a similar thing. I loved my little trike. It became whatever I wanted it to be. A racing car. A train. A tractor even.'

Sienna conjured up an image of Adam as a little boy. He would look just like Ethan did now, with dark springy hair and a wicked grin. She'd like to bet that he had lived life dangerously and always worried his parents.

'Does Ethan have a bike?'

'No.' She shook her head, her eyes vaguely sad. 'There was never anywhere for him to ride safely. He can ride a bike, of course, they have them at nursery, but Ethan's never actually had one.'

'So we'll have to see about getting him one, won't we?'

It was the way he said 'we' that got to her. She had expected him to state that *he* would buy Ethan a bike. That he would do it without consulting her. This was turning into a day that she would always remember. A surprisingly happy day.

After another energetic game of football Ethan grew tired and Sienna suggested they go home. He was asleep almost before they set off and she sat quietly too.

Inside her, hope began to grow that their relationship could be turned around. She was forced to admit that she was still very much in love with Adam, that she had actually never truly fallen out of love, despite everything. And Adam—well, he needed to learn that just because his father had gone to pieces after his mother's death, it didn't mean that every man was the same. Besides, she didn't intend leaving this mortal earth for many years yet. She wanted to live into blissful old age with Adam at her side.

That night their love-making was better than ever, as though the day they had spent together had somehow intensified their feelings. And in the days that followed she let him see in every way possible that she loved him.

And yet no words of love ever passed his lips. He wanted her, he enjoyed her, and he adored his son. He played with Ethan endlessly. He never worked late, he honoured her wishes, but she was forced to the sad re-alisation that everything he did was for Ethan's sake.

His grandfather remained in hospital but Adam rarely visited him, which Sienna found sad. 'Perhaps I should go to see him?' she suggested. They were sitting outside after dinner. The air was still, it was one of those warm, balmy summer evenings when the scent of roses filled the air and the birds sang their evensong. 'It can't be any fun lying in a hospital bed with no visitors to relieve the monotony.' Although Sienna had never had anything to do with Adam's grandparent, she did feel sorry for him.

But Adam shook his head. 'He wouldn't appreciate it.'

'Why not?' Her fine brows drew together in a frown. 'How do you know?'

Adam sucked in a lungful of air and seemed to be having difficulty in finding the right words. Eventually, though, he spoke. 'Because—because he's never liked you, Sienna. He never approved of you. It's the reason why he and I fell out.'

Sienna felt her heart stop and then race. 'He doesn't like me? What have I ever done to him?' It didn't make sense. All these years he and Adam hadn't spoken and she was the reason! She racked her brains, trying to recall whether she had ever said anything to cause offence. And came up with nothing.

Adam did not answer her question. 'It's all water under the bridge, Sienna,' he said instead. 'Grandfather and I will never see eye to eye. We're too much alike.'

Too pig-headed. Too proud. Too busy making money. His grandfather was a rich man. He'd made his money in advertising. Sienna had often wondered why Adam had not followed him into the business, the same as his father had done, why he had started up for himself in developing properties.

'Nevertheless, I don't like being the reason you and he fell out,' she declared strongly. 'I think I should go to see him after all and try to put matters right.'

'The hell you will, Sienna. It's too late, I tell you.' Adam's eyes grew starkly cold, filled with a sudden anger that she didn't understand.

That night they did not make love. Adam lay with his back to her, still and silent, and although Sienna wanted to put her arms around him and tell him that she understood and was sorry for him, sorry for his grandfather, too, she did not dare.

He had erected a barrier around himself and she knew that only he could take it down. It was a pity because they had been getting on so well. Adam had shown a warmth towards her that had been absent even in the early years of their marriage. It was as though being a father had made a world of difference to him.

Now all that had gone again. Simply because she had suggested going to see his grandfather. Why on earth hadn't he told her all those years ago that the old man didn't like her? Surely they could have sorted it out.

Adam slept little, knowing that he ought to try to make amends with his grandfather. When Ethan grew up and hopefully had children of his own he would be heartbroken if they hated him as much as he had hated his grandfather all these years. Admittedly the old man had brought it all on himself. But Adam felt differently now that he was a father and he actually did not want his grandfather going to his grave believing that no one loved him.

A few weeks ago he would never have dreamed that his feelings would change so dramatically. And he had Sienna and Ethan to thank. Sienna was teaching him that

relationships had to be worked at. Nothing came easily.
Not love or hate. They were each born of communica-
tion and honesty. And when that was lacking...

For all these years he had worked towards one goal,
he had let no one stand in his way. A selfish attitude and
it had cost him his wife and the first years of his son's life,
but changing was hard, especially since his visit to his
grandfather had dragged up old memories, old hatreds.

It really was not that simple to let go. Only in bed
with Sienna could he lose himself. Then the world was
a perfect place. He was never happier. Everything was
forgotten except that moment in time.

Last night had felt like hell.

CHAPTER ELEVEN

I'D LIKE to come with you,' said Sienna, her fine eyebrows lifted in hopeful anticipation. She didn't care that Adam's grandfather didn't like her. She simply felt that he ought to have more visitors.

'I don't want you leaving Ethan,' he told her firmly.

'Marie will look after him.' Marie was a woman who came in daily to do the jobs Sienna could easily have done for herself. It had been Adam's idea but she hadn't dared argue. And Marie had told Sienna that any evening she and Adam wanted to go out she would be more than willing to babysit.

'You really think my grandfather would be pleased to see you?' Adam's eyes were much darker than normal, even his body language told her that it was a definite no-no. He stood rigidly in front of her, almost challenging her to argue with him.

'Are you saying that he still hates me?' Sienna began to find the whole conversation bizarre. 'How can you be sure?'

'He doesn't know that we're back together.'

It was a plain, matter-of-fact statement, but it shocked

the hell out of her, made her heart pound. 'You haven't told him? He doesn't even know about Ethan?'

She saw a flicker in Adam's eyes, gone almost immediately, a blank expression taking its place. 'I saw no need to. He's very ill, Sienna, you seem to be forgetting that. I wouldn't like to distress him further.'

'Distress him?' It was impossible not to raise her voice. 'Why would telling him that he has a great-grandson distress him?' Surely it would give him the will to live? Or did he still hate her that much that it would kill him off altogether? Was that what Adam thought?

'You do not know my grandfather,' he replied bitterly. 'But if it will make you feel any happier, I will tell him tonight. Be prepared, though, to hear that he doesn't want to see either of you.'

'You are unbelievable,' she said. 'Your grandfather's unbelievable. What kind of a family have I married into?' She let her breath out on a long hiss of confusion and incredulity. In fact, she walked out of the house and into the garden, kicking at a blade of grass that had dared to grow on the immaculately mowed lawn.

They, of course, had a gardener, and a man to look after the pool. All of these things seethed in Sienna's mind now. Adam could afford to do anything he wanted, buy anything he wanted, and yet he was afraid to tell his grandfather that his wife was back and they had a child.

It made no sense. None of it made sense. Was the whole world going mad or was she the crazy one? She ought never to have walked back into Adam's life. She and Ethan had been happy as they were.

Actually, Ethan was still happy. Even happier. He loved his dad. He didn't see his faults, he was too young to understand. All he knew was that he had a father to play with him, to read to him, to buy him wonderful gifts. His world was rosy.

Adam knew that he owed it to Sienna to tell his grandfather but it was not that simple. Sienna did not know the whole truth. Neither did he ever want her to.

Not now that their marriage was beginning to mean something to him! He wanted nothing to ruin it. And the truth, if it came out, would spell the beginning of the end. He would lose her altogether. And possibly Ethan too, even though he would fight for him. But Sienna was a fighter too and she would not relinquish her son to anyone, not even to his father.

It would be a blood battle, and did he want that?

'So you've finally come to see me again?' Adam's grandfather was propped up with pillows, his face still pale and drawn but a surprisingly fierce light in his eyes. 'About time, too.'

Adam groaned inwardly. He was glad to see the old man looking a little better, but he didn't want a confrontation, not after he'd just walked away from one. 'I'm glad you're feeling better, Grandfather.'

'No thanks to you,' he growled. James Farley had wispy white hair and a pale complexion, with grey eyes not dissimilar in shape to his grandson's. 'What have you been doing instead of coming to see me?'

'I didn't think you were well enough for visitors.' Which was only half a lie.

'Poppycock! You'll do whatever you want and to hell with everyone else.'

'In that case, I take after you.' It was always the same

when they met. He had been prepared to talk quietly, to have the sort of comfortable conversation that grandfathers and grandsons should have, he'd been going to tell him that he had a great-grandson, but somehow in the space of a few seconds they had each managed to stir each other's blood.

'It's a pity your father didn't have the same backbone.'

Adam agreed with him. If his father hadn't gone to pieces after his mother had died, he would never have fallen out with his grandfather over Sienna. It was a vicious circle and he could see no way out of it.

Neither did he dare now to tell the old man that he was back with her or all hell would break loose. It might possibly kill him off altogether. And he didn't want that on his conscience.

Instead, he talked about the success of his business. 'I'm doing better than I ever expected. I'm in Europe and America. I'm expanding all the time.'

Instead of being impressed, the old man snorted. 'You wouldn't have done that if you hadn't got rid of Sienna. She would have held you back, your vision would have been clouded. It would be history repeating itself. Your father loved my daughter too much. He was no good without her. It's a case in point, Adam. You're better off without a woman in your life. You'd best remember that.'

Long after he had left the hospital his grandfather's words swam round and round in his mind. He had always believed that he had been better off without Sienna. He had got on with his life without her to hold him back, he had become the success that he was. But success hadn't bought him the happiness he expected. It had brought him loneliness instead.

Which he hadn't truly discovered until Sienna and Ethan had erupted into his life. He had thought he was happy but now he knew that it had all been a pretence. Nothing had prepared him for the joy he felt knowing he had a wonderful son like Ethan.

It gave life a whole new meaning. He loved lying on the floor with him, racing cars around a track, he loved swimming in the pool with him—he was a brave little swimmer already—and he truly loved hearing Ethan call him Daddy. It gave him a warm, comfortable feeling.

But even more than this he loved having Sienna back in his life.

He had never fully realised what he had been missing. She had brought a whole new meaning to the word marriage. She was sensational in bed but even better than that she kept his feet firmly grounded. She taught him that family life meant a whole lot more than making pots of money.

On that point alone he did not agree with his grandfather.

Sienna was waiting for Adam. She had spent her time imagining the conversation he would have with his grandfather. James Farley would be surprised to hear that they had got back together, maybe shocked even, but he would surely be pleased. She couldn't imagine that he would still hold his grievance against her— whatever it was. And he would be astonished to hear that he had a great-grandson. And once he'd got used to the idea, he would want to see Ethan.

Ethan, too, would be tremendously excited to find out that he had a great-grandfather. It would be a one-up on all of his friends who had grandfathers. A great-grand-father would be so much more important than a mere grandfather.

Her own father had gone to live in New Zealand after his divorce and she never heard from him. Her mother was remarried and had moved to Ireland but much to Sienna's disappointment they saw little of each other. She had never been able to afford to go over there, and her mother hadn't visited. They kept in touch by phone but that was all. It wasn't the same.

Adam looked tired, she thought, when he walked in. He had lines of strain on his face and didn't quite meet her gaze. She knew instantly what had happened.

'You haven't told him, have you?' she demanded fiercely and loudly, not even waiting for him to speak. 'After everything I've said, and after promising, you still haven't told him.'

Her anger triggered anger. Adam scowled, his eyes navy and savage, his thick brows jutting ever more fiercely over them. 'My grandfather's a very ill man.'

'And what's that supposed to mean?' She was fired up and ready to go. 'That it would be too a big a shock? I would have thought that hearing he had a four-year-old great-grandson would cheer him up. Not the other way round.'

Adam towered over her like an avenging angel. His body was taut, looking ready to snap. Even his nostrils flared.

Sienna sensed danger and knew that she ought not to press the issue but something drove her on. Ethan deserved to know his great-grandfather. And the old man deserved to know Ethan as well. It was as simple as that.

Why couldn't Adam see it? Why was he being so stubbornly obstinate? Why couldn't he see the wider picture?

'You can't go on ignoring the bond between you.' It was criminal that he was denying his grandfather the pleasure of young blood. 'Ethan will light up his life. You're being extremely unfair and negative about the whole thing.'

'You do not know what you are talking about, Sienna.' Adam rubbed the back of his neck and looked suddenly tired.

'Then tell me.'

The look he gave her suggested that she was being irrational but Sienna did not think so. As far as she was concerned, she had made a perfectly normal request—and he had failed to carry it out. When he turned away she accepted that there was nothing more she could do tonight. Continuing to protest most certainly wouldn't help matters.

In bed that night, when she had expected Adam to ignore her, he did nothing of the sort. He groaned and pulled her into his arms instead. 'It's been a hell of a day, Sienna. I need you like I've never needed you before.'

What she ought to have done was declare that she wouldn't allow him to make love to her again until he had told his grandfather. Except that his nearness drove her crazy. Her body melted against him and the instant his knowing fingers touched and tortured, everything else was forgotten, she wanted nothing but Adam's body beside her and inside her. She wanted everything he had to offer. And more importantly she wanted him to feel that way too. She wanted to help him forget his torment.

He made love without the usual preliminaries,

driving himself into her like a man who was having his last wish granted. And it was all the more exciting because of it. Sienna felt as though she had died and gone to heaven.

And later, when they had both regained their breath, he touched and stroked more gently, seeking out all her erogenous places. He knew precisely how to suck her nipples into his mouth and stroke them with his teeth until she bucked and wriggled and wanted him inside her again. He knew that to nibble behind her ears created a similar response. He knew that even her belly button was responsive to his touch.

So many places, so much mind-blowing pleasure.

When he wanted to enter her again she bucked away from him. 'Oh, no, Adam, it's your turn this time.' And she teased his nipples in exactly the same way, enjoying his reaction, the deep groans, the way his face screwed up as if he was in agony. Then she kissed her way down to his navel, exploring it with her tongue, then lower and lower.

Before she could reach her goal he hauled her on top of him. 'Take me inside you, Sienna. Do it now, do it quickly.'

With their positions reversed, Sienna guided him into her. It was the first time they had ever made love this way and it gave her a feeling of power. Until his groan rent the air and he quickly turned her over. Within the space of a heartbeat he lost control.

Sienna stretched languorously when she awoke the next morning. She felt good, she felt warm and happy and wanted Adam to make love to her again. But the bed beside her was empty, and a note on his pillow said that he had gone to work. She smiled at the thought of him writing the note, it was something he had never done before. Perhaps a turning point?

As she showered her thoughts turned to his grandfather. Maybe James Farley didn't like her, but was that any ground to hide Ethan from him? Adam was being pathetically cautious. There and then she made the decision to go and see him as soon as she had taken Ethan to nursery. She would deal with Adam's fury when the time came.

Her heart pounded as she entered the hospital, a private one naturally—would the old man go anywhere else? And when she announced who she had come to see she was taken to a pleasant room where she found him sitting in a chair near the window. A fountain played in the centre of a lawn and a dovecote was alive with white doves. It was a satisfyingly peaceful scene.

He looked at her long and hard, and Sienna began to wonder whether he recognised her, before he said gruffly, 'What are you doing here?'

Not a very auspicious beginning, thought Sienna, not the welcome she would have liked, but she ignored his beady stare and smiled instead. 'I thought you might be in need of some company.'

A snort followed her words. 'It depends who the company is.'

Meaning that she was not on his list of favourite people!

'Adam's at work. I thought—'

Another loud exclamation of disgust, a flash of pale eyes. 'So you've wheedled your way back into his life? How the hell did you manage that? He's a very busy man, he can do without distractions like you.'

Sienna was beginning to see why Adam had found it difficult to tell his grandfather about Ethan. James Farley had become more obstreperous with old age. He'd always been difficult but…

What did she do now? Did she blurt out the fact that she had borne Adam a son and that's why they were back together? Or did she try to get him onside first?

'I guess we never really stopped loving each other.' What a lie that was, but perhaps he didn't know about his grandson's incapacity to love.

'And it took you five years to discover that?'

James Farley might be old but his mind was still sharp. It hadn't taken him long to work out how long they'd been apart.

Sienna shrugged. 'We were both busy.'

'He's a fool.'

'I'm sorry if that's your opinion,' she said quietly. 'May I sit down?'

'Are you staying?'

'I'd like to.'

'Why?'

'Because we've never really got to know each other. I thought that—'

'You thought that you'd wheedle your way into my good books so that I'd leave you something in my will, is that it?'

Sienna shot her eyes wide. 'Of course not.'

'Good, because you're not getting anything.'

Such bitterness. Didn't old people usually mellow? Why was he like this? And would she be doing more harm than good if she told him about Ethan now? But this was her mission and he deserved to know. It might turn him around, give him something nice to think about, give him an incentive for living. It couldn't be easy, sitting here day after day with no company. Perhaps it was loneliness that was making him bad-tempered.

'If you really don't want my company, I'll go,' she said, thinking carefully as she spoke, already turning back towards the door. 'I was going to tell you something I really feel you ought to know, but—'

'Wait!' His voice wasn't strong but it was a command nevertheless. 'If you've come here for a specific purpose—apparently not simply to see me—then for pity's sake have the decency to tell me. Don't walk away like a coward.'

Sienna turned and fixed her blue eyes on James Farley's rheumy grey ones. Swallowing hard, she said, 'It's something Adam should have told you, but felt he couldn't. We have a son, Mr Farley. His name is Ethan and he's four years old.'

Silence followed. A long silence. And Sienna was afraid that she had gone too far, that he wasn't ready for such information. But amazingly his lips quivered, a smile followed. A weak one, a ghostly one, but a smile nevertheless.

'I have a great-grandson?'

Sienna nodded. And waited.

'Is he why you came back?'

'Yes,' she whispered.

'What took you so long?'

'Adam always put his work first. He's a driven man. I thought he would be angry and send me away again. At the very least he would have accused me of holding up his chances of success.'

'Which you would have done,' he announced bluntly.

'I'm aware of your feelings,' answered Sienna, keeping her chin high. 'It's why you've never liked me.'

'Adam told you that?' he asked, a frown now adding to the other creases on his brow.

She nodded.

'But it didn't stop you coming here today? You have guts, girl. In the end you thought Adam deserved to know. The same as you felt that I should know. I've underestimated you, Sienna. It must have taken a great deal of courage to come here. Does Adam know?'

'No,' she said softly.

'Why didn't he tell me himself?'

'Do you have to ask?' she questioned with a wry smile.

'I guess I wasn't very well disposed towards him. I'm in shock, Sienna. How about I ring for a pot of tea?'

Sienna was amazed at how well he had taken her news. She had expected to be shooed out. She had thought he would show no interest in his great-grandson, just as he'd had no interest in her. Instead, it appeared that finding out about Ethan had performed a miracle.

She stayed another hour, telling him about Ethan and the life they'd had together, and she promised that she would bring him on a visit one day.

When she got back to the house Sienna felt pleased with herself. She had actually achieved something today. But her happiness was short-lived when Adam came home and she told him where she had been.

'You did what?'

'I went to see your grandfather,' she repeated.

Adam groaned and closed his eyes and she knew exactly what he was thinking. 'Did he throw you out?'

'He wanted to at first when he found out that we were back together, but once I'd told him about Ethan we got on like a house on fire.' She almost laughed at the expression on Adam's face. 'Don't you believe me?'

'He wasn't angry?'

'Why should he be? When he learned that he had a great-grandson he went all soft.'

Adam's eyed widened. 'My grandfather soft? I don't believe you.'

'Well, perhaps not quite soft and mushy,' she agreed with a laugh, 'but he warmed towards me and he's looking forward to meeting Ethan. I thought perhaps we'd go at the weekend. What do you think?'

Adam did not know what to think. He had been horrified when Sienna had told him where she'd been, he had imagined all sorts of repercussions. And when she'd confessed to telling him about Ethan he'd gone cold all over. Much as he wasn't overly fond of his grandfather he had no wish to see him further displeased.

And yet here she was, saying that James Farley actually wanted to meet Ethan. The very thought sent his mind spinning out of control. Ethan had brought him and Sienna back together, now it looked as if he was going to do the same with his grandfather.

Did the boy have magic powers? Or were children naturally good ambassadors?

He shook his head. 'I cannot believe all that I am hearing.'

'Believe me, it's true,' Sienna told him with one of her incredible smiles. She slid her arms about his waist and turned her face up to his. 'This is one happy day.'

But her happiness did not last.

She said nothing to Ethan about his great-grandfather, she wanted it to be a surprise. She could imagine his pleasure, his whoop of joy, and if she told him too soon he'd be so excited that he would not sleep, and he'd keep pestering her as to when they were going to see him.

In the end Ethan never got to see his grandfather. Adam had a phone call on Friday evening to say that his grandfather had died. He'd suffered another heart attack.

CHAPTER TWELVE

Tears slid down Sienna's cheeks. She had been looking forward to getting to know Adam's grandfather, seeing more of him, introducing Ethan, watching the two of them interact and bond.

Now it was too late, it would never be. It was so sad and she couldn't help wondering whether her visit had had anything to do with it. Her heart felt heavy at the thought.

Adam turned away and Sienna wondered whether he was blaming her, as well. Or if he was wishing that he had tried long before now to make amends. The old man hadn't treated him fairly but even so he was Adam's only blood relative. She saw the way his shoulders sagged and she wanted to comfort him but didn't know how, whether it would even be welcome.

At least it had been quick, that was one consolation. James wouldn't suffer any more. But the sadness remained with them, and Adam had the job in the days that followed of arranging the funeral.

It was a quiet affair. His grandfather had outlived all of his cronies so there was no one except Adam and Sienna to stand by his graveside and wish him a last farewell. More tears rolled down Sienna's cheeks. What a sad ending to his life. She held Adam's hand tightly as they walked away. He didn't know it but she had seen a tear in his eye too.

Later that evening, after Ethan was in bed, unaware of the traumatic day they had had—Sienna hadn't thought it fitting to tell him about the death of someone he had never known—Sienna asked Adam why his grandfather had never liked her. 'It came across in waves when I went to see him, it was only after I told him about Ethan that he melted. It wasn't a comfortable feeling to be hated so much.'

Adam drew in a deep sigh and shook his head. 'It's not a story that you'd want to hear, not today anyway.' His lips thinned, his thoughts clearly flying back over the years.

But Sienna insisted. 'It can't make any difference now. I thought he was a lonely old man. I actually felt sorry for him.' And she knew that she wouldn't rest until Adam told her the whole story.

'You wouldn't feel sorry if you'd known him properly,' asserted Adam, jumping to his feet and striding across the room. He looked out across the gardens and Sienna knew he was fighting his demons.

The air was very still outside, the sky even at this hour an intense blue. It felt as though the world was holding its breath, waiting to hear about his grandfather.

'And since I didn't get to know him, I'm looking to you to tell me about him,' she added softly.

He turned then and looked at her with eyes that were filled with immense sorrow. Which Sienna found odd considering he had never liked the old man. Clearly a lot had gone on between them that she knew nothing about.

Finally he spoke. 'He said that you reminded him of my mother.' Adam's voice was so quiet that she had to strain to hear. 'And he wanted no reminders. He actually blamed her for dying, for the way my father went to pieces afterwards.'

Sienna saw raw emotion on his face, his eyes once again moist with unshed tears. Was she asking too much of him too soon? He had never spoken much about his mother but she knew that he had loved her dearly and had never got over her death. And his grandfather's attitude must have made it far worse.

Several long seconds passed. So many unhappy memories were flooding his mind that it was painful to watch and yet she knew that she had to ask the crucial question. 'So you went the opposite way and married me *because* I reminded you of your mother? You did it to spite your grandfather.'

His denial was instant and emphatic. 'That was not my reason.'

Of course he would say that. He wouldn't admit to such derisory grounds for asking her to marry him. There wasn't a cat in hell's chance of him admitting the truth. Sienna curled her fingers into her palms. This was not a day when they should be arguing and yet she could not help herself. He couldn't make such a profound statement and then expect her not to react.

'No?' she asked, her eyes wide. 'And yet you fell out with your grandfather because of me. It doesn't make sense, Adam.' None of it made sense. The whole thing was growing more bizarre by the second.

Adam drew in a deep breath, compressing his lips until they were almost non-existent, his whole being as still as the calm before a storm, and what he said next blew Sienna away.

'I fell out with him because he said that if I married you he would disinherit me.'

She stopped breathing.

'I couldn't believe he had said that.' Adam shook his head as if reliving the scene. 'Did he think I couldn't stand on my own two feet? That I couldn't make a go of my life without *his* money? And you can bet your life that I wasn't going to let him tell me who I could or could not marry.'

His words were suddenly harsh, his face flooded with anger.

Silence filled the air between them. A loud silence.

Sienna felt her head spin and thought she might faint.

Adam had married her simply to prove to his grandfather that he could do whatever he wanted! That he would not be dictated to.

Unbelievable!

It meant that there was no truth in his statement that he was unable to love because of what had happened to his father. The fact was he simply didn't love her!

The only reason he had married her was to prove himself to his grandfather. It had been a war between the two men.

She had been stuck in the middle!

And now she had marched right back into his life!

Adam closed his eyes, needing to block from his view Sienna's shocked face. It had been wrong to have this discussion today of all days. Today should have been a day of mourning, not disclosures.

He felt truly sorry now for having told her. He should

have waited, he should have left it. He shouldn't have mentioned it at all.

He hadn't realised all those years ago that his grandfather had been trying to protect him when he had declared that Sienna was wrong for him. That his grandfather simply hadn't wanted history repeating itself. He hadn't wanted Adam to love Sienna so much that if anything happened to her he would fall into the same trap as his father.

In that moment Adam realised that the incredible had happened. He was truly and deeply in love with Sienna. He was in that trap. He wouldn't be able to function without her.

But Sienna looked at him with eyes of stone. 'I cannot believe that I am hearing this. I rue the day I ever met you, Adam. I thought that we had married for love. I know I accused you of loving your work more than me but deep down in my heart I didn't mean it. I truly thought that you loved me. What a fool I was. I loved you more deeply than you'll ever know. But it's gone now. We're over, Adam. I wish that I'd never come to see you.'

'You cannot walk out, I will not let you.'

His voice was immediately strong and a fierce light shone from his eyes, a light that warned her, told her, that if she dared to attempt it he would be there to stop her. Well, let him try. He would soon discover how serious she was.

'Sienna…' Adam closed the space between them, ignoring the signs in her eyes, knowing only that somehow he had to make amends.

But Sienna was quicker, sidestepping away from him, darting to the other side of the room. Near the doorway. 'It's over, Adam. You have no idea how much I'm hurting. In fact, I don't think the hurt will ever go away. Not that you're worthy of such pain. I hate you, Adam, with the whole of my breaking heart.'

She ran out of the door and up the stairs, intent only on escaping him. She needed to be alone with her thoughts. Her heart was indeed breaking in two. Her whole world was crumbling around her. Hot, plump tears slid down her cheeks as she threw herself down on the bed.

It was amazing how one short declaration could change everything. She found it hard to believe that Adam had married her simply to spite his grandfather. What sort of a man did that? And what woman in her right mind would carry on living with someone who had made such an admission?

He hadn't been backwards in using her body. It had been the best part of their relationship. It was ironic that he had made her feel so very special when all the time it had been part of his devious plot to get one over on James.

Sienna clamped her lips tightly together, her mind going over and over the events of the last weeks. It had actually seemed as though everything was coming together, the future had looked rosy. And yet in an instant it had been shattered. It lay around her feet like shards of glass, like petals dashed from a rosebush by heavy rain. Never in her life had she felt so worthless.

The realisation dawned that Adam never actually kissed or cuddled her except when they were making love. Why hadn't she put two and two together and recognised that all he needed was a bed partner? It saddened her to accept that this was all he had ever wanted her for.

There was no doubt in her mind now that it was imperative she get out of here. Where she would go she had no idea. But escape was her goal. She had Ethan to think about too. He would be devastated if he thought he was losing the father he had only just found. All of this needed to be taken into consideration.

She expected Adam to come after her, was surprised when he didn't. But at least it gave her thinking time, planning time. How long she lay on the bed Sienna had no idea. At some stage she must have fallen asleep because she awoke shivering. She pulled the covers over her, still fully dressed, but did not go back to sleep.

The green glow from the clock told her that it was almost midnight—and the bed beside her was empty. Not that she cared. Adam could go to hell. She would never forgive him for the way he had treated her. Never!

The night was long and cruel, her mind tormented, but when morning came she had made her plans. Thankfully Adam had left for work by the time she got up, and after taking Ethan to school she began making phone calls.

For a few days they barely spoke. She slept in one of the other rooms, getting up early so that Ethan would not know there was anything wrong. Even Adam acted normally in front of Ethan, swimming with him, promising to take him out on his boat again, reading him bedtime stories, including Sienna in everything he did.

Sienna was suspicious. If he thought that by pretending nothing had happened it would all go away, he could think again. She kept cheerful for Ethan's sake but as soon as he was in bed and asleep she ignored Adam totally, usually shutting herself in her room, watching TV or reading a book.

Until the night Adam came to see her. He pushed the door open without even knocking. 'Things have gone on for long enough, Sienna. We need to talk.'

'About what?' she asked, her blue eyes coldly hostile. 'About the fact that you don't love me, never have and never will? That our marriage is a sham and Ethan is stuck in the middle? Is that what you want to talk about? Do you have a magic recipe to put everything right? I don't think so. You and I are finished, Adam. I'll soon be out of your hair.'

His nostrils flared as he stared at her for several long condemning seconds. 'And Ethan?'

'You'll have rights.' She noticed that he didn't say anything about her leaving, it was only Ethan who concerned him. Just as she had thought.

'Rights be damned! Ethan is not leaving this house. I've lost enough years already.' His eyes were cold and condemning, his chin tilted arrogantly, the cleft beneath his lips clearly defined. He was firmly of the belief that he could make this happen.

Sienna thought otherwise. 'If you really expect me to stay here, locked into a loveless marriage, Adam, you're crazy.'

Jutting black brows gathered fiercely together. 'We can work at it, for Ethan's sake.'

'Let's leave Ethan out of this.' Sienna kept her back ramrod straight, her eyes declaring war. Her chestnut hair was tousled where she had raked her fingers through it, but she did not care what she looked like. There was no way that she was going to give in. Her mind was made up.

She was leaving him.

And Ethan was going with her.

'How can we leave him out of it when he is a part of both of us?' Adam's voice had never been stronger. It was like steel and Sienna shivered as a chill ran down her spine. 'I will not stand by and let you take him from me.'

She would need to be careful. It had been wrong to tell him that she was planning to leave because he would now watch her like a hawk. She heaved a sigh. 'I guess I wasn't thinking straight.'

'Indeed you weren't.' Gruffness filled Adam's voice. 'We don't have to sleep together, Sienna, if you cannot face that, but Ethan has to be our main consideration.'

'Of course,' she said quietly, looking down at her feet, not wanting him to see that she was lying through her teeth.

'Then I will say no more.'

She had half hoped that Adam would go back to his apartment after their argument. It could actually work if they lived that way. She and Ethan in this house, Adam in his apartment. Then Ethan could see his father frequently and she would be happy with him out of her hair.

But dared she even suggest it? Or would the fact that she would still be forced to see him periodically make matters worse?

She guessed plan number one was the best. She had already warned her mother to expect her.

Happily Adam did not know in which part of Ireland her mother lived. And if he tried to find her it would be like looking for a needle in a haystack. She would be perfectly safe.

On the day they left she waited until Adam had gone to work before she packed their clothes and a few of

Ethan's toys, telling him that they were going to Ireland to visit his grandmother.

'How about Daddy?' he asked.

Not wanting to tell him an outright lie, Sienna said, 'Daddy has his work, he can't come with us.'

'But I will see him again soon?'

'Of course you will,' she assured him. Though she did not know how long it would be before she allowed that to happen. The way she was feeling at this moment it would be a very long time.

It wasn't being fair on Ethan, she knew that, and she didn't want him to forget about Adam altogether. They had had such a short time together it wasn't really fair on him, or Adam either. But how could she stay under the circumstances? It still made her hackles rise every time she recalled that he had married her simply to get one up on his grandfather. What sort of a man would do a thing like that? Had he ever meant to tell her, or had he planned to go through his whole life keeping it a secret?

There would come a time when they would need to see each other again, perhaps when she wasn't so angry, but meanwhile Ethan would be happy living in a new place with his grandmother. He'd have all sorts of new things to do, places to explore.

She had told them at the nursery school, though she hadn't said exactly where they were going as she did not want anyone passing the information on to Adam. And she had hired a taxi to take them to the airport, rather than using his driver. They were taking a flight to Dublin and she had paid cash for everything so that Adam could not track her movements. The account he had opened for her was the one thing she could thank him for. For once she did not have to worry about money.

Although Ethan had been fretful when they were leaving the house, excitement soon took over when he found out that he was going on a plane. 'Wow, Mummy!' he exclaimed when they reached the airport. 'Are we going on Daddy's plane? Is he coming with us?'

Sienna frowned. 'Daddy's plane?'

'Yes, he told me about it, he promised to take me on a ride one day if I was very good.'

This was the first Sienna had heard about it but she was not surprised. Whatever money could buy, Adam seemed to have. In her opinion it hadn't made him into a better person, though. He had ridden roughshod over her, buying the house, insisting they move in, spoiling Ethan terribly with all the presents he bought. Every night there was something different. It wasn't good for her son.

And Adam wasn't good for her!

'Well, we're not going on Daddy's plane today.'

Sienna suddenly realised how sharply she had spoken and softened her voice. 'We're going on a much bigger one. This is the biggest adventure of your life, Ethan.'

His little face split into a wide smile. 'Thank you, Mummy. And when Daddy comes, I'll be able to tell him all about it.'

'You certainly will,' she answered, grimacing inside, wishing that his hopes were not so high. Deep down she hated what she was doing to him. But for her own sanity she had to get away. She could not carry on living with a man who didn't love her, who had never loved her.

During their wait at the airport Sienna constantly

looked over her shoulder and it was not until they were on the plane that she was able to relax.

When they reached Dublin her mother was waiting. Sienna had tears in her eyes as they hugged. It wasn't until she had had Ethan that she had realised the power of a mother and child relationship. It was a bond too strong to break, and they hadn't seen enough of each over the years.

'And look at you, Ethan,' said his grandmother, folding him into her arms. 'How you have grown.'

'I'm four and a half,' said Ethan importantly.

'And do you go to school?'

'Yes.'

'Then you must tell me all about it when we get home.'

Home was a cottage on the coast. It was an hour and a half's drive away from Dublin and Sienna had never seen anywhere look more welcoming or peaceful. This was exactly what she needed. Somewhere remote, somewhere where Adam would never find them. What little bit of guilt she felt for taking Ethan away from him she quickly forgot once they settled in.

Her mother was a good-looking woman in her forties with blonde hair and grey eyes, still as slender as she had been in her teens, and was clearly happy with her life here.

Her husband, Niall, was an artist and had a studio at the bottom of the garden. He specialised in seascapes and Sienna could not think of a better place for an artist to live and work.

Ethan was fascinated with all the brushes and paints and poor Niall was soon being bombarded with questions, leaving Sienna time alone with her mother.

'Is there something wrong?' asked Anne. 'I didn't

want to question you before but as soon as you said you'd like to come and stay with us I couldn't help wondering.'

Sienna sighed, a heavy sigh that lifted her chest before relaxing again. 'I went to see Ethan's father.'

Anne's pale eyebrows rose. 'And?'

'We moved in together.'

'I see. I take it it's not working out?'

'Not at all,' declared Sienna, shaking her head. 'I thought he deserved to know about Ethan, but it was a mistake. Marrying him was a mistake. The biggest one I've ever made. Bigger than agreeing to move in with him again.'

Anne took her daughter's hands in hers. 'We all make mistakes, darling. It's how we deal with them that counts. Is running away the best solution, do you think? I met mine head on. I divorced your father. Why have you never wanted a divorce from Adam? Do you still love him?'

It took Sienna a long time to answer, and then all she said was, 'I don't know.' There were times when she did and times when she didn't. It was like riding a roller-coaster. There were so many ups and downs that she couldn't keep count.

'Which means you do still love him,' said her mother sagely. 'Otherwise it would have been a definite no.'

Adam was anxious to get home. As each day had passed and Sienna had still been there, he had counted his blessings. When she had announced that she and Ethan were going to walk out on him he had felt raw, as though he had been cut wide open. It had felt like salt being rubbed into a wound. And it had hurt like hell.

Thank goodness he had persuaded her to stay. He wanted her at his side for the rest of his life. He needed to be patient, though. He shouldn't have told her about his grandfather. It had been an insane thing to do. And now he had to find some way of making amends.

Simply telling her that he loved her wouldn't do. She wouldn't believe him, she would think that he was saying it to try and get her back into his bed. Which wasn't his main reason at all, even though it was one he would certainly enjoy. The nights had been hellish without her.

The house was quiet. Too quiet! It was too early for Ethan to be in bed, so where were they? Suspicion built in him and he raced up the stairs, taking them two at a time, calling out their names at the same time.

Her room was neat and tidy—and empty! The same with Ethan's. He snatched open wardrobe doors and saw nothing but more emptiness!

His heart slammed down into his feet.

She had gone! Despite her promise, she had left him. She had taken Ethan, his precious son, and they had gone God knew where.

In that split second Adam wanted to sit down and cry. He wanted to drop his head in his hands and sob. Nothing had ever made him feel like this before.

CHAPTER THIRTEEN

ADAM had had no idea that Sienna was still planning to leave. He should have been more alert. He thought that he had persuaded her to stay. How wrong could he be?

'I will not stand by and let you take him from me.' His own words came back to haunt him.

'I wasn't thinking straight.'

'Indeed you weren't. We don't have to sleep together, Sienna, but Ethan has to be our main consideration.'

'Of course.'

'Then I will say no more.'

She had looked truly contrite and he had been satisfied. He thought that she was of the same opinion as him, that Ethan needed both his parents.

And now she had gone!

Without leaving a single clue!

The first thing he did was try her mobile phone, but it was switched off. Every time he tried it, it was off. Then he phoned Maria, but he drew a blank there as well. It was her day off, he should have known. Sienna had cleverly waited until she knew that no one would see her leave.

He went to see Jo. Sienna's old neighbour was as

shocked as he to hear that Sienna had run away. 'I've not heard from her. I thought she was happy with you.'

'So did I,' he growled. 'Have you any idea where she might have gone?'

Jo shrugged. 'Not really. Anywhere, I suppose.'

Which was no answer at all! 'Does she have other friends?'

'I don't think so. She's never mentioned anyone special.'

Adam felt that he was getting nowhere fast and his blood pressure was rising. How could Sienna do this to him? And, more importantly, to Ethan? It was unfair on both of them.

Did she really hate him that much that she couldn't bear living with him any more? He shouldn't, of course, have told her the real reason he had married her. It had been a fatal mistake, a damning admission, and had damaged their relationship further.

But hadn't he shown her recently that he loved her? Surely she must have picked up on it? Did it matter what had happened in the past? Wasn't the present more important?

He realised how little he knew about Sienna. He had, by his own insensitive behaviour, sent her running. He felt terribly guilty. Everything was his fault. Every damn thing! And now he hadn't a clue where to start looking.

He checked her bank account and discovered that she had drawn out a huge amount of cash but paid nothing by cheque or on her card. He even checked Ethan's school in case Sienna had told them the reason she had pulled him out, perhaps left a forwarding address. But to no avail. So what did he do now? The driver he had put at her disposal said he hadn't been asked to take her anywhere—which meant she must have called a taxi.

She was clever. She had left no clues whatsoever.

By this time Adam was pulling his hair out. Sleep became impossible. How could he sleep without knowing where Sienna and Ethan were? And where did he begin his search? Because if he had to search every inch of the country, he would do so. Unless she had gone abroad, gone as far away from him as she could. Hadn't she once said something about a distant relative in Australia? He groaned.

The thought that she had put as much space between them as she could cut deep. It stopped him breathing. It was like a knife turning in a wound. If that was the case, it would be impossible to find her.

Except that nothing was impossible! He would check all the airports. See if she had been booked on any flight.

Didn't her mother live in Ireland? He was sure that she'd once mentioned it, many years ago when they had first met. Maybe they had gone there? He felt a brief glimmer of hope. As far as he knew, they never saw each other but where else would she go? Would it be a wild-goose chase? He had no address, nothing. He racked his brains to try and recall whether Sienna had ever dropped a clue. But he drew a blank.

Sienna was constantly on her guard, afraid that Adam would discover her whereabouts and come after her like a raging bull. She had done all she could to cover her tracks but was aware that Adam would leave no stone unturned.

Ethan, on the other hand, was in his element, learning to paint. Sienna was actually quite proud of him. He seemed to have a natural talent, which Niall said should be nurtured. He naturally kept asking where his father was, and Sienna's answer was always the same. 'Any day soon, my darling, you'll see him. Don't forget Daddy's a very busy man.'

She tried to ignore her own aching heart. Despite everything, despite vowing to hate Adam for the rest of her life, there was no hiding the fact that she was still crazily in love with him. Her wise mother had been right. There were times when she even wondered whether they ought to go back, whether putting space between them was worth all the heartache.

It was then that she had to remind herself that Adam wanted only his son—not her, never her. She was someone to be used in bed! Making love was magical, she was able to forget everything in those moments, but was it enough? Enough to survive on for the rest of her life, or at least until Ethan was grown up and left home?

Her heart simply couldn't take the pain.

'Adam!'

'Peter! What are you doing here?' The last person Adam had expected to see was Peter Wainwright. He had been in Ireland for two days but so far hadn't been able to pick up Sienna's trail. She had definitely flown to Dublin, that was as much as he knew. But no one remembered seeing a beautiful chestnut-haired Englishwoman with a young, dark-haired son.

Peter was a long-time business acquaintance who he sometimes met socially. He had even been at their wedding.

'Business, old boy. And I guessed you must be some-where around because I saw Sienna yesterday.'

Adam went very still. He even stopped breathing. But he gave nothing away. 'She never mentioned seeing you. Where was that?'

Peter smiled. 'She didn't notice me, she was too en-grossed in your son. You're a dark horse, Adam, you never told me you had a boy. I assume he is yours? He's fine looking without a doubt.'

'Of course he's mine.' Adam was swift to confirm it. Not many people outside his own immediate circle even knew that he'd been separated from his wife. But why hadn't Peter answered his question? He did not want to give away the fact that he was here looking for them, but he was anxious to find out where they were.

'They were going into that grocery shop down the road. Are you living here now?'

'Goodness, no,' answered Adam. 'We're visiting Sienna's mother.'

As soon as they had parted company Adam went into the shop in question and when he came out he was smiling.

'It's Daddy!'

'Don't be silly, Ethan, it can't be your daddy. He would tell us if he was coming.' Nevertheless, Sienna felt her heart miss a beat before starting to hammer alarmingly.

'But it *is*, Mummy.' Before she could stop him Ethan had run out of the house and down the path. 'Daddy, Daddy!' he cried, and threw himself into Adam's arms.

Through the window Sienna saw Adam swing Ethan up and hold him close. She saw their happiness.

Complete happiness. And in that instant realised how selfish she had been in keeping Ethan away from the father he had only just got to know. The father he loved with all of his dear little heart.

She had thought only of herself, and her hurt. She had ignored what she was doing to their son.

How Adam had found them was a mystery. He wore a black cotton shirt and jeans and looked relaxed, as though he was on holiday. And yet she knew that he would be far from relaxed. He had obviously been hell bent on finding them and with his determination had left no stone unturned. Though goodness knows what had brought him to this tiny corner of Ireland so quickly. Somehow, some way, she must have left a clue.

The smell of scones fresh from the oven filled the air. Ethan had helped her make them and they had been looking forward to a tasting session. Her mother had already taken a couple to her stepfather in his studio.

She saw Ethan chattering away to his father, saw his animated face, his arms linked around Adam's neck. And she closed her eyes. It was a scene that would remain etched in her mind for ever—no matter what the future held.

She moved to the doorway and her eyes met Adam's. She watched as he slowly walked towards her, Ethan still clinging happily to him. Her heartbeat accelerated and she felt a prickly heat all over her body.

This was a defining moment.

It was make-or-break time.

What the outcome would be she did not know. There would need to be a lot of changes before she went back to Adam. Even knowing that Ethan was the hub of their relationship, she could not see herself living happily as a family unless there was also love on Adam's side.

She needed to know whether he had come to take Ethan away from her, or whether he wanted her as well.

Her eyes remained on his face as he walked slowly up the narrow path. His expression was unreadable. He gave her no clue whatsoever as to what was going through his mind.

'Mummy, Daddy says he's come to take me home.'

Sienna's heart grew heavy. So he had come for Ethan alone! Her chin immediately lifted, her eyes hardening as they met Adam's. And she waited for him to qualify Ethan's statement. But not a word was spoken. His eyes locked with hers but they told her nothing.

He came to a halt in front of her and finally spoke. 'Aren't you going to ask me in?'

'How did you find us?' she asked, uncaring that her voice was sharp.

Adam shrugged. 'That's not important now. What is important is that we need to talk.'

Sienna reluctantly stepped back and allowed him entry. Then she walked through to the sitting room with its view down the garden to the sea beyond. It was normally peaceful sitting here but right at this moment everything inside her churned sickeningly.

She could see Niall's studio and her mother standing talking to him. What would her mother say, she wondered, if she knew that Adam was right here in her house?

'Ethan,' she said gently, 'why don't you go down and see Grandma and Grandad?'

'But—'

'Daddy and I need to talk.'

'I want to talk too. I've missed my daddy.'

'Ethan!' she warned, and he took one look at her face and fled.

Sienna knew that her mother would keep Ethan with them, giving her time to sort things out with Adam.

'You've been baking.'

Sienna nodded.

'It smells good.'

Such banal talk when she knew he must be dying to lash out at her, give her hell for running away, taking his son away from him.

'And you're looking good too, Sienna.'

That was a lie, she looked anything but. Her face was pale and drawn without a scrap of make-up and she looked nothing like the vibrant woman with whom he had once enjoyed mind-blowing sex.

Sex! It's all it had been. All it had ever been. She was a mad fool to still be in love with him. Simply looking at him drained the energy from her and she sat down.

Adam, on the other hand, remained standing, his eyes fiercely dark, almost black, thick brows beetling over them. 'Why did you run away?'

'Isn't it obvious?'

'You promised you would stay.'

Her eyes met his defiantly. 'What woman would want to live with a man who had married her for all the wrong reasons?' Only a woman who still loved him despite what he had done!

She watched the conflicting emotions cross his face. She saw grimness and doubt, she saw sadness, but she did not see what she wanted to see. There was no love, no tenderness.

What she would have liked was for him to say that he could not live without her. That he wanted to give their marriage another go. Actually, what she would have *really* liked was for him to say that he loved her.

'Were you being fair on Ethan?' Adam dropped down on the settee opposite, his knees apart, his elbows resting on them as he leaned towards her. His hands loosely linked.

He looked relaxed now and yet she knew that he wasn't. He was wired for an argument. He was damned angry with her and he was here to take Ethan home.

Over her dead body!

'Ethan hadn't seen my mother for a long time.' She tried to keep her voice reasonable. 'He's enjoying himself. He's not cried himself to sleep at night because he's missing his father, if that's what you're thinking.' She didn't tell him that Ethan constantly asked when he was going to see him again. No way was she going to put herself back in the firing line.

'And how about you? Have you cried yourself to sleep?'

His eyes locked with hers and Sienna felt a tingle run through her as though she had touched an electric wire. Damn! How could she still feel like this? Here was a man who did not love her. A man who enjoyed her body but nothing else. The fact that he was the father of her child was incidental.

'That will be the day,' she declared, hiding her feelings behind a strong contemptuous voice. 'I really don't know why we ever married. It was a disaster waiting to happen. You conned me, Adam. It's not something I can easily forgive you for. In fact, I might never forgive you.'

'You don't think that for Ethan's sake we—'

'Let's leave Ethan out of this.' Fire lit her eyes now, filled her belly. 'He is the innocent party. And I wish with all of my heart that he wasn't stuck in the middle.'

'We could make our marriage work.'

Sienna stared at him for several long seconds. 'You're kidding!'

'We'd both need to work at it, of course, but—'

'But what, Adam? We both know that you do not love me. You took *my* love and threw it back in my face. How are we supposed to ignore that? How are we supposed to live happily in front of Ethan if we hate the sight of each other?' She watched the play of shadows on Adam's face, could almost hear his brain ticking away.

'I do not hate you, Sienna.'

His voice was nothing more than a low growl now, coming from somewhere deep inside him. He was filled with an emotion that she did not understand.

'Whatever,' she snapped. 'It's not enough for me to move back in with you.'

'I love you.'

The whole world came to a standstill. Had Adam actually said that he loved her? And if he had, did he mean it? Or was it simply a ruse to get her back on side? He wanted Ethan and he knew that she would never be parted from him so he had to say something drastic.

Like he loved her!

'Yes, and the world's going to end tomorrow.' Her eyes flared magnificently. 'I'm not a fool, Adam, I know what your game is.' Love wasn't even a part of his vocabulary.

'I mean it, Sienna.'

His eyes met and held hers and a faint shudder ran down her spine. If only!

'I've not always loved you, I freely admit it. Though I was damned attracted to you.'

Yes, he had certainly proved that. He had invited her into his bed with the swiftness of a sparrowhawk catching its prey. And she had enjoyed every minute! But marriage wasn't totally about sex, it was about love and trust and honesty. They had been dismally absent.

'Asking you to marry me was an irresponsible thing to do. I wanted to get back at my grandfather and I've regretted it ever since. I've lived with that guilt. Every day of my life I've lived with it. Inevitably I pushed myself hard to become a success. I needed to prove to the old bastard that I could do it. And you took the brunt, I'm afraid. I'm sorry, Sienna. From the bottom of my heart I'm sorry.'

To give him his due he did look repentant, but Sienna wasn't fooled. 'It's not enough, Adam. Anyone can say they're sorry. I was in love with you. Really in love. Have you any idea how it makes me feel, knowing that I've been used?'

'Rock bottom, I guess.'

'To put it mildly.' Her eyes flashed into his. 'And when I found out that I was having your child, I wanted to kill myself.'

Adam groaned and she saw pain in his eyes but she did not care. He deserved it.

'Thank God you didn't,' he said hoarsely.

'I would never have gone through with it, I didn't have the courage,' she confessed, 'but it was how I felt at the time. Now Ethan is the biggest joy in my life. I love him to bits and when he was so poorly I nearly went out of my mind.'

'You shouldn't have had to suffer alone.'

'But I did, didn't I, Adam?' Her blue eyes blazed into his much darker ones. 'I've had years alone. And God knows why I ever thought I was doing the right thing in introducing you to your son. Because it's him you want now, isn't it? It's not me. You're saying you love me but—'

'*Sienna!*'

He spoke with such force that her words dried up in her mouth.

'Sienna, I do love you.'

Her eyes flashed strong disbelief. 'So what's happened to this afraid-to-love thing that you told me about?'

'I *was* afraid, because of my father, the way he reacted to my mother's death.' His voice was fierce and urgent, wanting her to believe in what he had to say. 'But I realise now that if you love someone, you love them no matter what.'

'You didn't love me when you married me.'

'No, that's true.' He winced as he said it. 'But I do now. I can't face the future without you, Sienna.'

Sienna saw the plea in his eyes, but still something held her back. How could she be sure? He could be saying all this just to get Ethan. His son had made such a difference to him. It had turned him into a different man. And that man she loved. But was he the true Adam? How would she ever know?

'I know I'll have to change. I know I need to regulate my working hours in order to spend time with my family. Actually,' he admitted with a wry grimace, 'my business can run perfectly well without me. I'm just a figurehead these days. My directors even tell me I put too much time in. But I enjoyed doing what I did. I had nothing else to do. But now I do have something, Sienna. I have a whole beautiful new life in front of me, with a son I adore and a wife I'm deeply in love with.'

There was such pain and honesty in his eyes that she finally accepted that he was speaking the truth. New life breathed into her body, she felt it creep up from her toes and fill every bone, every sinew, every vein, every artery. It heated her blood and threatened to engulf her.

'You really mean that?' Even her voice had grown stronger and she could not take her eyes away from his.

'More than you'll ever know.'

She heard sincerity, she saw clear truth in his eyes, and her heart felt like bursting.

Adam loved her!

He truly loved her!

A miracle had happened today, here in this beautiful corner of Ireland where the air was soft and the desolate beauty blew your mind away.

'I know that you don't love me any more, but—'

'Adam, I *do* love you.' She leaned forward and pressed the tips of her fingers to his lips. 'I've never stopped loving you.' Maybe she had told herself that she had but in truth her love for Adam had never gone away. There had always been a part of him in Ethan. And she loved her boy. 'You've made me laugh and you've made me cry, but I love you still.'

The look in his eyes, the incredulous look, made her smile.

'I don't deserve you,' he groaned.

His arms slid around her, pulling her gently against him where she could feel the frantic beat of his heart echoing the thud inside her own body.

'Tell me I'm not dreaming this.'

'You're not dreaming it.' Neither was she. There was fierce honesty in Adam's eyes, humility too, which was something she had never expected to see. Adam had been brought to his knees by love. She too was bowled over. It was as if a fairy godmother had waved her magic wand over them. The past was swiftly forgotten, all the pain and heartache. Their future was rosy.

Together, the three of them—and the new little life that was already forming inside her...

CAPTIVE IN THE MILLIONAIRE'S CASTLE

BY
LEE WILKINSON

Lee Wilkinson lives with her husband in a three-hundred-year-old stone cottage in a Derbyshire village, which most winters gets cut off by snow. They both enjoy travelling, and recently, joining forces with their daughter and son-in-law, spent a year going round the world 'on a shoestring' while their son looked after Kelly, their much loved German shepherd dog. Her hobbies are reading and gardening, and holding impromptu barbecues for her long-suffering family and friends.

CHAPTER ONE

FEBRUARY the fourteenth.

The headlines in the morning paper read:

A WELL-DESERVED VALENTINE FOR WELL-KNOWN AUTHOR. For the second year running, Michael Denver, who, according to some of the top literary critics, is unsurpassed in the field of psychological thrillers, has won the prestigious Quentin Penman Literary Award, this time for his new book, *Withershins*. This makes him one of the most celebrated authors of his day, with five award-winning novels to his credit.

In spite of this, Michael Denver, after hitting the headlines with a high-profile divorce from top model Claire Falconer, and subsequent rumours of a reconciliation, guards his privacy fiercely and refuses to be either interviewed or photographed.

His four previous books have been snapped up by Hollywood and three of them have already become major box-office successes. Having been widely acclaimed, and quoted as being 'his best so far,' *Withershins* seems likely to follow suit.

Michael replaced the receiver and ran his fingers through his thick dark hair. The phone call from his long-time friend, Paul Levens, had finally served to make up his mind.

Well, almost.

He could do with a PA, and if Paul was right and this girl was the treasure he claimed she was, she might be just what he wanted.

No, not wanted. *Needed*.

For quite a while, hating the idea of working with another person rather than on his own, as he was used to, Michael had put off the evil moment. But now, of necessity, he was having to think again.

When Paul, who had just reached the position of Associate Director at Global Enterprises, had casually mentioned that he knew of the ideal woman to fill the position, Michael had raised various objections, all of which—unusually for him— were anything but logical.

'Look,' Paul said, his blue eyes serious, 'I'm well aware that after the way women threw themselves at you following your divorce the entire female sex are anathema to you, but it isn't like you to let emotions, especially such destructive ones, overrule your common sense.

'You *need* a good PA. And I'm offering you the chance of a really first-class one. Believe me, Jennifer Mansell is as good as you're going to get.'

With devastating logic, Michael demanded, 'If she's that good, why are you letting her go?'

'Because I have little option. The powers that be have decided that in the present economic climate we *have* to trim staff wherever possible.

'Arthur Jenkins, the departmental boss she's worked for for more than three years, recently suffered a heart attack and is retiring on doctors' orders.'

in evidence. So far he'd only glimpsed her from a distance Tall and slim with dark hair taken up in an elegant swirl, she was wearing an ankle-length chiffon dress in muted, south-sea-colour shades of aquamarine, lapis lazuli and gold.

Paul, the only other person who knew he was there, had pointed her and Arthur Jenkins out to him.

'What did you manage to find out about her?' Michael asked quietly.

'Not a great deal,' Paul answered. 'The only information Personnel could give me was that she's twenty-four years old, quiet, efficient, and came to Global straight from a London business college.

'The people she worked with say she did her job well, and described her as having a friendly manner, but tending to keep herself to herself.'

'Anything else?'

'Very little's known about her private life but I did manage to pick up, from the grapevine, that for some time she wore an engagement ring.

'After she stopped wearing it, a few months ago, it appears that several of the men in the office tried their luck, but all of them were given a very cool reception, not to say the cold shoulder. It seems she's gone off men.'

Michael frowned thoughtfully. From that brief report, Jennifer Mansell sounded ideal.

However, reluctant to admit as much, he merely said, 'Thanks for the information.'

Paul shrugged heavy shoulders. 'Such as it is. Well, I'd better go and circulate. I take it you don't want to meet her now?'

Shaking his head, Michael answered, 'No.'

'Well, when you've managed to get a good look at her, if you do change your mind, just let me know.' Paul sketched a brief salute before heading for the stairs.

Michael was waiting only a minute or so when Arthur Jenkins and Jennifer Mansell came into view once again.

With no unseemly display of thigh or bosom, the simply cut dress she was wearing showed off her slender, graceful figure to perfection.

As she got closer he noticed that on her right wrist she was wearing a small watch on a plain black strap, and, on her right hand, a gold ring.

Her dark head was turned away from him as she conversed with her portly companion.

For some strange reason—a kind of premonition, perhaps—Michael found himself oddly impatient to see her face.

When she did turn towards him she was smiling, and he caught his breath. He *knew* that face, and not just because something about her reminded him of a young Julia Roberts.

Though they had never actually met, he had seen her before. But where and when?

And then he remembered, and he found his heart beating faster as he relived the little scene that had taken place at the castle, was it five years ago or six?

It had been late afternoon and, the only visitor still remaining, she had been standing in the cobbled courtyard, bright with its tubs of flowers.

Head tilted back, a coolish breeze ruffling her long dark hair, she had been watching some early swallows wheeling overhead, smiling then, as she was smiling now. He had been standing on the battlements, looking down. Still smiling, she had glanced in his direction. For a long moment their eyes had met and held, until, as though shy, she had looked away.

Though he hadn't had the faintest idea why, even then she had seemed familiar to him, as if he had always known her.

Seeing her start to head towards the main gate, he had turned to hurry after her. But by the time he had descended the spiral stone stairway of the north tower she had vanished from sight.

Impelled by a sudden urgency, he had moved swiftly across the courtyard and beneath the portcullis. At the bottom of the steep, cobbled path that led up to the castle gate, a car had been just pulling away.

He had tried to attract her attention, to no avail. As he had stood there the car had bumped down the uneven dirt road, turned right, and disappeared round the curve of the rocky hill.

Climbing up to the battlements again, with a strange sense of loss he had watched the silver dot take the picturesque coastal road that skirted the island, and head in the direction of the causeway.

To all intents and purposes the little incident was over, finished, but he had thought about her, wondered about her, and her face had stayed etched indelibly in his memory.

He had tried to play his disappointment down, to tell himself that he couldn't possibly feel so strongly about a woman he had only glimpsed, and never actually met. But wherever he went he had found himself scanning the faces of people passing by, unconsciously looking for her.

Over time, the impact she had had on him had gradually faded into the recesses of his mind, but he had never totally forgotten.

Now here she was again, as though fate had decreed it, and he was strangely shaken to see her once more.

In spite of his present aversion to women, he was tempted to go down, to see her at close quarters, to speak to her and hear her voice.

But common sense held him back.

Everything had changed. Instead of being a twenty-two year old with romantic ideals, he was older and wiser, not to say battle-scarred and bitter, with a newly acquired mistrust of women. And though her face was poignantly familiar, he didn't know what kind of woman she really was.

As he stood watching a tall, balding man detached her from Arthur Jenkins's side and led her onto the dance floor, where they were immediately swallowed up in the crowd.

Michael ran thoughtful fingers over his smooth chin. His inclination was to get to know her better, but, with all his previous reservations still intact, he didn't feel inclined to rush things…

He was standing staring blindly over the throng of dancers when Paul reappeared and remarked, 'So you're still here? I wasn't sure how long you intended to stay.'

'I was planning to leave shortly,' Michael told him, 'but I wanted another word with you first.'

'You've had a look at her, I take it? So what do you think?'

'From what I've seen so far, your recommendation appears to have been a good one, but—'

An expression of resignation on his face, Paul broke in, 'But you're not going to do anything about it! Oh, well, it's up to you, of course. But I personally believe it would be a mistake to let her slip through your fingers without at least taking things a step further.'

'I have every intention of taking things a step further,' Michael said quietly. 'But as this is neither the time nor the place, I'd like you to have a quick word with her and tell her…'

A group of chattering, laughing people paused nearby, and he lowered his voice even more to finish what he was saying.

'Will do,' Paul promised crisply as Michael clapped him on the shoulder before striding away.

Hearing a car turn into the quiet square lined with skeletal trees, Laura went to the window and peeped through a chink in the curtains.

She was just in time to see a taxi draw up in front of the block of flats, and Jenny climb out and cross the frosty pavement.

'Hi,' Laura greeted her flatmate laconically as she came into the living-room.

'Hi.' Tossing aside her evening wrap, and glancing at Laura's pink fluffy dressing gown and feathery mules, Jenny observed, 'I thought you'd be tucked up in bed by now.'

Her round, baby-face shiny with night cream, and the long blonde hair that earlier in the evening she had spent ages straightening once again starting to curl rebelliously, Laura agreed. 'I would have been, but Tom and I went out to Whistlers, and we had to wait ages for a taxi back.

'How did the party go?'

'Very well,' Jenny answered sedately.

Noting her flatmate's sparkling eyes and her barely concealed air of excitement, Laura asked, 'What is it? Did Prince Charming turn up and sweep you off your feet?'

'No, nothing like that.'

'So what's happened to make you look like the fifth of November? Come on, do tell.'

'I could do with a cup of tea first,' Jenny suggested hopefully.

'You drive a hard bargain,' Laura complained as she disappeared kitchenwards. 'But as I could do with a cup myself…'

Slipping off her evening sandals, Jenny settled herself on the settee in front of the glowing gasfire, stretched her feet towards the warmth, and hugged the bubbling excitement to her.

After starting the evening in low spirits, knowing that she no longer had a job, Jenny was now on top of the world, with the hope of new things opening up.

She hadn't felt so happy since Andy's perfidy had torn her world apart, making her feel betrayed and unwanted, worthless even.

Laura returned quite quickly carrying two steaming mugs.

Handing one to Jenny, she plonked herself down and urged, 'Right. Spill it.'

'You know Michael Denver?'

'You mean the writer? The one you've always been nuts about?'

'I wouldn't put it quite like that.'

'Why not? It's the truth…'

And it was. Since reading his first book, Jenny had been hooked, fascinated, not only by his intricate mind games and clever, complex plots, but by the brain behind them.

Yet for all their brilliance his books were easy to read, and his writing had compassion and sensitivity. His characters were real people with faults and failings and weaknesses, but also with courage and spirit and strength. People that his readers could understand and care about.

'So what about Michael Denver?' Laura pursued.

'He's in need of a PA, and I'm being interviewed for the job.'

Laura's jaw dropped. 'You don't mean interviewed by the man himself?'

Jenny nodded. 'Apparently.'

'When?'

'Eight-thirty tomorrow morning.'

'It's Saturday tomorrow,' Laura pointed out.

'Yes, I know. But it seems he's in a hurry to fill the post. He's sending a car for me. I can hardly believe it.'

'Neither can I. Are you quite sure you haven't had too much champagne?'

'Positive.'

'So how come?'

'It appears that Mr Jenkins, bless him, has sung my praises to Paul Levens, one of Global's directors, who happens to be a friend of Michael Denver's.

'When there was no available job for me with Global,

Mr Levens, who knew that Michael Denver needed a PA, suggested me.'

'And bingo!'

'It may not be that simple. I may not get the job. But I certainly hope I do. It would be a dream come true to work for someone like him.'

Laura grunted. 'Well, all I can say is, if he doesn't realize how lucky he is and snap you up, he's an idiot.'

Smiling at her friend's aggressive loyalty, Jenny said, 'Well, we'll just have to wait and see.'

Finishing her tea, she added, 'Now I'd better get off to bed, so I have my wits about me for the interview. I get the feeling that Michael Denver isn't one to suffer fools gladly.'

Pulling a disappointed face, Laura protested, 'Spoilsport. I was just going to ask you what you've found out about him.'

'Hardly anything. But I'll tell you what little I do know in the morning.'

'It's a deal! Sleep well.'

The following morning, after a restless night, Jenny was up early. By the time she had finished showering, her flatmate, who usually slept late on a Saturday, was already pottering round the kitchen making toast and coffee.

'Sheer nosiness,' she confessed in answer to Jenny's query. 'I couldn't wait to hear all about the man himself. And I wanted to be up just in case he came in person to collect you.'

'It's hardly likely,' Jenny said dryly.

'Well, at least I'll get to see his car... Now then, what about some toast?'

Shaking her head, Jenny admitted, 'I'm too nervous to eat a thing. But I will have a coffee.'

Laura poured two cups before asking with unrestrained eagerness, 'So what did you find out about him?'

'Very little, except that he lives in a quiet block of flats in Mayfair.' In a portentous voice, she added, 'These days everything about him is shrouded in mystery.'

Only half believing her, Laura asked, 'Honestly?'

'Honestly.'

'Why? There must be a reason.'

'Well, as most of it seems to be public knowledge already, I'll tell you what Mr Levens told me.

'When Michael Denver first shot to fame after winning his second award, he became an overnight celebrity. But it seems that he's a man who values his privacy, and he did his utmost to play it down and stay in the background.

'Then he met and married a top photographic model named Claire Falconer—'

'Oh, yes, I know her!' Laura exclaimed. 'Or rather I know *of* her.' Then impatiently, 'Go on.'

'Both "beautiful people" and celebrities, they seemed to be madly in love with each other and ideally suited.

'The media soon nicknamed them the Golden Couple, and followed them everywhere with their cameras. But while *she* enjoyed all the fuss and the media attention, *he* loathed it.

'The attention was just starting to die down when a story that she'd been seen in the bedroom of a secluded hotel with another man while her husband was away got into the papers. She claimed it was a lie. But a follow-up story included a photograph of the pair of them trying to slip out of the hotel the next morning.

'That gave rise to rumours that after only six months the marriage was breaking up, and the press had a field day. Michael Denver stayed tight-lipped and refused to comment, but his wife gave an interview in which she announced that she still loved him and was trying for a reconciliation. What he'd hoped would be a quiet divorce degenerated into a three-ringed circus—'

'Now you mention it, I do remember reading about it. At the time I felt rather sorry for him.'

'I gather from what Mr Levens told me that between his ex-wife, who continued to oppose the divorce, and the attentions of the gutter press, his life was made almost intolerable.

'His refusal to give interviews or be photographed just made the paparazzi keener, and in the end he was forced to move flats and go to ground.'

'It must have been tough for the poor devil.'

'I'm sure it was.'

'Do you know, in spite of all that press coverage I've no idea how old he is or what he looks like, have you?'

'Not the faintest,' Jenny admitted.

'My guess is that he'll be middle-aged, handsome in a lean and hungry way, with a domed forehead, a beaky nose and a pair of piercing blue eyes.'

'What about his ears?'

'Oh, a pair of those too. Unless he's a tortured genius like Vincent Van Gogh.'

'Fool! I meant flat or sticky out?'

'Definitely sticky out, large, and a bit pointed.'

'What makes you think that?'

'Because that's what a brilliant writer *ought* to look like.' Jenny laughed. 'Well, if you say so.'

'By the way, if you get back to find the flat empty, don't be surprised. It's Tom's parents' wedding anniversary, and later we're off to Kent to spend the day with them.'

'Well, I hope everything goes really well. Do give Mr and Mrs Harmen my best wishes.'

Her coffee finished, Jenny dressed in a taupe suit and toning blouse, swept her hair into a smooth coil, added neat gold studs to her ears and the merest touch of make-up.

With just a mental picture of Michael Denver, and no real

idea of his age or what he might want in a PA, she could only hope he would approve of her businesslike appearance.

The car, a chauffeur-driven Mercedes, drew up outside dead on time.

Laura, who was stationed by the window, exclaimed excitedly, 'It's here! Well, off you go, and the best of luck.'

Trying to quell the butterflies that danced in her stomach, Jenny picked up her shoulder bag, and said, 'Thanks. Enjoy your day.'

Outside, the air was cold, and Jack Frost had sprinkled the pavement with diamond dust and scrawled his glittering autograph over natural and man-made objects alike.

By the kerb, the elderly chauffeur was standing smartly to attention, waiting to open the car door for her.

As she reached him he bid a polite, 'Good morning, miss.'

Jenny returned the greeting and, feeling rather like some usurper masquerading as royalty, climbed in and settled herself into the warmth and comfort of the limousine.

By the time they reached Mayfair and drew up outside the sumptuous block of flats, she had managed to conquer the nervous excitement, and at least appear her usual cool, collected self.

Having crossed the marble-floored lobby, she identified herself to Security before taking the private lift up to the second floor, as instructed.

As the doors slid open and she emerged into a luxurious lobby she was met by a tall, thin butler with a long, lugubrious face. 'Miss Mansell? Mr Denver is expecting you. If you would like to follow me?'

She obeyed, and was ushered into a large, very well-equipped office.

'Miss Mansell, sir.'

As the door closed quietly behind her a tall, dark, broad-shouldered man dressed in smart casuals rose from his seat behind the desk.

A sudden shock ran through her, and though somehow her legs kept moving she felt as if she had walked slap bang into an invisible plate-glass window.

While she was convinced they had never met, she felt certain that she knew him. Some part of her *recognized* him, *remembered* him, *responded* to him…

But even as she tried to tell herself that she must, at one time, have seen his photograph in the papers, she felt quite certain that that wasn't the answer. Though there had to be some logical explanation for such a strong feeling.

Michael, for his part, was struggling to hide his relief. For a man who was normally so confident, so sure of himself and the plans he was putting into action, he had been unsettled and on edge. Half convinced that she wouldn't come, after all, and angry with himself that it *mattered.*

Now here she was, and though for some reason her steps had faltered and she had appeared to be momentarily disconcerted, she had quickly regained her composure.

Holding out his hand, he said without smiling, 'Miss Mansell… How do you do?'

His voice was low-pitched and attractive, his features clear-cut, but tough and masculine rather than handsome.

'How do you do?' Putting her hand into his, and meeting those thickly lashed, forest-green eyes, sent tingles down her spine.

She had expected him to be middle-aged, but he was considerably younger, somewhere in his late twenties, she judged, and nothing at all like the picture Laura had painted of him.

At close quarters, Michael found, she was not merely beautiful, but intriguing. Her face held both character and charm, and a haunting poignancy that made him want to keep on looking at her.

Annoyed by his own reaction, he said a shade brusquely, 'Won't you sit down?'

Despite the instant impact he had had on her, she found his curt manner more than a little off-putting, and she took the black leather chair he'd indicated, a shade reluctantly.

Resuming his own seat, he placed his elbows on the desk, rested his chin on his folded hands, and studied her intently.

Her small, heart-shaped face was calm and composed, her back straight, her long legs crossed neatly, her skirt drawn down demurely over her knees.

There was no sign of the femme fatale, not the faintest suggestion that she might try to employ any sexual wiles, which seemed to confirm that she was different from the women who had, in the wake of his divorce, seemed to think he was fair game.

Appreciating the natural look, after all the artificial glamour of the modelling world, he was pleased to note she wore very little make-up. But with a flawless skin and dark brows and lashes, she didn't need to.

Up close, the impact of those big brown eyes and the wide, passionate mouth was stunning. But though she was one of the loveliest and most fascinating women he had ever seen, it wasn't in a showy way.

Her hands were long and slender, strong hands in spite of their apparent delicacy, and he was pleased to see that her pale oval nails were buffed but mercifully unvarnished.

On her right hand he glimpsed the gold ring she had worn the previous night, but her left hand was bare.

Becoming aware that she was starting to look slightly uncomfortable under his silent scrutiny, and wanting to know more about her, he instructed briskly, 'Tell me about yourself.'

'What exactly would you like to know?'

She had a nice voice, he noted—always acutely sensitive to voices—soft and slightly husky.

'To start with, where you were born.'

'I was born in London.'

'And you've lived here all your life?'

'No. When I was quite small, we moved to the little town of Kelsay. It's on the east coast…'

With a little jolt of excitement, he said, 'Yes, I know it.' The fact that she came from Kelsay seemed to confirm— though he hadn't really *needed* any further confirmation—that she was the girl he had seen at the castle.

'So how come you're back in London?'

'When my great-grandmother, whom I was living with, died just a few weeks after I left school, I enrolled at the London School of Business Studies. Then when I had the qualifications I needed, I applied for, and got, a job with Global Enterprises.

'I started work in the general office, then became PA to Mr Jenkins, one of the departmental heads.'

'I understand from Paul Levens that Mr Jenkins is retiring, and that the department he ran is being merged with another. Which is why you're looking for a new position?'

'That's right.'

'He also mentioned that Mr Jenkins spoke very highly of you, praising your loyalty, your tact and your efficiency. All attributes that as far as I'm concerned are essential.'

When she said nothing, merely looked at him steadily, he went on to ask, 'What, in your opinion, is a PA there for?'

'I've always thought that a good PA should keep things ticking over smoothly and do whatever it takes to keep her boss happy.'

'Even if it includes running his errands and making his coffee?'

'Yes,' she answered without hesitation.

Thinking that after some of the women he had known she

was like a breath of fresh air, he asked, 'You wouldn't regard that as infra dig?'

'No.' Seriously, she added, 'I've always thought of a PA as a well-paid dogsbody.'

Managing to hide a smile, he said, 'Good. Though the majority of the work would involve taking shorthand then transferring it onto a word-processor, it's that part that slows me down, I'm looking for a PA who isn't going to quibble about exact duties.

'I also need someone who, as well as being efficient, is discreet and trustworthy.'

'Mr Levens explained that.'

'And you think you fit the bill?'

'Yes, I believe I do.'

'Though the monthly salary will stay the same, between books there may be longish periods when I won't need a PA at all.

'But I must warn you that when I *am* writing, I often work seven days a week, and should I decide to work in the evenings, I'll expect my PA to be available. Would you be happy with that kind of "all or nothing" arrangement?'

She answered, 'Yes,' without hesitation.

Michael was well satisfied with that firm 'yes'. If he did decide to give her the job, and it was still a big if, it sounded as if she might well take it.

CHAPTER TWO

JUST for a moment the thought stopped Michael in his tracks. Was he seriously considering letting a woman into his life again, even on a purely business basis?

He wished he could come up with a resounding *no way!* But somehow this woman was different. And he was strangely reluctant to let her walk away from him for a second time.

Glancing up, and finding Jenny was looking at him expectantly, he rounded up his straying thoughts and resumed his questioning. 'While you've been working for Global Enterprises, how many times have you been off sick?'

'None at all. Luckily, I'm very healthy.'

'Then we come to the question of salary, and holidays. The commencing salary would be…'

He named a sum so in excess of what she might have hoped for that she blinked.

'But I expect holidays to be fitted in during the slack periods. Any taken during the busy spells would need to be agreed on well in advance. Does that seem reasonable to you?'

'Perfectly reasonable,' she answered steadily.

Running lean fingers over his smooth jaw, he regarded her in a contemplative silence for a moment or two.

She was a very beautiful woman, and, even taking into

account a broken engagement, it was hard to believe that there was no current man in her life.

Deciding that that was one thing he ought to establish, he began carefully, 'Do you live alone?'

'I have a flatmate.'

'As distinct from a live-in lover?'

A little stiffly, she objected, 'I'm afraid I don't see why my private life is relevant.'

His face cold, he said, 'It's relevant on more than one count. Apart from the long hours which this kind of work sometimes involves, when I begin a new book I prefer to leave London and work in comparative isolation, where I can be quite free from any unwanted social distractions.'

'Oh…'

Deciding to spell it out, he added, 'Which means I need a PA who is free from any personal commitments or obligations.'

'I see,' she said slowly.

'Is that a problem for you?'

She shook her head. 'No, not really.'

No nearer to finding out what he wanted to know, he applied a little more pressure.

'Then you have no ties? For example, no fiancé, who would almost certainly object?'

'No.'

Well, that seemed decided enough. Though he knew to his cost that, if it suited them, some women could lie with composure.

'And you don't dislike the thought of having to leave London?'

'No, not at all.'

She sounded as if she meant it.

He was oddly pleased.

Claire had hated the thought of leaving the bright lights of

London and burying herself in what she referred to as 'the back of beyond', and after the first time she had refused point blank to go to Slinterwood again.

To please her, he had tried staying in town to finish writing *Mandrake,* but after several unproductive weeks he had given it up as hopeless.

With that important deadline fast approaching, she had suggested that he should go to Slinterwood while she remained in London.

Now, in retrospect, he could see that that had been the beginning of the end as far as their marriage was concerned...

Jenny was sitting quite still, but, sensing that she was once again growing uncomfortable with the lengthening silence, he went on, 'In that case I'm prepared to offer you a month's trial period.'

He hadn't *consciously* made up his mind, and his abrupt offer of a job had surprised even himself.

Jenny, also taken aback by the suddenness of the offer, hesitated, wishing she had more time to think.

Picking up the vibes, and sensing his earlier indecision, not to mention a certain amount of antagonism, she had expected further searching questions, and then a cool promise to 'let her know'.

She *wanted* the job, so she really ought to be over the moon, but she had found his attitude, and the intentness of his gaze, more than a little daunting.

But that wasn't insurmountable, she told herself stoutly. The important thing was that she had been offered the chance to work for a writer she admired enormously, and even if her job was only to transcribe his words she wanted to be part of the creative process...

Now, watching her hesitate, and suddenly concerned that

she was about to refuse after all, he asked brusquely, 'So what do you say?'

Telling herself that if it *did* prove to be a mistake, it was only for a month, she said, 'Thank you. I—I accept.'

He nodded. 'Good. Now the only thing is, how soon can you start?'

'Whenever you like.'

'Then let's say immediately.'

'You mean Monday?'

Deciding to strike while the iron was hot, he told her, 'I mean now.'

Sounding a little startled, she echoed, 'Now?'

'As I told you, when I begin a new book I prefer to leave London and work in comparative isolation. I was planning to go today. Seeing that you're free to start at once, it would be more convenient if you travelled with me.'

'Very well.'

'If my chauffeur takes you home, how long will you need to get organized and pack enough clothes for…shall we say…up to a month? Then we'll both be free to reassess the situation.'

'Half an hour at the most.'

'Excellent.

'By the time you get down to the lobby, the car will be outside, waiting. The car will drop you home and when you've had time to pack, I'll pick you up myself.'

'Thank you.'

Feeling as though she had been caught up and swept along by a tidal wave, she got to her feet and prepared to leave.

Wondering if he'd done the right thing, or if he'd allowed his subconscious feelings to hurry him into something he might regret, Michael rose to accompany her. If he found he *had* made a mistake he could always pay her for the month but get rid of her straight away.

Once again picking up the vibes, and not altogether at ease, Jenny headed for the door. Though at five feet seven inches she was tall for a woman, he was a good head taller, with a mature width of shoulder, and for once in her life she felt dwarfed, towered over.

As he opened the door the butler appeared as if by magic to escort her to the lift.

'I'll call for you in approximately an hour, depending on the traffic,' her new boss reminded her.

'I'll be ready,' she promised.

She had moved to join the manservant when a thought struck her, and, turning to Michael Denver, she began, 'Oh, by the way, where are we—?'

At the same instant the phone on his desk rang, and with a murmured, 'Excuse me,' he turned to answer it.

Oh, well, Jenny thought resignedly, she could find out exactly where they were going when he came to pick her up.

The Saturday morning traffic proved to be relatively light, and the drive back to her Bayswater flat was over quite quickly.

As good as her word, some half an hour after the chauffeur had dropped her Jenny's case was neatly packed with easy-care, mix-and-match stuff, and she was ready and waiting.

Smiling to herself, thinking of her flatmate's excitement when she read it, Jenny began to scrawl a hasty note.

Got the job, subject to a month's trial period. Will be starting immediately. Being whisked off to what I presume is his house in the country to begin work on his latest book.

Will be in touch. Jenny.

PS. The man himself is nothing like either of us

pictured. He's quite young and not bad-looking, but rather cold and unapproachable, so he might not be pleasant to work for.

She had just finished writing when, glancing out of the window, she saw a large black four-wheel drive with tinted windows draw up by the kerb. It seemed somewhat out of place in London, but no doubt it would have its uses in the country.

Picking up her case and shoulder bag, her coat over her arm, she brushed aside the niggling doubt that she was doing the right thing, and hurried out.

The air was still cold, but the sun was now shining brightly from a clear, duck-egg-blue sky, and reflecting in the car's gleaming paintwork.

As she walked across the pavement Michael Denver opened the car door and jumped out, and she felt the same strange impact she'd felt on first seeing him.

'Good timing,' he congratulated her as he came round to take her case, before opening the car door.

By the time she had climbed in and fastened her seat belt he had stowed her case and was sliding behind the wheel once more.

While he skilfully threaded his way through the traffic, she stayed silent and tried to relax, but she was very conscious of him and could only manage, at the most, an *appearance* of tranquillity.

It wasn't until they had reached the suburbs and were heading out of London that she broached the question that had been at the back of her mind. 'By the way, Mr Denver—'

'I'd prefer to be on first-name terms,' he broke in coolly, 'if that's all right with you?'

She had expected him to retain the formality of surnames,

at least for the time being, and, startled, she answered, 'Oh, yes. Quite all right...'

'Michael,' he prompted.

It seemed somehow momentous to be using his given name, and it took a second or two to pluck up enough courage to say, 'Michael.'

'And you're Jennifer?'

'Yes. But I usually get called Jenny.'

'Then Jenny it is. A nice old-fashioned name of Celtic origin,' he added. 'Now, you were about to ask me something?'

'Oh, yes... I still don't know where we're going. I presume you have a house somewhere in the country?'

'Yes, it's called Slinterwood.' His tone of voice holding an undercurrent of something she couldn't quite pin down, he added with apparent casualness, 'You know the Island of Mirren?'

'Of course.' Her voice held a little quiver of excitement. 'It's just down the coast from where my great-grandmother used to live.'

'Have you ever visited it?'

'I went once.'

'How long ago?'

'I was eighteen at the time. It was a short while before I moved to London.'

'You went to see Mirren Castle?'

'Yes. In those days it was open to the public at certain times.'

'What did you think of it?'

'I didn't see a great deal,' she admitted. 'I'd gone on the spur of the moment, quite late one afternoon, and I'd chosen the wrong day, which meant I couldn't go inside.

'But what I did see of the place was absolutely wonderful and I've never forgotten it. I had hoped to go back one day and see more of it.'

'And did you?' he pressed.

She shook her head. 'Things change, and by the time I had a chance it was too late. I heard that Mirren's new owner had closed the castle to the public and made it clear that visitors to the island were no longer welcome.'

'So you've never been back?'

'No.'

'Well, as you say, things change. But there's nothing to stop them changing again.'

She was wondering about that rather cryptic remark when he pursued, 'Did you ever find out who the new owner was?'

She shook her head. 'No. But I believe the island stayed in the hands of the same family. It was just a different policy in force.'

'A policy that caused you great disappointment?'

'Well, yes... Though I can't say I really blamed the new owner.'

In answer to her companion's questioning glance, she admitted, 'If it was mine, *I* wouldn't want visitors tramping around making a noise and dropping litter.'

When he said nothing, feeling the need to justify that remark, she added, 'I can't help but feel that a lot of the island's charm must lie in its isolation and the serenity that kind of isolation brings.'

Either her feelings echoed his own, or, he thought cynically, she was clever enough to realize that they were what his feelings *would* be, and to play up to him.

'Then you're not a gregarious creature?' he asked.

'No, not really.'

'Yet you chose to live in London.'

'I don't *dislike* London. It's an exciting, vibrant place to live, and of course it's where a lot of the jobs are.

'But after I'd left Kelsay I found I missed the sound of the sea and the dark night sky and the stars. With the glow from the street lamps it's not easy to see the stars in central London—' Suddenly realizing her tongue was running away with her, she broke off abruptly.

It wasn't at all like her to talk so freely to a man who was not only a virtual stranger but her new employer, and she wished she had been more circumspect, more restrained.

When he made no effort to break the ensuing silence, fearing she had already got off on the wrong foot, she apologized. 'I'm sorry, I'm afraid I was babbling. You can't possibly be interested in my—'

'Oh, but I am,' he broke in smoothly. 'And I found your "babbling", as you call it, quite poetic.'

Unsure whether or not he was making fun of her, she let that go, and, trying to get back to the more mundane, pursued, 'I presume from what you said just now that Slinterwood is somewhere near Mirren.'

'Slinterwood is *on* Mirren.'

'Sorry?'

He repeated, 'Slinterwood is *on* Mirren.'

Still unsure if she had heard correctly, she echoed, '*On* Mirren?'

'That's right.'

She caught her breath, bowled over by the thought of actually staying on Mirren.

For as long as she could remember, she had felt a strange affinity with the place, a secret fascination that almost amounted to an obsession.

She had thought of it as *her* island.

It drew her, called to her. Even when she and her parents had been living in Jersey, Mirren had often been in her thoughts.

Having decided to go back to Kelsay to take care of her

great-grandmother, she had made up her mind to ask the old lady—who had lived within sight of the island all her life—to tell her everything she knew about it.

But on the day before Jenny's arrival another stroke had left her namesake partially paralyzed and unable to speak coherently.

Now fate seemed to be offering a chance, not only to learn something about her island, but to *live* on it for a while.

She could barely restrain her surprise and delight.

Giving her a sidelong glance, he commented, 'You look pleased.'

Steadying herself, she said, 'I am rather.'

'And surprised?'

'That too. For one thing, I thought Mirren was still privately owned.'

'It is.'

So if he rented a house there, even if it was through an agency, he probably knew the name of the family who owned it.

She waited hopefully, but, when he volunteered no more information, unwilling to appear over-curious in case it stalled the conversation she refrained from asking.

No doubt she could broach the subject again, when they had got to know each other better.

Her restraint was rewarded when he went on, 'You said, "For one thing"... So what was the other?'

'I hadn't realized there were any buildings on the island, apart from the castle.'

'Oh, yes.'

'So where is Slinterwood, exactly?'

'It stands overlooking the sea, about a mile south of the castle.'

'How strange I never saw it.'

'Not really. I'm half convinced that, like Brigadoon, it's enchanted, and only appears from time to time...'

He sounded perfectly serious. But when she glanced sideways at him she saw the corner of his long, mobile mouth twitch

'Apart from that, until you actually reach it, it's hidden by a curving bluff and a stand of trees.'

'Is it the only house on the island?'

'No. There's a couple of farms, and about half a mile down the coast from Slinterwood there's a small hamlet that was built in the eighteen hundreds to house the estate workers.'

Seeing her puzzled frown, he went on, 'You wouldn't have noticed it—because of the lie of the land it's only visible from the seaward side.'

'Oh... Do people still live there?'

'Yes. Though the castle itself is no longer inhabited, the estate still needs its workers, most of whom have lived on the island for generations.

'Though, of necessity, the young, unmarried ones leave to look for partners, there's something about Mirren that seems to draw them back, and keeps the cycle going.'

He relapsed into silence, leaving her to mull over what she had learnt, which was both thrilling and a little disturbing.

Thrilling because she would be living on her dream island and working for a famous author. Disturbing because—though Michael Denver had told her from the beginning that he liked to work in 'comparative isolation'—she was just starting to appreciate exactly how isolated they would be, and to wonder, with the faintest stirring of unease, if she had been wise to come.

Slinterwood, it appeared, was on the opposite side of the island to the causeway, which meant that once she was there it was a long way back.

Added to that, the causeway itself, which for part of the time would be under water, was well over a mile long and only safe to cross at low tide and in good weather conditions. So with no transport of her own, she would be a virtual prisoner.

Oh, don't be so melodramatic! she scolded herself. All it amounted to was that she and Michael Denver were bound to be thrown together a good deal in relative isolation

But so what? A man of his standing was hardly likely to turn into a Jekyll and Hyde, or prove a threat in any way. And though the house *was* isolated, there must be a housekeeper or a manservant, someone to take care of the place and look after Michael while he was there.

But would he expect *her* to provide some companionship for the odd times he wasn't working?

It was a bit of a daunting prospect.

Though with his reputed aversion to women, he would hopefully prefer to spend his leisure time alone.

If by any chance he didn't… Well, she had taken on the job, and if providing some companionship while he was at Slinterwood proved to be a part of it she would just have to cope.

After all, she was getting very well paid. And if, at the end of a month, she wasn't happy with her duties, she could always say so and let someone else have the post.

Her thoughts busy, for the past few miles Jenny had been staring blindly into space, but now, her immediate concerns shelved, she was able to give her attention to the scenery.

They were travelling through pleasant rolling countryside where, in the shade, the grass was still stiff and white with frost, and the skeletal trees stood out black and stark against the pale blue of the sky.

Topping a rise, they ran into a small sunlit village with old mellow-stone cottages fronting a village green.

Standing opposite a duckpond, where a gaggle of white geese floated serenely, was a black and white half-timbered inn called the Grouse and Claret.

'I thought we'd stop here for lunch,' Michael said. 'If you're ready to eat, that is?'

'Quite ready. I didn't have any breakfast.'

'Why not? Pushed for time?'

She shook her head. 'To tell you the truth, I was a bit nervous.'

He found himself wondering about that rather naive statement. Had it been made for effect? To encourage him to think she was sweet and innocent?

When, his face cool and slightly aloof, he made no comment, she regretted her impulsive admission and wished she had simply said that she was hungry.

He drove through a stone archway into the cobbled yard of the inn, and, stopping by a stack of old oak beer barrels, came round to open her door.

Well, whatever faults he might prove to have, she thought as she climbed out, his manners, though quiet and unobtrusive, were flawless.

With the kind of surety that made her guess he had stopped here before, he escorted her through the oak door at the rear, and into a black-beamed bar where a log fire blazed and crackled cheerfully.

The bar, its low, latticed windows tending to keep out the sunshine, would have been gloomy if it hadn't been for the leaping flames. It was empty apart from a broad-faced, thick-necked, cheerful-looking man behind the bar, and two old cronies in the far corner who appeared to be regulars.

The landlord's hearty greeting proved Jenny's supposition to be correct.

'Nice to see you again, Mr Denver.'

'Nice to see you, Amos.'

'Me and the wife have been wondering if, the next time you came, Mrs Denver might be with you?'

Jenny saw Michael's jaw tighten, but his voice was still pleasant and level as he asked, 'And what made you wonder that?'

'Why, the newspaper stories that you and 'er were getting together again. You must have seen them.'

'I never look at the papers,' Michael told him. 'Half the stuff they print is suspect, to say the least. It pays not to believe a word.'

Amos grunted his agreement. 'We might not have done, but it sounded as though it was Mrs Denver herself who had told the reporters.'

'Well, whoever told them, there's not a word of truth in it,' Michael said shortly.

With an unexpected show of tact, Amos changed the subject to ask, 'So what's it to be? Your usual?'

At Michael's nod he enquired, 'And what about the young lady?'

'Miss Mansell is my new PA,' Michael answered the man's unspoken curiosity.

Then giving Jenny a questioning glance, he asked, 'What would you like to drink?'

As she hesitated, wondering what he would consider suitable, he suggested, 'A glass of wine? Or would you prefer a soft drink?'

Fancying neither, and having noticed a sign over the bar that announced, 'We Brew Our Own Ale', she abandoned the idea of 'suitable' and said, 'If it's all the same to you, I'd like half a pint of the home-brewed ale.'

'An excellent choice,' Amos said heartily. Then to Michael, who had managed to hide his surprise, 'No doubt you've been singing its praises.'

'I don't need to,' Michael answered gravely. 'I'm convinced that Miss Mansell can read my mind.'

'Dangerous thing, that,' the landlord remarked with a grin as he drew two half pints of ale. 'I'm only pleased my wife can't read mine. Though, mind you, she makes up for it by reading my letters and going through my pockets…

'Now then, you'll be wanting a good hot meal?'

'If that's possible?'

'It certainly is. My Sarah has her faults, but she's an excellent cook. I can recommend the rabbit casserole and the apple pie. If the young lady wants something lighter, we can always run to a salad.'

Used to Claire, who had needed to rigorously watch her diet, Michael turned to Jenny and lifted a dark, enquiring brow.

'The casserole and the pie sound great,' she said, surprising him yet again.

'Then make that two, please, Amos.'

Nodding his approval, Amos disappeared in the direction of the kitchen while, frowning a little, Jenny found herself having second thoughts.

Her new boss had obviously been a little startled by her robust choices, and she wondered if, in order to create a good impression, she should have gone for a more ladylike salad and a soft drink.

Oh, well, it was too late now to worry about it.

He carried both their glasses over to a table by the fire, and was about to settle Jenny in one of the comfortable, cushioned chairs when, seeing the firelight flicker on her face, he made to move it back. 'That might be too close for you…'

'No… No, it's fine.'

Hearing the hint of surprise in her voice, he explained, 'I suppose I got used to my ex-wife. She never liked to sit close in case the heat ruined her skin.'

When he said nothing further, deciding he was disinclined for conversation, Jenny turned her head and watched the leaping flames while she slowly sipped her drink.

Lifting his own glass to his lips, Michael found himself wondering why on earth he was talking about Claire, when for months he had done his best to avoid mentioning her name or even thinking about her.

Perhaps it was Amos's revelations that had brought his ex to the forefront of his mind.

He had little doubt that Claire's talk with the reporters had been deliberately staged. Though he was sure she no longer loved him, and probably never had, he knew that she couldn't bear to let go any man that she had once considered hers.

But she was wasting her time. He hadn't the slightest intention of taking her back. In the short time they had been married she had cuckolded him and almost succeeded in emasculating him.

Anything he had once felt for her had long since died, and when the divorce had been finalized, mingled with the pain and bitter disillusionment had been relief.

Unconsciously, he sighed, and with a determined effort he brought his mind back to the present.

His companion was sitting quietly staring into the fire. Watching the pure line of her profile, he noted that though she *appeared* to be at ease, she wasn't nearly as composed as she looked.

He was still studying her surreptitiously when their food arrived, and he suggested, 'Tuck in.'

It looked and smelled so appetizing that, in spite of her previous misgivings, when a generous plateful was put in front of her Jenny obeyed.

It was every bit as good as the landlord had boasted, the tender meat served with small, fluffy dumplings, a selection of root vegetables, and rich, tasty gravy.

Michael noted that she ate neatly and daintily, but with a healthy appetite. After getting used to seeing Claire toy with a salad and then leave half of it, he found it a pleasure to lunch with a woman who obviously enjoyed her food.

The pie that followed was just as good, with light, crisp pastry, tangy apples cooked to perfection, and lashings of thick country cream.

When Jenny had finished the last spoonful, she sat back with a satisfied, 'Mmmm…'

Watching her use the tip of a pink tongue to catch an errant speck of cream, he felt a sudden fierce kick of desire low down in his belly, and was forced to glance hastily away.

Since his divorce he hadn't so much as looked at another woman, and that sudden, unbidden reaction threw him off balance.

Seeing she was looking at him, and hoping his tension didn't show, he asked unnecessarily, 'I take it you enjoyed the meal?'

'It was absolutely delicious. I can quite see why you like to stop here—'

All at once she broke off, flustered, wondering if he'd thought her greedy.

She was trying to find some way to change what had become an uncomfortable subject when the landlord appeared to clear away the dishes and bring the coffee, sparing her the need.

'A grand meal, Amos,' Michael said heartily.

He sounded sincere, and, realizing that he too had enjoyed it, Jenny relaxed. Perhaps, because of what she saw as the newness and possible fragility of the relationship, she was simply being over-sensitive.

'I haven't tasted anything as good as that since I was here last.'

'I'll tell Sarah,' the landlord promised. 'She'll be pleased.'

For a little while they sipped their coffee without speaking, and, a quick glance at her silent companion confirming that he was once again in a brown study, she seized the opportunity to watch him.

His dark hair was thick and glossy, still trying to curl a little in spite of its short cut, and, though he lacked either charm or charisma, his face was interesting, lean and strong-boned, with a straight nose and a cleft chin.

It was the kind of face that wouldn't change or grow soft and flabby with age. At sixty or seventy he would look pretty much as he looked now.

His eyes were handsome, she conceded, long and heavy-lidded, tilted up a little at the outer edge, with thick curly lashes. His teeth too were excellent, gleaming white and healthy, while his mouth had a masculine beauty that made her feel strange inside.

Dragging her gaze away with something of an effort, she studied his ears, which were smallish and set neatly against his well-shaped head. A far cry from the large, sticky-out ears Laura had predicted.

Jenny was smiling at the remembered picture when he glanced up unexpectedly.

As he watched the hot colour rise in her cheeks, pointing to her guilt, she saw his eyes narrow.

He obviously thought she had been laughing at him, and, knowing how fragile a man's ego could be, she braced herself for an angry outburst.

But, his face showing only mild interest, he suggested blandly, 'Perhaps you'd allow me to share the joke?'

Seeing nothing else for it, she drew a deep breath and admitted, 'I was smiling at the mental picture my flatmate had painted of what you, as a successful author, ought to look like.'

'Oh? So what *should* a successful author look like?'

She repeated as near as she could remember word for word what had been said that morning.

His face straight, but his green eyes alight with amusement,

he said quizzically, 'Hmm... Large, pointed, sticky-out ears...
So how do I compare? Favourably, I hope?'

She smiled, and, relieved that he'd taken it so well, dared
to joke. 'Not altogether. After seeing some old reruns of *Star
Trek,* I've developed a passion for Mr Spock.'

Her lovely, luminous smile, the hint of mischief, beguiling and fascinating, hit him right over the heart, and for a
moment that vital organ seemed to miss a beat.

Striving to hide the effect her teasing had had on him, he
pulled himself together, and complained, 'Being compared to
Mr Spock and found wanting could seriously damage my ego.'

'Sorry,' she said, with mock contrition. 'I wouldn't want
to do that.'

'So you weren't suggesting that my ears aren't as exciting
as a Vulcan's?'

'I wouldn't darc.'

'I should hope not.'

His sudden white smile took her breath away and totally
overturned her earlier assessment that he lacked either charm
or charisma. Obviously he had lashings of both, hidden
beneath that cool veneer.

All at once, for no reason at all, her heart lifted, and she
found herself looking forward to the days and weeks ahead.

CHAPTER THREE

WATCHING her big brown eyes sparkle, Michael thought afresh how lovely she was.

He had been in Jenny's company now for several hours, and ought to be getting used to her beauty, almost taking it for granted.

But he wasn't.

In fact, just the opposite.

The fascination the first sight of her had aroused was still there, and growing stronger.

Which was bad news.

The last thing he wanted or needed was to be attracted to his new PA. That would be the ultimate irony, as Paul would be quick to point out.

That morning, when Paul had phoned to find out the result of the interview and Michael had admitted that Jennifer Mansell was on a month's trial, Paul had been quietly jubilant.

'I'm sure that in spite of all your doubts she'll prove to be just what you need.'

'We'll see,' Michael said cautiously. 'It depends on what kind of woman she turns out to be, and how I get on working with someone else.'

Paul grunted. 'Well, of course I can't answer for the latter, but, so far as Miss Mansell's concerned, I've heard nothing but good about her.

'Though I'll keep my ear to the ground, just in case, and if I *do* hear anything further I'll let you know. In the meantime stop being such a misogynist and give the poor girl a chance.

'She's known to be good at her job, and, as I said before, I don't think she's the kind to throw herself at you. If by any chance she does, for heaven's sake take her to bed. It might be just what you need to turn you back into a human being.'

'Thanks for the advice,' Michael said dryly, 'but I've had my fill of women.'

Now he found himself wondering how he would react if Jenny Mansell *did* throw herself at him.

So far she'd given not the slightest sign of wanting to do any such thing. Rather, she had trodden warily, as though negotiating a minefield, looking anything but comfortable whenever the conversation showed signs of straying into the more personal...

Becoming aware that time was passing, he swallowed the remains of his coffee and remarked, 'If you're ready, we really ought to be on our way.'

Jenny, who had been sitting quietly watching his face, wondering what he was thinking, said, 'Yes, I'm quite ready.'

'There would be no hurry if we didn't need to be over the causeway before the tide turns.'

His words reminded her of her earlier doubts about the advisability of being so isolated, and perhaps some of that uncertainty showed on her face because, frowning, he queried, 'Is there something wrong?'

She hesitated. If she did still have doubts, common sense told her she should voice them now, before it was too late...

He was watching her face, concerned that for some reason

she was going to back out at the last minute, and his voice was tense as he demanded, 'Well, is there?'

She lifted her chin, and, knowing that she was going anyway, regardless of doubts, answered, 'No, there's nothing wrong.'

'Then perhaps you'd like to freshen up while I pay the bill? I'll see you back at the car.'

As Jenny washed her hands and tucked a stray hair or two into the silky coil she rationalized her decision by telling herself that, having come this far, had she confessed to doubts he would have had every right to be angry.

She had a feeling that, in spite of his offer of a month's trial period, he hadn't been particularly keen to engage her in the first place, so he might have been glad of the opportunity to send her packing back to London.

Then not only would she have missed her chance to stay on Mirren, but it would have meant losing a job she'd really wanted without even starting it, and never seeing Michael Denver again.

The latter shouldn't really matter.

But somehow it did.

Though she was too aware of him to be altogether at ease in his company, she wanted the chance to get to know him better, to find out for herself just what kind of man he was, what made him tick.

When she made her way outside, he was waiting to settle her into the passenger seat.

The sun, though low in the sky, was still shining, but already the air seemed chillier, less clear, promising the onset of an early dusk.

'How long before we get to Mirren?' she asked as they left the Grouse and Claret behind them and headed for the coast.

'Half an hour or so.'

Unwilling to ask direct questions, she suggested innocently, 'Perhaps you could tell me something about the island?'

'What do you know already?'

'Apart from what I saw on that one short visit, and what you've already told me, nothing, really. I only know that it's always fascinated me.'

'Well, it's roughly nine miles long by three wide. The higher ground is interspersed with pasture land, and, apart from some stands of pines, the only trees are the ones around Slinterwood.

'Because the island has fresh water springs, it's been inhabited for centuries, and for most of that time it's been home to a rare breed of sheep similar to merinos, prized the world over for their fine, soft wool.

'These days a lot of the farmland has been turned into market gardens, which produce organic fruit and vegetables for the top London hotels.'

With a slight grin, he went on, 'At the risk of sounding like a guidebook, I'll just add that on the seaward side there are some pleasant sandy coves, ideal for summer picnics and swimming.'

'It sounds lovely.'

'It's certainly picturesque.'

She waited, hoping he'd tell her more about his connection with the island, and about the family who owned it.

But he changed the subject by remarking, 'One good thing about travelling at this time of the year is that there's not too much traffic.'

There proved to be less as they approached their destination. Even in high summer this part of the coast was relatively quiet, and now the coastal road was deserted in both directions as they joined the rough track that led down to the causeway.

Glancing at the water, Michael remarked, 'The tide must have turned some time ago.'

'How can you tell?' she asked.

'At low tide there are sand flats on either side of the causeway. Now they're almost covered, which means we're only just in time to get across.'

She felt another little shiver of pure pleasure at the thought of staying on the island she had always considered to be a special, enchanted place.

In the meantime, the here and now was magical. The early evening air was quite still, the water flat calm, the raised causeway, a shining ribbon edged by black and white marker poles, curled into the distance, where Mirren seemed to float, serene and enchanted, on a sea of beaten silver.

Dusk was already creeping in, veiling a sky of icy pearl with delicate wisps of grey and pink and the palest of greens.

Jenny found herself holding her breath as they started across the causeway, almost expecting the island to retreat before them like some mirage.

They were nearly halfway across when a slight change in the lie of the land brought into view the twelfth-century castle. Its towers and battlements silhouetted against the sky, it seemed to be part of the craggy outcrop of rock on which it stood.

As it had on her first visit, the sight brought a strange surge of emotion, and, feeling as if her heart were being squeezed by a giant fist, she sighed. It must have been wonderful to have lived there.

As though reading her thoughts, Michael remarked, 'It seems a shame that the castle is no longer inhabited.'

'Perhaps it's unsafe?' she hazarded.

He shook his head. 'Though the stone is crumbling a little in parts, it's still structurally sound.'

So *why* wasn't it still lived in? she wondered.

The question trembling on her lips, she glanced at him, but

something about his hard, clear-cut profile, the set of his jaw, convinced her that she had asked enough questions for one day, and, biting it back, she returned her attention to the view.

Leaving the causeway, where the impatient tide was already lapping at the marker poles, Michael took the road that she had driven up all those years ago.

Having reached the castle and passed the spot where she had parked previously, they carried on up the winding road, skirting a high bank on the right.

Growing on the rocky bank amongst the dried bracken were a straggle of gorse bushes, some of which were in full bloom.

As they drove up the hill, in the nearside mirror Jenny caught a glimpse of Mirren Castle from a new and intriguing angle, and asked impulsively, 'Would you mind very much if we stopped for a moment? I'd like to take a closer look at the castle.'

'Of course not.' He brought the car to a halt and climbed out to open her door. Then together they walked back a few yards to a natural vantage point.

The air was bitingly cold, and even in so short a time the sky was starting to lose its colour and get hazy, while a bank of cloud had appeared on the horizon behind the castle.

'It looks so different from here,' she exclaimed, after she'd studied it for a moment or two. 'I hadn't appreciated that the rear walls were built on a cliff that drops straight into the sea. It must have made it much easier to defend.'

'It was a virtually impregnable fortress in its day. The enemy got through its outer defences only once and that was due to an act of betrayal...'

Eager to hear more, she turned to look at him, her face expectant.

'One of the defenders, who had been bribed by the besieging army, crept down at night and raised the portcullis. But he didn't live to benefit from his treachery. It seems he was one of the first to be killed before the enemy were driven out.'

Seeing her shiver in the thin air, he broke off and said briskly, 'You're cold. We'd better get moving.'

As they walked back to the car, noticing the yellow gorse flowers glowing eerily now in the gathering dusk, she remarked wonderingly, 'Isn't it amazing how anything can bloom in such bitter weather?'

Reaching to open the car door, he said, 'Luckily, gorse blooms all the year round.'

She glanced up at him. 'Luckily?'

'Surely you've heard the old saying, "When gorse is in bloom, kissing's in season"?'

She smiled, and, glancing up to make some light remark, saw the sudden lick of flame in his eyes and read his intention.

But trapped between the car door and his tall, broad-shouldered frame all she could do was stand gazing up at him, her big brown eyes wide, her lips slightly parted, her wits totally scattered.

As he bent his dark head and kissed her mouth her eyes closed helplessly, shutting out the world and leaving only sensation.

Just at first his lips felt cold, then the coldness turned to heat as his mouth moved lightly against hers, making every nerve-ending in her body sing into life and sending her head spinning.

Though Jenny had been kissed many times, and though most of those kisses had been long and ardent, somehow they had failed to move her, leaving her feeling untouched, aloof, uninvolved.

Andy's kisses had been pleasurably different and exciting, yet even they had left some small part of her vaguely dis-satisfied.

But while Michael's thistledown kiss couldn't have lasted

more than a few seconds, by the time he lifted his head her legs would no longer hold her and her very soul seemed to have lost its way.

Opening dazed eyes, she became aware that he was half supporting her, and made an effort to find her feet and stand unaided.

Though he too had been knocked sideways, partly by her response, and partly by a torrent of feeling that had almost swept him away, his recovery was light years ahead of hers.

Cursing himself for a fool, he stepped back.

He hadn't meant it to happen. Kissing her had been a sudden impulse that he knew he ought to regret.

But somehow he couldn't.

Though if her office reputation was anything to go by, she should be angry at the liberty he'd taken, more than ready to slap him down.

But a quick glance at her face showed that she looked neither. She still appeared dazed, as if that kiss had shaken her as much as it had shaken him.

Seeing that she was starting to shiver, he opened the car door and, a hand beneath her elbow, helped her in.

Without a word, she sat down and fumbled for her seat belt. She still hadn't fastened it by the time he slid behind the wheel, and he leaned over to fasten it for her.

As his muscular thigh accidentally pressed against hers, though she said nothing, he felt her instinctive withdrawal.

While he started the car and put it into gear, Jenny made an effort to pull herself together and make sense of her feelings.

After all, what had happened really? Just a light, casual kiss to illustrate an old saying. A kiss that had clearly held no importance for him.

Yet remembering that little lick of flame in his green eyes before he had kissed her, she wondered if it *had* been quite that casual. Or had it been a preliminary? A chance to test the water, so to speak?

Though from what she'd heard, she had formed the distinct impression that after his disastrous marriage Michael Denver was reluctant to have anything to do with the female sex. And the vibes she had picked up during the interview had gone to support that.

Recalling how his jaw had tightened as though he was in pain when the landlord of the inn had mentioned his ex-wife and the likelihood of a reconciliation, she wondered if perhaps he still loved her.

From all accounts *she* had been the one to stray, and perhaps, when it was too late, she had found herself regretting that lapse.

After all, she had opposed the divorce. And she must believe he still loved her, or she wouldn't have talked to the press about the possibility of them getting back together.

True, he had denied it, but maybe it was only his hurt pride and anger that had so far prevented him from taking her back? Or maybe he was simply teaching her a lesson?

If he was, *while* he was, he might need a woman in his bed. Sex without strings or commitments, simply to assuage a natural appetite?

But in these days of sexual freedom and equality, many women felt the same.

And why not?

Except that personally she couldn't embrace that way of thinking. So if Michael Denver *was* hoping for someone to keep his bed warm while he was away from London—and that could account for the very generous salary—she might have a problem.

It was a far from reassuring thought, and she began to wish that she hadn't accepted his offer.

'Another minute or so and you'll be able to see Slinterwood Bay.' His quiet remark broke into her uneasy thoughts.

His tone was so down-to-earth, so mundane, that all at once her vision of having to fight him off dissolved into the absurd.

Talk about letting her imagination run away with her! It was just as well he didn't know what she'd been thinking, otherwise he would be wondering what kind of madwoman he had hired as his PA.

Still berating herself, she turned her attention to the scenery once more.

They had breasted the rise and were following the coast road that curled round behind the bluff. On their left the dimpled sea was spread like a sheet of pewter in the silver-grey dusk, the tide creeping up the smooth expanse of sand and eddying between low outcrops of rock in the small bay.

The sky was still clear enough to catch a glimpse of a thin silver crescent of moon, while far out to sea a bank of purple cloud formed a mountain range on the horizon.

'And there's Slinterwood itself.'

In a sheltered hollow at the foot of the hills, a stand of mixed trees, some deciduous, some coniferous, curved a protective arm around a long, low, creeper-clad house.

Wisps of pale smoke were curling lazily from two of its barley-sugar chimneys and hanging in the still air like twin genies.

Surrounded by a low-walled terrace, the house was built of stone, with crooked gables, overhanging eaves, and dormer windows. It looked as if it had stood in that spot since time immemorial.

On the seaward side, stone steps ran down to the beach where, well above the high-water mark, a small blue and white rowboat had been turned upside down.

They took the track through the trees that led to the front terrace, and came to a halt by an old oak door with a lighted lantern above it.

Jenny smiled. With an arched top, black iron studs and hinges, and wood bleached to a pale, silvery grey, it was the kind of enchanted door that was familiar from childhood fairy tales.

Either side of the door were long windows made of small, square panes of glass, the edges encroached on by trails of ivy.

When she had gathered up her coat and bag, Michael helped her out, before retrieving her case.

He appeared to have no luggage of his own, but of course, as he came here regularly, it would be like a second home.

Lifting his head, he asked, 'Can you feel how still it is?'

And it was. Nothing moved in the blue-grey dusk. Not a single twig stirred, not an ivy-leaf quivered. Everything was so calm and motionless it was as if the very air held its breath in anticipation of the coming night.

'Winter evenings on Mirren often bring this kind of stillness,' he added as they made their way over to the door.

Jenny had half expected the housekeeper to be waiting, but when no one materialized, apparently unsurprised, Michael produced an ornate key and turned it in the huge iron lock.

Then, swinging open the heavy door, he switched on the lights and ushered her into a panelled hall that ran the entire width of the house.

There were doors to the right and left, and at the opposite end—like a mirror image of the landward side—were a matching door and windows that looked towards the dusky sea.

The wide floorboards were of polished oak, and on the right a dark oak staircase climbed up to the second floor.

Since drawing up outside, and seeing that fairy-tale door, Jenny had felt as if she knew the place. Now, as she stepped over the threshold, she had the strangest feeling that she had been here before. That the old house had been waiting for her return, and welcomed her back.

Catching sight of her expressive face, Michael asked, 'What is it?'

'Nothing...' Seeing he wasn't convinced, she admitted, 'I just had the strangest feeling that I know the house. That it's familiar...'

He set her case down, and without believing it for an instant suggested, 'Perhaps you've been to Slinterwood before?'

'No, I'm sure I haven't. It must be déjà vu.'

Yet though she was quite certain she had never been here before, the feeling of warmth, of being made welcome, of coming home, persisted.

Michael, who had always believed that houses had their own aesthetic or emotional effect or appeal, an atmosphere that anyone sensitive could pick up as vibes, asked carefully, 'This feeling... Is it an unpleasant one?'

'No... No, anything but.'

'But quite strong?'

'Yes. Very.'

'When you say you feel you know the house, can you visualize the layout of the rooms?'

'No... I don't think so...'

Something impelled him to say, 'Try.'

Standing quite still, she closed her eyes. 'The doors on the same side of the hall as the stairs lead to a big living-kitchen and... I suppose you'd call it a morning room.

'Next to the kitchen there's a walk-in larder that has a green marble cold-slab, and a deep porcelain sink with an old-fashioned water pump over it.'

'Go on,' he ordered tersely.

With no idea where she was getting such clear mental pictures, she obeyed. 'Across the hall, there's a long living-room on the seaward side, and behind that a library-cum-study and a dining-room.'

'What about upstairs?'

Opening her eyes, she said, 'I'm not sure… I think there's a master bedroom above the living-room, and several smaller bedrooms with fireplaces, sloping ceilings, and polished floorboards.

'At the end of a corridor, there are two steps down to a big, old-fashioned bathroom, with a claw-footed bathtub…'

A curious note in his voice, he said, 'And you think that's an accurate description of the rooms?'

She shook her head with a self-deprecating smile. 'I'd be very surprised if it were.'

'Why?'

'Well, either it's complete guesswork, or it's something I've dreamt at one time or another.'

Though she tried to keep it light, the clearness and certainty of those mental pictures had shaken her somewhat.

With no further comment, he picked up her case and turned to lead the way up the stairs and along a corridor with polished oak floorboards.

'I understand from Mrs Blair that she's put you in the lilac room.'

He slanted her a quick glance, as if he expected some comment, but all she could think of to say was, 'That sounds lovely.'

It was a pleasant room on the seaward side of the house, with light, modern furniture, pale lilac walls, white paintwork and, rather to her surprise, an en-suite bathroom.

Except for the sloping ceiling, the polished oak floorboards and scattered rugs, it wasn't at all what she had visualized.

Knowing he was watching her face and aware of the relief she couldn't altogether hide, she observed, 'There's no fireplace.'

His voice level, he told her, 'At one time there were fireplaces in all the rooms. But apart from the one in the main bedroom, they were taken out some three or four years ago when oil-fired central heating and en-suite bathrooms were put in.'

'Oh,' she said, a shade hollowly.

Putting her case on an oak blanket chest, he offered, 'Before you make yourself at home, I'll show you the rest of the upstairs.'

Opening doors and switching on lights as they went, he told her, 'Next door is my room…'

The main bedroom was a large, attractive room with a black-beamed ceiling, polished period furniture, and a stone fireplace, in which a log fire had been laid ready.

'And across the landing,' he went on, 'there are three smaller bedrooms, pretty much the same as yours, and a bathroom.'

The bathroom, which was at the end of a short corridor and down two steps, had a claw-footed bathtub, just as she had described.

Seeing he was waiting for her to say something, she offered as carelessly as possible, 'A lucky guess.'

Though he frowned a little, he made no comment.

As they went back across the landing he suggested, 'When you've had time to freshen up, come down and we'll have a cup of tea before I show you round the rest of the house.'

Nodding her thanks, she returned to her room, where she gnawed her lip thoughtfully.

Common sense told her that it was silly to find herself still wondering if she'd been here before, when she knew quite well she hadn't.

So where had those vivid mental pictures come from?

Having seen the outside of the house—with its steep gables and plethora of chimney pots—the fireplaces and sloping ceilings were a logical deduction. While the position of the bathroom, and the steps leading down to it, *must* have been just a lucky guess.

But although she did her utmost to explain away what had happened, the feeling of *knowing* the house still persisted.

Oh, well, she thought, it was a warm, friendly feeling, so she wouldn't worry about it.

When she had washed her hands and tidied her hair she descended the stairs and crossed the hall, still with that feeling of being at home, and opened the living-room door.

It was a long spacious room with pale walls and a beamed ceiling, comfortably furnished and homely, as she had known it would be. It was lit by a couple of standard lamps and the glow of a log fire.

Pulled up to the hearth were two soft leather armchairs, and on a low table between them was a tray of tea and a plate of what appeared to be home-made scones, with small dishes of jam and cream.

Glancing up from the chair he was occupying, Michael invited, 'Come and join me.'

Once again rocked by the impact the sight of him always had on her, she obeyed, and, taking a seat opposite, remarked, 'Though the whole house is anything but cold, this is really cosy.'

'So long as the electric pump's working, the central heating keeps the place at a comfortable temperature,' he agreed.

'Strictly speaking,' he went on, 'the fires are only necessary when the electricity supply fails. But I love an open fire, especially in the winter.'

'So do I,' she agreed wholeheartedly.

'Why?'

'Why?' she echoed uncertainly.

'Yes, why?'

'Well, I—I find a fire is visually pleasing. It brings a room to life…'

'Go on.'

Somewhat fazed by his persistence, she attempted to put her feelings into words. 'As far as I'm concerned, a fire meets some primitive need that's made up of more than just the requirement for warmth.'

It was so close to his own feelings—feelings that Claire had neither understood nor shared—that he was taken aback, But all he could find to say was, 'Very nicely put.'

Unsure whether or not he was mocking her, and deciding to change the subject, she asked, 'Would you like me to pour the tea?'

'If you wouldn't mind,' he agreed smoothly.

Outwardly serene, she assembled fine china cups patterned with a ring of tiny flowers, and reached for the matching teapot. 'How do you like your tea?'

'A little milk, no sugar.'

Watching her calm face and graceful movements, he frowned a little. She both puzzled and intrigued him. The fact that she knew the house had taken him by surprise, and he wanted to see into her mind, to know how she had managed to come by such detailed knowledge and information.

There had to be some explanation, and sooner or later he would find it, he promised himself as, with a word of thanks, he accepted the cup and saucer she passed him.

Taking a sip, he added, 'It's nice to be waited on occasionally.'

Deciding to play the gracious hostess, if that was what he wanted, she offered him a plate and a scone.

His face straight but his eyes amused, as if he knew exactly what she was thinking, he accepted the plate and took a scone.

Watching her replace the rest, he queried, 'Won't you join me?'

As she started to shake her head he added persuasively, 'Mrs Blair is proud of her scones, and quite rightly.'

'They look very tempting,' Jenny admitted. 'But I don't think so.'

'Why not?' Recalling Claire's horrified expression when he'd suggested that she try one, he added, 'You're not worried about a few extra calories, are you? You're plenty slim enough.'

'No… Luckily I have the right kind of metabolism, so I don't need to worry about putting on weight. It's just that I had such a big lunch.'

'So did I. But we can't hurt Mrs Blair's feelings.'

He smiled at her, a white, slightly crooked smile that put fascinating creases beside his mouth, lit up his face, and warmed his green eyes. 'Tell you what, shall we share one?'

Beguiled by his smile and that teasing glance, and wondering how she could ever have thought him unattractive, she found herself agreeing. 'Why not?'

He split the light, floury scone in two and spread both halves with jam and a generous amount of cream, before cutting each piece into four quarters.

Then on an impulse, he picked up one of the pieces and reached across to offer it.

Without conscious volition she opened her mouth, and he fed it to her.

Thrown by the gesture, she sat like someone in a dream and watched him eat his own piece.

The little ritual was repeated until the scone was all gone.

Though she had told herself it was nothing, and tried to appear calm and unmoved, something about the unexpected intimacy had made her feel hollow inside, and her hand was shaking slightly when she lifted her cup to her lips.

CHAPTER FOUR

WATCHING Jenny, and seeing the slight flush on her cheeks, Michael wondered what on earth had impelled him to act in that way.

But whatever it had been her reaction had proved surprising. Any other newly hired PA would have either backed off or made a big deal of it.

She had done neither.

Though clearly taken by surprise, she had met the informality with a kind of sweet, slightly shy acceptance that he had found oddly moving.

Now she was avoiding his eyes, looking anywhere but at him, and he noticed that the hand holding her teacup wasn't quite steady.

He was wondering how best to restore the status quo when the lights flickered and seemed momentarily in danger of going out.

'It looks as though the generator is on the blink again,' he remarked, 'which can be a nuisance when I'm working.'

'It must be,' she agreed in a heartfelt voice.

'If the story's flowing,' he went on, 'I hate to be held up. That's one of the reasons I decided I needed a PA who can take shorthand.'

'Does it go on the blink often?'

'From time to time it gets temperamental and leaves us in the dark.'

Which no doubt accounted for the oil lamps she had noticed scattered around. 'And you've only that to rely on?'

''Fraid so. At the moment there's no national-grid electricity on the island. Nor are there any phone lines. Plans are under way to have both by next year, but at the moment a mobile is essential.'

'Oh, dear!' she exclaimed. In the excitement and the rush to get ready, she had left hers on charge.

'You have a problem?'

'It's only that I've just realized I've forgotten to bring mine.'

'Is there anyone you need to get in touch with?'

She half shook her head. 'Not at the moment. I left a note for my flatmate… It's just that I feel lost without my mobile.'

'Well, if the need arises, you can always borrow mine. More tea?'

'No, thanks. What about you?'

He shook his head, and, keen to see her reaction to the rest of the house, suggested, 'Shall we continue the tour?'

She rose and accompanied him to a door at the far end of the room that led through to a red-carpeted library-cum-study.

It was a large, handsome room with book-lined walls and a wide stone fireplace, in which a fire had been laid ready.

The fireplace itself was ornate, the stone surround decorated with mythical birds and beasts. In the centre of the mantel was a symbol she knew well, a phoenix rising from the ashes.

Perhaps that in itself wasn't remarkable.

What *was* remarkable was that she had *known* it was there even before she'd looked.

A little shiver ran down her spine.

But she was making too much of it, she told herself

sturdily. That kind of ornamentation was no doubt quite common. She could almost have expected it.

Realizing that Michael was waiting for her, she pulled herself together and prepared to move on.

He opened a communicating door, and ushered her through. 'At one time this was the dining-room, but it was so little used that I decided to make it into an office.'

It was clear that she had been mistaken in presuming he just rented the house. To be able to make that kind of major alteration, he must surely own it.

The office was sparsely furnished and businesslike, its windows fitted with slatted blinds. There was a smoke-grey carpet, a large desk on which sat a computer and a printer, a black leather swivel chair, a bookcase full of what appeared to be reference books, and a filing cabinet.

With no ornaments or pictures, it was clearly intended as a place to work without any distractions.

Leaving by a door on the far side, they crossed the hall and went through into a large living-kitchen, with comfortable-looking rustic furniture and a big, wood-burning range.

'As you can see, it's been brought up to date fairly recently,' Michael remarked.

Looking at all the mod cons, which included a microwave and a dishwasher, Jenny asked, 'And there's no problem with the power?'

'So long as everything isn't switched on at the same time, the generator, which is housed through here—' he let her peep into what had once been a stable block and was now garages '—manages to cope.

'Next door to the kitchen is the cold larder, which has been left more or less as it was…'

If the kitchen hadn't disturbed her serenity, the larder did. There were the shelves and cupboards, the green marble slab at the far end, and the deep porcelain sink with its old-fashioned water pump, just as she had visualized it.

'And it fits your description perfectly,' he went on softly, 'even to the pump.' Then, like a cobra striking, 'Do you think it works?'

'Oh, yes,' she said with certainty.

'You're quite right. But how did you know?'

Thrown, she stammered, 'Well, I—I didn't really.'

But when he'd asked the question, she had pictured clear water gushing from the spout when the handle was pumped up and down.

Until then she had been trying to treat the whole thing lightly, as though it was some game. Now the *strangeness* of it threw her, making her feel nervous, unsure, as though she were stranded on thin ice that might give way at any moment and plunge her into dark and unknown depths.

His eyes on her face, he queried, 'And you're *sure* you've never been here before?'

'Positive.'

She looked and sounded genuinely shaken, and for a moment he was almost tempted to believe her. But only for a moment, then common sense returned, making him wonder what kind of game she was playing.

After his divorce, some women had gone to great and diverse lengths to capture his interest, but none as intriguing or as well planned as this.

But how *could* she have planned it?

To have come up with such an accurate description of the house, she must have been here before, seen photographs of the place, or been told all about it. And she hadn't known where he was taking her until the very last minute.

Perhaps Paul had mentioned that he did his writing at Slinterwood, and given her detailed information about the place?

Knowing Paul, that didn't seem very likely, but it was the only logical explanation he could come up with. Unless she was clairvoyant.

'Perhaps you have second sight?' he suggested, half in earnest.

A little flustered by the concept, she assured him, 'No, not that I know of. But if I believed in reincarnation, I might think I'd lived here in some previous life.'

'And do you? Believe in reincarnation, I mean?'

'No.'

'So how do you account for it?'

She couldn't.

But still she tried. 'When I've had the chance I've always enjoyed visiting National Trust properties and stately homes... All I can think is, I must have seen, and half remembered, another house enough like Slinterwood to superimpose the two.'

It sounded weak even in her own ears, and a little defensively she said, 'I'm afraid it's the only explanation I can come up with.'

'There *could* be another one,' he mentioned, his voice even.

When she looked at him uncomprehendingly, he went on, 'Paul knows Slinterwood quite well—perhaps he told you all about it?'

She shook her head. 'No.'

Then, catching the fleeting expression of doubt that crossed his face, she added sturdily, 'You can ask him if you don't believe me. I'd never even *heard* of Slinterwood until you mentioned it earlier today.'

There was an unmistakable ring of truth in the words that brought him up short, and he found himself saying quietly, 'I do believe you.'

She relaxed a little as they moved on and came to a halt outside the final door.

'What you thought might be a morning room is actually the housekeeper's room. Or should I say it used to be, when there was a housekeeper.'

'But I thought… You mentioned a Mrs Blair. Isn't *she* the housekeeper?'

'Mrs Blair is the wife of one of the estate workers, and lives in the hamlet just down the coast. She cleans and airs the place when I'm in London and gets everything ready for when I'm coming down, while her son does the heavy work and takes care of the generator.

'But once I'm here I prefer to look after myself without interruptions, so she doesn't come in unless I ask her to.'

'Oh… Oh, I see…' Jenny said, all her previous doubts about the wisdom of being isolated here with him—especially now she'd discovered they were quite alone—flooding back.

He smiled a little, as if reading her thoughts, and assured her, 'Don't worry, even if we are here all by ourselves I'm not going to turn into an axe murderer or a dangerous psychopath.'

She flushed. 'I didn't think you were.'

And it was true. After her reaction to that earlier kiss, and the shared intimacy by the fire, her worries were of a different nature.

Once again reading her mind with deadly accuracy, he queried, 'But you do have other concerns?'

'Other concerns?' she echoed. Then hastily, 'No! No, certainly not.'

'Well, in that case,' he said blandly, 'I'll leave you to unpack and settle in while I make a phone call or two.'

Jenny climbed the stairs, her thoughts chaotic. Had she been wise to say she had no other concerns? After all, it could be interpreted in two ways.

Normally both her brain and her tongue were well coordinated and under control, but Michael Denver had the disturbing ability to scatter her wits and turn her into a gibbering idiot.

Thinking back to the original interview, she had foolishly stated, 'A good PA should do whatever it takes to keep her boss happy.'

Suppose he'd taken that to mean she was willing to share his bed? If he had, and he turned up the heat, where would that leave her?

Here. Quite alone with him. And vulnerable.

It wasn't that she was afraid he might overstep the mark. What shook her was the sudden realization that he might not need to, that it wasn't so much *him* she wasn't sure she could trust as *herself.*

But surely she would only have to remind herself of the past, of her humiliating failure at relationships, to enable her to keep the barriers firmly in place?

While she had waited for the right man to appear, she had been more than able to keep other males at bay with a cool reserve that had effectively frozen them off.

Then Andy had come along.

He had seemed to be the one, and, their wedding only a few weeks away, she had given in to his pleas to sleep with him.

Until the flat they were planning to rent became vacant, Andy had been sharing a flat with a man named Simon. A small flat with paper-thin walls and very little privacy.

Knowing that Simon might walk in at any moment had put Jenny on edge, and, despite Andy's assurance that his flatmate 'wouldn't give a toss', she had been unable to relax.

Though she had tried very hard to please him, to be everything he had wanted her to be, the experience had left her feeling bitterly disappointed and woefully inadequate.

She had hoped that Andy would understand and be patient. But, showing a less than pleasant side of his nature, a side she had never seen before, he had accused her of not caring enough, of lacking warmth and passion and being next door to frigid.

That night, back in her own bed, she had cried herself to sleep.

The following morning, rallying a little, she had tried to tell herself that things would improve once they were in their own flat and married.

But her confidence, both in herself and in Andy's professed love for her, had been badly shaken.

Then, not long afterwards, and quite by chance, she had discovered that he was two-timing her.

Their flat had finally been vacated, and she had been taking some things round when she had discovered him in what would have been their bed, with another woman, and the bottom had dropped out of her world.

She had thrown his ring at him, and, feeling used and betrayed, hurt and humiliated and bitterly angry, vowed never to trust another man.

Laura, ever practical, had said, 'You should thank your lucky stars that you found out what the swine was really like before you married him.'

While recognizing the sense of that, it had still taken her months to get over the hurt, to claw back some of her pride and self-respect, and bury her feelings of inadequacy.

So how could she think of herself as *vulnerable* when it came to a man like Michael Denver? A man who, apart from one brief kiss, had really shown no interest in her as anything other than his hired PA.

Yet somehow she did.

It made no sense, but that one light kiss had moved her in a way that no other man's kisses had.

Though that didn't mean she had to act like a complete numbskull, she scolded herself. She'd always been very successful at masking her feelings, a trait that had helped her enormously when it came to dealing with difficulties in either her personal or professional life, and that was what she would do with Michael, at least until she got her newly awakened libido under control!

Having succeeded in convincing herself that she'd been fretting over nothing, she pushed any remaining worries to the back of her mind, and, closing the heavy curtains to shut out the darkness pressing against the panes, set about unpacking.

Putting her nightdress and dressing gown on the end of the bed, she stowed the rest of her things neatly away in the wardrobe and the chest of drawers, while she debated changing out of the suit she was wearing.

A lingering caution suggested she should stick with the businesslike image. But while she could see the sense of that, she felt the need to change into something easier, slightly less formal.

Having decided, she stripped off the suit and hung it in the wardrobe before freshening up in the pretty lilac and white bathroom.

Then, making a positive statement, she chose a simple olive-green dress that Laura had disgustedly described as 'matronly', and slipped it on.

Somehow she had to get through their first evening alone together with the guidelines firmly in place and her composure intact.

Hopefully he would want to begin work as soon as dinner was over—she grasped at the prospect like a lifeline—and once their attention was fixed firmly on his next book it should make things a lot easier.

When she descended the stairs and made her way to the living-room, she found it was empty. Which might possibly mean he was already in his office working.

But that too was empty, as was the library.

She finally ran him to earth in the kitchen where, his

sleeves rolled up and a tea towel draped around his lean hips, he was using two wooden spoons to toss a green salad.

The oak table was already set with a fish platter, a bowl of what looked like home-made dressing, and a basket of crispy rolls. A bottle of white wine waited in a cooler.

Glancing up from his task, he said, 'Two things. I hope you like fish?'

'Yes, I do.'

'And I hope you don't mind eating in the kitchen?'

'No, not at all.' Glancing at the glowing range, which had been set in an inglenook fireplace, she observed, 'It's nice and homely.'

'I decided to keep the old range to sit in front of, and cook on if the generator fails.'

Her hair, he noted, was still in the businesslike coil and her dress, with its long sleeves, calf-length skirt and demure neckline, clearly wasn't intended to be provocative.

It didn't look as if she had any plans to vamp him, he thought with wry humour.

But though the dress was conservative, it was far from dull. The silky material clung lovingly to the curve of her bust and waist, and swirled becomingly around her slender legs when she moved.

Aware of his scrutiny, she asked quickly, 'Is there anything I can do to help?'

According to Claire, most women disliked having to get their own drinks, and, deciding to put her to the test, he suggested, 'Perhaps you wouldn't mind getting us both a drink?'

A loaded drinks trolley was standing to one side, and while she surveyed the various bottles he watched her.

When her inspection was over, appearing completely unfazed, she queried, 'What would you like?'

'A dry Martini with ice and lemon, please.'

'Shaken not stirred, presumably?'

He grinned. 'What else?'

Spooning crushed ice into a silver cocktail shaker, she teased, 'Your middle name doesn't happen to be James, by any chance?'

His face straight, so that she didn't know whether or not to believe him, he told her, 'As a matter of fact it does.'

With a composure that suggested she knew exactly what she was doing, she added measures of vodka and French vermouth to the ice and shook it thoroughly, before pouring the mixture into two Martini glasses and adding a twist of lemon to each.

Handing him one, she suggested, 'Try this and see if it's to your taste.'

'Thanks.'

As he accepted the glass their fingers brushed and a kind of electric shock tingled up her arm.

She had read about that effect in romantic novels, but had never believed it could happen in real life. Now, as she found it could, her composure abruptly deserted her.

He made no comment, but the gleam in his eye told her he knew.

When he'd taken a sip of the cocktail, he said, 'Spot on.' Then, with a lopsided grin, 'You may have just added bartender to the other things I expect my PA to do.'

She couldn't help wondering exactly what he meant by 'other things', but was too chicken to ask.

There was a pair of rocking chairs in front of the range with a low table between them, and, trembling inside, her legs none too steady, she took her own glass and went to sit by the fire.

When the salad was mixed to his satisfaction, he discarded the tea towel and joined her by the fire.

Glass in hand, he leaned back comfortably, his legs crossed neatly at the ankles. 'The meal's ready, but if you're in no hurry…?'

'Well, no, I'm not… But I—'

'Then I suggest we relax for a while and get to know one another.'

Judging by the expression on her face, Michael thought, she didn't welcome his suggestion.

That impression was amply confirmed when she hurried on, 'I thought you might want to eat straight away so you could work later?'

'No. I wasn't thinking of doing any work tonight.'

'Oh…' she said, her lifeline gone and her heart sinking. Then rallying, 'So what time will you want to start in the morning?'

He shook his head. 'I won't. After the pressures of London life, I usually take a day or two to relax and unwind while I mull over my next plot.'

'Oh,' she said hollowly.

If only he *would* get down to writing in earnest, she thought in helpless frustration. As soon as he had made a start and his book was absorbing all his attention, she would feel a great deal happier.

'And one of the best ways to do that, I find, is to go walking.'

Well, at least he'd be out.

'Do you like walking?'

Ambushed by the question, she answered truthfully, 'Yes.' Adding, 'Before I went to live in London I used to walk for miles along the beach—' Suddenly realizing where her answer might be leading, she broke off abruptly.

But her anxiety was put at rest when he merely said, 'Of course, at this time of the year it depends to a great extent on the weather. Rain's forecast, so if it happens to be heavy it might be expedient to find some other form of relaxation.'

The prospect of him ending up housebound because of the weather wasn't one that pleased her.

His face straight but a hint of amusement in his voice, he observed, 'You seem positively disappointed at the thought of not starting work straight away.'

She blurted out the first thing that came into her head. 'I—I've never worked for a writer before and I can't wait to see how a book comes to life, and to know I'm playing some small part in its creation.'

Then grasping at what, hopefully, would be a safe topic, she asked, 'Do you begin by plotting out the various chapters?'

Normally he never discussed his writing with anyone, but as they were going to be working together he decided to go along with it.

'No. I usually start with just a bare idea of the storyline. Then I concentrate on the characters, and their relationship to one other.

'Once I have those things clear in my mind, I start to make preliminary notes.

'If it begins to gel, I'm under way. If it doesn't, I start all over again...'

She soon found herself fascinated by what had begun as a mere expedient, and listened eagerly.

Although the conversation wasn't going along the lines he had planned, responding to what he recognized as a genuine and intelligent interest, Michael answered her questions freely.

Though she hadn't stated as much, from the questions she asked it soon became clear that she had read his books.

More than read them—*knew* them.

By the time he paused to suggest that it might be time to eat, Jenny had forgotten both her motive for starting the conversation and her earlier agitation.

When she was seated, he helped her to a selection of seafood and some of the crisp salad before pouring wine for them both.

While they ate a leisurely meal he kept the conversation light and impersonal, and she relaxed even more.

By the time they returned to sit in front of the stove with their coffee, she realized that their first evening alone together was almost over.

Though she was too conscious of him to be totally comfortable, she had not only survived the day, but in some respects thoroughly enjoyed it.

Their cups were empty, and she was about to mention that she would like an early night when, out of the blue, he remarked, 'I find it almost impossible to believe that a beautiful woman like you has no man in her life.'

When, flustered, she said nothing, he fished, 'But possibly you haven't met the right one yet?'

Uneasy about the direction the conversation was taking, but feeling the need to say something, she admitted, 'I was once engaged to be married.'

'Oh, when was that?'

'It ended six months ago.'

'May I ask what happened?'

Endeavouring to hide the feelings that, in spite of all her efforts, were still somewhat painful, she said flatly, 'I gave him back his ring when, a few weeks before we were due to be married, I found him in bed with another woman.'

'So presumably you don't believe in...shall we say...open-ended relationships?'

'I have some friends who do, but that kind of relationship isn't for me.'

'Even if you really loved the man?'

'*Especially* if I loved him.'

'And you haven't met anyone you could fall in love with since your engagement broke up?'

'No,' she answered.

Then before Michael could delve any further, she put her cup on the low table and rose to her feet. 'Now if you'll excuse me, it's been a long day, and last night I didn't sleep very well…'

It was the truth. Anxious about the forthcoming interview, she had been unable to settle, and had tossed and turned for a long time before finally falling into an uneasy doze.

'So I'm really tired,' she added.

He was about to try and persuade her to stay when, seeing her stifle a yawn and noticing that there were faint blue shadows beneath her eyes, he uncoiled his long length and agreed, 'Then bed it is.'

This wasn't at all what she had planned, and, disconcerted, she blurted, 'Oh, please… Don't let me disturb you.'

'You're not. I was rather looking forward to a reasonably early night, myself.'

The ground cut neatly from beneath her feet, she had no choice but to let him escort her upstairs, switching out lights as they went.

At her bedroom door he paused, and, blocking her way, stood looking down at her.

Taking a deep, unsteady breath, she stammered, 'Well, g-goodnight.'

Putting a single finger against her cheek, he said, 'Goodnight. Sleep well.'

As, his light touch rooting her to the spot, she gazed up at him like a mesmerized rabbit, he bent towards her.

The conviction that he was about to kiss her again galvanized her into action, and, flinching away, she brushed past him and fled into her room, followed by the sound of his soft laughter.

Once inside, her heart racing, her breath coming fast, she

leaned weakly against the door panels. A moment later she heard his light footsteps move away, and then the door of his room close.

Angry with herself, and even angrier with him when she recalled that mocking laughter, she wished fervently that, rather than panicking and running away, she had kept her head.

She should have stood her ground and made it plain that she had simply come here to do a job and wasn't in the market for a bit of light dalliance. Instead she had acted like a silly, immature schoolgirl.

But then that was the effect Michael Denver had had on her from the start.

She groaned inwardly. However was she going to face him in the morning?

But even as she quailed at the prospect, she realized that something about the little scene that had just taken place didn't quite add up.

Michael was a skilful, sophisticated man, not an inexperienced youth liable to dither, and there had been ample opportunity, not only for him to kiss her, but to start a big seduction scene if he'd really wanted to.

So why, instead of just getting on with it, had he telegraphed his intention?

Had he wanted to see her reaction?

Or had the whole thing been just a charade, a deliberate attempt to fluster her?

Oh, come on! Common sense stuck in its oar. Why should he *want* to fluster her?

Wasn't she, once again, letting her imagination run away with her? Wasn't it much more likely that she had been totally mistaken? That he hadn't intended to kiss her at all?

If she *had* misinterpreted what had been just an innocent movement on his part, and bolted, no wonder he had laughed.

She groaned again. It was a toss up which of the scenarios was worst, she thought as she picked up her nightie before heading for the bathroom to clean her teeth and prepare for bed.

Perhaps, in the morning, after making such a fool of herself, it might be better to tell him that she had had second thoughts and wanted to leave?

But did she really want to leave Slinterwood?

The answer had to be no.

Though the strange rapport she felt with the house made her extremely reluctant to leave it, she was forced to admit that the overriding reason for wanting to stay was Michael Denver himself.

Being in his company wasn't altogether comfortable, but it gave her a buzz, sharpened her perceptions, and made all her senses diamond-bright.

Love was supposed to have the same effect, she mused as she stepped out of the shower and began to dry herself. But though she had thought herself in love with Andy, he had never made her feel so aware, so *alive*.

Perhaps she had been turned on by the thought of working for a writer of Michael's calibre?

She had certainly *wanted* the job, but what she hadn't bargained for was her unprecedented reaction to the man himself.

Though surely she could keep that under control? she thought as she pulled on her nightdress.

Admittedly she had made a poor job of it so far, but the first day was over, and from now on things should get easier. All she needed to do was keep cool and not let him fluster her.

CHAPTER FIVE

JENNY awoke next morning to find it was almost nine o'clock. After lying awake for several hours the previous night unable to stop thinking about what a fool she'd made of herself, she had overslept.

It was just as well Michael didn't want to start work immediately.

Jumping out of bed, she drew aside the curtains and looked out of the window at the lovely, peaceful scene spread before her.

The sea resembled a slightly wrinkled sheet of silver paper with a lacy edging of filigree where the waves washed gently up the pale sand.

For as far as she could see in either direction the beach was deserted, the only sign of life a grey cormorant standing on one of the rocky outcrops, spreading out its wings to dry.

Despite the fact that rain had been forecast, the sun was shining and the sky was a clear baby-blue.

With a bit of luck, she thought, Michael Denver might take himself off for a long walk.

But even if he did, she would have to face him first, and, remembering his mocking laughter, she found it was a daunting prospect.

What was she to say to him? How could she excuse her stupid behaviour?

The answer was, she couldn't.

However, knowing it was no use putting off the evil moment, she went purposefully into the bathroom to clean her teeth and shower.

Having dressed for the day in tailored fawn trousers, a donkey-brown blouse and flat-heeled pumps, she coiled her hair, applied a little make-up and sallied downstairs before her courage failed her.

She found him in the kitchen breaking eggs into a pan. An appetizing smell of coffee and grilling bacon filled the air.

'Good morning.' His tone was measured, his manner practical, down-to-earth. There was no sign of the mockery or derision she had half expected.

Even so, she was unable to meet his eyes as she responded with a polite, 'Good morning.'

Noting that evasion, and guessing the cause, he smiled inwardly.

Last night, at her bedroom door, he had been very tempted to kiss her again, but then, reminding himself of all the problems such a move could cause, he had drawn back.

That hesitation had given her the chance to step in and show her true colours, but instead of reacting seductively her response had been to bolt like a startled rabbit.

Which could mean one of two things. Either she was as innocent and naive as she appeared, or she was playing some deep game.

Abandoning the puzzle for the time being, he asked, 'Sleep well?'

She picked up the slightest hint of amusement in the question—as if he already knew the answer—but, choosing to ignore it, she lied, 'Yes, very well, thank you.'

'If you'd like to sit down and pour the coffee, breakfast is almost ready.'

As she obeyed he queried, 'How do you like your eggs? Sunny side up? Or asleep?'

'Asleep, please.'

'Same here.' Expertly flicking fat over the yokes, he added, 'But then I was already sure that our two hearts beat as one.'

Her hand shook a little and some of the coffee she was pouring spilt into the saucer.

'Damn,' she muttered.

Hiding a smile, he turned away to dish up the crispy bacon and perfectly cooked eggs.

They ate without speaking, and only when Michael removed their empty plates to stack in the dishwasher did she find her voice and say, 'Thank you. That was very nice.'

'Toast and marmalade?' he offered.

'No, thanks, I've had quite enough.'

Resuming his seat, he refilled their coffee cups and observed, 'The rain seems to be holding off, so I think a good long walk is indicated.'

Unsure whether or not he was including her, and reluctant to say anything in case he hadn't been and she put the idea into his head, she made no comment.

A moment later he settled the matter by saying, 'It might be a good idea to bring your notebook and pencil just in case I need any notes taking.'

Then, catching sight of the expression on her face, 'You *did* say you liked walking?'

'Yes.'

'So you have no objection to accompanying me?'

Unable to think of a convincing reason to back out, after a moment or two she answered, 'No.'

If he noticed her brief hesitation, he gave no sign. 'Then

I'll pack a spot of lunch while you get your outdoor things. It's much colder than it looks, so wrap up well.'

Up in her room, she pulled on a pair of sturdy shoes, found a sweater to wear beneath her coat, and a woolly hat to pull down over her ears. She did enjoy walking, and at least being out in the open air and on the move would be preferable to staying cooped up indoors with him. And it would give her a chance to see something of her island.

When she descended the stairs she found he was waiting in the hall, also dressed for walking, and with a rucksack on his back.

Running an eye over her sensible shoes and clothing, he nodded, before asking, 'Any preference as to which direction?'

She shook her head. 'No, I'll leave it to you.'

'You mentioned that when you lived at Kelsay you used to enjoy walking along the beach…'

Surprised that he'd remembered, she said, 'Yes.'

'Then I suggest we follow the coastal path down as far as Gull Point, before striking inland and taking a shorter route back.'

'That sounds fine,' she agreed.

Grinning, he said a shade sardonically, 'Heaven be praised, an amenable woman!'

'Quite a lot of us are.'

'Not in my experience.'

'Then you've obviously been associating with the wrong kind of women.'

The teasing retort was out before she could prevent it, and, wondering what on earth had made her blurt out something that sounded so rude and insensitive, she bent her head and waited for the storm that was bound to come.

But all he said was, 'You may well be right.'

* * *

In spite of feeling she had got off to a bad start, Jenny found the walk both pleasant and invigorating. The heavens were cloudless, the scenery picturesque, and the salty tang of the sea air a long-missed and well-remembered pleasure.

Breathing in the cold air was like drinking sparkling champagne, and the light had that clear, diamond-edged sharpness that only winter days brought.

For the first hour or so they walked in silence, keeping up an easy pace that covered the miles seemingly without effort.

During that time, Michael had been trying to think up some interesting characters to people the plot that had begun to unfold in his mind. But more often than not his attention, rather than focusing on his book, had wandered to the woman by his side.

Though Jenny appeared to be quiet and reserved, she was far from dull, and she certainly didn't lack spirit. Yet when, after that first impulsive kiss, he had expected some display of coldness or anger, she had appeared dazed, quiescent.

Which failed to add up.

As did her pre-knowledge of Slinterwood.

Though even if they *were* both imponderables at the moment, there were bound to be answers…

But there he was, doing it again!

For the umpteenth time, he lassoed his straying thoughts, and, annoyed by his inability to concentrate, told himself irritably that he should never have engaged a PA. Particularly a female one, and, more especially, a female who intrigued and distracted him.

Unconsciously taking out his displeasure on her, he quickened his pace.

After half a mile or so, it became plain that she was having a struggle to keep up with him, but not a single word of complaint passed her lips.

Feeling like a heel, he slowed down and suggested, 'Shall we have ten minutes' rest and a cup of coffee?'

Sounding a little breathless, she said, 'A cup of coffee would be lovely.'

He led the way to a nearby outcrop of flattish rock, and, taking a Thermos from the rucksack, filled two cups and handed her one.

As they drank she asked, 'Any idea about the storyline yet?'

'The beginning of one,' he admitted grudgingly.

'What about the characters?'

He shook his head, his dissatisfaction with himself plain. 'I was wondering…'

Though he asked, 'What were you wondering?' his tone didn't sound as if he would welcome suggestions.

Though she doubted the wisdom of going on, having stuck her neck out, she felt she had no choice. Taking a deep breath, she asked, 'Have you ever considered carrying any of your previous characters over to another book?'

His attention caught, he queried, 'If by any chance I did, which of the characters would you advocate?'

Her face eager, she said, 'Two that I found particularly fascinating were Finn and Dodie…'

She had named two minor characters from his third novel, *Rubicon,* the fate of whom, to suit the plot, had been deliberately vague and inconclusive. Characters he had often thought he could have done a great deal more with.

'I've always wondered what happened to them after they left Orlando.'

The fact that she had spoken about them as if they were real people set off fireworks in his mind and sent his thoughts racing.

Watching his face grow aloof and distant, and only too aware of the lengthening silence, she lost countenance and said, 'I—I'm sorry. Please forgive me. I should have kept my suggestions to myself.'

'Far from it!' he exclaimed jubilantly, and, removing the empty cup from her nerveless fingers, set it down, and, taking her face between his palms, kissed her full on the lips. 'You've given me just the idea I needed.'

When he released her, flushed and breathless, she stammered, 'Oh… W-well, I only hope it works.'

'It'll work,' he told her with certainty.

Shaken by that kiss, but warmed by the thought that she'd been able to help in some small way, she watched him pack away the cups and the flask.

Shrugging the rucksack into place, he said, 'I suggest we have lunch at Gull Point, but first, as a reward, I'll take you to a secret cave with an answering echo.'

That day set the pattern for the days that followed. A stationary high pressure system kept the weather fine and dry, and while the book began to take shape they walked the length and breadth of the island.

Though Jenny ventured no further suggestions, rather to Michael's surprise he found himself talking to her about the emerging plot, finding it an advantage to have an intelligent listener to bounce his ideas off.

The days spent walking in the open air working up an appetite were followed by good and substantial evening meals.

Michael had been in touch with Mrs Blair, and while they were out that good lady made a daily visit to tidy up, lay the fires, and replenish the fridge.

Each evening, after their return, they would sit down to a pre-dinner drink and decide on a menu. At Jenny's suggestion, they now took it in turns to make dinner, and he was pleased to find that she was an excellent and inventive cook.

Dinner over, they spent their evenings by the fire, sometimes talking, sometimes reading, sometimes in what passed as a companionable silence.

On the surface everything appeared to be calm and contented, but beneath the surface there were still disturbing eddies and undercurrents.

Though Jenny *appeared* to be as ideal as Paul had suggested, along with his unanswered questions and reoccurring doubts Michael was struggling against a growing physical attraction that he was finding hard to control.

He tried to tell himself that it was nothing serious, simply a normal male's sexual response to a beautiful, desirable female, and that any other woman might have caused the same response.

But remembering the many attractive women who had vied for his attention after his divorce—all of whom had left him cold—somehow he didn't believe it.

Since that last, impulsive kiss, well aware that it would be playing with fire, he had been careful not to touch her, not even to let their fingers accidentally brush when he handed her a drink.

For her part, still plagued by that disturbing sexual awareness, and knowing how vulnerable she was, Jenny was grateful for his restraint.

Then the weather changed abruptly. Storm clouds rolled in over the sea, and that day, having walked the more hilly centre of the island, they were forced to battle their way back through heavy rain and a raging wind.

That evening it should have been Jenny's turn to cook, but seeing how tired she was after changing into dry clothes Michael had sent her to sit in front of the range while he made a seafood risotto.

Her hair was still damp, and she had left it loose around

her shoulders. It made her look about sixteen, he thought, and even more appealing.

After the meal they sat by the fire, sipping coffee and talking desultorily while they listened to the rain beating against the windows and the soughing of the wind in the chimney.

To all intents and purposes it was a quiet, contented, domestic scene.

A few weeks ago that thought would have made him laugh cynically. But now, to his surprise, rather than hating to have someone else here he was starting to look forward to the quiet evenings spent in Jenny's company.

He watched her face in the flickering firelight. Her eyes were half closed, and between softly parted lips he caught the gleam of pearly teeth.

His pulse rate quickening, he was forced to look away while he searched for some safe topic of conversation that would steer him well away from temptation.

By nine-thirty, noticing that she was having to stifle her yawns, he suggested that they both needed an early night.

She rose at once, and, having escorted her upstairs, Michael said an abrupt, 'Goodnight,' and disappeared into his own room before he gave way to the urge to kiss her.

Wondering at that sudden curtness, she went through to the bathroom to clean her teeth and shower.

Over the past week, though still plagued by that unbidden attraction and unable to totally relax, she had found the time spent in Michael's company both exciting and rewarding.

Though things had got off to a rocky start, she was beginning to feel that she had made the right decision after all, and to hope that by the time the month's trial period ended he might feel the same.

If he didn't, she knew she would be desolate.

She derived an immense amount of pleasure and satisfaction from the fact that he discussed his book with her and, from time to time, not only asked her opinion but appeared to listen to it.

Added to that she loved the island and the house, and knew that she would be happy to stay here in this lovely place for as long as he wanted her to.

Though they had covered a lot of ground there was still a great deal more to see, including a closer look at the castle, and she hoped that the storm would blow itself out before he began to work on his book in earnest, and they were tied to the house…

Her thoughts still busy, she had just returned to the bedroom when, without warning, the lights went out, plunging her into total darkness.

She had got used to the city, where there was always some degree of illumination, and the sudden complete absence of light came as a shock.

Taking a deep breath, she stood and waited for her eyes to adjust to the dark.

They didn't, and she soon realized that they weren't going to. The blackness was total. It wrapped her up and pressed against her suffocatingly, making her blind and helpless.

As though the absence of sight sharpened her other senses, she became aware of sounds that previously had stayed in the background—waves surging up the beach and crashing onto the rocks, wind buffeting the house, and rain lashing against the windows.

Enjoyable sounds, had she been tucked up cosily in bed. Not quite so enjoyable when she was standing in utter darkness, unsure of which way to move.

It had been a long and strenuous day, and, feeling bone-weary, she thought longingly of getting into bed and going to sleep, so that the absence of light wouldn't matter.

She made an effort to visualize the room before moving carefully towards where she thought the bed ought to be.

Only it wasn't.

There seemed to be a great deal more floor space than she remembered.

Altering direction, she tried again.

After another couple of fruitless attempts, totally disorientated, she admitted that she hadn't the faintest idea where the bed was.

If she could find a wall and follow it round... One hand held out in front of her, she began to move forward cautiously.

She had gone only a few steps when she stumbled into something she identified as the dressing-table stool, and knocked it over with a clatter.

As she fumbled to set it upright there was a light tap and the door opened. 'Having problems?' Michael's voice queried out of the darkness.

Her heart leapt in her chest, and even in her own ears her voice sounded husky and breathless as she answered, 'I was trying to find the bed, but I got disorientated and knocked over the dressing-table stool.'

'I know exactly where the dressing-table is,' he said reassuringly, 'so stay where you are, and I'll come and get you.'

Apart from the faint brush of his bare feet on the boards, he moved silently, and a few seconds later she jumped as an unseen hand took hers.

He must have eyes like a cat, she thought as he began to lead her unerringly through the blackness.

Wits scattered by his touch and his nearness, it took her a little while to realize that they had left her room and were heading down the corridor.

At the same instant that realization dawned she saw the half-open door of the next room illuminated by a reddish-gold glow.

'Why are you taking me to your room?' she demanded, hanging back.

'It seems the most sensible place for you to wait while I have a look at the generator,' he told her in a no-nonsense voice. 'Your room will soon start to get seriously cold, and there's a fire in mine.'

He gave the hand he was holding a little tug.

Unwilling to seem foolish by arguing, she bit her lip and followed him into the cosy bedroom, where an oil lamp glowed and a cheerful log fire blazed in the wide grate.

He led her to an armchair in front of the fire and pressed her into its cushioned comfort, before releasing her hand.

Feeling curiously shaky, her own hand still tingling from the contact, she looked up at him.

He was wearing a short navy dressing gown belted around his lean waist, and that seemed to be all. Through the gaping lapels she caught a glimpse of a smooth, olive-skinned chest and the strong column of his throat.

She felt a sudden, devastating urge to put her lips to the hollow at the base, and, feeling her colour rise, she hastily lowered her eyes.

His bare legs and feet, she noticed, were strong and well proportioned, and if feet could be said to be nice his were, with straight toes and neatly trimmed nails.

Noting her gaze, he remarked lazily, 'Fascinating things, feet, don't you think?'

Blushing harder than ever, she looked away, staring with some desperation into the flames.

Taking pity on her, he stopped his teasing, and asked, 'Would you like a nightcap of some kind while you wait?'

'No, thank you.' She was well aware that she'd sounded prim.

'Well, in case a story's flowing and I can't sleep, or I wake up and want to work during the night, I've had a coffee-maker installed…'

Of course. She remembered seeing it when he'd first shown her his room.

'So when I get back, if I've managed to fix the generator, we can have a hot drink.'

Bearing in mind that this was his bedroom, it sounded too intimate for comfort, and she told him quickly, 'All I really want is to get into my bed.'

Accepting her decision with good grace, he said, 'Well, if you're okay where you are for the time being, I'll pull on some clothes and get to work.'

While she sat and listened to his quiet movements and the rustle of clothing, she stared resolutely into the fire.

A minute or so later, fully dressed and wearing a thick Aran sweater, he picked up the oil lamp and headed out, closing the door quietly behind him.

Beginning to relax, she leaned back in the chair and watched pictures in the flames while she listened to the storm.

It was warm and comfortable, and in spite of her lingering agitation the flickering firelight had a soporific effect, and after a short time her heavy eyelids began to droop.

When Michael returned, Jenny was sitting bathed in a red-gold glow, fast asleep.

Though the neckline of her ivory satin nightie was modest by modern-day standards, it allowed an enticing glimpse of the upper curve of her breasts and the start of the shadowy cleft between them.

She looked like every man's dream, lovely enough to tempt even a saint, and he felt his heart start to beat faster.

He put down the lamp, tossed aside his sweater, and, irresistibly drawn, moved closer and stood gazing down at her.

Her head was tilted a little to one side, and beneath silky brows her long black lashes lay like fans against her high cheekbones. Even in sleep the pure line of her jaw and the curve of her chin showed character and determination, but her beautiful mouth looked soft and vulnerable.

He wanted to stoop and crush it beneath his own, to take her in his arms, to carry her off to bed and make love to her. But he knew instinctively that if he did, it wouldn't be just a one-night stand.

Even though he still had to solve the puzzle of what kind of woman she was, he was beginning to feel that she was destined to play some special kind of role in his life.

Perhaps Paul had already sensed that. Paul who had sounded a little anxious when, a few minutes before the lights went out, he had phoned to say, 'I'm sorry to call so late. But I wondered how you were getting on with Jenny Mansell.'

'No real problems so far,' Michael answered cautiously. 'What makes you ask?'

'Earlier tonight I went out for drink with Peter, one of the personnel bods from Global, and heard something a bit disturbing.'

'Go on,' Michael said evenly.

'Well, as it happens, Peter's sister, Lisa, is in the same department that Jenny used to work in. Apparently, soon after she'd left, Lisa overheard one of the men telling another that Jennifer Mansell's coolness was all put on, that once she was away from the office, she was "hot stuff".

'He boasted that on quite a number of occasions she'd taken him back to her place and acted "like some sex-starved nymphomaniac".

'When Lisa, who had apparently liked Jenny, asked him

why he hadn't said anything sooner, he protested that it was hardly the done thing to talk about a woman while she was still there.

'Lisa pointed out that it was hardly the done thing to talk about a woman behind her back. That shut him up temporarily. But only temporarily. Now rumours about Jennifer Mansell being predatory are rife.'

'Tell me something, do *you* believe the rumours?'

'I'm more inclined to believe that they're simply malicious, and spring from the fact that he'd made a pass at her in front of the entire office and been turned down flat. But I thought, having got you involved with the lady in question, I'd better let you know.'

'Well, thanks for the warning.'

'Sorry and all that. If there's anything I can do…?'

'As a matter of fact there is. Jenny once mentioned that she had a flatmate. Flatmates tend to know one another well, so if you could have a discreet word with her or him…?'

'Will do.'

'Oh, by the way,' Michael seized the opportunity to ask, 'when you first told her about this job, did you mention Slinterwood at all?'

'Slinterwood?' Paul sounded a bit blank. 'No, should I have done? Was there a problem?'

'No, no problem. I just wondered.'

'She didn't dig her heels in about going?'

'No, not at all. Look, I'll tell you all about it one of these days.'

'Right. I'll let you know what, if anything, the flatmate has to say.'

Frowning, Michael ended the call, his thoughts in turmoil. He didn't *want* to believe that there was any truth in the rumours. But though, up to press, she had shown not the slightest sign of coming on to him, in fact just the opposite, his brush with predatory women had made him wary.

However, sooner or later he'd find out the truth, but now he should wake her, and let her get to bed.

Thinking of Sleeping Beauty, he stooped and touched his mouth to hers.

Though her eyes remained closed, she gave a little sigh, her lips parted beneath that lightest of pressures, and her warm arms slid round his neck.

Without conscious volition, he lifted her to her feet while he deepened the kiss, and, like dropping a lighted match into a pool of petrol, passion exploded between them.

Fully awake now, and with no thought of past or future, of rights or wrongs or consequences, Jenny kissed him back, melting against him.

She was warm and fragrant in his arms, and while he kissed her his hands traced her slender curves, lingering over the enticing swell of her hips and buttocks, before following her ribcage upwards to the soft but firm curves of her breasts.

The touch of his hands made Jenny's pulse race madly and brought every nerve-ending in her body into singing life.

Through the thin satin of her nightdress his fingers found and teased the nipples, feeling them grow firm beneath his touch.

Transported by the exquisite, needle-sharp sensations he was arousing, she began to make little mewing sounds deep in her throat.

Those sounds inflaming him even further, he slipped the satin straps from her shoulders and bent his dark head to take first one, and then the other, of the pink velvety nipples into his mouth.

As he suckled sweetly she gasped and shuddered, the acute pleasure he was giving her almost more than she could bear.

When her nipples felt seductively ripe and swollen on his tongue, he slid the nightie down over her hips and let it pool around her bare feet.

Then, her arms still around his neck, he drew back a little and looked down at her. Her cheeks were flushed and her lips gently swollen.

His eyes dropped, and in the golden glow from the dying fire he saw her naked body for the first time.

She was graceful and perfectly proportioned, with a smooth, flawless skin. Her breasts were beautifully shaped, her waist slender above nicely rounded hips, her legs long and slim as a ballerina's.

Drawing her close again, he kissed her while he stroked his hand down her flat belly to the nest of black silky curls between her thighs.

She shuddered repeatedly as his long fingers found their goal and started to explore, luring all sensation downwards.

Normally his foreplay was both skilful and leisurely, a game he enjoyed and excelled at, a game he could play until he'd driven his partner almost wild with pleasure.

But no woman had ever affected him as Jenny did, and for the first time since he was a teenager he found it almost impossible to hold back, to keep his self-control.

When the little inarticulate murmurs she'd been making changed to pleas, shaken by the depth of his longing, he lifted her in his arms and carried her over to the bed.

Pulling aside the covers, he laid her down, and, with hands that weren't quite steady, stripped off his clothes before joining her.

She received him back silently, willingly, her arms going round his neck once more while she gladly welcomed his weight.

It was like making love to an eager flame, but after their first skyrocket trip to the stars he contrived to take it slower, delaying the climax, drawing out and intensifying the pleasure until it spilt over into ecstasy.

Temporarily spent and sated, his breath coming quickly,

his heart still racing, the blood still pounding in his ears, he lay quietly.

Blissfully happy, and loving the feel of his dark head pillowed on her breast, Jenny lifted a hand and stroked his hair tenderly.

Strangely content, he lay for a while before lifting himself away. Then, turning onto his back, he gathered her close and settled her dark head at the comfortable juncture between chest and shoulder.

Nestled against him, the steady beat of his heart beneath her cheek, she was fast asleep within seconds.

He could hear her light breathing, her breath occasionally fluttering in her throat as if she was still in the grip of some powerful emotion.

Having had his fill of women, he hadn't meant to get involved, and he should be regretting what had happened, what complications might ensue.

If it hadn't been for Paul's phone call, and the doubts it had raised, he would have sworn she was inexperienced.

But whatever the truth of the matter, what they had just shared had been shared on equal terms.

Jenny hadn't sought to make the running, nor had she merely surrendered, rather she had returned passion for passion in what had seemed to be an innocent, untutored way that had shaken him to the core.

Had she been an obviously worldly woman, and anyone other than his own PA, it would have been a sexual encounter he would never have forgotten.

As it was, with everything else that was involved in the equation, his feelings were in chaos, his well-ordered life turned upside down.

CHAPTER SIX

JENNY surfaced slowly, reluctantly, unwilling to break the spell of the previous night. Still half asleep and basking in the golden glow of the most wonderful experience of her life, she lay with her eyes closed, savouring the glory of it.

For perhaps the first time, she felt truly like a woman—contented, fulfilled, blissfully happy, as though she had finally found her heart's desire.

But as she became fully awake the reality of making love with Michael was dawning on her.

As she was shocked into complete wakefulness all the pleasure drained away, and she lay quite still, her body frozen, her mind jarred.

It was a few seconds before her brain accepted the fact that she was lying in Michael's arms, in Michael's bed.

Following her less than happy relationship with Andy, hurt, disillusioned, and bitterly humiliated, she had sworn never to get involved with another man.

Now, after months of keeping any would-be suitors at bay, she had gone to bed with her boss. A man she scarcely knew.

What on earth had made her do it? she wondered in growing horror.

Perhaps, because he had come to her and kissed her so

gently, so sweetly, her defences had been down, and before she had even started to appreciate the danger it had been too late.

Passion had flared between them, the kind of passion she had never felt before, the kind of passion that swept away any doubts or fears.

She had rejoiced in the certainty that here was the man she had been waiting for, that the two of them were meant to be lovers, meant to be together always.

But in the cold light of day she realized that that had been just a fantasy, an illusion.

In reality, passion—she shied away from the word lust—was all it had been.

In the past, when other girls had gone to bed with men they scarcely knew, she hadn't judged them, but she *had* wondered at the wisdom of their actions.

Now, without intending to, she had joined their ranks, and with a vengeance.

The whole episode had been a terrible mistake, something she could only regret.

Except that she *couldn't* regret it. It had been the most wonderful and earth-shattering experience, and she would never be the same again.

The memory of last night would stay with her for the rest of her life, even though Michael didn't care a jot for her, and had just wanted to use her.

But even as the charge went through her mind, she knew it was false. Though he couldn't possibly feel anything for her but lust, he had been tender and caring, *careful* of her…

In contrast to Jenny's slow awakening, Michael's brain was instantly alert, and even before he opened his eyes every minute of the preceding night was crystal-clear in his mind.

He hadn't meant it to happen, but he couldn't regret that it had.

Though by nature a caring, passionate man, in the past he had found love-making satisfying and pleasurable rather than earth-shaking.

With Jenny it had been an entirely new experience. She had burnt in his arms like an eager flame, arousing a storm of feeling that had rocked him to the core.

She was like no other woman he had ever met. From the moment he'd set eyes on her she had been special, his awareness of her so intense that at times he had felt almost befuddled.

And now he had once made love to her, he knew that he wanted her, craved for her and all she could give him, as an addict craved a drug.

Though she was lying quite still, he knew that she was awake, and he wondered what she was thinking, what the previous night had meant to her.

But of course that would depend entirely on what kind of woman she really was, what she wanted from him, and how she viewed their new relationship.

Did she still want him as much as he wanted her?

He felt instinctively that she did.

But there was one way to find out.

Jenny caught her breath as the arm that was lying over her tightened, and a warm hand closed lightly around her breast and began to stroke and tease the nipple into life.

She wanted to ask him to stop, to tell him that though she'd been foolish enough to let last night happen, it didn't mean that she was prepared to go on with it. But her heart was in her mouth and the words wouldn't come.

He raised himself up on one elbow, and his lips brushed her shoulder before travelling up the side of her neck.

As she shivered in response he turned her onto her back and smiled down at her.

In the morning light that filtered through the closed

curtains, she could see the creases either side of his mouth, the gleam of his white teeth, and the intriguing cleft in his chin.

He appeared fresh and vital, in spite of the dark stubble that adorned his jaw.

'You look beautiful,' he told her softly, 'all warm and seductive, just slightly tousled, and still flushed with sleep.'

He bent and touched his lips to hers.

His breath was fresh and clean, and though she longed to kiss him back she didn't want to be just his plaything, someone who filled a need while he was away from London.

Summoning all her will power, hoping to freeze him off, she kept her mouth firmly closed.

When he gave a slight sigh and lifted his head, she thought she'd succeeded.

But wanting, *needing,* to make her his again, to make her come to life and respond as completely and passionately as she had done the previous night, he returned to lay siege.

For a while his mouth played with hers, stroking, sucking, nibbling, bestowing little plucking kisses that coaxed and titillated and demanded a response.

A response she tried hard to withhold, and couldn't.

When her lips finally parted helplessly beneath his, he gave a little murmur of satisfaction and deepened the kiss, making her forget everything but the here and now, the delight and excitement his mouth was engendering.

Then his hands began to caress her, and in no time at all she was lost, mindless, any urge to resist swamped by the passion he was so easily arousing.

Using first his fingers, and then his mouth—the slight rasp of his stubble against her soft skin adding extra stimulation—he teased her nipples into life and found erogenous zones she hadn't even been aware of, before his hand slid down to the warmth of her inner thighs to bestow fresh delight.

The earlier urgency gone, he took his time about pleasuring her, finding his own pleasure in her little gasps and moans, and the knowledge that her body was so responsive to his touch.

Time and time again she thought herself sated, but each time he skilfully rekindled her desire, until finally he moved over her and joined her on that roller-coaster ride to the stars.

When she awoke for the second time she was alone in his bed. A fire was blazing in the grate, and above the sound of the wind and rain beating against the windowpanes she could hear the shower running and a faint, but tuneful whistling.

Her thoughts chaotic, she struggled to find some kind of mental stability and not condemn herself too much for what had just happened.

When she failed miserably on both counts, she bowed to the inevitable and admitted that she had made a complete hash of things.

Instead of freezing him off, she had kissed him back and triggered off a further bout of love-making that had shattered her good resolutions.

Though in the past she had never had to question her self-control, when it came to Michael she had thought of herself as vulnerable.

And rightly so.

He affected her like no other man she had ever met, and had he felt anything for her beyond lust she would have stayed for as long as he wanted her.

But he didn't.

Which made the situation impossible.

The only thing she could do was to leave.

Closing her mind to the fierce stab of pain that decision brought, she did her utmost to concentrate on practicalities.

He hadn't been planning to start work today, so she would

ask him to take her over to the mainland, where she could get some transport back to London.

Then the following morning she could call at her nearest employment agency and start looking for another position.

As if nothing had happened.

Whereas *everything* had happened, and she would never be quite the same again.

When, on her return home, she told Laura her flatmate would be both surprised and shocked.

Shocked, not for any moral reasons, but simply because she had known Jenny for long enough to be certain it wasn't in her nature to go to bed with a man she hardly knew, and her boss into the bargain.

Many a time, since her engagement had ended, Laura had urged her to loosen up, to find another boyfriend and have some fun.

'All this holding back gets you nowhere,' she said flatly. 'In fact that's probably what drove Andy to cheat on you in the end.'

Then quickly, 'Sorry, I shouldn't have said that.'

'Why not?' Jenny asked a shade bitterly. 'I've no doubt you're quite right.'

'Then why don't you let your hair down next time you meet a man you like? Live a little while you're still young?'

But with her own firmly entrenched standards of morality, Jenny found herself unable to follow that advice.

Laura's comment was, 'I can't say I expected you to. I only hope Mr Right comes along before you get too old and withered to make the most of it.'

However, nothing had been said about the possibility that Mr Right, when he *did* come along, might not fit into the role…

Becoming belatedly aware that the shower had stopped, and Michael might be back at any moment, Jenny slipped out of bed and, seizing her nightdress, which had been draped over a chair, was hurrying to the door when his voice stopped her in her tracks.

'Don't go…'

Clutching the nightie to her, she spun round to find he was standing there naked, his hair still damp, his jaw smoothly shaven, a towel draped around his neck.

Broad-shouldered and slim-waisted, lean-hipped and muscular, his belly flat, his legs long and straight, his smooth olive skin gleaming with health, he was so superbly *male* that she could hardly breathe.

'Brunch is all ready,' he went on, 'and I thought we might have it here by the fire…'

In the circumstances, eating together in his bedroom hardly seemed a sensible option, but her tongue refused to work.

Grinning at the expression on her face, he offered, 'If it seriously bothers you, I could put on some clothes first.'

When she continued to stand there struck dumb and unable to take her eyes off him, he went on, 'On the other hand, if you keep looking at me as though I'm Suleiman the Magnificent we could end up back in bed.' A gleam in his eye, he queried, 'Which option do you prefer?'

Blushing rosily, and hastily averting her gaze, she said, 'Brunch. With both of us dressed.'

She had meant to state it firmly, but it came out more like a plea.

He sighed. 'Well, in that case I expect the pancakes will wait ten minutes.' Then teasingly, 'But I'm getting hungry, so any longer and I might have to come and fetch you.'

Without further ado, still clutching her nightie, she turned and fled.

Her feelings all over the emotional map, she showered, cleaned her teeth, and brushed and coiled her hair.

Then, unconsciously hurrying, she found fresh undies, off-white slimline trousers, a fine wool shirt-blouse in olive-green, and a pair of low-heeled court shoes.

She debated briefly whether to stop and pack, then, deciding to do it *after* she'd told him her decision, she braced herself and went back to his bedroom, where she was greeted by the appetizing aroma of freshly brewed coffee.

A heated container, and a low table set with plates, cutlery, napkins, and everything necessary, had been assembled in front of the fire.

Thrown by the intimacy of the little scene, she wished she had stayed safely in her own room. But if Michael had followed through with his half-threat to come and fetch her, it might possibly have made things even more difficult.

Looking elegant in well-cut stone-coloured trousers and a fine black polo-necked sweater, he was pouring coffee.

Glancing up, he said quizzically, 'Just made it. Now come and sit down and tell me if you prefer honey or maple syrup.'

From the container he produced a plate of golden, delicious-looking pancakes.

She had intended to tell him straight away that she was leaving, but instead she found herself saying, 'Maple syrup, please.'

As she prepared to spread the syrup over one of the pancakes firelight glinted on the gold ring she wore on her right hand.

He had noticed the ring previously, but, his attention focused on other things, he had never really *looked* at it.

Now, suddenly, his interest roused, he found himself staring at the engraving, *recognizing* it.

His voice studiedly casual, he remarked, 'That's a most unusual ring.'

When, scarcely listening, mentally rehearsing how to break the news that she was leaving, she said nothing, he pressed, 'How long have you had it?'

'Sorry?'

'The ring you're wearing… How long have you had it?'

'Since I was eighteen.'

'May I ask where it came from?'

'It belonged to my great-grandmother.'

Noting her abstraction, and thinking it best, he dropped the subject for the time being.

The pancakes were every bit as delicious as they looked, and Jenny and her companion who, head bent, appeared to be deep in thought, cleared the plate and emptied the coffee pot while she tried to pluck up the courage to tell him what she had decided.

Breakfast over, and left with no further excuse for delay, she took a deep breath and blurted out, 'This isn't going to work.'

Jolted out of his reverie, he looked up.

Seeing she had his attention, she repeated desperately, 'This isn't going to work.'

He knew at once what she meant, and his heart sank. Clearly she was having second thoughts, regretting what had happened between them. And really he should have known there was a chance that that might happen.

Cursing the impulse that had made him rush her into his bed the previous night, he wished he had taken things more slowly.

Usually he was a great deal more sophisticated, more focused, more laid-back and in control of his actions. He'd always been able to hold back, to wait for something he really wanted.

But somehow Jenny had got under his guard, and he was having difficulty thinking straight and applying his usual self-control.

It was a moment or two before, pretending ignorance, he was able to ask evenly, 'What isn't going to work?'

'This…' She spread helpless palms. 'This whole thing… It should never have happened.'

'You mean sharing my bed?'

'Yes.' Feeling her colour rise, she went on, 'I've never done this kind of thing before. One-night stands and casual affairs aren't for me...'

He was inclined to believe her, which made him wonder just *why* she had responded to him so ardently. As though following his train of thought, she added jerkily, 'Nor is sleeping with my boss.'

'So you mean you won't be sleeping with me again?'

'No...'

He raised a dark brow.

Vexed with herself, she said sharply, 'I mean I want to leave.'

There was no way he could let her go.

Apart from wanting her in his life, the fact that she had known Slinterwood, taken in conjunction with the ring she was wearing, made him certain that she had some, as yet unexplained, connection with the house and the island.

Unwilling to show his hand until he had more to go on, he tried to settle on the best strategy to employ to keep her here.

Unable to decide, he said lightly, 'I thought you wanted to see how a book comes to life, to help in its creation.'

'I did,' she admitted, 'but now I think it would be best to go.'

'Why?'

'In the circumstances I really can't stay.'

'I don't see why not. If you don't want to share my bed, don't. It isn't compulsory.'

But she *did* want to share his bed, that was the trouble. He drew her, so that she was like the moon held by the earth's gravitational pull.

'If you would prefer to, we can forget everything that's happened between us,' he was going on mendaciously, 'and carry on simply as employer and employee.'

How could she possibly forget what had happened? The

memory would always loom between them, insoluble and embarrassing.

At least on her part.

But while it had been life-changing for her, clearly it had meant so little to him that, in order to keep an employee he needed, he was willing to brush it aside and forget it.

Which flayed her pride, making it even more impossible to stay.

She shook her head, and, taking a deep, steadying breath, said, 'If you could just take me across the causeway, I can find my own way back to London.'

If Michael refused to take her, she decided desperately, she would have to find some other means of getting over to the mainland.

However, he was too clever a tactician to precipitate matters by giving an out and out refusal. His tone eminently reasonable, he said, 'Look, don't decide this instant. Leave it until tomorrow and see how you feel then.'

She had opened her mouth to protest, when he added, 'For one thing, it would be highly dangerous to try to cross the causeway in this weather. By tomorrow the storm should have blown itself out, and if you *still* want to go back to London, I'll take you.

'In the meantime, twenty-four hours will give me a chance to try and line up a replacement PA.'

A sense of justice pointed out that she owed him that much. After all, she had agreed to take the job, and she couldn't deny that she was as much to blame for what had happened between them as he was.

Watching her hesitate, he added persuasively, 'If you stay at least for today it will give me an opportunity to show you round the castle.'

Much as she wanted to see the castle, she recognized the

offer as bait. Finding her voice, she pointed out, 'But it's raining heavily.'

'Which for the moment rather rules out the battlements. But you could still see the inside.'

'The *inside?*' She felt a quick thrill of excitement. 'Could I really?' Then doubtfully, 'Are you sure the owner won't mind?'

'Quite sure.' He spoke with certainty.

Even so, she knew she ought to refuse. But it seemed a terrible shame to throw away such a chance.

Reading her expression right, and suddenly more confident of success, he added lightly, teasingly, 'And just to set your mind at rest, I promise I won't do anything you don't want me to do.'

Recognizing that confidence, and fairly sure he was laughing at her, she gritted her teeth.

Of course she *could* shatter his assurance and have the last laugh by insisting on leaving the island immediately.

Only she was abruptly convinced that it would be a waste of time. He held the whiphand, and the gleam in his green eyes told her he knew it.

No matter how reasonable he might *appear,* if it came to the crunch she would get no help from him, and the sound of the storm raging outside emphasized the folly of attempting to walk.

Recognizing thankfully that for the moment her opposition was at an end, and promising himself that from now on he would take the softly-softly approach, he said briskly, 'So that's decided. Now I've a quick phone call to make…'

Presumably the phone call would be to an employment agency, in the hope of finding himself a new PA.

'So if you'd like to fetch a mac, I'll meet you downstairs in a few minutes.'

She rose to her feet, and, her legs feeling oddly shaky, went to do as he'd suggested.

Once again her feelings were in turmoil. Mingling with a

host of misgivings was a swift and fierce gladness that she wasn't going just yet.

Because of the weather, she had one more day on her island. One more day with Michael. She would forget her embarrassment, forget all her doubts, and do her best to enjoy it.

By the time she had washed her hands, belted a stone-coloured mac around her slender waist, and made her way down to the hall, he was standing waiting by the front door.

He had pulled the car in as close as possible, but even so by the time he had helped her into the passenger seat the shoulders of his short jacket were spattered with rain and his ruffled dark hair was dewed with drops.

A strong wind was buffeting the treetops into a frenzy of activity, and heavy storm clouds were being driven across the sky like a straggling flock of grey ragged sheep.

As they climbed towards the road, through the water that streamed down the windows she could see that the sea was a boiling mass of white-topped breakers.

From being a small child she had loved, and been in tune with, all aspects of the elements. Now something inside responded to the wildness of the weather and, her heart lifting, she wanted to laugh aloud.

As though he sensed and shared her feelings, Michael turned his head to smile at her.

The short drive along the coastal road was quite spectacular, and when they surmounted the ridge Jenny caught her breath at the sight of the castle, bleak and imposing against the stormy sky.

Looking at it, she found herself quoting, '"Four grey walls and four grey towers…"'

Slanting her a glance, Michael offered, 'But not too many flowers at this time of the year.'

She was still marvelling how quickly he'd picked up that

spur-of-the-moment quotation when he added, 'I see you know your Tennyson.'

'After we did "The Lady of Shalott" at school he became a firm favourite of mine.'

'Mine too.'

'You like poetry?'

'Yes.'

She was surprised that so masculine a man should admit to enjoying poetry.

Seeming to read her mind, he asked, 'Why not? As a writer I love language in all its forms.'

'Of course. Have you always liked poetry?'

Driving through the castle gatehouse and beneath the portcullis, he answered, 'Since reading my first nursery rhyme at the age of three, and progressing to Marvell and Donne, it's been only too easy to get drunk on words.'

Words were the tools of his trade, she realized, so it made perfect sense.

Close at hand, the castle looked even more stark and dramatic, with its rain-drenched cobbled courtyard and its high stone walls running in water.

As they drew up close to a huge, iron-studded door Michael remarked slyly, 'I've always rather liked Andrew Marvell's, "To His Coy Mistress".'

Watching the colour mount in her cheeks, he added, 'I see you know it.'

Then instantly contrite, he grimaced. 'Sorry, I shouldn't tease you. But you blush so beautifully that I couldn't resist it.'

He touched her cheek. 'Forgive me?'

The look on his face made him irresistible, and her heart turned over.

'There's nothing to forgive,' she said huskily.

'A truly generous woman,' he commented with a smile.

Then, taking a large key from his pocket, he instructed, 'Wait here.'

Having turned the key in the ornate iron lock, he hurried back through the deluge and held the car door against the strong gusts while she clambered out.

In the two or three seconds it took to get inside, the wind and rain beat into her face, almost stopping her breath and blowing loose strands of hair into wild disorder.

Closing the door behind them, Michael said, 'Phew!'

Strangely exhilarated, she raised a glowing face and smiled at him as she began to peel the stray tendrils of wet hair from her cheeks and tuck them back into the coil as best she could.

Thinking he'd never seen anyone more beautiful, he produced a spotless hankie and, shaking out the folds, used it to dry her face.

Her heart doing strange things and her smile dying away, Jenny stood rooted to the spot looking up at him, her lovely brown eyes wide and defenceless.

The urge to take her in his arms and cover her mouth with his was so strong it was like a physical pain, and he was forced to step back and remind himself firmly of the softly-softly strategy he had decided on.

Jenny had been convinced he was about to kiss her, and when he stepped back she sighed with what she told herself was relief.

But somehow it felt more like regret.

Though she knew, and admitted, it was the road to nowhere, she had *wanted* him to kiss her.

Once again she had demonstrated just how dangerous it was to be near him, and if she was to retain any remaining pride or self-respect she must leave as soon as the weather would allow.

As he returned the damp square of cotton to his pocket, and

smoothed back his wind-ruffled hair, Jenny took a deep, steady-ing breath, and transferred her attention to her surroundings.

They were standing in a huge, panelled hall, with a massive stone fireplace and a great oak staircase that climbed to a second-floor landing and a minstrels' gallery.

Picturing the hall with a blazing fire, the metal chandeliers lit with dozens of candles, a colourful throng of people, and the long table groaning with food and drink, she knew that in its heyday it must have been a magnificent sight.

But now, in the flickering grey light that filtered through long, leaded windows awash with water, it looked bare and bleak and deserted.

Even so, she felt a warmth, the same sense of belonging, of coming home, she had felt on seeing Slinterwood for the first time.

Despite that aura of welcoming warmth, the air itself was cold and dank, and as though in response to the realization she shivered.

Noticing that involuntary movement, Michael said crisply, 'There's been no form of heating in this part of the castle for donkey's years, so I suggest we get moving.

'How much of the place do you want to see?'

'I'd like to see it all,' she said, her eagerness and excite-ment returning with a bound. 'That is, if you don't mind?'

Secretly pleased by her enthusiasm, he said, 'I certainly don't mind, but if you get bored you'll have to tell me.'

How could she get bored when she would be seeing the place she had wanted to see for as long as she could remember, the castle of her dreams?

'I won't get bored,' she said with certainty.

He led the way across the hall and through a door at the end. 'This is the east wing. Neither this, nor the north wing, have been lived in since the early eighteen hundreds, and are empty apart from a few chests and settles and the odd four-poster bed.'

But, for Jenny, even the virtually empty rooms they walked through held an endless fascination, and she looked around her with unflagging interest.

When they reached the end of the north wing, Michael said, 'Beneath here are the dungeons. They're pretty grim-looking, but there's no record of anyone ever having died there.'

From the dungeons they made their way through archways and bare stone passages to the sculleries, kitchens, and store-rooms, the servants' quarters and the servants' hall.

Then, having shown her the gatehouse, which had once been used to house soldiers, the towers, with their arrow-slits and spiral stairways and, above the family vault, the beautiful little chapel—which he told her was still used on special occasions—they returned via backstairs dimly lit by cobwebby windows to the main hall.

As they approached a door near the huge fireplace, above the mantel, she noticed a shield with a familiar design, a phoenix rising from the ashes.

She turned to ask Michael about it, but he was going on, 'And through here is the west wing. It was occupied until the late eighteen hundreds, so the rooms are still fully furnished.'

He led her through a grand living-room, an elaborate music room, a dining-room, a library, and then a magnificent long gallery.

The gallery was elegantly proportioned, with deep, leaded windows made of uneven panes of pale-greenish glass, down which rain streamed incessantly, making the light dim and wavering and giving the place an eerie, under-water feeling.

'It's absolutely beautiful,' Jenny remarked.

'It's said to be haunted.'

'Haunted? By whom?'

He found himself smiling at the excitement in her voice. 'By a lady named Eleanor.'

'Why does she haunt the gallery?'

Lowering his voice to sepulchral tones, he said, 'It's a gory tale of love and hate and jealousy. Sure you want to hear it?'

'Quite sure,' she said.

CHAPTER SEVEN

SMILING at the eagerness in Jenny's voice, Michael began, 'When Lady Eleanor Grey was just eighteen, she fell in love with, and married, Sir Richard D'Envier and came to live at Mirren.

'For a few months they were extremely happy, but Charles, Sir Richard's younger brother, had also fallen in love with Eleanor, and each day he grew more bitterly jealous.

'Eventually, unable to stand it any longer, he hired a couple of cutthroats to waylay Sir Richard and kill him.

'But Richard, a courageous man, fought them off, and, though he was badly wounded, he managed to remount his horse and ride back to the castle, where he died in his wife's arms.

'They were perilous times, and because Eleanor was pregnant she was particularly vulnerable.

'As was the custom in those days, Charles, now head of the household, offered her and her unborn child his protection, if she would marry him.

'Still mourning her husband, Eleanor didn't want to marry again, but for the sake of her unborn child, she felt forced to seriously consider his proposal.

'What she didn't know was that one night after too much wine Charles had boasted that if the child was a boy, he would find some way of getting rid of it.'

Jenny, who had been listening with bated breath, urged, 'Go on.'

'Though Eleanor had never liked her husband's brother, she had almost decided that she had little choice but to accept his proposal when something happened to change her mind.

'Charles had made one serious mistake. Because he believed his ruffians had bungled the murder, he refused to pay them.

'One night, in their cups, the pair aired their grievances, and the news got back to Eleanor. Her dislike of Charles turned into a fierce hatred, and a strong desire for revenge.

'Unaware that she knew the truth, Charles was pressing her for an answer to his proposal, but she bided her time while she thought up a plan to get him away from the retinue that invariably surrounded him.

'Eleanor often walked in the long gallery, and one evening she sent Charles a flirtatious little note saying that if he met her here, she would give him her answer.

'He came, all smiles, and prepared to embrace her. He didn't see the jewelled dagger hidden in the folds of her gown until she plunged it into his heart.

'A bloody and melodramatic tale,' Michael added in his normal voice.

'Did she kill herself too?'

'No. Apparently she had half intended to, but the thought of her unborn child held her back. Luckily for her, there were many at the castle who were still loyal to Sir Richard, and when Charles was hastily buried, and the news spread that he had died of a fever, no one challenged the story.'

'So what happened to Eleanor?'

'Having given birth to a healthy son, whom she named Richard, she survived to see him grow into a fine young man, the image of his father.

'She lived to be forty-five, without ever remarrying, and

according to legend she still walks in the long gallery where she avenged the death of her husband.'

Jenny sighed. 'I'm pleased there's a happy ending after all.'

His smile just a little mocking, Michael asked, 'Don't you feel a spot of womanly pity for poor lovelorn Charles?'

'Certainly not,' she denied crisply. 'He only got what he richly deserved.'

Laughing at her honest indignation, Michael led her up to the top floor, with its dressing-rooms, retiring-rooms and magnificent bedchambers.

When she remarked on the fact that the rooms led straight into one another, he told her, 'At that time there were no upstairs corridors, which must have meant a distinct lack of privacy for any guests. Though they did manage to keep the servants well out of sight.'

'How did they do that?' she asked curiously.

'I'll show you.'

Crossing to one of the inner walls, he moved aside a hanging tapestry to reveal a small door.

'Where possible, the staircases and corridors used by the servants were built between the main walls, and the doors into the various rooms hidden behind hanging tapestries. That way a servant could slip in to make up the fire, and disappear again without being noticed.

'And, speaking of things being hidden, there's a secret passage I haven't yet shown you.'

'A secret passage?'

Jenny, who had been fascinated by the architecture of the old place, the archways and steps that seemed to lead nowhere, the huge fireplaces and the beautiful old windows, gave a shiver of excitement.

Misreading that shiver, he said, 'You're cold.'

She was, frozen through, but she'd been far too engrossed to heed the cold.

'Come on, let's get going.'

Thinking he intended to leave, she protested, 'I'd love to see the secret passage.'

'And so you shall.'

Taking her hand, he hurried her down the stairs and across the hall, and, coming to a halt on the far side of the fireplace, ran his fingers along the oak panelling just above head height.

There was a muffled click, and with a grating noise a section of the panelling moved to one side.

Peering excitedly into the cobwebby gloom, Jenny asked, 'Where does it lead?'

'The first short section leads to the south wing, which is where we're heading, and the second, much longer section, to an escape tunnel which goes down under the walls, through a gap in the rock, and eventually comes out about a quarter of a mile away.'

'Have you ever been through?'

'Oh, yes.'

'I've never been through a secret passage,' she told him. Then hopefully, 'If we're heading for the south wing, do you think we could go that way?'

Quizzically, he charged, 'You've been reading too much Enid Blyton.'

With a grin, she admitted, 'As a child, I loved her books… So could we?'

Amused, he agreed, 'We could. But it will be dark and rough underfoot, and all I have with me is a small pencil-torch.'

'I'm sure we'd manage,' she told him eagerly.

'What if I can't locate the lever that opens the panel to let us out?'

Looking anything but concerned, she suggested, 'Well, if

you can't, so long as you leave this panel open we could always retrace our steps.'

'Very well. You'd better follow me.'

As they stepped through the gap, reminding her to tread carefully, he took her hand.

Feeling a delicious thrill of adventure, she followed close on his heels.

The tunnel was narrow, the air cold and musty, the ground uneven beneath their feet.

As they moved away from the open panel, the torch a small spotlight in the surrounding darkness, the walls seemed to close in claustrophobically.

Unconsciously, she gripped his hand tighter.

'Do you want to turn back?'

His voice sounded strangely hollow, disembodied, but the fingers curled round hers were strong and reassuring, and she answered, 'No, no, I'm quite happy, really.'

Once or twice she stumbled, and he asked, 'Okay?'

Each time she answered, 'Fine, thank you.'

After what seemed an age, he said, 'If I remember rightly, we should be just about there.'

As they slowed to a halt he let go of her hand to release the lever. At the same instant she stepped on a loose piece of rubble, and gave a gasp as her left ankle turned painfully.

'What's wrong?' he asked.

'I've twisted my ankle,' she admitted ruefully.

He thrust the torch into his pocket, and his arms went around her.

Standing on one leg, storklike, she leaned against him, grateful for his support.

He could feel the slender weight of her body, smell the apple-blossom scent of her hair and the fragrance of her skin.

She heard the breath hiss through his teeth then, in the

darkness, his mouth found hers unerringly, and he was kissing her with a passion that swept her completely away.

How long they stood in the darkness kissing, Jenny never knew. She was in a blissful world of her own, everything else obliterated, forgotten, the touch of his lips and the feel of his arms all she had ever wanted or needed.

Overwhelmed with tenderness, she touched his cheek.

Even against the coldness of his face, he was aware that her fingers felt icy.

The realization waking him to practicalities, he lifted his head, and, one arm still supporting her, felt for the lever.

After a second or two, he found and depressed it, and with a grating sound the panel slid aside, letting in light.

'Can you walk?' he asked.

'Yes, I think—' The words ended in a little cry of pain as she tried to put her weight on her injured left ankle.

Unable to lift her in the narrow space, he ordered tersely, 'Stay where you are and keep that foot off the floor.'

Poised on one leg, one arm braced against the wall, she muttered, 'This is ridiculous.'

'If you attempt to walk on it, it'll only make matters worse.'

Seeing the sense of that, she stopped arguing and did as she'd been bidden.

He went through the opening first, then turned, and, stooping, said, 'Put your arms around my neck and duck your head.'

She obeyed, and, one arm encircling her waist, his free hand shielding her head, he helped her clear of the panelling and swung her up into his arms.

They had emerged into what seemed to be a small inner hall, with a row of high internal windows on one side.

In spite of the turmoil caused by that kiss, and being held against his broad chest, she noticed that the air felt appreciably warmer.

He opened the nearest door into a red-carpeted room with dark oak panelling, and carried her over to a leather couch set in front of a stone fireplace, and put her down amidst the cushioned comfort.

She was surprised to see a fire was already laid in the grate and a box of matches lay waiting. To one side of the hearth a large wicker basket was piled high with logs.

As soon as she was settled with her back against a pile of cushions he pulled off her shoes, dropped them by the old-fashioned fender, and stooped to strike a match.

When the kindling flared and caught hold, he rose to his feet and said with satisfaction, 'There, that should soon be burning nicely. Now you stay here and get warm, and I'll be back in a minute.'

He disappeared through a door in the far wall.

Already able to feel the welcome warmth of the fire on her icy feet, Jenny glanced around her curiously. The room seemed to be a combination of living-room and study, its long, arched windows looking out onto a rain-swept inner courtyard.

Michael had told her the castle was no longer inhabited, but, attractively furnished and homely, with books and ornaments and a grandfather clock that chimed melodiously, this room showed every sign of being lived-in.

A silver-framed photograph standing on the nearby bookcase caught her eye. It was of a handsome man with clear-cut features, blue eyes beneath still dark brows, and iron-grey hair. He looked aristocratic, and she found herself wondering if *he* owned Mirren.

All at once she felt distinctly uncomfortable, an intruder, as if the man might walk in at any moment and demand to know what she was doing here.

It was something of a relief when, a short time later,

Michael returned. He had discarded his jacket, and was carrying a first aid box under his arm and two steaming mugs.

'Warmer?' he queried.

'Much. I don't really need this now.' She began to wriggle out of her coat.

He put everything down on a low table that stood close by and helped her.

Tossing it over one of the high-backed chairs, he remarked, 'I thought we could do with a hot drink, as soon as I've had a look at that ankle.'

Sitting down on the edge of the couch, he grimaced. 'I'm afraid it's already starting to swell. We'll just have to hope there's nothing broken.'

Though he was as gentle as possible, she winced as his fingers began to probe

After a moment, he announced, 'There doesn't seem to be, thank the Lord.' Taking a can of analgesic spray from the first-aid box, he added, 'But your feet are like ice.'

The fine spray felt colder still.

'There, that should help to curtail the pain and prevent any further swelling.

'However, a bit of support wouldn't be a bad idea...' Producing a crêpe bandage, he bound her ankle neatly and efficiently.

'Thank you,' she said, when he'd finished. 'That's starting to feel better already.'

He handed her one of the mugs, and, taking a seat in a nearby chair, remarked, 'I'm afraid there's no fresh milk, so I hope you don't mind having your coffee black?'

'No, not at all.'

His eyes on her face, he asked, 'So what's wrong?'

'Nothing,' she assured him. 'I'm fine.'

'You're lying,' he said shortly. 'Apart from your ankle, something's bothering you.'

'I just feel I've no right to be here,' she admitted in a rush. 'If the owner should—'

Something about the look on his face stopped her short, and, light suddenly dawning, she said almost accusingly, '*You* own the castle.'

'That's right,' he agreed.

'The island too?'

'Yes.'

'Why didn't—?' She bit her tongue.

'I tell you?' he finished for her.

'I'm sorry,' she said in confusion. 'Of course you had a perfect right to keep it to yourself.'

'How kind of you to say so.'

Though she felt sure the gentle sarcasm wasn't meant to wound, emotionally friable, she flushed, and her eyes filled with unbidden tears.

He rose to his feet, instantly contrite. 'I'm sorry.' Reaching for her hand, he raised it to his lips and kissed it.

His lips felt warm against her palm, and a shiver ran through her.

'Now, why don't you relax and drink your coffee?'

But his touch had ruffled her even more, and he realized it.

Cursing himself for a fool, he released her hand and began to sip his own coffee.

The fire was blazing merrily now, throwing out a circle of heat. After adding some more logs, he queried, 'Feet warmer?'

Her voice a little stilted, she answered, 'Yes, thank you, warm as toast now.'

Then, sounding more like herself, 'In any case it was well worth getting cold for. The castle is absolutely wonderful.'

Pleased and relieved that she wasn't the kind to bear a grudge, he said, 'I'm very glad you think so. I've always loved the old place.'

'Do you know its history?'

'Oh, yes, it's all in the family archives. Following the battle of Hastings, William the Conqueror gave the island, and a large chunk of the surrounding countryside, to Michel D'Envier, a young Norman duke who had helped raise an army to fight alongside him.

'After Michel fell in love with, and married, the daughter of an English nobleman, he started to build the castle, and it's been home to the D'Envier family since it was completed in the early part of the twelfth century.

'Though internally it's been altered a lot over the years, the outer walls and the battlements, the towers and the gatehouse date from then. That's why I've done my best to maintain the place in good order and keep it structurally sound.'

'That can't be easy.'

'It isn't. Luckily I have the money now, but in the past it's been a big drain on the family resources. That's one of the reasons my father, after being approached by the local historical society, decided to open the unoccupied wings to the public.'

Embarrassed to recall her own comments about visitors dropping litter, she wished she had kept her opinions to herself.

'Oh, I see,' she said a shade awkwardly.

'Personally,' Michael went on, 'I never liked the idea, and after my father died and probate was granted, I reversed that decision.'

A gleam of devilment in his green eyes, he added, 'So you see you have me to blame for your disappointment all those years ago.'

Forgetting her embarrassment, and picking up on his mood, she assured him lightly, 'Well, as you've more than made up for it today, I forgive you.'

'How very magnanimous.'

This time she only smiled.

It was still raining hard, and what little light there had been was fading. Beyond the fireglow that enclosed them in their own little cocoon of well-being, the room was growing dusky.

As soon as she had finished her coffee, he put his own empty cup down, switched on a couple of standard lamps, and, resuming his seat, queried, 'Feel any better now?'

'A lot.' She moved her foot experimentally.

He shook his head. 'I meant now you know you're not trespassing do you feel more relaxed, more comfortable about being here?'

'Oh… Yes… Yes…'

'You don't sound at all sure.'

She wasn't. It was much too cosy. Too intimate. Remembering his kiss in the secret tunnel and her own helpless reaction to it, how could she feel relaxed and comfortable? She ought to be heading home to London, well away from temptation.

After a moment, needing to break the lengthening silence, she remarked, 'Though you told me there was no one living at the castle, it looks and feels as if there could well be.'

'My parents lived here until my mother died some six years ago, and my father followed her less than a year later. Soon after his death, all that remained of the staff—three old family retainers, a man, his wife, and daughter—who had worked at the castle all their lives, decided to retire and go to live in one of the cottages on the estate.

'I didn't want this wing to get damp and neglected, so I arranged with Mrs Blair to come in regularly to clean and air the place and make sure the radiators are working properly.'

'It seems strange to talk about radiators in a castle this old.'

'Castles this old tend to be cold, draughty places, and to

make it liveable in the entire south wing was refurbished early in the nineteen hundreds, and a generator and a central-heating system installed.

'It's all very old-fashioned now, but it still works, and hopefully should last until I've drawn up plans to have the whole thing modernized.'

'Why don't you—?' She stopped short.

His eyes on her face, he urged, 'Feel free to ask anything you want to know.'

Encouraged by his words, but determined to be cautious all the same, she admitted, 'I was wondering why, when you come to the island, you don't live here? Or perhaps you do, sometimes?'

He shook his head. 'I used to visit often when my father was alive, and when I'm on the island I still come to spend a day or two and sometimes the odd night here. There's one bed always kept aired. But I haven't actually lived at the castle since I left to go to university. If I'd returned to Mirren after graduating, I would probably have followed the family tradition and taken up residence at Slinterwood.

'You see it was originally intended to be the home of the family's eldest son, that is, until his father died. Then, if his mother was still alive, *she* would move into Slinterwood, while he and his family were expected to take over the castle.'

'So you're the eldest son?'

'I'm the only son.'

Fascinated by what he was telling her, and forgetting her earlier resolve to be cautious, she said, 'But you didn't take over the castle when your father died?'

'No, the circumstances weren't right. I was unmarried and living in London, still trying to find my feet as a writer. However, I decided that one day, if my wife was willing, I *would* move back, as my father had always hoped.'

His voice flat, dispassionate, he added, 'But when I did eventually get married, after coming here on a couple of occasions Claire decided that she hated the island.'

So even if he and his ex-wife did get back together, the castle wouldn't be lived in...

As the silence stretched, knowing that he must be thinking much the same, Jenny made an effort to change the subject.

Indicating the photograph she'd noticed previously, she asked, 'Who's that?'

'My father. I took that picture of him when he was about sixty.'

'A nice-looking man,' she commented. Adding, 'Though your eyes are a different colour, I can see the likeness now.'

'All the D'Envier males seem to have dark hair and that kind of bone structure.'

Which meant that if he ever had children, his sons would probably look like him...

Sighing a little, she pictured two small boys with Michael's clear-cut features, cleft chin, and thick dark hair.

Watching her face grow soft, he wondered what she was thinking.

Since that impulsive kiss in the darkness of the secret passage, his mind had been only partly on what was being said, his concentration seduced by memories of her response. How willingly her cold lips had parted beneath his, how pliantly her body had moulded itself against his body, how eagerly her arms had welcomed him and held him close...

Jenny looked up suddenly, a question trembling on her lips, and their eyes met.

She saw the darkness in his, darkness that held a fierce flame of desire in its depths, and, shaken rigid by that look, and her own response to it, she glanced hastily away.

A log settled in the grate with a rustle and a spurt of orange sparks, and the grandfather clock ticked away the seconds.

'You were about to ask me something?'

Michael's tone held no trace of any emotion other than a kind of casual friendliness, and just for an instant she wondered if she could have imagined that blazing look.

But she knew she hadn't. The memory of it was burnt indelibly into her brain.

Afraid to look at him, she fumbled around for the question that had been on the tip of her tongue.

'I presume, from what you were saying, that the name D'Envier has been anglicized?'

'Yes. My father decided it was time to become totally English, to drop the apostrophe and change the spelling.

'But enough of me and my family. Tell me about yourself and *your* family. You told me you were born in London and went to live at Kelsay when you were quite young?'

'Yes…'

'Why?'

'My father left when I was two years old, and as my grandparents had been killed in a car crash the previous year my mother took me to live with my great-grandmother.'

'Go on.'

'I really liked living at the seaside, and I loved Gran dearly. Possibly because I was named after her, we seemed to share a special bond.

'But when I was seven, my mother remarried, and took me to live in the Channel Islands. I was very sad to have to leave Gran. I missed her a lot. We stayed in Jersey for nine years, then my parents decided to move to France.

'I'd never got on particularly well with my stepfather, so I chose to go back to Kelsay and live with Gran. By this time she was very old and frail and had recently suffered a stroke.

So for the next two years, while I finished my schooling, I helped to look after her...'

Though she had talked, obediently following his lead, right from the start part of her mind had been taken up by her companion.

Or rather by her *awareness* of him.

Though she avoided looking at him, she was conscious of every single thing: his light breathing, the slight rise and fall of his chest, the movement of his hands, the flick of his dark lashes when he blinked, and the faint, masculine scent of his aftershave. She was even convinced she could hear the beat of his heart.

'You mentioned that the ring you're wearing had belonged to your great-grandmother?'

'Yes.'

Reaching across the table he took her hand, and twisting the ring between his finger and thumb, remarked, 'A beautiful old signet ring like this is bound to have a fascinating history. What exactly do you know about it?'

Her heart lurching drunkenly at his touch, she half shook her head. 'Well, nothing, really...'

Sounding a little breathless, she added, 'I know Gran always wore it. I recall seeing it on her finger when I was quite small.'

Making a determined effort, she withdrew her hand, and went on, 'When I went back to nurse her, she was still wearing it. I would have liked to have asked her where it came from, but the stroke, as well as leaving her partially paralyzed, had made her practically unintelligible, and trying to talk upset her.'

'So after her death you inherited the ring?'

'Not exactly. The night she died I was sitting with her. In the early hours of the morning, she awakened from a doze. Seeing I was there, she pulled the ring off her finger, and pressed it into my hand.

'She tried very hard to tell me something, but the words

were garbled. To save her any further distress, I pretended to understand. I put the ring on my own finger, and promised to always wear it. Then I laid her hand on top of it, sandwiched between my own two hands…'

Michael got a vivid mental picture of a very old wrinkled hand, held lovingly between two young, strong hands, and felt a lump in his throat.

'She gave a little, contented sigh, and a short time later slipped peacefully away. I wish she *had* been able to tell me what she so obviously wanted to tell me. If there really is a story attached to the ring, I would have liked to have heard it.'

'Presumably you know what the engraving is?'

'Oh, yes, it's a phoenix. I noticed several as we walked round the castle, and there's a similar one carved on the mantel in the library at Slinterwood. I believe in the past mythical birds and beasts were often used for ornamentation.'

'You're quite right. And of course they were frequently used in heraldry, and sometimes to illuminate manuscripts and old family trees.'

'Such as yours, presumably?'

'Yes.' Casually, he added, 'One day I'll show you.'

But she wouldn't be here 'one day'. The thought was like a physical pain.

Watching her face, noting the spasm that crossed it, and guessing the cause, he decided the time had come to dig a little deeper.

'How much do you know about your ancestry?' he asked evenly.

'Not a great deal. I really can't go very far back at all.'

'Then start with your great-grandmother. Where was she born and bred?'

'To the best of my knowledge Gran was born in Kelsay and lived there all her life.'

'Tell me about her.'

Knowing it was safer to keep talking, she went on, 'Gran was a lovely person, warm-hearted and generous, with a sense of humour and a belief in the goodness of life that somehow managed to survive losing the one man she really loved...'

His interest quickening, Michael asked, 'How did that happen?'

'When she was only eighteen she fell deeply in love and got engaged to be married. But, tragically, her fiancé died.'

'Do you know his name, or where he came from?'

'I'm afraid not. The only thing I recall my mother telling me was that he was a widower with a young son, and about ten years older than Gran. But apparently they had adored each other and she mourned him for years...'

With an effort, Michael bit back his excitement. What Jenny had just told him had made a nebulous idea that had been forming at the back of his mind crystallize into something like a certainty.

All he needed now was proof. And he thought he knew exactly where to find it, but that would have to wait until the next day.

Bringing his mind back to the present, he said, 'But presumably she married sooner or later?'

'Oh, yes... Eventually she met and married a man named Charles Peacock, and Margaret, my grandmother, was born three years later.'

'Go on.'

'Margaret married George Rider, and had my mother, whose name is Louise. When my mother was twenty-two she married my father, Jonathan Mansell, and I was born a couple of years later.

'I'd never really thought about it before,' she added, 'but it seems strange that for the past three generations only single girls have been born.

'I know my mother would have liked another child, but my stepfather, who had two children by a previous marriage, didn't want any more.'

'What about you?' Michael asked. 'Do you intend to have children?'

The question took her by the throat. Swallowing hard, she answered jerkily, 'I'd always hoped to…'

She stopped speaking as, outside in the darkness, a fierce squall of wind and rain battered against the windowpanes.

'It still sounds rough out there,' Michael remarked. Adding, after a moment, 'The coastal road can be tricky in the dark and in this kind of weather, so I think it might make a lot of sense to stay here for the night.'

CHAPTER EIGHT

'STAY here?' Jenny's voice sounded high and panicky.

'Why not? After all, there's nothing really to go back for. Though there's no fresh food, there's plenty to eat in the store cupboard, so we won't starve by any means.'

'I'm sure food's not a problem, but...'

Her apprehension was palpable, and hovered between them like a chaperon.

Michael glanced at her from beneath long, thick lashes. 'You're worried about the sleeping arrangements?'

'You said there was *one* bed kept aired.'

'Which of course you can have, if you prefer. But I was going to suggest that you might like to sleep in front of the fire?

'You see, the couch you're on is a bed-settee. To the best of my knowledge it's nice and comfortable, and should be a great deal cosier than the bedroom.'

Jenny thought quickly. Because of her damaged ankle, staying here might prove to be the lesser of two evils.

If they went back to Slinterwood, apart from getting to and from the car there would be stairs to climb, and Michael might insist on carrying her.

Just the idea of being carried up to bed in his arms sent a quiver through her.

'So what do you think?'

She swallowed, then said, 'I'm quite happy to stay here tonight, so long as tomorrow morning I can be back at Slinterwood in good time to pack.'

He sighed. So she was still bent on leaving.

'Well, if that's what you really want,' he agreed evenly. 'But I was rather hoping you might have changed your mind.'

Trying to sound cool and decided, she said, 'No, I haven't changed my mind.'

In spite of all her efforts, Michael heard the quiver in her voice, and, knowing she was nowhere near as unmoved as she was endeavouring to make out, smiled to himself.

'Well, in that case,' he said smoothly, 'I think, as we only had a light brunch, it might be a good idea to eat before too long, then we can get an early night. Don't you agree?'

She had been prepared for him to argue, and, both surprised and relieved that he had put up no further opposition, she nodded.

'Let me know when you're starting to feel hungry.'

Eager to get the evening over, she told him, 'I'm ready to eat whenever you are.'

'Then I'll go and see what I can rustle up.'

'Do you need any help?'

He shook his head. 'We have the remains of a hamper from Fortnum and Mason, so I should be able to manage a meal of some kind.

'There's a dining-room next door,' he added, 'but in the circumstances it might be better to eat on our knees in front of the fire.'

'That suits me fine,' she agreed.

Rising leisurely to his feet, he tossed some more logs onto the fire, sending a shower of bright sparks crackling up the chimney, and, having collected the coffee mugs, went through to the kitchen.

While he was sorting through the cupboard and assembling a meal of sorts, his thoughts were even busier than his hands.

Though with so many unanswered questions, so much at stake, he had absolutely no intention of letting Jenny leave at this stage in the game, he knew it would pay to tread carefully.

To start with, he warned himself, he must hide his desire for her. He had seen how very uncomfortable any sign of its existence made her.

He was practically sure of three things, however.

Firstly, that she wanted *him* as much as he wanted *her.* All her actions seemed to prove it.

Secondly, that her discomfort was almost certainly due to the fact that it went against both her nature and her convictions to indulge in what she regarded as casual sex.

And thirdly, that even though she felt it was completely wrong to sleep with her boss, she couldn't trust herself to hold out against him.

The latter conclusion caused a storm of feeling and a surge of sexual excitement that he had to struggle hard to stifle.

At first, his distrust of the female sex had made him try to ignore an attraction he had told himself was purely physical.

But he no longer believed that that was all it was. What he felt for Jenny, while he hesitated to put a name to it, went a great deal deeper. Somehow it had quietly taken over and become a force to be reckoned with, a fever in his blood.

His thoughts turning to the coming night, and recalling her warmth, her sweetness, her innocent passion, he felt a strong urge to throw caution to the winds and make her his once more.

But was that passion as innocent as it seemed? Suddenly recalling what Paul had told him, he found himself wondering if perhaps there might be some truth in the rumours.

No, he couldn't believe it.

Or was it simply that he didn't *want* to believe it?

Though not much time had passed, knowing Paul never let the grass grow under his feet, and in need of some kind of re-assurance, he took his phone out of his coat pocket and rang Paul's mobile.

When there was no answer, he left a cautious message asking if there were any results yet from 'the enquiry'.

He was just about to drop the phone into his trouser pocket when it buzzed.

'That was quick,' he said. 'So where were you?'

'I don't know who you were expecting to call,' Claire's clear, light voice said, 'but I don't suppose it was me.'

'No, it wasn't,' he told her flatly.

'You don't sound very pleased to hear from me,' she said plaintively.

Ignoring that, he asked, 'Why are you calling?'

'I wanted to talk to you.'

'We've nothing left to talk about.'

'But of course we have. The press seem to believe that we're getting back together.'

'Could that be because you told them we were?'

'Darling, don't sound so cross. I only mentioned it as a pos-sibility. I still love you, and I miss you so. I didn't realize just how much I loved you until it was too late.

'Look, suppose I came to see you? We could discuss things, sort out exactly where we stand—'

'My dear Claire, I already know exactly where *I* stand. As far as I'm concerned our marriage is over. Finished. Nothing you can say or do will alter that—' But Michael was talking to himself.

Slipping the phone into his trouser pocket, he grimaced. He didn't believe for one instant that Claire still loved him; in fact he'd come to the conclusion that she never had.

A career as a photographic model was a notoriously precarious one, and at twenty-six she might soon be replaced by a fresh and dewy seventeen-year-old.

Added to that, her former lover had proved to be fickle and moved on, so no doubt she was regretting even more the ending of her marriage and the loss of a lifestyle that had been very much to her taste…

In the other room, sitting gazing into the flames, her thoughts on the coming night, Jenny tried to tell herself that there was no need to be worried.

She had little doubt that, as far as it went, Michael would keep his mocking promise not to do anything she didn't want him to do.

But that left her wide open.

And suppose he decided to test her? Suppose he kissed her goodnight?

She could tell him to stop, of course, but he was a sophisticated man, skilful and experienced, a man who might choose to ignore what she *said* and judge solely by her reactions.

If he did, she would be lost, and she knew it.

It was her inability to trust herself to say no, and mean it, that had renewed her determination to leave in the morning.

But first she had to get through tonight…

The door opened and Michael came in wheeling a trolley loaded with food and a bottle of white wine.

Her pulse began to race just at the sight of him.

The sleeves of his black polo-necked sweater were pushed up to his elbows exposing muscular forearms, a chef's apron was tied around his lean waist, and there was a dark smudge on his cheek.

It made his hard face look oddly boyish, and her heart melted like candlewax in a flame.

At that instant, as though becoming aware of it, he raised

a hand and rubbed the mark off, before saying, 'I'm afraid it's not exactly what you'd call a *usual* meal, so a nice bottle of Chablis might help it down.'

He put the trolley near to the settee, drew his own chair closer, and reached to open and pour the wine.

She watched his hands, strong, well-shaped hands, with long fingers, and neatly trimmed nails, and a teasingly light touch.

How gently they had stroked and caressed her, how tenderly they had cupped the weight of her breasts and teased the nipples into life, how delicately they had traced the skin of her inner thighs, before going on to explore the slick warmth that awaited…

All at once Michael glanced up, and, feeling the hot blood pour into her face, she stared into the flames.

Looking at her half-averted face he saw that she was as scarlet as a Judas flower and the tip of one small ear glowed red.

When, a moment or two later, she sneaked a glance at him, hoping he would put her high colour down to the heat of the fire, she saw he was smiling a little, as if he knew quite well what erotic thoughts had caused that burning blush. But to her great relief he made no comment.

When he handed her a glass, she took a sip of the cool, smooth wine while he spread a napkin on her knee and helped her to a plateful of food.

The meal, which proved to be surprisingly tasty, was comprised of spicy chicken breasts, tinned asparagus, and artichoke hearts. It was followed by bottled apricots in a creamy brandy sauce.

Apart from the odd remark they ate in a silence that, in spite of both their efforts to lighten the atmosphere, was weighted with sexual tension.

When they had finished eating, Michael stacked their dirty dishes on the trolley and took them through to the kitchen.

He returned quite quickly with a tray of coffee and Benedictine, and thin, gold-wrapped mints.

Her mind had been on other things, and as he unloaded the contents of the tray onto the table Jenny said a somewhat belated, 'Thank you very much for the meal.'

Imagining Claire's reaction had she been presented with what, in effect, was a scratch meal out of tins, Michael said ruefully, 'I won't ask if you enjoyed it, but at least it should keep the pangs of hunger away until the morning.'

'As a matter of fact I thoroughly enjoyed it.'

She sounded as if she meant it, and, marvelling at her good temper and adaptability, he smiled at her.

Riveted by the warmth of that smile, she sat quite still gazing at him.

Her eyes were soft and luminous, and held a mixture of emotions that he didn't dare try to decipher, but that drew him like a magnet.

As though under a spell of enchantment, he rose to his feet, knowing he simply *had* to kiss her.

He had taken just one step when the spell was broken by the buzz of his mobile phone.

Wishing he'd switched if off, he turned away with a murmured, 'Excuse me.'

Shaken by how near she had come to disaster—if he'd touched her it wouldn't have stopped at kissing, she knew—and still quaking inside, Jenny turned away to stare into the fire once more.

Flicking open the phone, Michael said a curt, 'Hello?'

'Hi.' It was Paul's voice. 'Sorry I missed your call earlier, but I was on my way to Bayswater. As it was a delicate matter, I decided it would be better to handle things myself.

'I began by phoning Miss Mansell's flat and talking to her flatmate, whose name is Laura Fleming. When I told Miss

Fleming who I was and mentioned that there were some rather unpleasant rumours being circulated about Miss Mansell, she asked me to go over.

'She turned out to be a pleasant, down-to-earth girl, and while we chatted I discovered that I know her boyfriend, Tom Harmen. We both go to the same leisure centre. In fact on a couple of occasions we've played squash together when our respective partners failed to show up.

'But to get to the point, when I told Miss Fleming what was being said about her flatmate she was both furious and indignant. She knows Miss Mansell well, they've been friends and flatmates for a number of years, and she categorically denied that there was a word of truth in those rumours. In fact she was all for coming into Global and laying into the man responsible for them. But I assured her that now I knew they were lies, I would deal with the culprit myself and make sure that the rumours were scotched.

'So all in all, I think you can rest assured that your new PA is squeaky clean.'

'Thanks,' Michael said, 'I appreciate all the trouble you've gone to.'

'Any time. Now I must dash, I'm taking Joanne out to supper. Take care!'

'And you.'

Michael dropped the phone back into his pocket and resumed his seat.

Jenny, who had been in a brown study, looked up.

Though she had guessed that he intended to kiss her and known she should stop him, she had sat helpless and waiting.

When the phone had distracted him, aware that she should feel relieved, she had felt anything but.

But somehow, for her own sake, she *had* to find a way to conquer this weakness. If she gave in to him tonight, it would be total surrender. She wouldn't have the strength to leave in the morning, and they both knew it.

Then she would become his plaything, his temporary mistress, someone who meant nothing to him apart from a little easy pleasure while he taught his ex-wife a lesson, before taking her back.

No! She couldn't do it. *Wouldn't* do it.

Glancing up, she noticed that he was watching her intently, as though endeavouring to read her thoughts.

It unnerved her, and, needing something to occupy her hands and help to hide her feelings, she reached to pick up the jug of coffee and fill two cups, while Michael opened the Benedictine and poured a measure of the golden liqueur into a pair of brandy glasses.

Sitting in the warmth of the fireglow, they drank their coffee and sipped the sweet liqueur in silence.

But while neither of them spoke, she was only too aware that his eyes seldom left her face.

In the aftermath of the phone call, she had noticed that he seemed to be more relaxed, more certain, as though some private worry had been resolved and he could see his way forward.

Now, his mouth firm, the light of conquest in his eye, he looked like a man who intended to storm the fortress and succeed at all costs.

Feeling the vibes, and sensing that she was the object of his planned siege, she felt shivers begin to chase down her spine.

Telling herself she was being a fanciful idiot, she struggled to dismiss the idea.

As the grandfather clock chimed nine-thirty, he remarked, 'Well, if we are going to have an early night, it's about time I was starting to make up the bed-settee.'

She found herself holding her breath when he rose, and,

taking the empty glass from her nerveless fingers, set it down, before moving the table against the far wall.

When he turned back his face was bland, anything but threatening. And as if to prove that she really *had* let her imagination run away with her, he said, 'If you'd like to use the bathroom while I do it, you'll find a robe and plenty of toilet things.'

Glancing down at her bandaged ankle, he added, 'My bedroom has an en-suite, so there's no need to try and hurry.'

He stooped purposefully, and before she could tell him she didn't need any help he had slid an arm behind her back and one under her knees and lifted her into his arms.

Carrying her through to a bathroom that, though old-fashioned, was warm, well equipped and spotlessly clean, he lowered her carefully onto a cork-topped stool.

Then, opening the door of an airing cupboard, he took out some towels and a pile of bedclothes before asking, 'Will you be able to manage?'

There was a another stool in the shower cubicle, and several handgrips, and she answered hastily, 'Oh, yes, thank you.'

'Well, call if you need me.' He hung the towels over the rail and departed with the bedclothes, leaving her to prepare for the night.

Perched on the stool, she managed to wriggle out of her clothes with relative quickness and ease, but because of the need to manoeuvre to keep her bandage dry it took a lot longer than usual to shower.

When she had finished and dried herself, she stood up carefully, and, taking her weight on her good foot, hopped to the sink.

Amongst an array of toiletries, there were tubes of toothpaste, several plastic-encased toothbrushes, and a hairbrush and comb.

A coffee-coloured satin robe lay folded on a nearby shelf, but, guessing that it must have belonged to his ex-wife, she was reluctant to use it.

Having washed and cleaned her teeth, she brushed out her dark hair, and, leaving it to curl loosely around her shoulders, debated what to sleep in.

The thought of Michael seeing her in her skimpy undies threw her into a tizzy, and she decided she had very little option but to borrow the robe.

She had just belted it around her waist and folded her clothes when there was a tap at the door, and Michael's voice queried, 'Are you about ready?'

'Yes, quite ready, thank you. But I really don't need any help.'

Ignoring that obvious untruth, he came in.

It must have taken her even longer than she had realized, because he was wearing a short silk robe and was clearly fresh from the shower himself.

He carried her through to the living-room where the lamps had been switched off, the fire was burning brightly, and the bed-settee, with its pretty, sprigged duvet and plumped up pillows, looked cosy and inviting.

Settling her back against the soft pillows, he sat down on the edge of the settee and smiled into her eyes.

'Don't!' she begged huskily.

Lifting a dark brow, he asked, 'Don't what?'

'You promised you wouldn't do anything I didn't want you to do.'

'And I have every intention of keeping that promise,' he assured her silkily. 'But I'm quite sure you want me to do this.' Tilting her chin, he kissed her with slow deliberation.

His kiss was so feather-light that he could feel her lips trembling beneath his own.

When she made an effort to draw away, he took her face between his hands, and continued to kiss her, little plucking kisses that coaxed and tantalized and beguiled, yet somehow she managed to keep her lips closed against him.

Instead of forcing the issue, his mouth began to stray over her face, planting soft, baby kisses on her cheeks, the tip of her nose, her closed eyelids, and the smooth skin beneath her jawline.

Feeling the way her pulse was racing, he began to nuzzle her neck, and she started to shudder helplessly as, using his lips and teeth and tongue, he delicately nibbled his way down to the warm hollow at the base of her throat.

When his mouth returned to hers once more, and the tip of his tongue stroked across her lips, they parted beneath his coaxing as if there were no help for it.

Even when he deepened the kiss, it was slow and careful, as if the gift of her mouth was infinitely precious to him. She had no defences against the sweetness and tenderness of that gentle seduction.

He continued to kiss her, and soon she was drifting in a kind of blissful daze where neither the past nor the future existed, and nothing in the world mattered but this Michael's touch and his kisses.

She was hardly aware that his hands had left her face and his fingers had pushed aside the satin lapels of the gown.

It was only when he bent his dark head to take a velvety nipple in his mouth that, panic-stricken, she jerked into life.

If she didn't stop him now, she was lost.

Twining her fingers in his hair, she tugged.

He drew back, and just for an instant she glimpsed a look on his face that echoed the kind of bliss she had been feeling before that sudden attack of panic.

'What's wrong, my love?'

There was no trace of the anger she had expected, and his quiet endearment made her heart stop.

Dragging the lapels together over her breasts, she said hoarsely, 'I don't want you to make love to me.'

He shook his head. 'All your reactions tell me plainly that you *do* want me to make love to you.'

'I *don't*,' she insisted.

Sounding completely unmoved, he said quietly, 'You're lying.'

Gritting her teeth, she said, 'I told you before, I've never believed in casual sex, and I don't want to get involved with my boss.'

'You're already involved,' he pointed out flatly.

'That was a mistake I'm bitterly sorry for. I only wish it had never happened…'

Just for an instant he looked as if she'd struck him, and her heart turned over.

'For one thing,' she ploughed on desperately, 'there's your wife—'

'My ex-wife,' he corrected. 'And as far as Claire's concerned I'm—'

'Don't tell me,' Jenny broke in bitterly. 'You're in no hurry to take her back until you're satisfied that she's learnt her lesson. Well, I've always believed that if you marry someone you should be faithful to them—'

She stopped abruptly, biting her lip. 'I'm sorry, I shouldn't have said that. It sounds terribly strait-laced and judgmental.'

His expression unreadable, he said, 'That kind of thinking certainly sounds a little old-fashioned in this day and age. However, that isn't to say I think you're wrong…'

He took her hand and held it, his thumb stroking over the palm.

'Though no doubt Claire would. Her attitude has always been a great deal more worldly. She regards the body simply as something to dress up and get pleasure from.

'And if by any chance we *did* remarry, when the honey-moon period was over, I'm sure she would want to revert to a "modern" relationship.'

She snatched her hand free. 'Well, *she* may be happy with that, but I wouldn't want any part of it. I don't intend to end up as a temporary plaything, "a bit on the side".'

'Who said anything about a plaything, or "a bit on the side"?'

Realizing that he wasn't about to take no for an answer, desperate now, and suddenly seeing a way out, she lied unsteadily, 'In any case there's someone else to consider...'

His eyes narrowed to green slits. 'Really? So who else is there, may I ask?'

'Someone who... It doesn't really matter.'

'Oh, but it does.'

She had hoped not to have to say any more, but the intentness of his gaze told her that there wasn't a cat in hell's chance of leaving it like that.

'So who is this *someone?* A secret boyfriend perhaps?'

'Not exactly secret,' she said.

'But a boyfriend you failed to mention?'

'Well, yes.'

'At the interview you led me to believe there was no one of any importance in your life.'

When she said nothing, he pursued, 'So if you expect me to believe in this man's existence you'll have to tell me more about him. To start with, what does he do?'

Pushed into a corner, and thinking of Laura's boyfriend, Tom, she answered, 'He works for one of the smaller airlines.'

'How long have you two been going out together?'

'Quite a while.'

'Is it serious?'

After a momentary hesitation, she said, 'Yes.'

Watching her face closely, and almost certain that she was

lying, he queried, 'How serious? He hasn't by any chance produced a ring and proposed?'

'As a matter of fact, he has.'

'So why did you lie to me at the interview?'

'I… I didn't,' she denied.

'You told me you hadn't a fiancé.'

Hoping Laura would forgive her, she said, 'I haven't. I didn't accept his proposal.'

'Why not?'

'I—I needed time to think it over.'

'So you decided to take the job until you'd made up your mind?'

'Yes.'

'Didn't he object to you leaving London?'

'He doesn't know anything about it. He's abroad on business for the next few weeks, and we agreed not to contact each other while he was away.'

'But presumably he'll be expecting an answer when he gets back?'

'Yes.'

'What do you intend to tell him?'

Deciding to stall, she said, 'I still haven't made up my mind.'

'What's he like?'

'Kind and thoughtful and generous.'

'Describe him.'

A little wildly, she said, 'He's in his early twenties, blond, handsome, fun to be with, and loaded with charm.'

'Every girl's dream,' Michael commented sarcastically. 'You said he was generous. Does that mean he buys you presents?'

Growing increasingly stressed, she said, 'He bought me a gift for St Valentine's day.'

'What kind of a gift?'

'A bracelet watch.'

'I haven't seen you wearing it.'

'It's too dressy for work. It's the kind of thing you'd wear in the evening, or for special occasions.'

'So why weren't you wearing it at Mr Jenkins's retirement party?'

'How do you know I wasn't?' Then almost accusingly, 'You were there!'

'For a short time.'

It gave her a strange feeling to realize that he had been at the party and she hadn't even seen him.

'But it was only for Global's staff and employees,' she protested, 'so how did you—?'

Breaking off, she answered her own question. 'Of course, you're a friend of Paul Levens.'

Then recalling Michael's reputation for being antisocial, she asked, '*Why* were you there?'

'I came especially to have a look at you.'

For a moment she was taken aback, then realization dawned. 'You mean before you asked Mr Levens to set up the interview?'

A gleam in his eye, he asked, 'Can you blame me?'

'No, I suppose not.'

Returning to the attack, he said, 'But we were discussing your boyfriend. Do you and he sleep together?'

'No.'

'Why not?'

Desperate to get the interrogation over, she said, 'Until now I haven't been absolutely sure of my feelings.'

'*Until now*... Does that mean you've finally made up your mind?'

She swallowed, then, knowing she had to sound convincing, said, 'Yes. I love him.'

Momentarily, Michael's certainty that she was lying was rocked.

Then the way she was avoiding his eyes made him wonder, and he returned to the attack once more.

'If you had been sure of your feelings previously, would you have slept with him?'

'I—I might have done.'

'But you would have to love a man before you went to bed with him?'

'Yes.'

'By the way, you still haven't told me what this boyfriend of yours is called.'

Her mind went completely and utterly blank.

Seeing he was waiting, and knowing that everything depended on being able to answer convincingly, she blurted out, 'His name's Tom Harmen. Now I refuse to answer any more questions.'

All uncertainty set at rest, Michael felt a surge of mingled relief and triumph.

'Just one last thing. How do you feel about me?'

'What?'

'I asked how you felt about me? Do you love me?'

'No—no, of course not,' she stammered.

'So why *did* you go to bed with me?'

'I've told you,' she cried jerkily. 'I hadn't intended it to happen.'

'You couldn't help yourself?'

When she failed to answer, just stared at him, he smiled, a slow smile of satisfaction that made her blood run cold, and she heard the clang of the trap closing behind her even before he drew her close and kissed her.

CHAPTER NINE

THOUGH Jenny wanted so badly to stay in Michael's arms, somehow she gathered the will power to pull herself free. 'No. I can't let this happen. I—'

'If you're going to tell me again that you have a boyfriend you love, you're wasting your time. I know you're lying,' he added flatly.

She half shook her head, then said in despair, 'No, that isn't it.'

'So what is?'

'You know perfectly well.'

'Tell me something. If Claire wasn't still in the picture, would you feel the same?'

'But she *is*.'

'That's just it, she isn't. You see—'

'How can you say that? If you think for just one moment that I—'

Putting a finger against her lips to stop the indignant flow of words, Michael said patiently, 'Will you please listen to me? I have absolutely no intention of taking Claire back. Everything was absolutely over, finished, when I divorced her.'

He paused to let that sink in while she stared at him, her

lovely brown eyes mirroring her hopes and fears and remaining doubts.

'Over?'

'Over.'

Hardly able to believe it, she whispered, 'You won't be taking her back?'

'No matter what lies she may be feeding to the newspapers, I *won't* be taking her back.'

Then with soft impatience, 'Now will you be still and let me make love to you before this wanting burns me up…?'

He wasn't taking his ex-wife back. *He wasn't taking her back!*

Jenny gave a little sigh, and as he bent his head her eyes drifted shut, and her chin rose to expose the long line of her throat.

Running his fingers into her dark, silky hair, he held her face between his palms and kissed her with a passionate tenderness.

It was all over between them. She heard the angels singing as she kissed him back.

For a while they just kissed. Then kissing was no longer enough, and, having removed her robe, he tossed aside his own and stretched out beside her.

While the fireglow warmed her and gilded her skin, his hands began a slow journey of exploration, caressing every inch of her body, finding all her secret places and making every nerve-ending sing into glorious life.

When his mouth followed his hands, she began to shudder as, whispering how beautiful she was, how much pleasure she gave him, how much he wanted her, he brought her to a fever pitch of desire.

Then he paused, supporting himself on one elbow while he gazed down at her.

Opening dazed eyes, she stared up at him.

There was a strange expression on his face, a look of hope, a kind of expectancy, as if he was waiting for something.

Her heart answered that look, and, smiling at him, she put her arms around his neck and heard his sigh of contentment and pleasure as she pulled him down into the cradle of her hips.

He made love to her in silence—tender, passionate love that needed no words.

Somehow that silence made the other sensations grow stronger, more intense, and while they moved in unison stars seemed to rain down on them like sparks, making them burn with ecstasy.

In the aftermath of their love-making, when she lay limp and quivering, her eyes closed, he drew her into his arms and, knowing beyond a shadow of a doubt that he had made the right decision, *she* was the woman he wanted, held her against his heart until she fell fast asleep.

Then he lay looking down at her lovely, peaceful face—the dark curve of her brows and the long sweep of lashes, the small straight nose and the wide, passionate mouth, the high cheekbones and the firm chin that gave her face so much character—and wondered at that indefinable quality that made a set of features unique and beautiful.

Features that had already been familiar to him the first time he'd set eyes on her.

And suddenly, the knowledge swimming from the depths of his mind, he knew exactly why.

When he eventually slipped into sleep, the final parts of the jigsaw had been fitted together and made a clear and fascinating picture.

Jenny awoke in the morning to instant remembrance and a surging happiness. It was all over between Michael and Claire. He wasn't going to take her back.

Hopes and dreams for the future danced in her mind as bright and entrancing as fireflies, and, smiling a little, she stretched luxuriously.

The grate had been cleared and a fresh fire was burning cheerfully, only to be diminished somewhat by pale winter sunshine slanting through the mullioned windows, its brightness matching her mood.

She had slept cradled in Michael's arms, and earlier he had kissed her awake and made love to her again. Long, slow, delectable love that had left her feeling treasured and beautiful and desirable.

Things she had never felt before. Things that, after Andy, she had never even *hoped* to feel.

And perhaps even more important, he had given her a sense of safety and fulfilment, as though she had at last found her true home in his arms.

But for the moment she was alone, and the smell of percolating coffee was drifting in.

Pushing back the duvet, she sat on the edge of the bed and gingerly tested her ankle.

Finding the night's rest had made all the difference, and though still a trifle painful it took her weight, she unwound the bandage and made her way into the bathroom.

When she had showered, she pulled on her clothes, cleaned her teeth, brushed her hair, and, eager to be with Michael, went through to the kitchen.

It was a pleasant enough room, with a wood-burning stove standing in a stone fireplace, an oak table and chairs, and, though they were somewhat out of date, 'all mod cons'.

There was a glass jug of coffee keeping hot on the stove, along with a dish of something that smelled extremely appetizing, but to her disappointment there was no sign of Michael.

Returning to the living-room, she folded the bedding and

left it in a neat pile on the settee, then, favouring her damaged ankle, went exploring.

From the inner hall they had come in by, an archway led to what appeared to be a formal drawing-room, and beyond that a butler's pantry. Further on still was a small oak door, which, when she tried it, opened into the main courtyard.

Outside it seemed reasonably mild, and, deciding that she didn't need a coat, she set off across the cobbles, pausing by the old metal-capped well to look around her at the picturesque scene.

The storm had passed through in the early hours of the morning, giving place to a relatively bright, sunny day.

Everywhere still looked freshly washed. The cobblestones gleamed and a million raindrops glittered on sills and guttering, the bonnet of Michael's car, and the ivy that festooned the southern wall.

She sighed with pleasure.

A seagull circled, calling raucously, and, tilting back her head to follow that beautiful, effortless flight, she noticed a figure on the battlements.

As she looked up their eyes met and held.

She had the strangest feeling of déjà vu.

Only it *wasn't* déjà vu, she realized as she absently watched the seagull settle on the cover of the well, its beady eyes fixed on her, its yellow webbed feet looking clumsy on so graceful a bird; this had really happened.

On her very first visit to the castle, she had looked up and seen a man with dark, wind-ruffled hair standing on the battlements.

Their eyes had met and held, and as though something momentous had happened her breath had caught in her throat and her heart had started to throw itself against her ribs.

Flustered both by the strength of her reaction and the intensity of the man's gaze, she had looked away.

It had been quite late, and, knowing herself to be the only visitor still there, she had wondered if the environs of the castle were closed and she should have been gone.

That thought in mind, she had started across the courtyard towards the main gate, but something had impelled her to pause just briefly and turn to look up at the battlements once more.

They were empty. The man who had had such an impact on her had vanished.

But the little incident had stayed in her mind for a long time afterwards.

Now she was sure that it had been Michael she had seen all those years ago, and, wondering at the strangeness of fate, she looked up to wave to him.

The battlements were empty. He had vanished once more.

She felt a sense of loss like a blow over the heart, a sudden panic, a fear that history was repeating itself.

Then, just as the seagull took to the air with a squawk, Michael's tall figure appeared from the north tower and started to cross the courtyard towards her.

Filled with gladness, she literally threw herself into his arms.

He gave a little grunt as he took the unexpected impact, and held her close.

When she'd been thoroughly kissed, a twinkle in his eye, he told her gravely, 'Now that's what I call real enthusiasm.'

Blushing a little, she murmured, 'Sorry.'

'There's no need to be sorry. I only hope I can look forward to a greeting like that every morning. I just couldn't help but wonder what brought it on.'

'I know it sounds silly, but I thought for a minute that you'd gone.'

'Gone?' he echoed blankly.

'Disappeared… Like you did the first time. You see, when

I looked up and saw you standing on the battlements, the scene was familiar to me. I thought for a moment that it was déjà vu, then I realized it really had happened. The first time I visited the castle I saw you standing in almost the same spot. You won't remember, but you looked at me, and—'

'As a matter of fact I remember very well.'

'You do?'

'I also remember that you appeared to be shy. You looked away, then turned to go back to your car.'

'I was the only visitor still there and I thought maybe I should have already left.'

'So you ran, without looking back.'

'No. When I reached the gateway I *did* look back, but you'd gone.'

'I was hurrying down the tower steps. I wanted to talk to you, to stop you leaving.' He sighed. 'But I was too late…'

She had stopped in her tracks and was gazing at him, wide-eyed.

'Then when I saw you again at Arthur Jenkins's retirement party—'

'But surely you didn't recognize me after all those years, when you'd caught only one brief glimpse of me?'

'As a matter of fact I'd never forgotten you, and I knew you almost at once.'

'Is that why you gave me the job?'

'Partly,' he admitted.

'You never mentioned we'd seen each other before.'

'I wondered if you might remember.'

'I did… Sort of… I felt as if I knew you, but I didn't know why. I wondered if I might have seen your photograph somewhere…'

Then wonderingly, 'It's all so strange.'

'The Turkish and Arabic people call it kismet.'

'That's exactly what it feels like,' she said, and leaned against him contentedly, her head fitting snugly beneath his chin.

He kissed her hair, breathing in the fragrance of it, and feeling as though his heart were too big to fit into its allotted space.

Then, not wanting to appear soft, he returned to the practical. 'How is the ankle today?'

Straightening up, she smiled at him. 'Almost as good as new. The spray you put on seems to have worked wonders.'

'I'm pleased about that. Though I admit I was quite looking forward to carrying you again.'

With a seductive glance from beneath long lashes, she told him demurely, 'I dare say I'll need some help by tonight...'

He laughed joyously.

'In the meantime,' she added prosaically, 'when I looked in the kitchen, whatever you'd been cooking smelled delicious.'

'Hungry?'

'Ravenous.'

An arm around her slender waist, he commented, 'Unromantic but reassuring. Let's go and eat. Then when we've finished breakfast, if you think your ankle will stand it I'll take you up on the battlements.'

'I'm sure it will,' she said happily.

After a tasty breakfast at the kitchen table, Michael fetched their outdoor things.

'I know you're eager to do this,' he said as he helped her on with her coat, 'but promise you'll tell me if your ankle starts to hurt.'

Feeling cherished and cared for, she gave her promise, and they climbed the steps of the north tower and emerged onto the battlements.

The air was clear and fresh and the pale sunshine held more than a hint of warmth as, hand in hand, they walked slowly round the battlements. The views over the gleaming silver sea, the mainland coast, and the sweep of pale sand either side of the causeway were serene and beautiful.

Looking over the island's fertile countryside, she could see a collage of green fields and hills dotted with the orangey-yellow of gorse, and an occasional farmhouse, and on the seaward side the deserted beaches and rocky coves she and Michael had walked beside.

From the battlements, Slinterwood appeared to be quite close, and a little further on along the coast Jenny could see a farm and a hamlet of cottages, grey smoke rising from their tall chimneys and hovering, serene and orderly as a gathering of quakers.

After gazing at the picturesque scene for a while in appreciative silence, a catch in her voice, Jenny remarked, 'It must be wonderful to live here and to know all this beauty is yours.'

'I've always considered that in most respects I was a very lucky man,' Michael answered seriously. Then giving her a squeeze. 'And now I'm convinced that I'm the most fortunate man alive.'

That remark earned him a kiss, which he returned with interest.

After a while, becoming aware that her ankle was starting to throb, but reluctant to move, she shifted her weight onto her good foot.

Noticing that small movement, and appreciating the cause, he said firmly, 'We'd better be starting down. You can come up here as much as you like when your ankle is fully mended.'

Glowing at the thought, she allowed herself to be shepherded to the tower steps which, with his help, she managed to get down with comparative ease.

As they crossed the courtyard he glanced at his watch. 'I'd like to be back at Slinterwood before too long, so it might be a good idea for you to get straight into the car…?'

Wondering if he was planning to start work, she nodded, and allowed herself to be helped in.

'This way you can rest your ankle while I just make sure everything's safe. Mrs Blair will be over some time this afternoon to tidy up after us…'

When he came back he was carrying a large manilla envelope, which he tossed onto the back seat before sliding behind the wheel.

'All set?' he queried.

She nodded, and a moment later they were heading for the gatehouse.

It would have been a wrench leaving the castle had she been leaving for good. But the situation having altered so dramatically, and comparing how things were now to how they had seemed on her arrival at the castle yesterday, she left with a smile hanging on her lips.

The journey back to Slinterwood along the high coastal road was spectacular, and Jenny thoroughly enjoyed it.

Wondering what the actual distance was between the castle and Slinterwood, she remarked, 'It must be quite a long way for Mrs Blair to walk.'

'It would be by road, but when the weather's fine she takes a short cut.'

He pointed. 'See the stand of pine trees on the right? There's a path runs through them that leads first to the castle, and then down to the causeway.'

'What about when it's wet?'

'Oh, she doesn't walk then.' Michael grinned. 'She has a little car. She pops over to the mainland regularly to shop and play bingo.'

When they reached the house, once again it seemed to welcome her, and Jenny went inside as if she were coming home.

Everywhere was clean and tidy, and the fires had been lit, proving that Mrs Blair had been and gone.

As Michael helped her off with her coat Jenny said, 'Earlier you mentioned that you wanted to get back. Does that mean you're planning to start work?'

'No, not just yet. There's something I want to do first. Do you mind if I leave you for a short time?'

Though a little surprised, she answered, 'No, of course not.'

Settling her comfortably on the couch in front of the living-room fire, her shoes off and a selection of books by her side, he explained, 'I want to call on old Martha before lunch.'

At Jenny's questioning glance, he went on, 'Martha is well into her nineties. She used to work at the castle until my father died. Then she, along with her husband, Noah, and daughter, Hannah, finally decided to retire. Noah was almost a hundred years old when he died last year.'

'Does she live alone now?'

'No. After her husband's death, she went to live with her daughter... Now, you're quite sure you'll be all right?'

Touched by his concern, she answered, 'Quite sure.'

He stooped and kissed her lingeringly, as if he could hardly bear to leave her. Then, straightening, he headed for the door. His hand on the knob, he turned to smile at her and say, 'I won't be long.'

A few moments later she heard his car door slam, the engine start, and the car draw away.

For a while Jenny sat thinking over all that had happened while they had been at the castle, and marvelling at the way fate worked.

Yesterday morning she had been determined to leave both Michael and the island. But now, only twenty-four hours later, she was deliriously happy at the prospect of staying.

Though it was only a short time since they'd met, it was as if she had known and cared for him all her life. The thought was like a flare going up, making clear feelings she hadn't yet faced, and could hardly credit. How could she possibly love a man she had only just met?

Yet she did.

One day, if she was very fortunate, he might come to feel the same way about her, but at the moment all that really mattered was that he had no intention of going back to his ex-wife, that it was *her* he wanted with him.

Things had happened so quickly between them, and even though no word of commitment had been spoken, and no promises made, she was content.

Although she wanted his love more than anything in the world, at the moment it was enough that he was tender and caring.

She was still savouring that newly found contentment when she heard the sound of the car returning and pulling up outside.

A minute or so later, to her surprise, there were voices in the hall, then the living-room door opened and Michael appeared, an old lady on one arm, and the manilla envelope he'd left in the car tucked under the other.

'Jenny, I'd like you to meet Martha... Martha, this is Jenny Mansell.'

Jenny swung her feet to the floor, but Michael said quickly, 'No, don't get up. Stay where you are. I've told Martha about your sprained ankle.'

Remaining seated, Jenny said with a smile, 'It's nice to meet you, Martha.'

As Martha gave a respectful nod Michael added, 'Martha has been with the family all her life.'

The old lady was tall and spare and dressed in black from head to toe. She wore long jet earrings and her pure white hair was in a neat bun. Though her face was as wrinkled as a walnut, her dark eyes were bright and alert, and she appeared to still have her own teeth.

When Michael had helped her off with her coat and she was settled in a chair by the fire, he suggested, 'What about a spot of brandy to keep out the cold?'

Then with a grin, 'And don't try to tell me I'm leading you astray, because Hannah mentioned that you always have a drop of "medicine" before lunch, to settle your stomach.'

Martha gave a cackle of laughter. 'And so I do.'

When Michael had supplied the old lady with a generous measure of cognac, he went to sit on the settee beside Jenny and explained, 'There's something I'd like you to hear, and, though Martha doesn't get out much these days, she offered to come and tell you first hand.'

As Jenny looked at him, puzzled and expectant, he took her hand and, twisting the heavy gold ring on her finger, went on, 'I'll start from when I first noticed the seal on your signet ring and recognized it as part of the old family crest. It was then I began to get an inkling of what might have happened.

'This morning, before I went up on the battlements, I had a quick look in the castle archives for some photographs I could vaguely recall seeing, and these are what I found. Martha recognized them both immediately.'

Reaching for the manilla envelope that he'd dropped on the coffee table, he opened it and passed her an old-fashioned, unframed, sepia photograph.

She found herself staring at a studio portrait of a young man sitting rather self-consciously beside a potted palm, his hands spread on his thighs.

Michael.

Only of course it couldn't be Michael.

Though the lean, strong face, the handsome eyes, and the well-shaped head of thick dark hair were identical, the moustache and the high, winged collar looked as if they belonged in the nineteen-twenties.

'Who is it?' she asked.

'My great-grandfather, Michael. I was named after him. Now take a good look at his right hand. See the signet ring on his little finger? Well, with a magnifying glass I was able to make out that the seal is a phoenix.'

Jenny was still puzzling over it when he handed her another photograph. Sitting in the same chair, by the same potted palm, was a young woman with dark eyes and dark hair, wearing a high-necked blouse and a long string of pearls.

Herself.

But again it couldn't be.

So who was it?

Almost immediately light dawned.

Watching her expressive face, he said, 'You've guessed it. Your great-grandmother, Jenny. The photographs must have been taken before she and Michael got engaged.'

'Engaged! So it was your great-grandfather who was the love of her life…'

Swallowing past the lump in her throat, she asked, 'What makes you think the photographs were taken before they got engaged?'

'Because he was still wearing the signet ring. When she agreed to marry him, he gave *her* the ring. However, before they could make any kind of formal announcement, he went down with flu. It turned to pneumonia, and within three days he was dead.

'As you know, he was a widower with a young son. He had married his own cousin when they were both very young, and after a brief and not particularly happy marriage his wife died in childbirth.

'When Michael became ill so suddenly and unexpectedly, his parents were away. They'd taken the child to Scotland to visit his maternal grandparents, and when they were summoned back it was to find that their only son was dead.

'Perhaps you can't blame them for being insular in their grief, but Jenny, who was heartbroken, found herself shut out, almost ignored.

'The only person who was sorry for her, and went out of her way to be kind to her, was Martha, who at that time was a young maid, about the same age as Jenny herself.

'Utterly devastated, as soon as Michael had been interred in the family vault your great-grandmother left, apparently for good.

'Martha told me all this before we set off for Slinterwood.'

There was silence for a time, then Jenny said slowly, 'I've often wondered if Gran had any connection with the island, and why I always felt it drew me. And now I know everything—'

'Not quite everything.'

She looked at him, her beautiful brown eyes fixed on his face.

'Remember the first time you came to Slinterwood, how familiar it was?'

'Yes,' she breathed.

'Well, of course your great-grandmother knew it well, and had Michael lived to marry her she would have gone there as a bride...'

'You're not saying her spirit...?'

He shook his head. 'No. Something altogether more mundane. But Martha will tell you the rest.'

While Michael replenished the old lady's glass, Martha took up the tale. 'One day, when you were a small child and living with your great-grandmother, she took you with her when she went shopping in Kelsay. After the shopping was finished, she put it in her car and took you into The Tudor Rose café, to buy you some lunch.'

The old lady's voice was a little croaky, as if she wasn't used to speaking so much these days.

She took a sip of her cognac before going on, 'Quite by chance, I was there with my daughter, Hannah. Though quite a lot of years had passed, your great-grandmother hadn't changed all that much, and she and I recognized one another, and got talking.

'While we chatted, your great-grandmother happened to mention that it had been her dream to see Mirren and Slinter-wood again before she died.

'As luck would have it, the family were away, Slinterwood was standing empty, and Hannah and I were looking after things.

'So I suggested to your great-grandmother that she should follow us back across the causeway, and take this chance to see both the castle and the house. She was only too delighted, and when we took her into the castle just briefly, and then over to Slinterwood, you came as well. You couldn't have been more than about three and a half, but you were a beautiful, intelligent little girl, who took notice of everything.

'I remember you were fascinated by the castle, and you loved Slinterwood. One thing that particularly took your fancy was the old pump in the larder, so Hannah primed it and pumped it to show you how it worked…'

Jenny smiled mistily. 'Though I've no recollection of actually going, that's obviously why everything was so familiar to me, why the house seemed to welcome me back…'

Getting to her feet, she went over to the old lady and, taking her hand, said sincerely, 'Thank you for coming spe-cially to tell me. And thank you for being kind to Gran when she needed a friend. I was very fond of her.'

'Bless you, but you don't need to thank me,' Martha said. 'Your great-grandmother was a very nice lady. I only wish the young master had lived to marry her.

'Well, I'd best be getting back, otherwise I'll be catching it off Hannah for keeping lunch waiting.'

'We mustn't have that.' Michael rose and helped her into her coat.

Then, having put more logs on the fire, he turned to Jenny, and said, 'I'll be back as soon as I've seen Martha safely home. In the meantime I suggest you stretch out on the settee and put your feet up.'

As the pair reached the door Martha turned and said, 'You're very much like your great-grandmother, but I feel in my bones that you'll be a great deal luckier in love than she was.'

With that pronouncement, the old lady allowed herself to be escorted out.

The fire was blazing cheerfully, and, leaning back against the cushions, Jenny put her feet up as she had been bidden, and sighed contentedly.

It had been a strange and eventful morning, but it couldn't have been a more wonderful one, she decided as she went over in her mind all that Michael and the old lady had told her.

Now she knew why the ring had meant so much to her great-grandmother, and why the island had always seemed to draw her...

Perhaps her destiny lay here with Michael. Perhaps they had been fated to meet, fated to carry on the love story that their great-grandparents had begun... Sighing, she stretched like a sleek and contented cat. She had never in her wildest dreams imagined being this happy...

Her thoughts grew scrappy as the warmth of the fire made her feel soporific, and, cocooned in a golden haze of euphoria, her eyelids drooped and she drifted into a doze...

CHAPTER TEN

JENNY awoke with a start to find she wasn't alone in the room. A woman was standing looking at her, a woman with blonde hair and blue eyes, wearing sheer silk stockings and a designer suit.

Jenny knew that face. She had seen it on the covers of glossy magazines.

But it couldn't be, she thought in confusion. Claire was in London.

Still her eyes continued to confirm what her brain was refusing to take in, that, far from being in London, Claire was right here.

And looking startlingly beautiful.

Jenny stared at her numbly, conscious of only one thing: Michael had lied to her. He'd told her that the relationship was over, but Claire's presence at Slinterwood went to prove the opposite.

'Who are you?' the newcomer asked sharply. 'What are you doing here?'

Pride insisting that she mustn't give herself away, Jenny found her voice and managed, 'I'm Mr Denver's new PA.'

'Then why are you lying down?'

'I've twisted my ankle, and Mr Denver told me to rest it.'

Clearly dismissing Jenny as any kind of competition, Claire relaxed and said, 'Oh, I see. What a nuisance for you.'

She sounded quite human. Almost pleasant.

As Jenny sat up and swung her feet to the floor, Claire queried, 'Incidentally, where *is* Michael? He doesn't seem to be around.'

'He's taking Martha home.'

The blonde grimaced. 'Any idea when he'll be back?'

'He said he wouldn't be very long.'

'He will be if Hannah gets talking to him. That woman could talk the hind leg off a donkey.'

'If he knows you're coming—'

'He doesn't know. I just made up my mind to come on the spur of the moment. It never occurred to me that he might not be here.'

Dropping into one of the armchairs, she put her handbag down, crossed her shapely legs, and, her voice not unfriendly, went on, 'I've an overnight bag with me if I don't manage to catch the tide, but I was hoping to be back in London by tonight.'

Then, her tone confiding, 'To tell you the truth, island life bores the hell out of me. Though I may need to be here a lot more after Michael and I are married again. Still,' she added reflectively, 'it should be worth it.'

Feeling hollow inside, Jenny made no comment, and after a moment or two Claire asked, 'How long have you been on the island?'

'Just over a week.'

'Do *you* find it boring?'

'No.'

'So how is the new book going?'

'It's beginning to take shape.'

'But he's not settled down to any actual writing?'

'No.'

'That's good. He hates to be disturbed once he's started. Has he taken you to see the castle yet?'

'Yes. We went yesterday.' To Jenny's eternal credit, her voice was steady.

'A cold, draughty hole, isn't it?'

'I thought it was beautiful,' Jenny said quietly.

'Oh, well, everyone to their taste.'

Then, discarding the jacket of her elegant suit, 'I stopped on the way for an early lunch, but I didn't have a drink so I'm *gasping* for a cup of tea.'

Heading for the kitchen, she added over her shoulder, 'Want one?'

Jenny shook her head. 'No, thank you.'

As the door closed behind the other woman, in a mad scramble to get away, Jenny pulled on her shoes, found her shoulder bag and mac, and, her only thought to escape before Michael came back, let herself out.

A red sports car was standing outside.

Following a sudden impulse, she tried the door.

It opened.

However, her hopes of using it to escape were dashed when the ignition keys proved to be missing.

Recalling the handbag Claire had left by the chair, she hesitated.

But going back into the house was too much of a risk. Michael might turn up at any moment and try to stop her leaving.

Paying no heed to her ankle, she hurried up the drive and along the road, glancing anxiously behind her from time to time.

When she reached the little copse that Michael had pointed out that morning, she veered off the road and took the cross-country path.

Only when she was hidden amongst the trees did she start to feel somewhat safer.

Where the sun hadn't penetrated, everywhere was still dripping, and the ground, thickly carpeted with brown pine needles, was wet and spongy beneath her feet and littered with storm debris, which made it slow going.

Her earlier numbness was still with her, the pain of Michael's treachery yet to come. As if she were slowly bleeding to death inside, all she could feel was a strange weakness, a lethargy. She longed to lie down on the saturated ground and find the blessed oblivion of sleep.

But she couldn't sleep until she was safely across the causeway.

Put to the test by the unstable ground, her ankle was throbbing badly now, but she almost welcomed the pain as an antidote to that terrible numbness.

After what seemed an age, she reached a point where a path went off to the right, and, looking through the trees, she could see the bulk of the castle on its rocky promontory.

Ahead she could make out the crescent of sea divided by the causeway, while in the far distance the mainland basked in the pale sunshine.

It looked a long way, and she admitted to herself that starting out on foot had been madness.

But she had had no choice.

Coming across a fallen tree, she sat down for a moment or two to rest her ankle.

Even that proved to be a mistake.

As though she had lost the will to battle further, she was overcome by a leaden sense of hopelessness and despair.

Only the thought of possibly having to face Michael again provided the necessary stimulus to bring her to her feet, settle her bag on her shoulder, and make herself go on.

She was descending the gentle slope that ran down to the road and the causeway when, on her right, a red sports car came into view.

Claire. The other woman was clearly on her way back to London.

Raising her hand, Jenny waved frantically, and, ignoring the pain, began to run. She had only gone a short distance when her ankle gave way and she went sprawling on the wet, uneven ground.

As she struggled to her feet the car flashed past, the driver looking straight ahead. By the time she'd picked up her bag and hobbled to the road, the vehicle was the size of a red toy car in the distance.

But that disappointment was almost instantly superseded by an even worse realization.

The tide was coming in. And fast. The sandy areas were almost covered. But she couldn't turn back now.

Picking up a length of old broken branch to use as a stick, she covered the last few hundred yards in record time.

Once she had set foot on the causeway, clearing her mind of everything but the necessity to get over as quickly as possible, she made what speed she could.

In what seemed to be an impossibly short space of time the tide, which had been rising stealthily, was starting to lap at the raised edges of the causeway.

She was still only about halfway across when the water began to swirl and eddy over the surface of the road, washing around her feet and wetting the bottoms of her trousers.

Looking at the far shore, she knew that at this rate she would be lucky to make it. But as both shores appeared to be almost equidistant, there was no point in turning back.

Her heart racing, she told herself firmly that she *had* to make it. There was no choice.

By the time she'd gone another couple of hundred yards, the water was starting to swirl around her ankles, dropping back a little between each assault, but returning with an inevitability that brought a surge of fear.

She tried to push herself into a splashing run, but at the added strain the stick proved to be brittle and snapped, making it too short to be of any use.

Dropping the useless piece into the swirling water, and trying not to give way to the panic that filled her, she stumbled on as best she could.

When Michael returned to Slinterwood, his contented mood was blighted by the sight of Claire's sports car standing near the front door.

That she should come to Slinterwood at this time was the last thing he had wanted or expected.

Wondering just how long she had been here, and what she might have said to Jenny, he drew up alongside the red sports car, switched off his ignition, and jumped out.

The house seemed quiet and there was no sound of voices as he let himself into the hall. He hurried through to the living-room to find that the couch was empty and there was no sign of either of the women, but an expensive suit jacket was tossed over a chair.

He was about to go upstairs to look for Jenny when Claire came in from the kitchen carrying a round tray of tea. Putting it down on the low table, she said, 'So you're back.'

Without preamble, Michael demanded sharply, 'What are you doing here?'

'I wanted to talk to you.'

'I thought I'd made it clear that as far as I'm concerned there's nothing left to say.'

'Darling, don't be horrid.'

Ignoring that, he asked, 'Have you seen Jenny?'

'Your PA? She was here a little while ago. I asked her if she wanted some tea, but she said no thanks. I brought an extra cup in case she'd changed her mind.'

'So where is she?'

'How should I know? Probably in her room.'

'What exactly did you say to her?'

Frowning, Claire answered, 'Not a great deal. I asked her how the book was going, and if she'd been over to the castle.

'She said yes she had, and she thought it was beautiful.'

'What else?'

'Only that I wanted to talk to you.'

'Go on.'

'I told her that I wasn't planning to stay, and if possible I wanted to be back in London tonight.'

'And that's all?'

'That's all. Though I don't see why it matters.'

He was breathing a silent sigh of relief when she added, 'I might have been jealous, only she's so obviously not your type.'

Then coaxingly, 'Why don't you sit down and have some tea?'

'I'll dispense with the tea, thanks. I had a cup with Martha. So suppose you start talking.'

Reaching to fill one of the teacups, she said, 'I know the break-up was all my fault, but honestly I've learnt my lesson.'

When there was no response, she persevered. 'What we had at the beginning was really good, wasn't it?'

'But it only lasted until someone you fancied more came along.'

Sounding defensive, she said, 'I was bored out of my mind. You can't blame me for needing some fun while you were working...' Then, her tone softening, 'But you must know it was always you I loved, and still do.

'Give me another chance and I promise things will be different next time.'

He laid it on the line. 'I'm sorry, Claire, but there's going to be no "next time". Everything's over between us, and has been since I filed for divorce.'

'Don't say that,' she pleaded. 'I know you still love me and it's only your pride that won't let you admit it.'

'That's where you're mistaken. I *don't* still love you. When we were first married I thought I did, but what I felt for you soon died when I realized just what kind of woman you really were.'

'I can't deny I was unfaithful, but Jerry was very attractive, and because I was bored I let myself—'

'Don't take me for a fool.' Michael's curt voice cut across her words. 'I know quite well that Jerry wasn't the only one, that in the short space of time we were married you had a string of lovers.'

'None of whom meant anything to me.'

'Whether or not they meant anything to you is beside the point. I wanted a wife I could trust to keep her wedding vows. Not one that every time she was out of my sight I was forced to wonder whose bed she was in.'

'If I promise to change, won't you give me another chance?'

'It may sound trite, but leopards don't change their spots.'

'So this really is goodbye?'

'You'd better believe it.'

She sighed. 'Oh, well, I thought it was worth a try before I agreed to marry Marcus Conran.'

'Marcus Conran? By all accounts he's a lecherous old devil who's been married at least five times.'

'But he's stinking rich and quite besotted. And while the lump sum you settled on me was generous, it's dwindling fast, and a girl has to think about her future.'

With a glance at her watch she got to her feet, pulled on

her jacket, and picked up her bag. 'I checked the tide-table, and if I get straight off I should just about make it.'

With a feeling of relief he showed her out.

As she got into her car her parting shot was, 'I won't invite you to the wedding.'

He watched the red car climb to the road and disappear in the direction of the causeway, before hurrying upstairs to look for Jenny.

Though all her things were still there, he could find no sign of her.

A hasty search proved she wasn't in the house, and the shoes and mac she had been wearing were gone. Her injured ankle seemed to preclude the idea of a walk for pleasure, and the fact that her handbag too was missing told him the worst.

Badly shaken, he tried to tell himself that she wouldn't attempt to *walk* across the causeway. In her semi-crippled state, and with the tide on the turn, it would be utter madness.

But coming from the opposite direction, he'd seen no sign of her.

Hurrying out to the car, he wondered frantically just how long she'd been gone.

He didn't need to ask himself *why*.

His fingers fumbled when he tried to switch on the ignition, and, as though to underline his state of mind, he clashed the gears as he turned the car.

When he reached the road he put his foot down hard. With a bit of luck she wouldn't have reached the causeway yet.

As he flashed past the stand of pines, recalling that morning's conversation, he wondered if she had taken the cross-country route.

If she had, though the ground was uneven and the terrain rough in places, it was very much quicker than going by road.

He groaned.

Please God, let him be in time to stop her setting foot on that damned causeway.

During the brief time the castle had been open to the public, one couple had lingered too long and then attempted to drive through the rising water.

They had had to be rescued by boat—it had been summer and there had been plenty about—and their car retrieved at low tide the following day.

Then a walker trying to make a last-minute crossing had been swept away. Fortunately a strong swimmer, he had just managed to reach the shore.

The memory of those near tragedies pounding in his brain, Michael rounded the bluff and took the serpentine road down the hill and past the castle at top speed.

Though the bends masked a great deal, there appeared to be no one on the road ahead.

Catching brief glimpses of the causeway, he could see that grey water was already swirling over it. He tried to tell himself that, surely, with an injured ankle, she wouldn't have attempted to cross.

Perhaps she was sitting down in the wood somewhere in too much pain to go on?

Well, if she was, at the very least she was safe, and if she hadn't strayed from the path he could find her quite quickly.

As he approached the start of the causeway, another possibility struck him: Claire might have picked her up. He would call Claire—hopefully she would stop long enough to answer it—and put his mind at rest.

Rounding the final bend, he brought the car to a skidding halt. He was pulling his mobile from his pocket when the sight of a figure some halfway across the causeway stopped his heart.

'Oh, dear God,' he breathed. Once the water was this deep, it came in with terrifying speed. If he took the car, even though it was a four-wheel drive and fairly high, it was doubtful whether he'd be able to get it back.

But even as the thought went through his head he knew he had no choice. He'd never be able to reach her in time on foot.

It might not even be possible by car.

Every nerve in his body tense, he drove down the incline and onto the causeway, his speed causing a wake of water on either side, and headed for that distant figure.

Her darkened gaze fixed on the far shore, which appeared, if anything, to be getting further away, Jenny battled on. But she knew herself to be going slower and slower.

The water was now almost calf-deep, and it was like trying to wade through treacle. Her feet and legs were numb with cold, but even through the numbness each step was a small agony.

Though she felt dazed, incapable of coherent thought, a small part of her mind knew with dreadful clarity that she wasn't going to make it.

Then, through the blood pounding in her ears, she heard what sounded like a car engine and someone shouting, calling her name.

Knowing she must be hallucinating, she ignored it and kept on as best she could.

There was a splashing noise, as though someone was running, a hand seized her arm and swung her round and strong arms swept her up.

A moment later she was bundled unceremoniously into the front seat of Michael's four-wheel drive, water that had washed in over the sill when he'd opened the car door slopping round her feet.

His face pale and set, he slid behind the wheel, and without a word carefully and deftly turned the big car, and started back to the island, steering between the marker poles.

All his instincts screamed at him to hurry, but, knowing that if water got into the engine they would be finished, he engaged a low gear, and, keeping up the revs, crept forward through the rapidly rising water both as fast and as slowly as he dared.

It was touch and go, and when they reached the shore, hardly able to believe they'd made it to safety, he drove up the incline before stopping to fasten their seat belts.

Clenching her teeth to stop them chattering, Jenny managed hoarsely, 'Thank you… I wouldn't have made it if you hadn't—'

Turning on her, he demanded with a kind of raging calm, 'Have you no sense at all? What in heaven's name made you do such an idiotic thing?'

Though he didn't raise his voice, his white face and the grimness of his mouth told her that he was absolutely *furious*.

'I—I'm sorry,' she stammered.

'And so you should be! Another minute or so and it would have been too late.'

Shrinking away, she bit her lip to hold back the weak tears that threatened. So she'd been stupid. But she was damned if she'd let him see her cry.

Without another word, he started the car, and they drove on in silence.

Shock had set in, adding to the cold and fatigue, and he could feel her shaking uncontrollably. A quick sideways glance showed him her eyes were closed and her face was ashen.

Seeing the unmistakable traces of tears on her cheeks, he berated himself for being such a brute to her. But he'd been so terribly afraid that he was going to lose her after all, and when he'd known for certain that she was safe all his previous fear had metamorphosed into anger.

By the time they reached Slinterwood, Jenny was barely

conscious and only vaguely aware of being helped from the car and carried into the house and up the stairs.

He brought her night things from her room, and as gently as he could, stripped off her clothes, dried her wet feet and legs, helped her into her nightdress, and tucked her up in his bed.

Almost before her head touched the pillow, she was fast asleep.

As he stood looking down at her small face, with its black fans of lashes and pale lips, he thanked God that she was safe.

Now he'd found her again, it would have finished him to lose her.

Jenny awoke with a start and sat bolt upright with a little cry, her heart throwing itself against her ribcage like a crazy thing.

It took a second or two to realize she was safe in bed. Then, her panic subsiding, and reassured by the sight of the familiar room, with its shaded lamps and blazing log fire, she leaned weakly back against the pillows while her heartbeat returned to normal.

Though her ankle throbbed dully, physically she felt almost as good as new, whereas mentally, recalling how Michael had lied to her to get what he wanted, she felt churned up and desolate.

But, having been brushed by the wings of death, she knew she owed him a big debt of gratitude, even if the future did look bleak and empty.

Recalling how quietly furious he'd been, she wondered if he was still mad with her.

Anticipating some degree of relief that she was safe, she had been totally floored by his unexpected anger.

Now, thinking about it, she suddenly recalled an incident she had witnessed some years ago, but that had stuck in her mind.

A mother, holding a little boy by the hand, had been

waiting at a busy crossing when a fellow pedestrian had spoken to her. Temporarily distracted, she had relaxed her hold, and the boy, seeing a friend on the opposite pavement, had pulled free and run into the road. Brakes squealing, the car had managed to stop with just inches to spare.

As the boy had begun to howl with fright, the mother had dragged him to safety. But instead of hugging and kissing him, as Jenny had expected, she had shouted at him and shaken him angrily, before bursting into tears of relief.

But surely that reaction would only happen if you loved the person involved, and Michael didn't love her, she thought bleakly. He loved Claire.

At that instant the door opened and Michael himself came in, carrying a large tray.

He was dressed in stone-coloured trousers and a fine polo-necked sweater in a dark green that picked up the colour of his eyes.

Her heart turned over at the sight of him, and she caught her underlip in her teeth and bit hard to hide the surge of emotion.

'So you're awake—that's good. I thought you should have some food inside you before settling down for the night.'

He both looked, and sounded, himself again.

Putting the tray on the table by the fire, he came over to the bed and, studying her closely, asked, 'How are you feeling now?'

'Fine, thank you,' she answered.

'Would you like to eat in bed or by the fire?'

Though she wasn't hungry, she answered without hesitation, 'By the fire.'

Then, deciding to take the bull by the horns, she added jerkily, 'And then I'd like to sleep in my own room, in my own bed. Alone.'

'Very well, if that's what you still want to do once we've had a chance to talk.'

What could he possibly say? she wondered dully. After Claire's visit, he couldn't very well deny he had lied about taking her back.

Turning down the bedclothes, he helped her out of bed and into her gown. Then, having carried her over to the fire, he settled her in one of the comfortable armchairs, and queried, 'Warm enough?'

'Oh, yes, thank you.'

Putting a napkin over her knee, he filled a plate with lamb casserole and handed it to her, before taking a seat opposite and serving himself.

The casserole, which proved to be good and tasty, was followed by fresh fruit and cheese.

In spite of her inward misery, once she had forced down the first mouthful she managed to eat a reasonable meal.

Though the air was thick with unspoken questions and recriminations, they finished eating without a word being spoken.

Only when they reached the coffee stage did Michael break the silence to ask a question he was sure he already knew the answer to. 'So why did you run away?'

'You know perfectly well!' she cried. 'You deceived me, told me a pack of lies, just to get me into bed again!'

'I did no such thing,' he said flatly. 'When I told you that Claire and I were finished—'

'You were lying!' she choked.

'I was *not* lying,' he denied quietly.

'But she *told* me that you and she were getting married again.'

'That was what she was *hoping,* but it was far from the truth.'

'Oh,' Jenny said in a small voice.

'When I told you the relationship was over, I meant every word. I had absolutely no intention of taking her back. As a matter of fact until I saw you again at Jenkins's retirement party I had no intention of *ever* remarrying.'

Jenny caught her breath, wondering if he could possibly mean what she thought he meant.

But, his voice level, he was going on, 'And Claire didn't really want *me* back. All she wanted was a secure meal ticket, and she saw me as a slightly better bet than the next candidate she has lined up.'

'The next candidate?'

'An old roué with five failed marriages behind him, a penchant for young, beautiful women, and unlimited millions to buy himself what he wants.'

'And you're not upset about it?'

'I might be if Claire was some innocent ingénue. But she isn't. Claire knows quite well what she's doing, and presumably she thinks it'll be worth it.'

Cynically, he added, 'So long as he keeps the cash supply flowing, and gives her plenty of freedom, it will probably work quite well until she becomes a rich widow.'

Still hardly able to believe it, Jenny persisted, 'You're not sorry it's finally over?'

He shook his head. 'Anything but. I've always believed that marriage vows should be meant and kept, and that children should be born into a home that was loving and stable. It would never have been that way with Claire.'

Jenny sighed. 'It's just that the ending of a relationship can be sad.'

'Personally I regard this as a happy ending.' He took her hand. 'Or, rather, the beginning of a new relationship. One that I hope and believe is destined to go on and last a lifetime and beyond.'

'You don't mean...' She stopped, afraid to put it into words.

'That's exactly what I mean!'

He lifted her hand to his lips and dropped a kiss in the palm, before going on, 'How could you think for one instant that after all we've shared I would take Claire back? It must have been obvious that I wanted you, needed you, so much that I couldn't think straight.

'It's been like that since the first moment I set eyes on you. All those years ago, when I saw you standing in the castle courtyard, you seemed achingly familiar, as if I'd always known you, as if I'd been waiting all my life for you.

'Then as I watched your car drive away that first time I felt empty, desolate, as though I was losing something that was infinitely precious. For months you haunted me. I saw your face in my dreams, and wakened with it still in my mind's eye. I found myself looking for you everywhere I went, in London's bustling shops and stores, on the busy pavements, in passing cars, the reflections in shop windows, and in the quiet park.

'For perhaps the first time I fully understood the meaning of the word *desideratum*—something desired as necessary. When I failed to find you, I felt an emptiness, a need, that took a long time to lessen. Seeing you again and getting to know you brought all those emotions back in force, and I feel more strongly than ever that we belong together.

'How do you feel?'

As those forest-green eyes looked into hers she said softly, 'The same.'

'That's good, because there's nothing we can do about it. It's destiny. You do believe in destiny?'

'Yes. I felt as if I was destined to come to the island, to the castle, and Slinterwood, as if I belonged here.'

'I'm quite certain you do. And I'm equally certain that it's our destiny to complete the love story our great-grandparents began. Though they weren't fated to be happy together, we'll make up for it.'

Lifting her, he settled her on his lap, and for a long time, his cheek against her hair, they sat in contented silence.

Eventually, when the fire began to die low, he said, 'Time for bed, don't you think?'

At her nod, he asked wickedly, 'Do you still want to sleep in your own bed, in your own room? Alone?'

'That depends.'

'On what?'

'On what inducements you can offer.'

'Well, let me see… I could…' Putting his lips close to her ear, he whispered erotic suggestions that made her toes curl and heat run through her.

Feigning indifference, she said, 'I suppose that *could* be worth staying for.'

'I'll make sure it is,' he promised.

Having set her carefully on her feet, and stripped off her night things and his own clothes, he carried her back to bed and got in beside her.

While his lips traced the pure line of her jaw and his hands started to caress her, she asked, 'Is your middle name really James?'

Stopped in his tracks by the unexpected question, he promised, 'You'll find out when we get married.'

'Are we getting married?'

'We're not only getting married, but in our very own chapel.'

'How wonderful…' Then dreamily, 'How many children would you like?'

Against her throat, he said, 'To begin with, I want you all to myself for a while, then perhaps we could start with a little girl just like you.'

'I was thinking of a couple of boys first… But perhaps it wouldn't be a bad idea for them to have an older sister. Then—'

A finger to her lips, he said, 'Whoa there!'

'You don't want a big family?'

'I'd love a big family.'

'That's good, because I—'

Stopping her lips once more, he said severely, 'But it may never happen if you don't stop talking and let me get some practice in.'

As she started to laugh, his heart swelling with love, he kissed her.

For a time the only sounds in the room were the rustle of logs settling in the grate and her little gasps and moans as, with hands and lips and tongue, he followed through with his whispered suggestions.

Both were conducive to practice.

Join our *EXCLUSIVE* eBook club

FROM JUST £1.99 A MONTH!

Never miss a book again with our hassle-free eBook subscription.

★ Pick how many titles you want from each series with our flexible subscription

★ Your titles are delivered to your device on the first of every month

★ Zero risk, zero obligation!

There really is nothing standing in the way of you and your favourite books!

Start your eBook subscription today at www.millsandboon.co.uk/subscribe

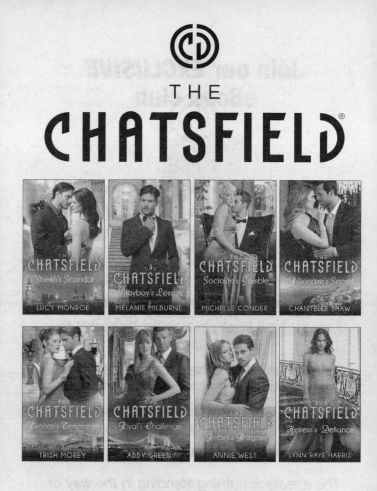

THE CHATSFIELD®

Enter the intriguing online world of
The Chatsfield and discover secret
stories behind closed doors...

www.thechatsfield.com

Check in online now for your exclusive
welcome pack!

Discover more romance at

www.millsandboon.co.uk

- ❤ WIN great prizes in our exclusive competitions
- ❤ BUY new titles before they hit the shops
- ❤ BROWSE new books and REVIEW your favourites
- ❤ SAVE on new books with the Mills & Boon® Bookclub™
- ❤ DISCOVER new authors

PLUS, to chat about your favourite reads, get the latest news and find special offers:

- 📘 Find us on facebook.com/millsandboon
- 🐦 Follow us on twitter.com/millsandboonuk
- ❤ Sign up to our newsletter at millsandboon.co.uk

Welcome to your new-look By Request series!

Wedding Wishes
LIZ FIELDING · CHRISTIE RIDGWAY · MYRNA MACKENZIE
By Request

Royal Seductions: Diamonds
LUCY MONROE · LUCY GORDON · NATALIE RIVERS
By Request

Misbehaving with the Millionaire
KIMBERLY LANG · MARGARET MAYO · LEE WILKINSON
By Request

RELIVE THE ROMANCE WITH THE BEST OF THE BEST

This series features stories from your favourite authors that are back by popular demand— and, now with brand new covers, they look even better than before!

See the new covers now at: www.millsandboon.co.uk/byrequest

0614/05/MB473